Prai

SUZANNE BROCKMANN

"Zingy dialogue, a great sense of drama,
and a pair of lovers who generate enough steam heat
to power a whole city."
—*RT Book Reviews* on *Hero Under Cover*

"Brockmann deftly delivers another testosterone-
drenched, adrenaline-fueled tale of danger and desire
that brilliantly combines superbly crafted, realistically
complex characters with white-knuckle plotting."
—*Booklist* on *Force of Nature*

"Readers will be on the edge of their seats."
—*Library Journal* on *Breaking Point*

"Another excellently paced, action-filled read.
Brockmann delivers yet again!"
—*RT Book Reviews* on *Into the Storm*

"Funny, sexy, suspenseful and superb."
—*Booklist* on *Hot Target*

"Sizzling with military intrigue and sexual tension,
with characters so vivid they leap right off the page,
Gone Too Far is a bold, brassy read with a
momentum that just doesn't quit."
—*New York Times* bestselling author Tess Gerritsen

"An unusual and compelling romance."
—*Affaire de Coeur* on *No Ordinary Man*

"Sensational sizzle, powerful emotion and sheer fun."
—*RT B*ody *Language*

SUZANNE BROCKMANN

TALL, DARK AND DARING

HQN™

Recycling programs for this product may not exist in your area.

ISBN-13: 978-0-373-77624-5

TALL, DARK AND DARING

Copyright © 2011 by Harlequin Books S.A.

The publisher acknowledges the copyright holder of the individual works as follows:

THE ADMIRAL'S BRIDE
Copyright © 1999 by Suzanne Brockmann

IDENTITY: UNKNOWN
Copyright © 2000 by Suzanne Brockmann

This edition published by arrangement with Harlequin Books S.A.

For questions and comments about the quality of this book please contact us at Customer_eCare@Harlequin.ca.

® and TM are trademarks of the publisher. Trademarks indicated with ® are registered in the United States Patent and Trademark Office, the Canadian Trade Marks Office and in other countries.

www.HQNBooks.com

Printed in U.S.A.

CONTENTS

THE ADMIRAL'S BRIDE

For Nancy Peeler.
We miss you guys!

PROLOGUE

Vietnam, 1969

SERGEANT MATTHEW LANGE had been left to die.

His leg was badly broken and he had shrapnel embedded in his entire right side. It hadn't hit anything vital. He knew, because he'd been hit hours ago and he wasn't dead yet. And that was almost a shame.

His morphine wasn't working. He not only hurt like hell but he was still alert enough to know what was coming.

The soldier next to him knew, too. He lay there, crying softly. Jim was his name. Jimmy D'Angelo. He was just a kid, really—barely eighteen—and he wasn't going to get any older.

None of them were.

There were a dozen of them there, United States Marines, hiding and bleeding in the jungle of a country too small to have been mentioned in fifth-grade geography class. They were too badly injured to walk out, but most of 'em were still conscious, still alive enough to know that sometime within the next few hours, they were going to die.

Charlie was coming.

Probably right before dawn.

The Vietcong had launched a major offensive yesterday morning, and Matt's platoon had been one of several trapped by the attack. They were now God knows how many clicks behind enemy lines, with no chance of rescue.

Hours ago, Captain Tyler had radioed for help, but help wasn't coming. There were no chopper pilots insane enough to fly into this hot spot. They were on their own.

But then the bomb dropped—close to literally. Well, at least it would be dropping literally, come morning. The captain had been ordered out of the area. He was told that in an attempt to halt the Vietcong, the Americans would be napalming this very mountain in less than twelve hours.

There had been twenty injured men. They'd outnumbered the uninjured by more than two to one.

Captain Tyler had played God, choosing the eight least wounded to drag out of there. He'd looked at Matt, looked at his leg, and he'd shaken his head. No. He'd had tears in his eyes, not that that helped much now.

Father O'Brien had been the only one to stay behind.

Matt could hear his quiet voice, murmuring words of comfort to the dying men.

If Charlie found them, he'd use bayonets to kill them. He wouldn't want to waste bullets on men who couldn't fight back. And Matt couldn't fight back. His right arm was useless, his left too weak to shoulder his weapon. Most of the other guys were worse than he was. And he couldn't picture Father O'Brien picking up someone's machine gun and giving Charlie a mouthful of lead.

No, bayonets or burning. That's what their future had come down to.

Matt felt like weeping along with Jimmy.

"Sarge?"

"Yeah, Jim. I'm still here." Like Matt might've walked away.

"You have a family, don't you?"

Matt closed his eyes, picturing Lisa's sweet face. "Yeah," he said. "I do. Back in New Haven. Connecticut." He might as well have said Mars, it seemed as far away. "I got two boys. Matt, Jr., and Mikey." Lisa had wanted a little girl. A daughter. He'd always thought there'd be plenty of time for that later.

He'd been wrong.

"You're lucky." Jimmy's voice shook. "I don't have anyone besides my ma who's gonna remember me. My poor ma." He started to cry again. "Oh, God, I want my ma...."

Father O'Brien came over, but his calm voice didn't cover Jimmy's sobbing. The poor bastard wanted his ma.

Matt wanted Lisa. It was the stupidest thing. When he'd been there, back in that stifling little crummy two-bedroom apartment in one of the worst neighborhoods in New Haven, he'd thought he'd go absolutely mad. He hated working as a mechanic, hated the way his money was already spent on groceries and rent before he even brought home his paycheck. So he'd re-upped. He'd told Lisa he'd reenlisted for the money, but the real truth was he'd wanted to get the hell out of there before he suffocated. And he'd left, even though she'd cried.

He'd married too young—not that he'd had a real choice about it. And he'd liked it, at first. Lisa, in his bed every night. No need to worry about getting her pregnant, since he'd already done that. He'd loved the way she'd grown heavy with child, with *his* child. It made him feel like a man, even though at twenty-two, fresh out of the service, he'd been little more than a child himself. But when the second baby had come right after the first, the weight of his responsibilities had scared him to death.

So he'd left. He'd come here, to Nam.

It was much different from his first tour, when he'd been stationed in Germany.

And right now all he wanted was to be back in Lisa's arms. He was the stupidest fool in the world—he didn't realize how much he had, how much he truly loved that girl, his wife, until he was hours away from dying.

Bayonets or burning. "Dear God."

Father O'Brien's soft voice had quieted Jimmy, and he now turned to Matt. "Sergeant—Matthew. Would you like to pray?"

"No, Father," he said.

Not even prayer could help them now.

"THEIR CAPTAIN JUST LEFT them there?" Lieutenant Jake Robinson kept his voice even, kept his voice low, even though he absolutely could not believe what his chief had just told him. Wounded marines, left behind by their CO in the jungle to die. "And now the good guys are going to finish them off with friendly fire?"

Ham nodded, his headphones still plugged into the radio, his dark eyes grim. "It's not as heartless as you're thinkin', Admiral. There's only a dozen or so of them. If Charlie isn't stopped before he gets to the river, we'll have casualties in the thousands. You know that." He spoke in a barely audible voice, too.

The enemy was all around them tonight. And well they should know. Jake's team of Men with Green Faces, U.S. Navy SEALs, had spent the past twenty-four hours marking the Vietcongs' location in this target area. They'd radioed the info in and now had exactly four hours to get out before the bombing raid began.

"Only a dozen men," Jake said. "Or so. Any chance of giving me an exact number, Chief?"

"Twelve wounded, one priest."

Fred and Chuck materialized from the jungle. "Only

nine wounded now," Fred corrected him in his soft Southern drawl. "We found 'em, Admiral. Near a clearing, like they hoped a chopper would be able to come in and grab 'em. Didn't approach—didn't want to get their hopes up if we didn't think we could help. What we could see, three of 'em are already KIA."

KIA. Killed in action. It was one of Jake's least favorite acronyms. Along with POW and MIA. But he didn't let his aversion show on his face. He never let anything like that show. His men didn't need to know when he was shaken. And this one had shaken him, hard. The commanders-in-chief knew those men were there. U.S. Marines. Good men. Brave men. And those commanders had given the order to proceed with the bombing regardless.

He met Ham's eyes and read the skepticism there.

"We've pulled off some tough missions before," Jake said. His words were as much to convince himself.

Ham shook his head. "Nine wounded men and seven SEALs," he said. "Against thirty-five-hundred Vietcong? Come on, Lieutenant." The chief didn't need to say what he was thinking. This wasn't just a tough mission, it was insanity.

And the chief had called Jake by his true rank, a sign of his disapproval. It was funny how accustomed he'd become to the nickname this team of SEALs had given him—Admiral. It was the ultimate expression of respect from this motley crew, particularly since he'd gone through BUD/S cursed with the label Pretty Boy, PB for short. Yeah, he liked Admiral much better.

Fred and Chuck were watching him. So were Scooter and the Preacher and Ricky. Waiting for his command. At age twenty-two, Jake was one of the two old men of the team—a full lieutenant having served three back-to-back tours of duty in this hell on earth. Ham, his chief, had been there with him for the last two. Steady as a rock and, at twenty-seven years of age, as gnarled and ancient as the hills. But he'd never questioned Jake's authority.

Until now.

Jake smiled. "Nine wounded men, seven SEALs and one priest," he pointed out lightly. "Don't forget the priest, Ham. Always good to have one of them on our side."

Fred snickered, but Ham's expression didn't change.

"I wouldn't leave *you* to die," Jake quietly told the man who was the closest thing to a friend he had in this armpit of a jungle. "I will not leave those men out there."

Jake didn't wait for Ham's response, because frankly, Ham's response didn't matter. He didn't need his chief's approval. This wasn't a democracy. Jake and Jake alone was in command.

He met Fred's eyes, then Scooter's and Preacher's and Ricky's and Chuck's, infusing them all with his confidence, letting them see his complete faith in their ability as a SEAL team to pull off this impossible task.

Leaving those poor bastards to die was not an option. Jake couldn't do it. Jake *wouldn't* do it.

He turned to Ham. "Get on the radio, Chief, and find Crazy Ruben. If anyone'll fly a chopper in this deep, it'll be him. Pull in all those favors he owes me, promise him air support, and then get on the wire and get it for him."

"Yes, *sir.*"

Jake turned to Fred. "Go back there and get their hopes up. Get them ready to move, then get your ass back here on the double." He smiled again, his best picnic-in-the-park smile. The one that made men under command believe they'd live to see another sunrise. "The rest of you gentlemen get ready to cut some very long fuses. Because I've got one hell of a plan."

"THEY MUSTA PARACHUTED IN!" Jimmy had real excitement in his voice. "Listen to that, Sarge! How many of 'em do you think are out there?"

Matt painfully pulled himself up, trying to see something, *anything* in the darkness of the jungle. But all he could see were the flashes in the sky from an enormous battle just off to the west. Deep in VC territory. "God, there must be hundreds."

Even as he said the words he couldn't believe it. Hundreds of American soldiers, appearing out of nowhere?

"They had to've dropped 'em in," Jimmy said again.

It seemed impossible, but it must have been true—because there came the air support, then, big planes screaming overhead, dropping all kinds of nasty surprises on Charlie.

Two hours ago a big, dark-skinned man had appeared, rising out of the jungle like an apparition, his face savagely painted with green and brown, a cammy-print bandanna tied neatly around the top of his head. He'd ID'd himself as Seaman Fred Baxter of the U.S. Navy SEALs.

Matt had highest rank among the men left behind, and had asked what the hell a sailor was doing this far inland?

Apparently there was a whole group of sailors out there in the jungle. A team, Baxter had said. Jake's team, he'd called them, as if that meant something—whoever the hell Jake was. And they were going to get Matt and Jimmy and the rest of 'em out of there. Stand ready for extraction, Baxter had said, and he'd disappeared.

Matt had been left wondering if the entire conversation hadn't been some weird morphine hallucination. Seals. Who would name a special forces group after a circus animal? And how the hell was an entire *team* of them going to get out of the jungle with nine wounded men?

"I've heard of the SEALs," Jimmy said, as if he'd somehow been able to follow Matt's drug-hazed thoughts. "They're some kind of demolitions experts. Even under-water, if you can believe *that*. And they're kinda like ninjas—they can move right past Charlie—within *feet* of Charlie—without being seen. They go miles behind the line in teams of six or seven men and blow stuff up. And I don't know what kind of voodoo they use, but they always come back alive. *Always*."

Six or seven men. Matt looked up at the flashes of explosions lighting the sky. Demolitions experts... No. Couldn't be.

Could it?

"Chopper!" Father O'Brien shouted. "Praise our Lord God Almighty!"

The roar was unmistakable. The hurricane-force wind from the blades felt like a miracle. Holy Jesus, they actually had a chance.

Tears were running down the padre's round face as he helped the medics lift the wounded men up and into the chopper. Matt couldn't hear him over the roar, over the sound of weapons discharging as the men with green faces suddenly appeared, keeping Charlie back, away from the clearing. Matt didn't need to hear O'Brien to know that his mouth was moving in a continuous prayer of thanks.

But Matt wasn't Catholic, and they hadn't made it out yet.

Someone lifted him up and the sudden knifelike pain in his leg made him scream.

"Sorry, Sergeant." The voice held the quiet confidence of a seasoned officer. "No time to ask where it hurts."

And then the pain was worth it, because he was inside, his cheek pressed against the olive-drab U.S.-made riveted metal of the chopper floor. And then they were lifting up and away, on an express flight out of hell.

But fear cut through his waves of relief. Dear God, don't let them have left anyone behind!

He forced himself over, onto his back, and the pain nearly made him retch. "Head count!" he somehow managed to shout.

"We got all of you, Sarge." It was the steady voice of the man who'd carried him aboard. He was crouched by the open doorway, a grenade launcher in his arms, aiming and firing even as he spoke. He was younger than Matt had imagined from his voice. He wore no insignia, no rank, no markings on his camouflage gear at all. Like the other SEALs, his face was streaked with green and brown, but as he turned to glance over his shoulder at the wounded men, Matt could see his eyes. They were an almost startling shade of blue. And as he met Matt's gaze, he smiled.

It wasn't a tense, tight grimace laced with fear. And it wasn't a wolfish expression of adrenaline-induced high. It was a calm, relaxed, "let's get together and play softball sometime" kind of smile.

"We got everyone," he shouted again, no room for doubt in his voice. "Hold on, Sergeant, it's going to be a bumpy ride, but we *will* get you out, and we *will* get you home."

When he said it like that, as if it were an absolute truth, even Matt could believe him.

THE HOSPITAL WAS THE PITS, filled with pain and stink and death, but Matt knew he was only going to be there a little while longer.

He'd been given his orders, his medical discharge. He was going home to Lisa.

He was going to walk with a limp, probably for the

rest of his life, but the doctors had managed to save his leg. Not bad for a guy who'd been left for dead.

"You're looking much better today." The nurse that stopped by his bed and checked his leg was a pretty brunette with two deep dimples in her cheeks when she smiled. "I'm Constance. You can call me Connie for short."

He hadn't seen her before, but he'd only been here about forty-eight hours. He'd spent most of that time in surgery and recovery.

"Oh, you're one of Jake's Boys," Connie said as she checked his chart, her Georgia peaches-and-cream accent suddenly hushed with respect.

"No," he said, "I'm not a SEAL. I'm a sergeant with—"

"I know you're not a SEAL, silly." She dimpled up again. "Jake's SEALs don't turn up in our hospital beds. We sometimes have to give them extra penicillin, but perhaps I shouldn't mention that in mixed company." She winked.

Matt was confused. "But you said—"

"Jake's *Boys*," she repeated. "That's what we call you— the wounded men that Lieutenant Jake Robinson brings in. Someone started keeping count here at the hospital about eight months ago."

At his blank look, she tried to explain. "Jake has developed the habit of resurrecting U.S. soldiers from the dead, Sergeant. Last month, his team liberated an entire prisoner-of-war camp. Don't ask me how, but Jake and his team came out of that jungle with seventy-five POWs, each one looking worse than the last. I swear, I cried for a week when I saw those poor souls." She shook her head. "I think there were ten of you this time, weren't there? Jake's up to…let's see…I think it's four hundred and twenty-seven now." She dimpled again. "Although if you ask me, he should get extra points for the priest."

"Four hundred and..."

"Twenty-seven." Connie nodded, taking his blood pressure, her touch businesslike, impersonal. "All of whom owe their lives to him. Of course, we only started counting eight months ago. He's been in-country much longer."

"A lieutenant, huh?" Matt mused. "My *captain* couldn't get even get one single chopper to fly in to pull us out."

Connie bristled. "Your captain is a word I will not use because *I* am a lady. Shame on him for leaving you boys that way. He better not come to *this* hospital for his annual checkup. There are a dozen doctors and nurses who are *dying* to get a chance to tell him to turn his head and cough."

Matt laughed, but then winced. "Captain Tyler tried," he said. "I was there. I know he tried. That's what I don't understand. How could this lieutenant make things happen when a captain couldn't?"

"Well, you know Jake's nickname." Connie looked up from her gentle but methodical checking of his shrapnel wounds. "Or maybe you don't. His teammates call him Admiral. And it wouldn't surprise me one bit if he made it to that rank someday. He's got something about him. Oh, yes, there's something very special in those blue eyes."

Blue eyes. "I think I met him," Matt said.

"Sergeant, you wouldn't just *think* it if you'd met him. You'd know it. He has a face like a movie star and a smile that makes you want to follow him just about anywhere." She sighed, then smiled again. "Oh, my. I am getting myself worked up over that young man, aren't I?"

Matt had to know. "So how *did* a lieutenant manage to get all those soldiers dropped into the area? There must've been hundreds of them, and—"

Connie laughed but then stopped, her eyes widening as she looked at him. "My goodness," she said. "You don't know, do you? When I heard about it, I didn't quite believe it, but if they managed to fool *you,* too..."

Matt just waited for her to explain.

"It was a ruse," she said. "Jake and his SEALs rigged a chain of explosives to fool the VC into thinking we'd launched a counteroffensive. It was just a distraction so he could get Captain Ruben's chopper in to pull you out. There weren't hundreds of soldiers in that jungle, Sergeant. What you saw and heard was solely the handiwork of seven U.S. Navy SEALs, led by one Lieutenant Jake Robinson."

Matt was floored. Seven SEALs had made him believe there was a huge army out there in the darkness.

Connie's dimples deepened. "Gracious, that man might be more than an admiral someday. He just might go all the way and become our president." She raised her eyebrows suggestively. "I'd give him *my* vote, that's for sure."

She made a note on Matt's chart, about to move on to the next bed.

"Connie?"

She turned back patiently. "Sergeant, I can't give you anything for the pain for another few hours."

"No, that's not... I was just wondering. Does he ever come around here? Lieutenant Robinson, I mean. I'd like to thank him."

"First off," she said. "As one of Jake's Boys, you and he are on a first-name basis. And secondly, no. You won't see him around here. He's already back out there, Sergeant. He's sleeping in the jungle tonight—that is, if he's sleeping at all."

CHAPTER ONE

Washington, D.C., today

THE PENTAGON.

Dr. Zoe Lange gazed out the window of the limo as the driver pulled up to the *Pentagon.*

Damn.

She was way underdressed.

Her boss, Patrick Sullivan, had told her only that she was a candidate for an important and potentially long-term assignment. Zoe had figured that appropriate dress for such a meeting meant comfortable—blue jeans, running shoes, a T-shirt with a little blue flower print, and hardly any makeup. She was who she was, after all. If she were going to join a long-term mission, everyone might as well know exactly what to expect right from the start.

She didn't dress up unless she had to.

Unless she were going someplace like, oh, say, the Pentagon.

If she'd known she was coming to the Pentagon, she would have put on her skintight black cat suit, her three-inch heels, dark red lipstick and worn her long blond hair in some kind of fancy French braid, rather than this high-school cheerleader ponytail she was wearing. Because men in the military tended to think female agents who looked like Emma Peel or one of James Bond's babes could hold their own when the going got tough. But little blue flowers, nuh-uh. Little blue flowers meant they'd have to hand her hankies to mop her frightened tears. Never mind the fact that little blue flowers didn't compromise her ability to run hard and fast, the way three-inch heels did.

Well, okay. She was here now. The little blue flowers were going to have to do.

She put on her sunglasses and picked up her oversize handbag that doubled as a briefcase and let herself be escorted by the guards into the building, through all the security checkpoints and into a waiting elevator.

Down. They headed down, further even than the B that marked the basement floor. Even though no more letters or numbers flashed on the display over the door, they kept sinking. What could possibly be this far down besides hell?

Zoe smiled tightly at the idea of being summoned for a meeting with the devil himself. In her line of business, it was entirely possible. She just hadn't expected to meet him here in D.C.

Finally the elevator stopped and the doors opened with a subdued chime.

The hallway was a clean off-white and very bright, not the dimly lit, smoky magentas and red-oranges of hell. The guards waiting for her outside didn't carry pitchforks. Instead they wore naval uniforms. Navy, huh? Hmm, wasn't *that* interesting?

U.S. Navy Lieutenant Clones One and Two led her down that nondescript corridor, through countless doors that opened and closed automatically. Maxwell Smart would've been right at home.

"Where are we heading, boys?" Zoe asked. "To the Cone of Silence?"

One of the lieutenants looked back at her blankly,

either too young or too serious to have seen all those late-night *Get Smart* reruns she'd watched as a kid.

But as they stopped at an unmarked doorway, Zoe realized her joking question had been right on the mark. The door was ridiculously thick, reinforced with steel, layered with everything else—lead included, no doubt—that would render the room within completely spy-proof. No infrared satellites could look through *these* walls and see who was inside. No high-powered microphones could listen in. Nothing that was said inside could be recorded or overheard.

It was, indeed, the equivalent of Maxwell Smart's Cone of Silence.

The outer door—and it was only the first of three she passed through—closed with a thunk, followed by the second. The third door was like a hatch on a ship—she had to step over a rim to get inside. It, too, was sealed tightly behind her.

Apparently, she was the last to arrive.

The inner chamber was not a big room. It was barely sixteen by thirteen, and it was filled with men. Big men, wearing gleaming white naval dress uniforms. The glare was intense. Zoe resisted the urge to pull her sunglasses down from where she'd pushed them atop her head as they all turned to look at her, as they all rose to their feet in a unison display of chivalry.

She looked at them, scanning their faces, looking for someone, *anyone* familiar. The best she could do was count heads—fourteen—and sort through the various ranks on their uniforms.

"Please," she said, with her best professional smile. "Gentlemen. No need to stand on my account."

There were two enlisted men, four lieutenants, one senior chief, two commanders, a captain, a rear admiral lower grade and three—count 'em, *three*—full-grade admirals, complete with scrambled eggs on the hats that were on the table in front of them.

Seven of the men were active-duty SEALs. Two of the admirals wore budweisers, as well—the SEAL pin with an anchor and an eagle in flight gripping Poseidon's pitchfork in one talon and a stylized gun in the other—which meant they'd been SEALs at one time during their long military careers.

One of the SEALs—a blond lieutenant with an even, white-toothed smile and a much too handsome face, who looked as if he might've come straight from the set of *Baywatch*—pulled out a chair for her. Nodding her thanks, she sat next to him.

"Name's Luke O'Donlon," he whispered, holding out his hand.

She shook it quickly, absently, smiling briefly at both O'Donlon and the SEAL on her other side, an enormous African-American man with a shaved head, a diamond stud in his left ear and a wide gold wedding band on his ring finger. As she set her bag down in front of her, her attention was held by the men on the other side of the big table.

Three admirals. Holy Mike. Whatever this assignment was, it required this spy-proof room and three full-grade admirals to launch it.

The admiral without the budweiser had snow-white hair and a face set in a permanent expression of disgust—as if he carried bad fish in his inside jacket pocket. Stonegate, that was his name. Zoe recognized him from his newspaper picture. He was always showing up in the *Washington Post*. He was part politician, something she didn't quite approve of in a man of his rank and standing.

Beside her, O'Donlon cleared his throat and gave her his most winsome smile. He was just too cute, and he knew it, too. "I'm sorry, miss, I didn't catch your name."

"I'm afraid that info's need-to-know," she whispered back, "and probably beyond your security clearance level. Sorry, sailor."

The senior chief next to her overheard and deftly covered his laughter with a cough.

The admiral who had reclaimed his seat next to Stonegate had a thick head of salt-and-pepper hair. Admiral Mac Forrest. Definitely a cool guy. She'd met him at least twice in the Middle East, the last time just a few months ago. He nodded and smiled as she met his eyes.

The admiral on Mac's left—the man directly across the table from her—was still standing, his face hidden as he quickly rifled through a file. "Now that we're all here," he said, "why don't we get started."

He looked up then, and Zoe found herself looking into eyes that were amazingly, impossibly blue, into a face she would've recognized anywhere.

Jake Robinson.

The one and only Admiral Jake Robinson.

Zoe knew he was in his early fifties—he had to be unless he'd performed his heroics in Vietnam as a twelve-year-old. Still, his hair was thick and dark, and the lines around his eyes and mouth only served to give his handsome face strength and maturity.

And handsome was a complete understatement. Jake Robinson was *way* beyond handsome. He needed a completely new word invented to describe the sheer beauty of his face. His mouth was elegant, gracefully shaped and ready to quirk up into a smile. His nose was masculine perfection, his cheekbones exquisite, his forehead strong. His chin was just the right amount of stubborn, his jawline still sharp.

Lieutenant Cutie-Pie sitting next to her—now *he* was

merely handsome. Jake Robinson, on the other hand, was the Real Deal.

He was looking around the table, quickly making introductions that Zoe knew were mostly for her benefit. Everyone else here knew each other. She tried to listen. The two enlisted SEALs were Skelly and Taylor. One was built like a pro football linebacker, the other looked like Popeye the sailor man. Which was which, she didn't have a clue. The African-American senior chief was named Becker. She'd met O'Donlon. Hawken, Shaw, Jones. Try as she might to memorize names, to attach them permanently to faces, she couldn't do it.

She was too busy flashing hot and cold.

Jake Robinson.

Great glorious God, she was being given a chance to work a long-term assignment under the command of a living legend. His exploits in Vietnam *were* legendary—along with his more recent creation of the Gray Group. Robinson's Gray Group was so highly classified, so top secret, she could only guess the type of assignments he handed out. But she *could* guess. Dangerous. Covert. Intensely important to national security.

And she was going to be part of one.

Zoe's heart was pounding as if she had just run five miles. She took a deep breath, calming herself as the admiral introduced her to the rest of the room. By the time fourteen pairs of very male eyes focused on her, she was completely back in control. Calm. Cool. Collected. Positively serene.

Except thirteen of those fourteen pairs of very male eyes didn't seem to notice how absolutely serene she was. Instead, they all focused on her ponytail and her little blue flowers. She could read their speculation quite clearly. She was the secretary, right? Sent in to take notes while the big strong men talked.

Guess again, boys.

"Dr. Zoe Lange is one of *the* top experts in the country—possibly in the world—in biological and chemical weapons," Jake Robinson told them in his husky baritone voice.

Around the room, eyebrows went up. Zoe could almost smell the skepticism. Across the table, the admiral's eyes were sparkling with amusement. Clearly, the skepticism's stench was strong enough for him to smell it, as well.

"Dr. Lange works for Pat Sullivan," he added matter-of-factly, and the mood in the room instantly changed. The Agency. He didn't even need to say the name of the organization. They all knew what it was—and what she did for a living. Admiral Robinson had known exactly what to say to make them all sit up and take notice of her, little blue flowers or not. She sent him a smile of thanks.

"I truly appreciate your being able to join us here today, Doctor." The admiral smiled at her, and it was all Zoe could do not to melt at his feet.

It was true. Everything she'd ever read or heard about Jake Robinson's smile was absolutely true. It was warm and genuine. It was completely inclusive. It lit him from within, made his eyes even more blue. It made her want to follow him anywhere. *Anywhere.*

"It's my pleasure, Admiral," she murmured. "I'm honored that you invited me. I hope I can be of assistance."

"Actually—" his face sobered "—it's unfortunate that we need your assistance." He looked around the table, all amusement gone from his eyes. "Two weeks ago, there was a break-in at the Arches military testing lab just outside of Boulder, Colorado."

Zoe stopped watching the man's eyes and started paying attention to his words. A break-in. At Arches. Holy Mike.

She wasn't the only one shifting uneasily in her seat. Beside her, Senior Chief Becker was downright uncomfortable, as were most of the other SEALs. Like Zoe, they all knew what was tested at Arches. They all knew what was *stored* there, as well. Anthrax. Botulinum toxin. Sarin. The lethal nerve gas VX. And the newest manmade tool of death and chemical destruction, Triple X.

The last time Zoe had been in Arches, she'd written a hundred-and-fifty-page report on the weaknesses in their security system. She wondered now if anyone at all had bothered to read it.

"The break-in was done without force, without forced entry, even," the admiral continued. "Six canisters of a deadly nerve agent were removed and replaced—it was only by dumb luck we discovered the switch."

Zoe couldn't stand it a minute longer. "Admiral, what exactly was taken?"

Stonegate and several of the other high-ranking officers were looking at her as if she deserved to get her mouth washed for speaking out of order. But she didn't give a damn. She needed to know. And Jake Robinson didn't seem to mind.

He met her gaze steadily, and she saw the answer in his eyes even before he opened his mouth to speak. It was the worst possible scenario she could imagine.

Trip X. *Six* canisters? Oh, God.

She realized she'd said the words aloud as he nodded. "Oh, God is right," he agreed with rather grim humor. "Dr. Lange, perhaps I could impose upon you to explain exactly what Triple X is, as well as our options for dealing with this little problem."

Little problem? Holy Mike, this was no *little* problem.

"Our options for dealing with it are extremely simple, sir," she said. "We have only one option—there are no choices here. We need to find and regain possession of the missing canisters. Believe me, gentlemen, Triple X is not something we want floating around out there. And particularly not *six* canisters' worth." She looked at the admiral. "How in God's name did this happen?"

"How's not important right now," he told her almost gently. "Right now we need to focus on *what*. Please continue, Doctor."

Zoe nodded. The thought of six canisters of Triple X set loose on the unsuspecting world made her blood feel like ice water as it flowed through her veins. It was terrifying. And she wasn't used to feeling terrified, even though her job was a frightening one most of the time. She spent hours upon hours learning the awful details of all the different weapons of mass destruction that were out there, ready to wreak havoc on the planet. But she'd learned to sleep dreamlessly at night, untouched by nightmares. She'd learned to sit impassively while reading reports of countries that tested chemical weapons on prisoners and the infirm. Women and children.

But six missing canisters of Trip X…

That scared her to death.

Still, she took a deep breath and stood up, because she'd also learned how to give tight, to-the-point, emotionless information even when she was badly shaken.

"Triple X is currently the nastiest chemical weapon in the world," she reported. "It's twenty times more potent than the nerve agent VX, and like VX, it kills by paralysis. Get a noseful of Triple X, gentlemen, and you choke to death, because your lungs, like the other muscles in your body, slowly seize up. Trip X or Tri X or T-X. It's all the same thing—airborne death."

Zoe moved around the table to the whiteboard that was on the wall behind Admiral Robinson. She picked up a marker and scribbled the two chemical components on the board, labeling them A and B.

"Trip X is a triple compound, which makes it far more stable to store and transport. It also makes it far more adaptable as a weapon." She pointed to the board. "These two compounds are stored dry, in powder forms that are, on their own, relatively harmless. But just like Betty Crocker's dromedary gingerbread mix, just add water. And then it's time to put your gas mask on. Instant poison. It's that easy, boys. You get me two balloons, about a teaspoonful each of Trip X compounds A and B, both harmless in dried form, remember, and a little H_2O laced with some acid or lye, and I can make a weapon that will take out this entire building—the entire Pentagon—as well as a good number of people on the street. Water sealed in one balloon, which is tucked inside of the other, which is also filled with air and that little bit of compounds A and B. A little acid or lye in the water eats through the rubber. Balloon springs a leak, water hits old A and B. It causes a chemical reaction that creates both a liquid and a gaseous form of Triple X, sending it out into the air, and eventually through the building's ventilation system, killing everyone who comes into contact with it."

The room was dead silent as she put the marker down.

Jake Robinson had taken his seat as she'd started her little lecture, turning to face her as she'd stood in front of the whiteboard. She was directly in front of him now. He was close enough to reach out and touch. And smell. He wore a subtle amount of Polo Sport—just enough to smell completely delicious.

She drew in a deep breath to steady herself—and to remind herself that although her world was fraught with evil, there *was* good in it, too. It held men like Jake Robinson.

"That's what two teaspoons of Trip X can do, gentlemen," she said. "As for six *canisters*..." She shook her head.

"I know it's hard to imagine a disaster of this magnitude," the admiral said quietly, "but in your opinion, how many thermos-size canisters would it take to wipe out this city?"

"Washington, D.C.?" Zoe chewed her lower lip. "Rough guess? Four? Depending on which way the wind was blowing."

He nodded. Clearly he'd already known that. And *six* were missing.

She looked around the room. "Any other questions?"

Senior Chief Becker lifted his hand. "You said our only option was to find the Triple X and regain possession of it. Is there any way to destroy it?"

"The two powders can be burned," she told him with a tight smile. "Just don't put the fire out with water."

Lieutenant O'Donlon raised his hand. "I have a question for Admiral Robinson. After two weeks, sir, you must have some idea who was behind the theft."

The admiral stood up. He towered over her by a solid six inches. She started toward her seat, but he caught her elbow, his fingers warm against her bare skin. "Stay," he commanded softly.

She nodded. "Of course, sir."

"We *have* identified the terrorist group that stole the Trip X," Jake told them, "and we also believe we've found the location of the missing canisters."

Everyone started talking at once.

"That's *great*," Zoe said.

"Yeah, well, it's not as great as it sounds," the admiral told her in a low voice. "Nothing's ever that easy."

"When do we ship out?" she asked just as quietly.

"I'm guessing our destination is somewhere in the Middle East."

"Guess again, Doctor. And maybe you should wait for all the facts and details before you agree to sign on. I've got a feeling you're not going to like this assignment very much."

Zoe met his steady gaze with an equal air of calm. "I don't need to know the details. I'm all yours—if you'll have me."

It wasn't until the words left her mouth that she realized how dreadfully suggestive they were.

But then she thought, why not? She was attracted to this man on virtually every level. Why not let him know it?

But something shifted in his eyes, something unidentifiable flitted across his face, and she realized in another flash that he wore a wedding band on his left hand.

"I'm sorry, sir," she said swiftly. "I didn't mean for that to sound—"

His smile was crooked. "It's okay, I know what you meant. It's a juicy assignment. But you won't be going to the Middle East." He turned and knocked on the table to regain the room's attention. "The terrorists who took the Triple X live right here in the United States. We've traced the canisters to their stronghold in Montana. They're U.S. citizens, although they're trying hard to secede from the union. They're led by a man named Christopher Vincent, and they call themselves the CRO, or the Chosen Race Organization."

The CRO.

The admiral glanced at her, and Zoe nodded. She knew all about the CRO. And this was what he'd meant about waiting to find out the details. The CRO was mysogynistic as well as being neo-Nazi, antigovernment and downright vicious. If Jake Robinson's plan was to send her into the CRO fortress as part of an undercover team assigned to retrieve the Trip X, it wasn't going to be fun. Women were treated little better than slaves in the CRO. They served, silently, tirelessly, unquestioningly. They were treated as possessions by their husbands and fathers. And they frequently were physically abused.

Jake was passing around satellite photos of the CRO headquarters—a former factory nestled in the hills about two miles outside of the tiny town of Belle, Montana. Zoe was familiar with the pictures, and with the extensive high-tech security the independently wealthy CRO leader, Christopher Vincent, had set up around the place.

If the lab in Arches had had even *half* the security of the CRO headquarters, this wouldn't have happened.

"We don't want to get in by force," the admiral was saying. "That's not even an option worth considering at this point."

Admiral Stonegate spoke up. "Why not simply evacuate the surrounding towns and bomb the hell out of the bastards?"

Admiral Forrest rolled his eyes. "Yeah, Jake," he said. "That worked so well at Waco."

"Surround 'em, then," Stonegate suggested, unthwarted and possibly even unaware of Mac Forrest's sarcasm. "Give our soldiers gas masks and let the CRO use the Triple X to wipe themselves out."

Admiral Robinson turned to Zoe as if he'd sensed her desire to respond.

"There are a number of reasons we wouldn't want to risk that," Zoe explained. "For one, if they waited for the right weather conditions—strong winds or even rain—the amount of Trip X they've got could take out more than just the immediately surrounding area. And then there's the matter of runoff. We don't know what would happen if that much Trip X got into the groundwater. We don't have enough data to know the dilution point—or, to be perfectly honest, if there even *is* a dilution point." The room was silent, and Zoe knew they were all imagining a lethal poison spreading through the groundwater of the country, making its way down to the Colorado River…. She took a deep breath. "I'll say it again, gentlemen, our sole option in this situation is to retrieve—or destroy—the six canisters of Triple X in its powder form."

"My plan is to continue surveillance," Admiral Robinson said. "I've already got teams in place, watching the CRO fort, trailing everyone who goes outside of their gates. We'll continue to do that, but we'll also be sending someone inside to track down the exact whereabouts of the Triple X. That's not going to be easy. Only CRO members are allowed in."

Senior Chief Becker lifted his hand. "Permission to speak, sir?"

"Please. If we're going to work together as a team, let's not stand on formality."

Becker nodded, but when he spoke, it was clear he chose his words carefully. "I think it's obvious that I'm not likely to be accepted as a member of the CRO any time in the near future. Seaman Taylor, here, either. And as for Crash—Lieutenant Hawken—his face may be the right shade of pale, but it's only been a year since he was on the national news. He's got to be too well-known. And while my intent is not to suggest that lieutenants O'Donlon, Jones and Shaw aren't capable of a mission of this magnitude, sir, it seems to me we might want to have a team leader with more experience. I'm sure either Captain Catalanotto or Lieutenant Commander McCoy of Alpha Squad would appreciate the chance to be included in this op."

The admiral listened carefully, waiting courteously until the senior chief had finished, despite the fact that

Zoe could tell from his body language that everyone he
wanted to be part of this operation was already right here
in this room.

"I appreciate your thoughts, Senior Chief. And I'm
aware of both Joe Cat and Blue McCoy's well-deserved
reputations." He paused, glancing around the room before
he casually dropped his bomb. "But I'll be leading this
team, hands-on, from out in the field. And I'll be the one
gaining entry into the CRO fort."

CHAPTER TWO

JAKE LIFTED HIS HANDS, halting the words of outrage, doubt and concern. He was too old to go into the field. He was too out of touch. It had been years since he'd last been in the real world. It was too dangerous. What if he were killed? What if, what if, what if?

"Here's the deal," he said. "I know Christopher Vincent. I met him about five years ago—he had a book published by the same company who released my wife's art books. We met at a party in New York, and I talked to him for a very long time. He's extremely dangerous, a complete megalomaniac. And it just so happens that he liked me. I know with a little help and the right cover story, I can get us inside."

"Admiral, this is highly irregular and—"

Jake cut Stonegate off. "And six missing canisters of T-X isn't?" He looked around the room. "I didn't call you here to ask your permission. *I* run the Gray Group. *I* call the shots. And this *is* a Gray Group mission. The president gave me this assignment with a direct order not to fail. Those of you who haven't worked for the Gray Group before need to know that I don't take that order lightly. What I need right now from the SEALs and from Dr. Lange is to know whether or not you want to be part of my team."

He hadn't even put the final *m* on *team* before Zoe Lange spoke up, her clear alto voice ringing out into the room. "I'm in and I'm behind you one hundred percent, Admiral."

She was just too cute, standing there in her blue jeans and blue-flowered T-shirt. She looked like a college student, but Jake knew better. She was Pat Sullivan's top operative. She'd come highly recommended. She was bright, she was beautiful and she was so freshly young it almost hurt to look at her.

Her hair was blond, long and straight. She wore it in classic California-girl style, with no bangs to soften her face. But she had a face that didn't need softening—it was already soft enough. She had baby-smooth skin, a face that was nearly a perfect oval, and equally perfect, delicately shaped features. From her fair skin and her light coloring, he'd expected her eyes to be blue. But they weren't. She had brown eyes. Not a light, hazel shade of brown, but deep, dark chocolate brown.

Was it possible for someone with eyes that dark to be a natural blonde? He knew exactly how to find out.

I'm all yours—if you'll have me.

Don't go there, pal! She hadn't meant it that way.

Jake focused his attention on his SEAL team. Harvard Becker. He'd never worked with the African-American senior chief, but when it came to electronic surveillance, he was the best. And right now Jake needed the best.

Seamen First Class Wesley Skelly, short and skinny, and Bobby Taylor, built double-wide, could've been any of the enlisted guys he knew back in Nam. Loyal to the bitter end, they drank too much, played too hard and were always right where you needed them, when you needed them. Right now, their loyalty was to Harvard, though, and they waited for their senior chief to nod his acceptance before they, too, agreed to sign on.

Lieutenant Billy Hawken, nicknamed Crash, was Jake's wife, Daisy's, cousin. Jake had helped raise him from the time the boy was ten. He thought of him as a son, but there was real reservation in the kid's eyes as he gazed at Jake across the table. *Are you sure you know what you're doing?* He could read the words in Billy's eyes as clearly as if he'd spoken them aloud.

Jake nodded. Yeah. He knew exactly what he was doing. He'd thought about it long and hard. This was more than just an excuse to get back into the real world. Although—he couldn't kid himself—he did want to do it just a little too much. Still, the timing was right and he trusted himself, trusted his instincts.

Billy turned to look at Lieutenant Mitchell Shaw, sitting on his right. Mitch and Billy had both worked for Jake's Gray Group more times than any of them could count. Mitch had been there at the conception of the group. He'd been part of the first mission. At five feet ten, he was shorter than most of the other SEALs, lean and compact, with long, dark hair and hazel eyes that gave nothing away.

Including his doubt.

His silence broadcast that, though, loud and clear.

Jake knew how Mitch thought, and he could practically see the progression that led to the lieutenant's short nod. He was in—but only because Mitch believed he and the rest of the SEALs would be able to keep Jake out of harm's way.

Jake was going to have to set him straight, but not here, not now.

"I'm in," Lieutenant Luke O'Donlon announced, his words echoed by Lieutenant Harlan Jones. Lucky and Cowboy. Both blond and blue-eyed, Jake had chosen them based on their fair-skinned complexions as well as their reputations. Both were hotshots, that title well earned, and both would be accepted into the CRO as easily as possible, if they had to go that way.

And that was that. He had his team. The SEALs had all agreed, if not quite as enthusiastically as Zoe Lange.

"Gather your gear, gentlemen—and Doctor," Jake said, glancing at the young woman. "And prepare to meet at Andrews in two hours. Bring a sweater or two. We're going to Montana."

Senior Chief Harvard Becker was the first to reach the door. He hit the buzzer that signaled the guards in the outer chambers and the hatch swung open. The SEALs cleared out, none of them uttering another word.

They probably knew Admiral Stonegate would handle all the uttering necessary.

"I will be registering my official protest," he told Jake stiffly. "An admiral's place is not in the field. You are far too valuable to the U.S. Navy to put yourself into a position of such high risk that—"

"Didn't you hear anything Dr. Lange said?" Jake asked the older man. "With the magnitude of this kind of potential disaster, we're all expendable, Ron."

"It's been years since you've been in the field."

"I've been keeping up," Jake told him evenly.

"Mentally, perhaps, but physically, there's just no way—"

Since he'd gotten out of the hospital, Jake had put himself into the best physical shape he'd been in since Vietnam. "I can keep up physically, too. Ron, you know, fifty-three's just not that old—"

"Dammit, this is all John Glenn's fault."

Jake had to laugh. "Excuse me for laughing in your face, pal, but that's ridiculous."

Stonegate was offended. "I *will* be registering a protest."

"You do that, Admiral," Jake said, tired of the noise. "But not until this mission is over. Everything you've heard today in this room is top secret. You leak *any* of it—even in the form of a protest, and I will throw your narrow-minded, pointy ass in jail."

Well, that did it.

Stonegate stormed out.

Mac Forrest followed. "And I'll help," he murmured to Jake with a wink. "Anything I can do, Jake, you just let me know."

The room was finally empty.

Jake drew in a deep breath and let it all out in a rush as he collected and organized his notes and papers.

That had gone far better than he'd hoped. He'd been sure his age was going to be an insurmountable issue, that none of his first choice of SEALs would accept the assignment. He'd gone so far as to have his hair colored for the occasion, covering the silver at his temples with his regular shade of dark brown. He'd figured looking as young as possible couldn't hurt.

And it *had* made him look younger, there was no doubt about it.

He'd liked the way his colored hair looked more than he cared to admit. But he had admitted it. He'd forced himself to confront the issue. He hated the thought of growing old. He'd fought it ever since he'd turned thirty with every breath he took, cutting red meat and high-cholesterol-inducing foods out of his diet. Eating health foods and seaweeds and exercising religiously every day. Aerobics. Weights. Running.

He hadn't lied to Ron Stonegate. He *was* in top-notch, near-perfect shape, even for a man fifteen years his junior.

There was only one type of exercise he no longer participated in regularly and that was—

Jake closed his briefcase with a snap and turned around and found himself staring directly into Zoe Lange's eyes.

Sex.

Yes, it had definitely been nearly three years since he'd last had sex.

Jake swallowed and forced a smile. "God, I'm sorry," he said. "How long have you been standing there? I didn't realize you were still in the room."

She shifted her briefcase to her other hand, and Jake realized that she was nervous. He made Pat Sullivan's top operative nervous.

The feeling was extremely mutual—but for what had to be an entirely different reason. He found her attractive, college-girl getup and all. *Much* too attractive.

"I just wanted to thank you again for including me in this assignment," she said, all but stammering. She was trying so hard to be cool, but he knew otherwise.

"Let's see if you're still thanking me after you get an up-close look at the CRO compound." Jake headed for the door to get away from her subtle, freshly sweet scent. She wasn't wearing perfume. He had to guess it was her hair. Hair that would slip between his fingers like silk. If he were close enough to touch it. Which he wasn't.

"I've spent years in the Middle East. At least I won't have to walk around wearing a veil in Montana." She followed, almost tripping over her own feet to keep up. "I'm just…I'm thrilled to be working with you, sir."

He stopped in the corridor just outside the third door. There was no doubt about it. "You've read Scooter's damn book."

For seventeen years, that book had been coming back to haunt him. Scoot had written his memoirs about his time in Nam. Who knew the monosyllabic, conversationally challenged SEAL was a budding Hemingway? But he'd written *Laughing in the Face of Fire* both eloquently and gracefully. It was one of the few books on Nam that Jake had actually almost liked—except for the fact that Scooter had made Jake out to be some kind of demigod.

Zoe Lange had probably read the damn thing when she was twelve or thirteen—or at some other god-awful impressionable age—and no doubt had been carrying around some crazy idea of Lieutenant Jake Robinson, superhero, ever since.

"Well, yeah, I've read it," she told him. "Of course I've read it." She was looking at him the way a ten-year-old boy would look at Mark McGwire or Sammy Sosa.

He hated it. Hero worship without a modicum of lust. What the hell had happened to him?

He'd turned fifty, that's what. And children like Zoe Lange—who hadn't even been born during his first few tours in Vietnam—thought of him as someone's grandpa.

"Scooter exaggerated," he said shortly, starting down the hall toward the elevators. He was mad at himself for giving a damn. So what if this girl didn't see him as a man? It was better that way, considering they were going to be working together, considering he was *not* interested in getting involved with her. *"Extensively."*

"Even if only ten percent of the stories he told were true, you would still be a hero."

"There's no such thing as a Vietnam war hero."

"You don't really believe that."

"Yeah? You can't be a hero alone in a room. You need the crowd. The ticker-tape parade. The gorgeous blonde rushing the convertible to kiss you silly. I know—I've seen pictures of U.S. soldiers coming home after the Second World War. *They* sure as hell didn't get egged by college students."

"The Vietnam era was a confusing time in history."

Jake winced. *"History.* Jeez, it wasn't *that* long ago. Make me feel old, why don't you?"

"I don't think you're old, Admiral."

"Okay, then start by calling me Jake. You're on my team, we're going to get to know each other pretty well by the time this is over." Jake stopped at the elevators and punched his security code into the keypad. "And I am old. I've been around a half a century, and I've seen more than my share of terrible, violent, monstrous acts. The things people do to each other appalls me. But I'm going to use that in my favor. Everything I've seen and learned is going to help me keep Chris Vincent and the CRO from doing some awful, permanent damage to this country that I love."

She laughed. Her teeth were white and straight. "And you claim you're not a hero." The elevator doors slid open and she followed him inside. "I think you're wrong. I think you *can* be a hero alone in a room. I think you would've shied away from the ticker-tape parade anyway."

"Are you kidding? I would've eaten it up with a spoon." He punched in the code that would take them to the ground floor. "Look, Doc, I appreciate your support, I do. Just…don't believe everything you read in Scooter's book."

"Four hundred and twenty-seven."

"Four hundred and twenty-seven what?"

"Men."

His first thought was surely a sign that he'd had sex on his mind far too frequently of late. But there was no innuendo in Zoe Lange's face, no hint of a suggestion in her eyes that she wanted Jake to be number four hundred and twenty-eight in a very, very long line. In fact, such a long line, it was preposterous. He tried not to laugh and failed. "I cannot begin to guess what you're talking about. I mean, I'm trying, but…" He laughed again at his own cluelessness. "You've lost me, Doctor."

"My father was number four hundred and twenty-seven," she said quietly. "He's one of Jake's Boys."

Jake didn't know what to say.

It happened sometimes. Someone would come up to him with emotion brimming in their eyes and shake his hand, whispering that their husband or son or father was one of Jake's Boys. As if he still had some kind of hold over them. Or as if, upon saving their lives, he'd somehow become responsible for them until the end of time.

He'd learned to be courteous and brief. He'd shake their hand, touch their shoulder, smile into their eyes and pretend he remembered Private This or Corporal That. The truth was, he didn't remember any of them. The faces stuck in his mind were only of the men he hadn't been able to save. The men who died, who were already dead. Empty eyes. All those awful, empty eyes...

"Sergeant Matthew Lange," she told him. "He was with the forty-fifth—"

"I don't remember him." He couldn't lie to this woman. Not if she was going to be on his team.

She didn't even blink. "I didn't expect you to, sir. He was only one out of hundreds." She smiled and reached out to take his hand, to squeeze his fingers. "You know, I owe *my* life to you, as well. I wasn't born until a year after he came home."

Which meant her father was probably younger than Jake was.

Perfect.

His one completely loyal ally, the one person on his team who honestly didn't have any reservations about his age or ability, had just managed to make him feel undeniably old.

And not just old, but *nasty* and old. Like some kind of complete degenerate.

As he gazed into her perfect brown eyes, as she held

on to his hand and he felt the warmth and strength of her fingers, the smoothness of her skin against his palm, he forced himself to admit that for the first time in the two and a half years since Daisy had died, he'd finally met a woman he could imagine himself making love to.

And he didn't want that. He didn't want to imagine himself capable of wanting anyone but the only woman he'd ever loved, the woman he *still* loved. But he couldn't deny that he missed sex, that he wanted sex. And he didn't know how to reconcile his physical needs with the indisputable fact that Daisy was forever gone.

Forever, permanently gone. And she wasn't coming back.

For just a second, he let himself really look at Zoe Lange. She was brilliant, she was brave, she was tough, yet her beauty held a sweetness to which he was powerfully drawn. Her eyes were alight with intelligent wit, her mouth quick to smile. Her laughter was contagious, and her body...

Jake let himself look, for just a second, at Dr. Zoe Lange's near-perfect body. Her legs were long, her jeans slightly loose on her hips and thighs. She was not particularly tall, not particularly short, but average wasn't a word that could ever be used to describe her. Her arms were well toned, lithe. She was trim in all the right places, and, God, all right, *yes,* he *was* a breast man, and she had a body that pushed all his buttons in a very big way. Her T-shirt clung to her full figure enticingly, making her demure little flowered print look decadent and sexy.

In a flash, in his mind's eye, Jake saw her, tumbled back on his bed with him, her T-shirt and jeans gone, his mouth locked on hers, her perfect breasts filling his palms, his body buried deeply inside her as they moved together and...

Oh God, oh God, oh *God.* Sheer wanting slammed into

him so hard he nearly gasped aloud. But that wanting was followed just as quickly by guilt and shame.

He still loved Daisy. How could he still love Daisy and want someone else so badly?

Sweet Lord, he missed her so much.

The hole in his gut that he'd been trying to heal for nearly three years tore wide open.

And he released Zoe's hand and took a step backward, bumping awkwardly against the elevator wall. He realized almost instantly that he was well on his way to becoming completely aroused. Ah, jeez, terrific. Just what he needed—a souvenir from his little guilt trip.

He didn't know whether to laugh or cry.

So he did neither, casually holding his briefcase in front of him.

Zoe kept her eyes carefully on the numbers above the elevator door, and he knew she'd seen something in his eyes that embarrassed her. No wonder—he'd been eyeing her like the hungry old fox checking out the gingerbread girl. Good job, Robinson. Way to feel even older and nastier. And somehow it was even worse since his attraction was clearly one-sided.

But when she turned toward him, she was the one who apologized. "I'm sorry," she said. "I didn't mean to embarrass you. You must get approached by people all the time and—"

"I like it when they've done something really right with their lives—the way your father obviously did. He must be very proud of you. God knows I'd be proud as hell if you were *my* kid." He tried his best to sound fatherly. But all he sounded was pathetic.

She smiled tentatively. "Well, thanks."

The elevator opened, and this time Jake stood back, courteously letting her out first. She looked both ways, up and down the deserted corridor as the elevator doors closed behind them.

"Exit to the street's down that way." Jake pointed. "Take the—"

"First right," she said. "I know, thanks. Listen, Admiral—"

"Jake," he said. "Please."

"Actually, Admiral works a little better for me."

"All right," he said quickly. "That's fine. It's not like I'm ordering you to call me Jake or anything. It's not like—"

"I know." She tried to meet his gaze, but couldn't hold it this time. She was nervous again. "I was just... I can't help but wonder about your willingness to put yourself at risk. I mean, you've earned the right to sit back and command safely from behind a desk, sir. And I can't imagine your, um, wife is very happy about your decision to go back into the field. Particularly after that assassination attempt a few years ago. You were in the hospital for months."

Jake had been around long enough to recognize a fishing expedition when he heard one. But what information exactly was Zoe Lange fishing for? Was she looking to find his motivation for taking the mission or his reason for looking at her as if he wanted to eat her alive?

He had no need to hide anything from her—well, except for the extremely unprofessional fact that nearly every time he looked at her, he pictured her naked. And even if thoughts of Daisy didn't stop that, all he really had to do was think about those missing canisters of T-X. *That* cooled him down pretty damn instantly.

"I know that's an extremely personal question," she continued quickly, "and you can tell me it's none of my business if you want and—"

"Daisy, my wife, died of cancer," he told her quietly. "It'll be three years ago this Christmas."

"Oh," she said. "I'm so sorry. I didn't know."

"And I think you're probably right. If she were still alive, I'd be thinking long and hard about the risks of this mission. But even if she were still alive, I wouldn't be able to avoid the fact that I've got a connection to Christopher Vincent. I know I can get into the CRO's inner sanctions. It's just, this way, it makes the choice a complete no-brainer."

She was looking at him with compassion in her eyes, and he glanced away, unable to bear the thought of looking closer and seeing her pity.

"You better go pack," he said brusquely. "We go wheels up in ninety-eight minutes. If you make us wait for you, trust me, the team will never let you live it down."

"Don't worry, Jake," she said. "I'll be the first one on the plane."

He watched her walk away, and before she took that right corner, she looked back and gave him a smile and a little wave.

And it wasn't until he was in his office, changing out of his ice-cream suit and into black BDUs, that he realized she'd called him Jake.

CHAPTER THREE

ZOE ITCHED TO CALL PETER.

Five months ago, she would have. She would have called on a secured line and she would have said, "What does it mean—a man's been a widower for nearly three years, and he still wears his wedding ring?"

Peter would've said, "That's obvious. He uses the ring to keep women from coming too close."

And *she* would have said, "I think he still loves her."

And Peter would've snorted and said, "Love's a myth. He just hasn't met anyone who could replace his dead wife. But you better believe when he does, that ring will come off faster than you can spit. The hell with him. What do you say you and I meet in Boston next weekend and set the Ritz-Carlton aflame?"

But that's what Peter would've said five months ago. Before he'd discovered that love was indeed *not* a myth.

Her name was Marita and she was a TV news anchor based in Miami. She was of Cuban descent and lovely, but Zoe wasn't even remotely jealous. Well, maybe she was a *little* jealous—but only of the fact that Peter, restless, hungry, insatiable, cynical superagent Peter McBride had finally found complete inner peace.

Zoe was jealous of that. She'd liked Peter—she'd even loved him more than a little, but she knew just from one conversation with him after he'd met Marita that he finally had a shot at true happiness.

And Peter deserved that.

Zoe had liked talking to him, liked the way he could always make her laugh. And she had liked making love with him the few times a year that their work for the Agency brought them into each other's presence.

But she'd known from the start there could be no permanence in their relationship. She was too like him. Too restless, too hungry, too damned insatiable, too jaded by a world bent on destroying itself.

She hadn't spoken to Peter in five months, assuming his new bride wouldn't appreciate his getting phone calls from a former lover. But she missed his friendship. She missed talking to him.

She missed the sex, too. It had been safe. She'd never once been in danger of completely losing her heart.

"So," she said to Peter, even though he wasn't there, "what does it mean that I'm packing my sexiest underwear and this little black nightgown?"

"To wear in Montana in September?" he would have mused, lifting one elegant eyebrow. "You're in trouble, Lange."

"You wouldn't believe the way he looked at me in that elevator." Zoe closed her eyes, momentarily melting just from the heat of the memory. "Dear God, I *am* in trouble."

"Doing your boss is bad office politics," Peter would have reminded her. "But on the other hand, he's not really your boss, is he? Pat Sullivan is. So, go for him. You've been fantasizing about the guy for years—how could you not go for him? And if he's looking at you like that... I'm surprised you didn't make a move right then and there. It wouldn't've taken much to disable the security cams in the elevator and..."

"He'd been giving me go-away signals from the moment we met." She pulled her warmest sweaters from her closet shelf. Her warmest sweaters—and her skimpiest tank tops. Shorts. Her bathing suit even. It was a bikini— Rio cut. Not quite a thong, but not quite demure, either. Maybe she'd get lucky and they'd have Indian summer. "Besides, at the time I thought he was still married."

"Ooh, there are those upright, golden, Girl Scout morals, shining through again." When Peter said it like that, it was as if it were something she should be ashamed of.

"He seemed so embarrassed by the fact that he finds me attractive. As if it made him feel, you know, *guilty.*" She'd come full circle. "He definitely still loves her. In his mind, he *is* still married."

"So what are you going to do?" Peter would've asked.

Zoe zipped and shouldered her bag. "He's a really good guy, Pete. I'm going to try to be his friend."

He'd always hated it when she called him Pete. "And for that you definitely need all that underwear from Victoria's Secret?"

"Six missing *canisters* of Trip X," she said, and Peter's evil spirit was instantly exorcised, instantly gone.

She had a job to do. A very, very important, life-or-death job.

Zoe grabbed her briefcase, grabbed her laptop and locked her apartment door without looking back.

DAY TWO. OH-THREE-HUNDRED.

Jake had been out most of the night, silently creeping along the perimeter of the CRO compound with Cowboy Jones. Lieutenant Jones's father was a rear admiral. Jake had figured that out of everyone on the team, Jones would be most at ease with buddying up with a man of his rank.

He'd been wrong.

Ever since they'd inserted in Montana, his entire team had been treating him with kid gloves. Let me carry that for you, Admiral. I'll take care of that, Admiral. Why don't you just stand aside and let me handle that, Admiral. Sit down, Admiral. You're getting in the way.

Well, okay. No one had said that last bit, but Jake knew they'd been thinking it.

Even Billy Hawken, the closest thing to a son Jake had ever been blessed with, had pulled Jake aside to tell him in a low voice that the technological advances in the surveillance gear in just the past few years had changed both the hardware and the software completely. If Jake needed any help understanding the readouts or if he needed any assistance with the equipment, Billy was standing by.

And no doubt if Jake needed helped cutting his food, Billy would do that for him, too.

What, was he suddenly ninety years old? And hell, even if he *was* ninety years old, that didn't automatically mean his brain had turned to oatmeal.

As they'd done the sneak and peek, Jones kept asking him if he'd seen enough, if he'd wanted to turn around and head back to camp.

The night had been crisply cold, but Jake had wanted to examine every square inch of the CRO compound he could see from the outer fence. He'd squinted through his night-vision glasses until his head had ached, and then he'd squinted some more. He'd done a complete circuit, and he'd lingered longer than he otherwise might have at the main gate, simply to show Jones he was capable of doing a complete, thorough job.

Except Lucky and Wes had been sent after them, to see what was holding them up. Jake and Cowboy had run into the pair on the trail. It was obvious that his team had sent them out as a search-and-rescue party to drag the old admiral in from wherever he'd gotten himself entangled in barbed wire.

It was discouraging, to say the least.

Jake needed these men to trust him. He needed their support, one hundred percent.

Because he *was* going in there. He'd figured out a plan—and Zoe Lange's somewhat different surveillance tonight had given him cause to believe it would work.

She sat across from him now, in the main trailer.

Bobby and Wes had gotten hold of four beat-up old recreational vehicles that afternoon, and the SEALs had already outfitted them with enough surveillance equipment to make a destroyer sit low in the water. They were parked in a KOA campground fifteen miles south of Belle—just a group of happy campers, in town to do some hunting.

Zoe stood up and opened the refrigerator, helping herself to a can of soda. Something without caffeine. She didn't look tired despite the late hour, but then again, he hadn't expected her to.

Jake had been taking care to keep his distance from her from the moment he'd stepped on the plane at Andrews. He hadn't gotten too close, had barely let himself look at her. But he allowed himself to watch her now as she spoke.

"The name of the bar is Mel's, and it's owned by Hal—Harold—Francke, spelled with a c-k-e. I didn't meet him. Apparently he doesn't come in often on Wednesday nights. The waitress I did meet was named Cindy Allora. She said Hal's always looking for new hired help." She smiled. "I guess he's a dirty old man with a wandering pair of hands, and the turnover rate of waitresses at Mel's is high."

A dirty old man. Jake tried not to wince visibly as she sat at the table.

Zoe looked different tonight. The flower-print T-shirt was gone. She was dressed all in black. Slim black flares, black boots, black hooded sweatshirt that slipped off one shoulder to reveal her smooth tanned skin and a body-hugging black tank top, its thin straps unable to hide the straps of her black bra.

She was wearing quite a bit of makeup, too. Dark liner around her eyes, thick mascara, deep red on her lips. She wore her hair down, loose and windswept around her shoulders.

She looked dangerous. Wild. Completely capable. And sexy as hell. Hal Francke would hire her on the spot. And then he'd be all over her.

"Maybe this isn't such a good idea," Jake said. "Maybe you could get a job working checkout at the supermarket."

She lifted an eyebrow lazily. "And I could communicate with you by semaphore flags when you came into town?" She leaned forward slightly. "You know as well as I do the CRO men come to town and go to the bar. Only the women go into the supermarket."

Jake refused to let himself look down her shirt. He kept his gaze staunchly focused on her dark brown eyes. "It just…it seems unfair. A scientist of your knowledge and ability. I'm not only asking you to wait tables, but virtually guaranteeing you're going to get groped as well."

She laughed. "You haven't worked with women much, have you, sir?"

"Not as team leader, no."

"Let's just say if it happens, it won't be the first time I've been groped while on assignment. And if letting Hal Francke cop a feel in the back alley helps keep me where I'll be of most assistance to you…" She spread her hands in a shrug.

Jake laughed in dismay. "God. You're serious."

"It's no big deal." She took a sip of her soda. "You know, Jake, I just don't take sex as seriously as I think you do."

Sex. God. How did their conversation get onto *that* topic? She was more than just dressed differently tonight, she was looking at him differently, too. Just a few days ago he'd felt bad because there hadn't been a bit of attraction in her eyes. Now she was holding his gaze rather pointedly. Now she was smiling just a little bit too warmly.

It made him nervous as hell.

And they were talking about sex. But he couldn't steer the conversation in a safer direction. Not yet. First he had to ask. "Are you telling me you'd *sleep* with this guy?"

"I think of my body as just another of my assets," she told him, a small smile playing about the corners of her lips. "I don't mind showing it off if it gets me closer to my goal. It's amusing, actually, to see the way men can be manipulated—" she leaned closer again and lowered her voice "—just by the whispered suggestion of sex." She laughed, and her eyes seemed to sparkle. "Look at you. Even *you* aren't immune."

"Me? I'm… I'm…" His face was heating in a blush, as if he were fourteen again. How did she know? He'd been purposely playing it super cool. Mr. Extra Laid Back. It had required superhuman effort, but he *hadn't* looked down her shirt. His gaze slid there now, and he quickly shut his eyes. "I'm only human." Damn, and he'd been trying so hard not to be.

"Try human *male*," she said, laughter in her voice. "I swear, men fall into one of two categories. You have the men who are totally controlled by sex, and you have the men—like you—who spend all their time trying to protect women from the men who are totally controlled by sex. Either way, it's a complete manipulation."

She stood up, peeling off her sweatshirt. "I walk into Mel's bar dressed in my little tank top. You're sitting at the bar, and maybe you're not controlled by sex per se.

Maybe you *don't* catch sight of me in the mirror and try to imagine me naked."

Jake did his best not to react. How could she know? There was no way she could have read his mind.

She sat next to him, sliding onto the bench beside him. "Maybe I sit down next to you and you glance over, and you think, gee, what's that nice woman doing in here alone? Maybe you don't notice what I'm wearing, maybe it has no effect on you, and you think, gee, she has pretty eyes." Her smile clearly said, *yeah, right.* "And you look up, and you notice about five big drunk guys getting ready to approach me, and you think, she's not going to like it when those clowns put their hands all over her. And you stand up, you move closer. You're ready to save the day."

She smiled. "Like it or not, notice 'em or not, babe, you've just been manipulated by my breasts."

Jake had to laugh. He put his head in his hands.

"God, the awful thing is that you're absolutely right. I just never thought of it that way." He looked at her from between his fingers. "Look, we need to focus on how you're going to get that waitressing job at Mel's, and what's going to happen after you're established there."

She stood up, slipping her sweatshirt over her shoulders. "Cindy invited me to a party at her friend Monica's house on Saturday afternoon. Hal Francke is going to be there. I thought it would be smart to manipulate him into approaching and asking me to work for him. That way if anyone in the CRO gets suspicious and starts checking into me, they'll find out I'm just another girl Hal found at some party. It's a little less suspect than if I go into Mel's and fill out a job application."

"It's also a little less certain," Jake pointed out. "I mean, you don't know for sure he's going to offer you the job."

Zoe gave him a look. "It's a hot tub party, Jake. He'll offer me the job."

Hot tub. Jake cleared his throat. Hot tub.

"Don't worry, I'll keep my bathing suit on," she assured him with a smile.

Somehow that didn't make him feel any better.

"So after I get this job waitressing at Mel's, what then?" she asked. "I mean, obviously, I'll be in place to act as a go-between for any communication between you and the rest of the team."

He nodded. "It might be a while before I can come into town. I know the CRO rules are pretty complicated—I might have to pass some sort of loyalty test before I have free run of the place. But once I do come into the bar, I'll, um…" He managed a weak smile. "Well, I'll hit on you. I'm sorry—but I think that's the cleanest way to explain why we're going to spend so much time whispering into each other's ears. If you could set it up—tell people you're a little older than you really are, they might believe there could be something between us."

Zoe's heartbeat tripled in time. Jake Robinson was going to hit on her. They were going to spend time cozied up together. True, it was only to pass information, but she could go far on a fantasy like that. She kept her voice low and controlled. "I think we can make them believe we're attracted to each other. Our difference in ages is not that big a deal."

"I'm old enough to be your father."

"So what? You can pretend you're going through some kind of midlife crisis, and I'll let everyone know I prefer more mature men. Experienced men." Gorgeous, incredibly buff, blue-eyed, heroic men…

"I just don't want it to come off as such an obvious setup. You know, the first time I come into the bar… A beautiful young woman like you…"

"Jake, the first time you go into that bar, the women are going to be lining up to meet you. I'll have to fight to get to the front of that line." She laughed in disbelief at the look on his face. "You'd think after fifty-three years of looking into the bathroom mirror every morning, you might've noticed you're the most handsome man on the planet."

His laughter was tinged with embarrassment. God, he really didn't know what he looked like, did he?

"Well, thanks for your vote of confidence, but—"

Zoe wanted to reach for his hand to squeeze it, to reassure him that this would work, but she didn't dare touch him.

"I'll set everything up," she said. "I'll set up the fact that I'm looking to have a fling, too."

"Not just a fling," he corrected her almost apologetically. "I'm going to need a way to get you into the CRO compound. I'll need your expertise in there to help me find the missing canisters of T-X. And the only way for a woman to get inside is…"

"Through marriage."

Her laughter sounded almost giddy to her ears. This assignment was a dream assignment to start with, Hal Francke's anticipated groping aside. She was working with Jake Robinson, the man who had always been her own personal poster model for the word *hero*. Whenever she'd imagined her perfect man, he'd always had Jake's steely nerve, his long list of achievements, and, yes, his deep blue eyes.

And now this dream assignment was going to have her pretend she was marrying her hero. He was going to have to kiss her, hold her in his arms. To *marry* her. Could it possibly get *any* better?

Yes, he could kiss her, and mean it. And maybe, just maybe she could make that happen.

"It won't be real," he told her hastily, misreading her laughter. "The way I understand it, Christopher Vincent performs any wedding ceremonies among his followers. There's no paperwork or licenses filled out. They don't believe in state intervention when it comes to marriage."

He looked at his hands, at the wedding ring he wore.

"It won't be real," he said again, as if he were trying to convince himself of that fact.

Zoe sat across from him, her elation instantly subdued. "Are you sure you want to do this?" she asked him quietly. "You'll have to take off your wedding ring."

Jake looked at his left hand again. "I know." He fingered it with his thumb. "That's okay. It doesn't really mean anything anyway. We were only married a few days before she died."

Wait a minute… "Crash told me you and Daisy were together for just short of forever."

"Daisy didn't believe in marriage," he told her simply. "She only married me at the end, because it was the only thing she had left to give me." He took off the ring, letting it spin on the table in front of him.

"You must really miss her."

"Yeah. She was pretty incredible." He caught the ring deftly, midspin, and slipped it into his pants pocket. "I should probably get used to not wearing this."

He looked so sad, Zoe ached for him. "You know, Jake—we could think of another way to do this."

He met her eyes. "I suppose I could call Pat Sullivan and see if Gregor Winston's available to take over for you."

Zoe reacted. "Gregor's not *half* as qualified as—"

Jake was smiling at her. "As you are," he finished for her. "Yeah, that's why I requested you."

"But he's a man," she pointed out unnecessarily. "He could get into the CRO without having to marry you."

"Thank goodness." Jake's smile faded as he gazed at her. "Look, I'm all right with this, Zoe. But if it makes *you* feel uncomfortable…"

She looked at his hands, now ringless. He had big hands, with neat nails and broad, strong fingers. She even found his hands outrageously attractive.

Uncomfortable was not the word to describe the way she felt about this assignment.

She tried to make a joke. "Are you kidding? I have no problem letting Hal Francke grope me. Why should it bother me if I have to let you do the same?"

It wasn't true. The part about Hal. Despite what she'd told Jake, she hated it when men touched her, when she had to use her body in any way while on the job. But there were times when dressing seductively got her further. And as for letting men touch her…

She'd learned to pretend it was nothing, to be flip about it. She was a tough, professional Agency operative. She shouldn't give a damn about something as meaningless as that. And although she also pretended her casualness extended all the way to the act of sex, she'd always drawn the line well before that. Always.

"Are you telling me you'd *sleep* with this guy?" Jake had asked about Hal Francke.

She'd purposely sidestepped his question, avoiding a direct answer. It wouldn't do her a bit of good to make her team leader believe she needed to be protected. As nice as it might be in some fantasy to have Jake ready to rush to her side, to protect her from the Hal Franckes of the world, this was reality.

And if he thought she was weak—in any way—she'd spend this entire mission inside the safety of the surveillance van.

"I'm going to have to make it look real," he told her. "You know, when I come into the bar."

"I will, too," she told him. "So don't freak out when I grab your butt, all right?"

He laughed, but it was decidedly halfhearted, and she knew what he was thinking. The last woman to grab his butt had been his wife.

Zoe pushed herself up and out of the booth, tossing her empty soda can into the recycling bin. "Do you want..." She stopped. It seemed so forward of her to ask—and that wasn't even considering her suggestion implied a lack of ability on the admiral's part.

But he could read her mind. "You're afraid I'm going to get stiff," he said, then winced realizing his poor word choice. "Tense up," he quickly corrected himself. "You're afraid I'm going to tense up."

Zoe couldn't keep from laughing, and Jake joined in, shaking his head. "Jeez," he said. "This *is* awkward, isn't it?"

She held out her hand to him. "Come here."

He hesitated, just looking at her, a curious mix of emotions in his eyes. He shook his head. "Zoe, I don't think..."

"Just come here."

With a sigh, he slid from the booth, the powerful muscles in his arms standing out in sharp relief as he pushed himself up. Dressed the way he was in a body-hugging black T-shirt and black BDU pants, she could see he was in better shape than most men half his age. He looked like some kind of dream come true. Why couldn't he see that?

"I don't need to, you know, practice this," he said, even as he took her hand. "It's not like it's something I've forgotten how to do."

"But this way, the mystery's gone," she told him. "This

way you don't have to spend any time in the bar thinking about the fact that Daisy was the last woman you held in your arms. This way you'll be able to concentrate on making it look real, on getting the job done."

She slipped her arms around him, but he just stood there, arms at his side, swearing very, very softly.

"Come on, Jake," she said. "This is just make-believe." She said it as much to remind herself of that fact.

He smelled too good. He felt too good. His body fit too perfectly with hers.

And slowly, very slowly, he put his arms around her.

Zoe rested her head on his shoulder, aware of the solidness of his chest against her breasts, the tautness of his thighs against hers, the complete warmth of his arms.

He slowly rested his cheek against her head, and she felt him sigh.

"You all right?" she whispered.

"Yeah." He pulled back, away from her, forcing a smile. "Thank you. This was a...smart idea. Because I *am* a little tense, aren't I?"

"You should probably kiss me."

He looked as if she'd suggested he use the neighbor's cat for target practice. "Oh, I don't think—"

"Jake, I'm sorry, but you are not a *little* tense, you are *so* tense. If you come into that bar and hold me so politely like that, as if I'm your *grandmother...*"

He couldn't argue, because he knew it was true. "I'm not sure I'm ready to—"

"Then maybe we better come up with another plan. Maybe we should be trying to figure out a way to get Cowboy or Lucky into the CRO compound. If you can't handle this—"

Something sparked in his eyes. "I didn't say I couldn't handle this. I meant that I wasn't ready to deal with this *right now.*"

"If you can't do it now, how're you going to do it in a week or two?" she asked. "Come on, Jake. Try again. And this time hold me like you want to be inside me."

The something that had sparked in his eyes flared into fire. "Well, hell, that shouldn't be too hard to do."

He pulled her to him almost roughly and held her tightly, his thigh between her legs, her body anchored against him by his hand on her rear end.

She felt almost faint. "Much better," she said weakly. "Now kiss me."

He didn't move. He just gazed at her, that hypnotizing heat smoldering in his eyes.

After several long moments, he still didn't move, so she kissed him.

It was a small kiss, a delicate caress of his beautiful mouth with her lips. And he *still* didn't move.

But he was breathing hard as she pulled back to look at him, as if he'd just run a five-mile race. His eyes were the most brilliant shade of blue she'd ever seen in her life.

She kissed him again, and this time he finally moved.

He lowered his head and caught her mouth with his and then, God, he was kissing her. *Really* kissing her. *Soul* kissing her.

She angled her head to kiss him even more deeply, pulling his tongue hard into her mouth, wanting more, *more*.

He tasted like sweetened coffee, like everything she'd ever wanted, like a lifetime of fantasies finally coming true.

He pressed her even more tightly against him as she clung to him, as still he kissed her, harder, deeper, endlessly, his passion—like hers—skyrocketing completely off the scale, his hands skimming her body as she strained to get closer, closer….

And then Jake finally tore his mouth away from hers. "My God." He looked completely shocked, thoroughly stunned.

Zoe still held on to him tightly, her knees too weak to support her weight. "That was…very believable."

"Yeah," he agreed, breathing hard. "Very believable."

"Good to know we can make that seem…so believable."

He pulled free from her embrace and turned away. "Yeah. That's good to know."

She had to lean against the counter.

"Look," he said, his back to her, "it's really late and I have some things I need to do before morning, so…"

He wanted her to leave. Zoe moved carefully toward the door. "I hope sleep is on that list." She tried to sound lighthearted, tried to sound as if her entire world hadn't just tilted on its axis.

He laughed quietly. "Yeah, well, sleep's pretty low priority these days. If I don't get to it tonight, there's always tomorrow."

She paused with her hand on the doorknob. "Jake, that kiss—it wasn't real. We just made it *look* real."

He turned and gazed at her then, the expression in his eyes completely unreadable.

"Yeah," he said quietly. "I know that."

CHAPTER FOUR

"LET'S DO IT!" HARVARD SAID, but stopped short as he caught sight of Jake. "Admiral. You're joining us for a run this morning, sir?"

"Do you have a problem with that, Senior Chief?"

"Well…no, of course not, sir." Harvard didn't say the word *but*. He didn't have to. It was implied.

Jake held on to the side of the team's beat-up station wagon for balance as he stretched the muscles in first one thigh and then the other. He kept his expression pleasant, his voice easygoing. "Say what you're thinking, H. If we're going to be a team, we can't keep secrets from each other."

"I guess I was thinking, sir, that if *I* were an Admiral, you wouldn't find me volunteering for PT at oh-seven-hundred on a morning after I'd been out on a sneak and peek until oh-*three*-hundred."

Jake looked at the faces of his men. And woman. Zoe was there, dressed in running gear that might as well have been painted on to her. He looked away from her, refusing to let himself think about last night. Refusing to think about that incredible kiss.

"Cowboy here was out as late as I was," he pointed out. "Lucky and Wes, too. In fact, who here closed their eyes last night before oh-three-thirty?"

No one.

Jake smiled. "So like you said, Senior, let's do it. I'm as ready as you are."

Harvard looked at Cowboy, and Cowboy nodded, very slightly.

The message couldn't have been more clear if he'd signaled with flags.

Don't let the old man hurt himself.

Jeez.

Harvard set the pace, taking the road that led in a two-mile loop around the campground at an unchallenging jog.

And no one complained. In fact, they hung way back, letting Jake be way out ahead, up with Harvard.

Not a single one of 'em thought Jake could keep up with them. Not even Billy or Mitch.

It would have been funny if it weren't so damned sobering. If his team didn't think he could keep up with them on a morning run, there wouldn't be much they'd trust him to do.

But then Zoe broke free from where she'd been blocked in, in the back, kicking her pace until she'd moved up alongside Jake. She didn't say a word. She just made a face, clearly scornful of the slow and steady pace. And then she lifted one eyebrow, her message again quite clear. *Shall we?*

Stop thinking of that kiss. God, he had to stop thinking about that kiss. Shall we *run?* she'd meant. As in run *faster.*

Jake nodded. Yeah. He turned and gave the senior chief his best-buddy smile. "Hey, H, how many times around this loop do you figure you'll go?"

Harvard smiled back. He clearly liked Jake. But this wasn't about being liked. "Oh, I figure twice'll do it, sir."

"And at this pace, that'll take you, what? About forty minutes?"

"A little less, I think."

"Dr. Lange and I are going to push it a little bit faster," Jake said, "and a little bit farther. We're going to do three loops in about two-thirds the time. Just let us know when you get back to camp."

Zoe was ready, and as Jake jammed it into higher gear, she was right beside him.

"Hey!" he heard Harvard say as they left him in their dust. He put on a burst of speed, hustling to catch up. "Admiral, this isn't necessary. You don't need to prove anything here."

"Obviously, I do."

"We're all tired this morning—"

"Speak for yourself. I'm an old man—I don't need much sleep."

Harvard looked pained. "I assure you, sir—"

"Save your breath, Senior. You're going to need it if you want to keep up." And Jake ran even faster.

ZOE STOOD UNDER THE campground shower and let the water stream onto her head.

She hadn't run a race like that in a long time. And it *had* been a race. Three times around the KOA campground driveway. At least six miles. At top speed.

It had been some kind of macho showdown, and Jake had come out on top. He was a good runner—he held something back, something in reserve for the end of the race. While everyone else was working overtime to keep up the pace for that last quarter mile, Jake had pulled a sprint out of his back pocket.

She shut off the shower and toweled herself dry.

The other SEALs had tried valiantly to keep up with

the admiral, but Harvard was the only one who'd stayed neck and neck.

And when it was over, Jake had been able to carry on a conversation. Bobby and Wes had been gasping for oxygen like fish on the deck of a boat, yet Jake had calmly given out orders, flashing that incredible smile of his at the pack of them.

At everyone but Zoe.

She slipped on her robe and wrapped her towel around her shoulders, using it to reach up and rub her wet hair as she headed toward the trailers.

The smile he'd sent in her direction had been self-conscious, and she knew he couldn't so much as look at her without thinking about that kiss they'd shared last night.

He was obviously embarrassed. It was clear he didn't know what to say to her, obvious that she'd overstepped the boundaries of propriety.

That was just perfect. She'd been trying to help, but all she'd done was make things awkward between them and…

Zoe had to laugh at herself—at her self-righteous attempt to justify what she'd done last night.

The truth was that she'd kissed Jake Robinson because she'd *wanted* to kiss Jake Robinson. Badly. She'd wanted to kiss him since she'd first found out about kissing, back in seventh grade.

She'd pushed too hard too fast, and now she was paying for it.

As she went up the steps to her private RV, she saw Jake standing with Bobby and Wes at the door to the main trailer.

He was watching her, but instead of holding her gaze, he looked away.

His message couldn't have been more clear. This

assignment was going to be neither easy nor fun for him. He'd prefer to keep whatever it was that had made him kiss her the way he had locked deep inside of him forever.

He was still in love with his wife, and a man like Jake Robinson would never cheat, not even on a memory.

LIEUTENANT LUCKY O'DONLON burst into the surveillance trailer as if his pants were on fire.

He skidded to a stop next to Bob Taylor and furiously whispered into the big enlisted man's ear. Lucky was gone as quickly as he came in, and now it was Bobby's turn to stand up.

Moving with the agile speed and grace of a ballet dancer, the six-feet-five-inch-tall, seemingly six-feet-wide SEAL pirouetted elegantly over to his swim buddy, Wes Skelly, and, glancing almost nervously at Jake, he leaned over and whispered something into Wes's ear.

Another graceful leap and Bobby, too, was out the door.

Wes knocked all the papers from his file onto the floor in his haste to get to his feet. He scooped them up, tossed them on the table in random order and scurried toward Cowboy, Crash and Mitch.

As he spoke to them, his voice was too low for Jake to hear, but he gestured with his thumb toward the door, then scrambled after Bobby.

Jake looked at Harvard, who was fine-tuning the programming for their satellite access computers. The big senior chief frowned as he watched Mitch rise to his feet and saunter out the door. He turned and met Jake's eyes and shook his head, anticipating the admiral's question.

"What the hell is going on?" Jake stood up for the first time in what seemed like hours, stretching his legs and heading toward the door.

Cowboy had crossed to the window and stood looking out.

Crash glanced out the door. "Apparently Dr. Lange has returned from her pool party."

"Yes," Cowboy said from the window. "She's definitely wearing a bikini. And she's definitely...wearing a bikini."

Jake opened the door, and stepped outside, intending to go out there and kick some ass. The male members of his team had no right to ogle Zoe, bikini or...

No bikini.

What she was wearing was, in fact, almost no bikini.

Two very small triangles of black fabric stretched across her full breasts, attached with a string that tied around her neck and around her back.

Oh, God, he was staring. Just like Lucky and Bobby and Wes and even unflappable Mitch Shaw, Jake was standing there and staring. He forced his eyes from her breasts and encountered her perfect rear end.

She was wearing some kind of a sarong-style cover-up around her hips, but it was white and completely wet and did little in the way of covering her.

In fact, it clung to her, outlining every detail of her black bikini bottoms, which weren't much in the way of bottoms at all. They were cut high on her legs, high on her rear. Oh, yeah, there was no doubt about it. Zoe Lange had a world-class rear end.

But Jake already knew that. He'd had his hands all over it just a few nights ago.

And he'd been avoiding her ever since.

"Isn't anyone going to get me a towel?" she asked.

Jake realized with a jolt that her hair was soaking wet. She was carrying a towel, but it was drenched and dripping, as was her bag and a pair of jeans she had over her arm. She still had beads of water on her shoulders and chest and…

The late afternoon air had an autumn chill. It was blatantly obvious that she was freezing.

He quickly lifted his gaze to her face. "What happened?"

"I got pushed into the pool on my way out of the party. Hal didn't want me to leave. But things were getting a little…too friendly." She was trying to be flip, trying to be tough and matter-of-fact. "It's no big deal. I got a little wet."

Lucky bounded over, a dry white towel in his hands, as Mitch reached to take her wet things.

"I'll hang these up for you," Mitch said.

It was amazing. Jake knew that after only three days of working together as a team, Lucky O'Donlon was hot for Zoe. But *Mitch?* Lieutenant Mitchell Shaw was not human when it came to distractions. He was the only man Jake had ever met who was completely nondistractable. Or so Jake had believed.

Lucky wrapped his towel around Zoe's shoulders, gently rubbing her arms, but she quickly backed away.

"Don't touch me!" Zoe's outburst surprised them all—herself included. She forced a smile. "Whoa. Where'd *that* come from? Sorry, Luke. I guess my whole afternoon was just a little too intense."

"Yo," Harvard said from the trailer door. "How come you guys don't throw *me* a welcome home party every time I come back to camp? We've got two months of work to do in two days and I see people standing around. Check the pay stubs in your wallets, please, and unless your pay grade is admiral, get your butts back inside."

"I need a shower, Senior Chief," Zoe said. "Give me twenty minutes to get cleaned up." She glanced at Jake as she wrapped her towel more tightly around her. "If that's okay, Admiral, I'll give you a full report then."

Admiral. It was her acknowledgment of his attempt to put a little space, a little formality between them since that night they'd kissed.

Hold me like you want to be inside me.

He wanted. Despite Daisy's memory, despite his and Zoe's age difference, despite the fact that she was at least partly under his command, a member of his team, he wanted her.

Keeping his distance seemed the smartest option under the circumstances. They were going to be forced into close quarters soon enough.

"A full report after you shower would be fine, Doctor."

Jake watched her turn away, watched her head toward the small RV that held her private quarters. But then he saw it. Bright red on the white of the towel.

He caught up with her quickly. "Zoe, you're bleeding."

She looked at the towel, pulling it back to reveal a nasty-looking scrape on her right elbow. Jake lifted the towel to reveal a lesser abrasion on her other arm. They were the kind of scrapes a woman might get from being pushed down, hard, onto her back. "Wow," she said. "I didn't even realize…."

"I think I need at least some of that report now," he said tightly.

She lifted her chin. "It wasn't anything I couldn't handle."

He still held her wrist. "And that's why you're shaking?"

"I'm freezing," she lied. He knew she was lying. Whatever had happened *had* shaken her up.

"'Too friendly,'" Jake remembered. He gestured to her elbow. "Is this the result of someone being too friendly?"

She gently pulled herself free. "It was Monica's boyfriend. I think he was coked up. I handled it, Jake. His family jewels are now lodged somewhere between his tonsils and his sinuses."

"Note to myself," Jake said. "Don't ever get Zoe angry."

She laughed as he'd hoped she would, but then abruptly turned away—but not before he saw the sudden welling of tears in her eyes.

"I'll tell you everything," she said, "but *after* I shower, okay?"

"Yeah," Jake said, fighting to hide the sudden rush of anger and protectiveness that made him want to seek out and destroy this Monica's boyfriend. "I'll get you something hot to drink. And meet you back in your trailer."

"Thanks, Jake," she whispered. "That would be very nice."

CHAPTER FIVE

ZOE KICKED OFF HER SHOWER slippers as she came inside her RV. She'd cranked the heat before she'd left for the bath house, and it was now close to roasting in the small trailer. But that was nice. She hadn't been truly warm in what felt like hours.

And she felt warmer still when she saw that Jake was, indeed, waiting for her in the small living area. He sat somewhat stiffly on the cheap foam seats of the built-in couch, three mugs of coffee on the table in front of him, and...

Three?

Mitch Shaw was sitting across the room, his medical kit on his lap.

Jake had brought a chaperone. He was probably going to pretend he'd only brought Mitch along as a medic, to make sure Zoe's elbows were cleaned and bandaged properly, but she knew better. He was afraid to put himself in a position in which he might kiss her again.

She smiled at Jake to make sure he knew that she knew better.

But he was in heavy team-leader mode, frowning slightly and very intense as he handed her one of the mugs and gestured toward Mitch. "I've asked Lieutenant Shaw to take a look at your elbows, Doctor."

Zoe gave the darkly handsome lieutenant a smile as

she sat down next to him. "Mitch and I are on a first-name basis, Admiral."

That one actually got her the ghost of a smile. "Any time you're ready," Jake said, "I'm ready to hear your report."

She took a sip of her coffee and pushed back the sleeves of her robe.

"First things first—I accomplished my mission this afternoon," she said as Mitch looked closely at her left elbow and then her right. His hands were warm, his touch gentle, almost soothing. "Hal Francke offered me the job."

"Great," Jake said. "When do you start?"

"I didn't take it."

As she watched, Jake struggled to understand. "Why not? Because of what happened at the party? I mean, don't get me wrong, if you don't think it's safe for you to be there, or—"

"I didn't take the job because I didn't want to seem overeager," she explained. "I told Hal I'd think about it. I'll go into Mel's in a day or so and let him ask me again. I'll make sure a ton of people overhear, and I'll make him beg. Ouch." She involuntarily jerked her arm free from Mitch. Holy Mike, that had hurt!

"Sorry," he murmured, his dark hazel eyes apologetic. "There're still a few pieces of dirt—something that looks like very fine gravel—that I should remove. I don't think I can do it without hurting you at least a little. But if I don't get it out…"

"Just…try to do it quickly." She gave him her arm, aware that she was perspiring from the anticipated pain, sweat beading on her upper lip. "Admiral, can you do me a favor and shut off the heat?"

"What, you changed your mind? You no longer want to simulate the conditions on Venus?"

"Ha, ha. *You* try getting dumped into a fifty-degree swimming pool and then driving fifteen miles in some trash heap of a car that doesn't have a working heater." She clenched her teeth against the pain.

Jake smiled as he turned down the heat. "Someday we'll have to tell her about BUD/S Training, huh, Mitch?"

Mitch was completely focused on cleaning her arm. "If you can't handle cold, don't become a SEAL."

"A major portion of Hell Week—the fifth week of SEAL training—is spent freezing your butt off," Jake told her. "You get wet early on and stay wet for the entire week."

"Yeah, I've heard about that." Zoe closed her eyes. Damn, whatever Mitch was doing hurt like hell. "I read in some magazine article about Hell Week that you guys pee on yourselves to stay warm while you're in the water."

"Yeah, sure." Jake snorted. "*That's* what reporters find important. That we pee on ourselves. Forget about the hours and hours of training we go through, the endurance tests, the underwater demolition, the HALO training. That's not half as interesting as peeing on ourselves. Jeez."

Zoe sensed more than felt Jake sit down beside her. But she opened her eyes when he took her other hand.

"Squeeze," he told her. "And keep your eyes open. If you close your eyes and shut everything else out, it's just you and the pain. And that's never good."

"I'm really sorry," Mitch murmured. "You must've landed on this arm pretty hard to get this stuff embedded so deeply."

Zoe took a deep breath and let it out in a whoosh. Jake's eyes were so blue and so steady. She held his gaze as if it were a lifeline.

"What happened at this party?" he asked. "Keep talking."

"I arrived a little after noon," she told him, gripping his hand more tightly and biting back the urge to shriek as Mitch probed particularly deeply. "Everyone was drinking pretty hard. Mostly just beer. But about five people went into the house, and when they came out, it was pretty obvious they'd done a few lines of cocaine. Hal Francke was one of them. This other guy, Wayne, Monica's boyfriend—God, what a jerk! He's one of those former high-school football-star types—he used to be big man on campus, but now he's just big and fat and mean. He went inside, too. A few different times."

She squeezed Jake's hand harder. "Ow. Ow, ow, *ow!*"

And just like that, the pain let up.

"Got it." Mitch was done. He was perspiring nearly as much as she was, his eyes filled with apology and an echo of her pain.

"I just have to put some antibacterial ointment on it and bandage it up. The other one looks clean."

Zoe tried to hide that she was shaking. "Well, that was fun. Thanks so much."

"So how'd this happen?" Jake asked. She had to give him credit. He was obviously trying really hard not to look as if he wanted to go out and hunt down Monica's boyfriend, Wayne.

The stupid thing was, she liked it. She liked the idea of this man being her hero. God knows there was a point this afternoon where she would have been plenty thrilled to see Jake parachuting down from the sky, coming to save the day.

She wasn't used to working in a team, like the SEALs. In her job, she often had herself, and only herself, to rely on.

She gently pulled her hand free from his grasp. "I went further out in the back of the yard," she told him as Mitch bandaged her arm, "looking for Monica. There was a path that led down to a stream, and some of the party had moved in that direction. I was getting ready to leave—I wanted to tell her I was taking off. But she must've been inside the house—everyone else who'd gone down to the stream was gone, too. Except for Wayne, who'd followed me. Like I said, he was on something nasty, and he got a little rough." It was an understatement, and she could tell from his eyes that he knew it. "But it was no big deal," she continued. "I handled it, I handled him."

She was stretching the truth pretty thin there. Because it *had* been a big deal. Zoe could still feel the man's hands on her breasts, still smell the alcohol on his putrid breath. He'd been a behemoth of a man, and when he'd tackled her, when the weight of his body had crushed her against the grass and gravel, for one awful moment she'd been afraid he'd actually be able to overpower her.

It was an awful feeling, that helplessness.

But he was stoned and stupid, and she'd used her brain and her ability to aim with a solid knee kick and she'd gotten away.

Hal Francke had been with a group of men by the pool, and they, too, had had far too much to drink. Zoe had picked up her towel and her bag, extremely shaken and ready to leave without even saying goodbye to the hostess, when one of the men grabbed her and tossed her into the pool.

Hal had jumped in after her, rescuing her even though she damn well hadn't wanted or needed it. He'd put his hands all over her as he pulled her to the side of the pool. It had taken every ounce of restraint she had not to kick *him* in the family jewels, as well.

The water had been freezing. Her towel and clothes had been soaked.

Hal had thought that was funny as hell. He'd invited her to dinner, invited her to stay at his fishing cabin for the rest of the weekend, subtly insinuated that he'd all but pay her to have sex with him. She'd told him she'd consider the *waitressing* job, thanks, but that she'd have to get back to him.

And then, elbows stinging and dripping wet, Zoe had gotten the hell out of there.

"It was no big deal," she said again. She was lying.

And Jake knew she was lying. But he didn't press her for more details.

"As far as what the locals think about the CRO—" she continued with her report "—most of the people at the party don't know anything about them. All they know is the old Frosty Cakes factory's finally been sold, and that the people who bought it mostly keep to themselves. They wish it had been bought by someone wanting to get back into production—they'd hoped for more jobs in this area. They know about the electric fence around the compound, but not much about the rest of Vincent's high-tech security system. And that's about it."

"That's it for me, too," Mitch said, finishing bandaging her arm. He held on to her hand several moments longer than he had to. "Again, I'm sorry I hurt you, Zoe."

"It's all right." She smiled at him. "I forgive you."

Mitch's eyes were warm as he packed up his medical kit. "Good."

Jake cleared his throat.

Mitch stood up. "If you don't need me any further, Admiral…"

"Thanks, Mitch. I'll be along in just a minute."

Zoe watched the lieutenant let himself out, then glanced

at Jake, wondering what he could possibly have to say to her that needed privacy. Why lose the chaperone now?

"Are you really okay?" he asked. He touched her with just one finger beneath her chin, turning her head so that she was forced to meet his eyes.

Silently, she nodded.

"Why do I get the feeling that you're not being completely honest?" he asked. "Look, let's make a deal. Right now. You don't lie to me, and I won't try to tell you what you should or shouldn't do. I won't make judgments about what might be too dangerous for you because you're a woman. But in return, you have to be brutally honest with me. You have to be able to pull your own plug, to pull yourself off some assignment that might get too uncomfortable for you for any assortment of reasons. Does that sound fair?"

Zoe nodded. Provided he could really do it. His instincts were to protect—anyone, really, but probably women in particular. He would need to be a truly exceptional leader to overcome his inherent prejudices in that regard.

But if anyone could be that kind of leader, Jake Robinson could.

"You've got a deal," she said.

"So. Honestly. Are you really okay?" His gaze was so intense, she could have sworn he was trying to read her mind. "What really happened, Zoe? Did this guy do more than just push you down?"

"Have you ever had your chute fail—you know, skydiving?" Zoe asked.

He gazed at her for several long moments, but then apparently decided to let her answer his question in her own way. It was a tough question, and if she had to go in circles to answer it, that was okay with him.

"Skydiving, huh?" Jake laughed softly. "Funny you

should mention that. Jumping is one of those things I've always hated. I mean, I've *had* to do it as a SEAL. It's part of the package. But some guys'll jump every chance they get. I've always had to force myself to do it." He paused. "And yes, I've had to cut myself free from the main chute more than once. It was pretty damn terrifying."

"You know that feeling you get right before you pull the backup chute—that sense of complete helplessness? Like, if *this* doesn't work, it's all over?"

Jake nodded. "Oh, yeah. Personally, I like being in control, which is why I probably don't like jumping."

"That's what it felt like today," she told him. "When Wayne was…" She closed her eyes. "When he was on top of me, tearing at my bathing suit."

Jake swore softly.

"You want honesty, Jake? For one awful moment, I thought I was going to be raped and that I wasn't going to be able to do anything to stop it. That kind of helplessness is not a really nice feeling, so you're right, I'm still a little shaken. But I'll be fine."

She opened her eyes to find Jake watching her, a mixture of emotions on his face. Anger. Remorse. Regret. Attraction. The power of his other feelings made him unable to hide his attraction. "Zoe, I'm so sorry this happened."

"It's really no biggie. I mean, I was the one who wasn't being careful. I should have known this particular guy would be trouble. And then I made a second mistake by letting him get too close. I definitely underestimated the situation. If I'm paying the right amount of attention, I'm completely capable of taking care of someone that size. But I messed up. And I almost paid for it."

"What's his last name?" Jake asked. "Wayne what?"

"No," Zoe said. "Sir. No disrespect intended, but I'm not going to tell you."

"You were sexually assaulted." His voice broke. "This is not something to just say oh, well about and let go."

"What are you going to do, Jake? Find him and beat him up? And maybe blow our cover when he recognizes you in a few weeks when you walk into Mel's bar with Christopher Vincent? Or maybe you think I should press charges? I'm supposed to be a drifter, right? My cover is that I've had my share of trouble with the law, that I'm jaded with the system—ready to be enlightened by the CRO's doctrine. Somehow it doesn't fit for me to go running to the police and shouting for justice."

He knew she was right. She could see it all over his face. He had such an expressive, wonderful face.

She leaned closer. "Our job here is to regain possession of that Trip X. That takes priority over everything. Even this."

Jake exhaled in frustration. "I just… I know. I just hate not being able to *do* anything."

She gave him a shaky smile. "You want to do something? You could put your arms around me for a minute."

He didn't need more of an invitation than that. He reached for her, and she found herself wrapped in his arms.

He smelled so good and felt so familiar—as if she'd been in his arms far more than just that one other time.

His arms were warm and so solid as he held her tightly, as he stroked her hair. It was funny how much better that made her feel.

It didn't mean she was weak. It didn't mean she wasn't strong. She didn't need him to hold her, but it sure was nice that he was there.

Zoe closed her eyes, not wanting this minute she'd asked for to end.

She felt him sigh and braced herself, waiting for him to pull away. But he didn't. And she didn't.

"God," he finally said on another sigh, still holding her tightly. "This just feels too good."

Zoe lifted her head and found herself gazing directly into his eyes. "You say that as if it's a bad thing."

He pushed her damp hair from her face. "It feels inappropriate," he whispered. "Doesn't it?"

She gazed at the graceful shape of his mouth. "Not to me."

"I'm not going to kiss you again," he said hoarsely, pulling away, pushing himself off the built-in couch and all the way across the tiny room. "Not until I have to."

Zoe tried to smile, tried to make a joke as he slipped on his brown leather flight jacket and prepared to leave. "Gee, I didn't realize kissing me would be such a negative."

He turned to give her a long look. "You know damn well that I liked it. I know it wasn't real, but nevertheless, I liked it too much. I'm leaving tonight," he added.

Zoe stood up. "*Tonight?* But…"

"I'm ready as I'll ever be and this…this is getting crazy. You be careful working at Mel's," he ordered. "With luck, I'll see you in the bar in a few weeks."

"Jake."

He stopped with his hand on the doorknob and looked back.

Zoe's heart was in her throat. He'd liked kissing her. Too much. "I liked it, too," she said, adding, "kissing you." As if he'd needed her explanation.

Another man might've stepped toward her, pulled her into his arms and kissed her until the room spun. But Jake just gave her a crooked smile that was overshadowed by the sadness in his eyes.

"Be safe," he said, and walked out the door.

JAKE KNEW FROM THE WAY Harvard cleared his throat that the moment of truth had arrived.

It was time for him to leave. So if anyone was going to try to make him change his mind, it was now or never.

Jake had kind of hoped it would be never.

So much for hoping.

"Permission to speak freely, sir."

Jake looked from Harvard to all four of the lieutenants, and then at the enlisted men. They were all there but Zoe. She wasn't part of this. Or maybe the men had intentionally excluded her.

"This isn't a democracy, Senior," Jake said mildly.

"At least hear us out, Admiral." Admiral. When Billy called him admiral, it meant he was dead serious.

Jake sighed. "I don't need to hear you out," he said. "You don't think I'm up for this. You think it's been too long since I've seen action, since I've been out in the real world. You don't think I can keep up, despite the fact that every time we've run together, *you've* had to fight to keep up with *me*."

"This is different than running, and you know it," Billy said. "Yes, you're physically fit for—" He broke off.

Jake bristled. "Go on, say it. For an old man. Right?"

"Jake, I love you, and I'm worried about you," Billy said, cutting through to the bottom line, the way he always did so well. "I don't know why you're doing this when any one of us could find a way to get inside the CRO—"

"Because I can walk through those gates in the morning," Jake told Billy, told them all, "and have dinner at Christopher Vincent's private dining table by night. If you or Cowboy or Lucky were to go in there, God knows how many months it would take you to work your way up to just being able to stand guard outside the dining room door."

He looked them all directly in the eyes, one at a time.

Billy. Cowboy. Mitch. Lucky. Harvard. Bobby. Wes. "We don't have months, gentlemen. The CRO could decide to do a test run of the Triple X at any time, in any city." They all had family, friends living all over the country, and his unspoken message cut through, loud and clear. Until they regained possession of the T-X, no one was safe.

Jake shouldered his bag of gear. "Now, who's taking Mitch and me to the airport?"

THE AIR FORCE FLIGHT TO South Dakota seemed to take forever.

Mitch slept for most of it, only waking as they began their descent.

Jake was sick and tired of thinking about the way his team had questioned his plan. He'd worked hard over the past week to gain their respect. He'd thought his physical stamina, his ability to run hard and fast, had won them over. Obviously, he'd been wrong.

His team thought of him as an old man.

He wished Billy was with him instead of Mitch. He'd wanted to talk to the kid about Zoe, find out if he was shocked by Jake's intention to pretend he and the young doctor were romantically involved.

But Jake's plan had called for one of the SEALs to wind up arrested, thrown into jail for conspiracy and charges of aiding and abetting the escape of a suspected felon. Both Mitch and Billy had volunteered, but Jake knew that playing this role would be hitting a little too close to home for the kid. It hadn't been that long since Billy had spent time in prison, facing very similar charges for real.

So Jake was here on the plane with Mitchell Shaw. A man he'd always thought of as a friend.

A man who—just a few hours ago—had lined up with the rest of the team and questioned Jake's command.

Right now, CNN was announcing a late-breaking story of conspiracy and intrigue in the U.S. military. As the story went, Admiral Jake Robinson had escaped from house arrest. He'd been confined to his quarters after being charged with conspiracy, allegedly leaking top secret military information to several extreme right-wing state militia groups. Those militia groups had been lobbying for fewer federal regulations, less control by the federal government. Allegedly there were tapes, and the words Jake had spoken could be interpreted as treasonous.

The military had been attempting to keep the entire affair from the public eye, since as an admiral in the U.S. Navy, Robinson *should* have been among the staunchest defenders of the federal government. But four days ago, as the story went, Robinson had escaped his guards with the help of three unidentified men, and now the incident was national news.

All four of the men were currently at large.

To help this cover story along, Mitch and Jake were going to be spotted in South Dakota, and Mitch was going to be apprehended while Jake once again made an escape.

Jake was then going to proceed, by car and on foot, to Montana, leaving a trail that the CRO could trace if they tried. And they would try—particularly after he showed up on their doorstep, seeking asylum.

Within a few days, CNN would stop carrying the story—Admiral Mac Forrest would see to that. And after several weeks of hiding in the CRO compound, Jake would be able to leave hiding and venture into town.

And then he'd see Zoe again.

Zoe. Who'd liked the way he'd kissed her.

Mitch shifted his jaw, expertly popping his ears as the plane continued its descent.

"Hey, Mitch," Jake said.

"Yes, sir?"

"No," he said, "not sir. I've got something I need to discuss, and I need you to talk to me as a friend."

Mitch nodded, completely serene. "I'll do my best."

"It's about—"

"Zoe." Mitch nodded. "I figured you were going to say something. I'm sorry if I got in your way. I honestly didn't think you were interested in her—you've been avoiding her all week." He smiled slightly. "You know, Jake, I've found it's far easier to get a woman into your bed if you actually interact with her."

"I don't want to get her into my…" He couldn't finish the sentence—it wasn't true. He exhaled noisily in exasperation. "God, she's too young for me. How could I even be thinking about that?"

"She doesn't think she's too young." Mitch smiled again. "I've been hanging out with her. Telling her stories about *you*. She's yours if you want her, Admiral. And if you don't, I'm hoping I might be next in line."

Jake had to know. "She's beautiful and she's smart and she's *very* sexy, but…you've had the opportunity to meet plenty of beautiful, smart, sexy women, and as far as I've seen, you've never given any of them a second glance. So why Zoe? What is it about her?"

Mitch gazed thoughtfully out the window at the approaching runway for several long moments. "She's one of us," he said simply, turning to look at Jake. "I get the sense that she wants the things I want from a relationship—no strings, no promises, no regrets. Just good, clean, healthy fun. Sex that's just that—sex. No more, no less." He laughed softly. "To be painfully honest, Jake, I tend to stay away from most women because I'm afraid of hurting them when I leave. And you know in our line of work, we always leave. We disappear on some assignment, and who knows when we'll be back. But Zoe…" He laughed again. "Zoe would never expect anything long term. Because she leaves, too. And she'd probably leave first."

The plane touched down on the runway with a jolt.

"I know you miss Daisy," Mitch said quietly. "I know how you felt about her. But you're not dead. And Zoe might be just what you need. It won't have anything to do with what you and Daisy had. It doesn't have to go too deep."

Jake sighed. "Just thinking about it makes me feel unfaithful."

"To whom, Jake?" Mitch asked gently. "Daisy's gone."

CHAPTER SIX

WEEKNIGHTS WERE THE WORST. Weekends were no picnic, but at least on Friday and Saturday nights, Mel's was crowded and Zoe was kept busy.

But on a Tuesday night like this one, Zoe sat at the bar with old Roy, who sat nursing a beer on the same stool every night and could have been anywhere from eighty to a hundred and eight, and Lonnie, who owned the service station on the corner of Page Street and Hicks Lane and was probably older than old Roy.

On Tuesday nights, Hal Francke had his bowling league, so even he wasn't around, trying his damnedest to brush up against her.

And Wayne Keating—Monica's boyfriend, the one who'd nearly overpowered Zoe—had been arrested for DUI. It was his third offense, and he was being held without bail. So there was no chance of him staggering into the bar and livening things up.

No, it was just another deadly boring Tuesday night in Belle, Montana.

Zoe was definitely going to go mad.

Two weeks had come and gone and come and gone and here she was, well into week five in her new career as barmaid, with no sign of Jake.

He'd gotten into the CRO compound. She knew that. She'd seen surveillance tapes of him being let inside. Even taken from a distance, she'd clearly recognized him. The way he walked, the way he stood.

According to the team, he'd been spotted from time to time within the confines of the electric fence.

But he hadn't come out.

Each time a car or van left the CRO gates and headed toward town, Harvard or Lucky or Cowboy would call, and Zoe's silent pager would go off. And she would know to be ready.

Maybe Jake would show up *this* time. Maybe…

But even though Christopher Vincent himself had come into Mel's a number of times, and always with an entourage, Jake had been nowhere in sight.

Zoe was completely frustrated. And getting a little worried.

Had something gone wrong? She called Harvard every night on the pretense of checking in, but in truth to find out if Jake had been spotted again during the course of the day.

What if he'd gotten sick? Or injured? What if Vincent knew he was only there to find the Triple X? What if Jake were locked in the factory basement, beaten and bleeding and…

Oh, dammit, and the really *stupid* thing was that beneath her worries and her frustration at this endless inactivity was the unavoidable fact that she missed him.

She *missed* the man.

She missed his smile, his solid presence, his calm certainty, the sweet sensation of his arms around her.

Zoe groaned, resting her forehead on the bar atop her folded arms. He'd only kissed her once, but she missed that, too. Holy Mike, when had she become such a hopeless romantic? And hopeless was the key word here.

This foolish schoolgirl crush she was experiencing was definitely one-sided.

Yes, the man had kissed her. Once. And afterward, he'd run screaming as hard and as fast as he could in the opposite direction. And when he kissed her again, it was going to be because he *had* to. He'd told her as much.

"Ya gonna do that singing thing tonight?" Lonnie leaned over and asked.

He was talking about the karaoke. Last Friday, Hal had bought a karaoke system secondhand and very cheap from a guy going out of business over in Butte. Zoe had been the only member of the wait staff brave enough to give it a try. The songs were mostly all retro dance hits, with a bunch of old country songs thrown in.

Zoe lifted her head to look in the mirror on the wall behind the bar. Besides Lonnie, old Roy, Gus the bartender and herself, there were only three other people in the place.

"I don't think so," she told Lonnie. "There's not much of a crowd."

Old Roy was already leafing through the plastic-covered pages that listed the song titles available on this karaoke system. "I love this old Patsy Cline song." He blinked at her hopefully. "Will you sing it? Please?"

It was the same song he played over and over on the jukebox at least three times every single night. "The record sounds much better than I do," she told him. "Here, I'll even front you a quarter."

"But we like it when *you* sing it." Now Lonnie was giving her *his* best kicked-puppy look. "I'd like to hear the other songs you did on Saturday night, too."

Zoe sighed.

"Please?" they said in unison.

She should really clean the bathrooms. God, she hated cleaning the bathrooms.

"Sure. Why not?" She went behind the bar to the stereo system and powered up the karaoke player. "But if I'm going to do this, I'm going to do it right." She untied the short apron that held her ordering pad and change. She set it down, picked up the karaoke microphone and switched it on. "Ready for this, boys?"

Both Roy and Lonnie nodded.

She used the remote to turn on the TV behind the bar, setting it to receive the signal from the karaoke system. She put in the right CD and programmed the machine and...

Thunderous strains of pedal steel guitar came pounding out of the speakers. Old Roy and Lonnie both clapped their hands over their ears.

"Sorry!" she shouted, turning the volume down by a full half.

The words on the screen turned color, and she sang them into the mike. "Crazy..."

Old Roy and Lonnie sat paying rapt attention—the president and vice-president of her personal fan club— as Zoe did her best country diva imitation, singing to an imaginary crowd of thousands.

One song became two, then three and four. Each time it ended Roy and Lonnie gave her a standing ovation.

"Sing mine again," Old Roy requested.

When Zoe looked to the bartender for help, Gus just smiled. "I like that one, too."

"Last one," Zoe said. "Last time."

She didn't need the words on the screen this time as she sang. "Crazy..."

It was her finale, and she went all out this time, exaggerating all the moves. Roy and Lonnie grinned at her like a couple of two-year-olds.

And during the instrumental break and the subsequent key change, she climbed up to sing while standing atop the sturdy wooden bar, and they gave her a two-man wave.

Zoe knew it wasn't so much her voice that got them going. Her voice was pleasant enough, and she could certainly carry a tune, but she was no Patsy Cline. No, Roy and Lonnie were fans of her tight blue jeans and her low-necked tank tops.

She closed her eyes, threw her head back and struck a pose for the last chorus of the song, letting a very country-sounding cry come into her voice as she sang about being crazy for crying, crazy for trying, crazy for loving you.

As the last strains of music faded away, the room was filled with applause. Way too much applause for just Old Roy and Lonnie.

Zoe opened her eyes.

And looked directly down at Christopher Vincent.

The CRO leader was standing near the door, surrounded by about fifteen of his disciples.

She'd had no warning, no time to prepare, but then again, she'd taken off her apron—and in it, her pager—at least five songs ago.

"That was just beautiful," Vincent said. "Just beautiful."

She gave a sweeping bow. "Thank you."

"Someone want to give her a hand down from there?"

"Yeah, I'd love to."

Jake.

He pushed his way out of the crowd and stood smiling at her.

She didn't faint with relief, didn't gasp, didn't reveal in any way that she recognized him. Instead she looked at him very deliberately, as if she were checking out the new man, the handsome stranger in town.

He was dressed the same as the rest of the men, in blue jeans and a worn denim work shirt. But the faded jeans hugged his thighs, and the shirt fit perfectly over his very broad shoulders. He was heart-stoppingly, impossibly beautiful, his eyes an incredible shade of molten hot blue.

During the past four and a half weeks, she'd forgotten just how amazingly blue his eyes were.

He'd been looking her over as thoroughly as she had been looking at him, and now he smiled.

Jake Robinson had a vast collection of smiles in his repertoire, but this one was very different from any she'd seen in the past. This one was as confident and self-assured as all the rest, but instead of promising friendship or protection, this smile promised complete, mind-blowing ecstasy. This smile promised heaven.

Damn, he was good. He almost had *her* believing that she'd lit some kind of fire inside of him.

Christopher Vincent noticed it, too. Noticed it, and recognized it. And wasn't entirely thrilled by it.

Zoe held Jake's gaze, lifting an eyebrow in acknowledgment of the attraction that simmered between them and giving him an answering smile that promised maybe. A very *definite* maybe.

"Zoe." Gus was completely overwhelmed behind the bar.

Jake reached for her, and she leaned down to give the microphone to Lonnie before bracing her hands on Jake's shoulders. He held her by the waist and swung her lightly to the floor, making sure that before her feet touched the ground, every possible inch of her that could touch every possible inch of him was, indeed, doing so.

And oh, God, it felt so incredibly good. She wanted to hold him tightly, to close her eyes and press her cheek against his shoulder, hear the steady beating of his heart beneath the soft cotton of his shirt. He was safe, he was whole, he was finally here. Thank God, thank God, thank *God*.

She wanted to hold on to him for at least an hour.

Maybe two. Instead she touched the side of his face and held his gaze for just a second longer, hoping he could read her mind and know how very glad she was to see him.

His arms tightened around her for just a second in an answering embrace before he, too, let her go.

"I'm Jake," he told her, with another of those killer smiles.

"And I'm Zoe," she said as she went behind the bar. "Welcome to Mel's. I'll be your waitress tonight." She slipped her apron around her waist, and sure enough—inside the pocket, her pager was silently shaking. She quickly shut it off. "What can I get you?"

He sat on the bar stool directly in front of her. "What kind of beer do you have on tap, Zoe?"

He said her name in a way that called up all kinds of erotic images, in a way that made her mouth go dry.

She leaned toward him, gesturing for him to come closer, and she felt his gaze slip down her shirt, nearly as palpable as a touch. "I recommend bottled beer," she told him. They had a little problem with roaches. She didn't know how they got into the tap hoses, but they did, and... yuck.

"Then definitely make it bottled," Jake said. He was close enough so his breath moved her hair. "Whatever you bring me will be fine."

As she turned around and reached into the cooler, she could feel him watching her. Make-believe, she told herself. It was all part of act. Jake Robinson wasn't really drooling over her rear end. He was just pretending to.

She opened the beer—a Canadian import—and set it down in front of him. "Glass?"

"I don't need one, no."

"Zoe, two pitchers, one light, one regular!" Gus called.

"Don't go anywhere," Zoe told Jake.

She could feel his eyes on her as she filled both pitchers.

He was still watching as she carried them with a stack of plastic cups to the tables where Christopher Vincent and most of his men were sitting.

"What brings you boys out on a Tuesday night?" she asked.

"My friend Jake's been going a little stir-crazy," Christopher told her. "He's been…keeping a low profile. You don't recognize him from anywhere, do you?"

Zoe glanced at the bar where Jake was sitting, still watching her. "He looks like a movie star. Is he a movie star?"

"Not exactly." Chris looked around. "Where's Carol? I wanted to introduce him to Carol. I thought they would hit it off."

"She's off tonight," Zoe said. "Some kind of program going on over at her daughter's school."

"Maybe tomorrow then."

"Tomorrow will definitely be too late," Zoe told him. "Finders keepers, and all that—because *I* definitely saw him first. He's adorable."

Chris didn't look happy. But Chris rarely looked happy.

Considering he was the leader of the so-called chosen race, Christopher Vincent was not a particularly attractive man, mostly due to the grim expression he wore on his face nearly all the time, and partly due to his thick, dark eyebrows, which grew almost completely together in the middle. He was tall and beefy with long dark hair, which he wore pulled back into a ponytail. He kept his face hidden behind a thick, graying beard, and he usually wore tinted glasses over his dark brown eyes. He looked over the tops of them as he gazed at Zoe.

They were definitely the eyes of a fanatic—the eyes of a man who wouldn't hesitate to use the Triple X he'd stolen if he thought it would further his cause.

He was volatile, with a very short fuse.

"I saw *you* first," he pointed out.

Oh, brother, this was a complication she hadn't anticipated. Somehow over the past few weeks, she'd managed to catch Christopher Vincent's eye. "You're married," she told him, trying to sound apologetic and even regretful. "I have a personal rule about married men. I don't touch 'em. See, I want to get married myself, and since married men are already married…" She shrugged.

"I've been thinking about taking another wife."

"Another…?"

"The federal government has no right to force us to follow its restrictive rules about marriage and family. A man of power and wealth should take as many wives as he pleases."

Oh, yeah? "What does your wife think about that?" Zoe asked.

"All three of my wives are kept very satisfied."

Holy Mike. If they ever got desperate, they could bust this guy for polygamy. "Wow," she said. "Well. It's hard enough being a second wife when the first one's not around. I don't think I could handle the competition."

"Think about it."

"I don't need to, hon," she said. "I'm the jealous type. I wouldn't want to share."

"You could have my baby."

And that was supposed to entice her? A baby with a single eyebrow with a complete lunatic for a father? "Well, it's tempting," she said. "But I really want to be someone's number-one wife."

He gestured for her to lean closer. "We sometimes

share wives in the CRO," he said in a low voice. "You could marry someone like Jake and still have my baby."

Ooo-kay. "Jake doesn't strike me as the kind of man who'd want to, you know, *share*."

"He's very generous," Christopher Vincent told her. He looked up, past her, and smiled. He had a smile like a wolf—lots of teeth, more vicious than happy. "Hey, buddy, we were just talking about you. Zoe here wants to marry you."

Zoe held up her hands. "Chris. Wait. I never said that." She turned to Jake. "He's just teasing. He's crazy, you know—"

It was the dead wrong thing to say.

Christopher exploded, reaching out with one hand and grabbing the front of her shirt, pulling her down so that they were nose to nose, so that she was practically lying on the table in front of him, so that her tray clattered onto the floor. "Don't *ever* call me crazy!"

"Hey," Jake said. "Whoa. Take it easy, Chris. Come on, pal, I'm sure she didn't mean to offend you."

Zoe felt him right behind her, his arms around her as he tried to pry the other man's fingers from her shirt.

Vincent released her, pushing her away from him, and she would have fallen over had Jake not been there.

"Dammit, Chris," Zoe said, refusing to let him see how badly he'd frightened her, how completely he'd freaked her out. "You ruined my shirt." She had to hold the front against her, he'd stretched it out so badly. He'd bruised her, too, by grabbing more than just her shirt. Way to woo a new wife, baby.

Gus had come out from behind the bar, and he was hovering nearby. "Everything okay over here?"

"I don't know," Zoe said. "Chris, are you done grabbing me?"

Jake's hands tightened on her in warning, but she didn't

give him time to answer. "I've got to go change my shirt." Pulling free from Jake, she picked up her tray and handed it to Gus, then headed for the back room.

She sensed more than saw Jake follow her. And she wasn't surprised, after she fished a T-shirt from her backpack, to turn around and see him standing there, door tightly shut behind him.

He looked really upset.

Zoe wasn't sure who moved first, and it didn't matter. As she reached for him, he lunged for her, and then, God, she was in his arms, just holding him as close as she possibly could.

"Are you all right?" He didn't release her to ask, he just kept holding her as tightly as she was holding him. "When he grabbed you like that..."

"I'm okay," she told him. And she was. Despite the bruises Christopher Vincent had just given her, she was more okay than she'd been in a long time. She pulled back to look at him. "Are *you?*"

"This isn't going to work." The tone of Jake's voice matched the intensity in his eyes. They'd turned into steel—hard and cold, with a razor-sharp edge. "The plan. I've got to come up with something else because I'm *not* letting you go in there."

"But—"

"He's dangerous, Zoe. He's completely unhinged. The whole organization's seriously off balance. Getting you inside as my wife is no longer an option. I don't want you anywhere near there. Besides, it's just not feasible, from what I've found out."

"Dammit, Jake—"

He kissed her. One moment, he was glaring at her, and the next his mouth was hard against hers, his tongue sweeping past her gasp of surprise.

Zoe felt herself sway, caught off balance for the briefest

moment, before she clung to him, kissing him back with as much passion, angling her head to grant him deeper access.

He was kissing her. Jake Robinson was kissing her because he wanted to, not because he had to. Tears stung the inside of her eyelids, and for the first time she let herself acknowledge that she wanted Jake Robinson more than she'd ever wanted any man. He was her hero, her commander and in many ways her deity. She worshipped him, on every possible level.

He pushed her back so she bumped against the concrete block of the storage-room wall as still he kissed her. His hands were all over her as he pressed himself hard between her legs, pulling her thigh up along his as he strained to get closer, even closer, playing out her wildest fantasy. But when he cupped her breast far more roughly than she would have expected, she opened her eyes in surprise.

And saw Christopher Vincent standing at the half-open storage-room door, his hand on the knob as he looked in at them.

He pulled the door shut behind him, and when he did, Jake stopped kissing her. He took his hand from her breast but otherwise just stood there, eyes closed, breathing hard, forehead resting against the wall beside her.

She'd been wrong. Jake hadn't really been kissing her. Somehow he must've heard the door open. Somehow he'd known that Christopher was there.

It wasn't a want-to kiss, after all. It was a had-to kiss.

Zoe drew in a very shaky breath. "Oh, *God*."

Jake pulled away from her, his eyes dark with apology. "I'm sorry—did I hurt you?"

She tried to joke. "Are you kidding? That was more fun than I've had in weeks."

He turned slightly away from her, and she realized that her shirt was hanging open in the front where Chris had stretched it, revealing the entire top edge of her very low-cut bra. She picked her T-shirt up from the floor, and turning her back to Jake, she quickly changed.

"We've got too much to talk about, too much to decide," Jake told her. "So I'm going to go home with you tonight."

She turned to face him, her heart in her throat despite the fact that she knew nothing would happen between them even if he *did* spend the night in her trailer. He'd *had* to kiss her. God, she was such a fool for thinking otherwise.

"I don't think that's a good idea. Why would you marry me if you can just get some whenever you want? Besides, I've set up my cover so that everyone out there in that bar *knows* that I'm looking to get married. What are they going to think if I just suddenly settle for casual sex?"

"I'm sorry," he said. "But I've changed my mind about the whole marriage thing. Zoe, this guy is *nuts*. The entire organization is screwy. The way they treat women is criminal. I can't let you do this."

"Jake, you *promised* that you'd let *me* decide—"

"That was before I knew how bad it would be. On top of that, Vincent's got security cameras everywhere. I found at least three in my bedroom. How the hell can I bring you there? Don't you think it would look a little suspicious when I don't make love to my gorgeous young wife?"

"So bring me there and make love to me." Zoe couldn't believe she was actually bold enough to say the words aloud.

Jake was silent, looking at her, looking hard into her eyes as if trying to see if she'd really meant what she'd just said.

She held his gaze, pretending she was as flip and blasé about the idea of being intimate with him, pretending she could shrug it off as just another job requirement, pretending it would mean no more to her than a way to find that missing Trip X.

It's no big deal, she told him with her smile, even as her heart was pounding.

"Even if you would do that," he finally said, "I wouldn't. I *couldn't*." He turned away. "That's not an option."

Zoe felt like crying. He honestly didn't want her. Even with necessity as a solid excuse, he couldn't acknowledge that any of the passion that sparked between them when they kissed was genuine. And maybe it wasn't. Maybe he was the best actor she'd ever met, and all of the real passion was her own.

God, she was pathetic.

But that was just too bad. Because she had a job to do and no time to feel sorry for herself.

She took a deep breath. "So you're just going to do this by yourself—find the Triple X on your own? All alone?"

"I need to get a message to Harvard. I think there's a way to intercept the images from the security cameras—but I'll need some equipment from him. If I can do that, you'll be able to see inside the CRO compound from the safety of the surveillance trailer."

"What if that's not enough? Jake, you *know* it's going to be easier for me to help you find the Trip X if I'm there with you. I think we've got to leave our options open. So I'm not going to let you pretend to come home with me, in case we need to use the marriage thing in the future." And wouldn't *that* be fun? Living with him twenty-four seven, pretending to be lovers, all the while knowing that she was about the farthest thing possible from the woman he truly wanted?

She handed him her ordering pad and pen. "Write Harvard a message," she continued. "Write down whatever equipment you need. Whatever *he* needs to know. I'll see that he gets it."

There was a knock on the door and old Roy stuck his head in. "Zoe, Gus is looking for you. Hal's bowling team just showed up." He frowned at Jake. "Say, young fellow, you're not supposed to be back here." He stepped farther into the room. "Everything all right, Zoe?"

Zoe gave the old man a reassuring smile. "Everything's fine, Roy. Tell Gus I'll be right there."

She looked at Jake as the door closed behind Roy. "I better get out there."

He couldn't hide his frustration. "There's more we need to discuss."

Zoe started for the door. "Load the jukebox with quarters, then buy another round for your friends. As soon as there's a lull, ask me to dance. Hal doesn't mind if the waitresses dance with the paying customers. We can talk more on the dance floor. Just make sure the songs you pick are ballads." She paused, her hand on the door. "I know this is distasteful for you, but I can't think of any other way for us to have a private conversation."

"Zoe—"

She closed the door behind her and hurried to the bar.

CHAPTER SEVEN

JAKE MADE A QUICK SWEEP of the room as he headed for the jukebox. The bar wasn't filled to capacity, but compared to when he'd first come in, it was hopping.

A tall man with long, greasy salt-and-pepper hair and a droopy mustache was behind the bar with Zoe and the bartender. He had to be Hal Francke. Sure enough, he didn't move past Zoe in the crowded space without touching her in some way.

So bring me there and make love to me.

Jake shook his head to exorcise Zoe's husky voice. She'd been serious. He'd seen it in her eyes. She would have had sex with him, in front of those cameras, to boot, in order to get this job done.

He stared sightlessly at the listing of songs on the old-fashioned jukebox, wishing he had some of her recklessness, her impetuousness, her careless youth. Wishing he could break away from everything that held him to the past, but knowing that even if he could forget for one night, for one *hour,* even if he could lose himself completely in this woman's sweet arms, he'd wake up and be right back where he'd started in the morning.

Or maybe even in a worse place.

I know this is distasteful for you.... Zoe had said that as she walked out the door. He had to set her straight. He couldn't have her continue to believe that. There was a lot about this assignment that was distasteful, but being with her was not.

Like he'd told her nearly five weeks ago—he liked kissing her. Too much. And even after all this time apart, he still liked it. Still much too much. He'd thought the distance would be good, that it would give him some perspective, some sense of reality. But all those weeks he'd dreamed about her in ways that were outrageously inappropriate.

He'd started out dreaming of Daisy, erotic, sensuous dreams of lovemaking filled with heat and light and such vivid sensations. But his dream would shift and change, the way dreams often do, and then Zoe would become the woman in his arms, her body wrapped around him.

He'd wake up, dizzy and out of breath and achingly, painfully alone.

Jake forced himself to focus and fed the jukebox dollar bills, punching in all the slow romantic ballads he could identify. He'd just picked a LeAnn Rimes song when he saw Christopher Vincent approach, his image shimmery but unmistakable in the curved glass.

He felt himself tense and worked hard to keep the smile on his face a pleasant one. God, when Christopher had grabbed Zoe, Jake had had to physically restrain himself. He'd come damn close to picking the man up and throwing him across the room.

"I guess our new little waitress likes you," Christopher said.

Jake pushed the buttons for a Garth Brooks song, not even looking up. "Oh, is she new here?"

"She came into town a few weeks ago. Hal met her at some party. Don't worry. I've checked her out. She's exactly what she says she is."

"Well, that's good to know." Jake smiled at Chris. "But no real surprise. I mean, she doesn't come across as some kind of rocket scientist or—I don't know—some kind of biochemical engineer. Can you imagine her in a lab coat?"

Christopher laughed, and Jake laughed, too, knowing that the real joke was on the CRO leader. God, it was going to be so good to nail this guy....

"Yeah," Chris said, "I can imagine her wearing *only* a lab coat." He laughed again. "She is some hot ticket."

Jake turned to the jukebox, uncomfortable with Christopher's openly lascivious appraisal of Zoe, not wanting to be a part of it in any way.

"I've seen her counting on her fingers," Chris continued, "but with a body like that, it's almost better that she's not too bright." He looked at the bar, watching Zoe as she poured another pitcher of beer. "Oh, yeah. She's choice."

As if she were a cut of meat. Jake felt his smile turning even more brittle and he stared at the jukebox, reminding himself why he couldn't simply beat the hell out of Christopher Vincent right here and right now.

"Just so you know not to get your hopes up too high," Christopher told him before he walked away, "she's holding out for marriage, our little Zoe is. You'd have better luck with Carol."

Jake glanced at the bar, but Zoe was gone. He quickly scanned the room, found her making the rounds of tables, double-checking that everyone had all the beer and liquor they needed to get them through the next few minutes.

She looked up, caught him gazing at her, and for a fraction of a second, he saw a glimmer of uncertainty in her eyes. Distasteful. Did she honestly think he found this part of the set up *distasteful?*

But just like that the uncertainty was gone and she smiled.

It was a very inviting, very warm smile, complete with

a very slow, very appreciative up-and-down look that was totally lacking in subtlety. It was a look he might've gotten back in high school, and his body responded in a way far more appropriate for a seventeen-year-old than a fifty-something grown man.

Jake moved toward her as surely as she made her way toward him. It was as if they both were magnetized, as if they couldn't have stayed apart from one another even if they'd tried.

Zoe set her tray on top of an empty table.

He slipped his hands into the back pockets of his jeans, afraid if he didn't he wouldn't be able to keep himself from reaching for her.

"I didn't buy another round yet," he told her. "When I came out, someone else had just—"

"It's okay." She looked away, as if suddenly shy. "You know, if you don't want to dance, we could try sitting at a table toward the back. But Gus and Hal might—"

He took his hands out of his back pockets, and just like that, he had her by her hand and was pulling her toward the dimly lit dance floor next to the jukebox. Just like that she was in his arms and swaying gently in time to the music.

"You should talk fast," she told him. "I don't know how long I'll have before Gus needs me."

He pulled her closer. "This is not distasteful," he murmured into her ear. "Let's start with that, all right?"

Zoe shook her head. "Jake, you don't have to—"

"It's just…" He searched to find the words that would explain. "It's very…weird for me. I was with only one woman for nearly thirty years—nearly your entire lifetime. Can you even imagine that?"

Silently, she shook her head.

"I'm going to make everyone in this bar believe that I've got a major thing for you," he told her. "And doing that will *not* be distasteful. I'd be lying if I told you I haven't spent the past weeks looking forward to this. Looking forward to it, and dreading it, all at the same time. You're a great kid, Zoe, and a beautiful woman and… And I'm sorry if I can't be as blasé about any of this as you, and I'm sorry in advance if I somehow make you feel bad. Holding you, even dancing like this, hurts a little bit. But it feels good, too. Really good. Which in turns hurts a little bit more. Does that make any sense at all?"

She nodded. "I'm sorry if I—"

"Let's not apologize to each other anymore. We've got to do what we've got to do, right?"

She lifted her chin. "*I* think one of the things *I've* got to do is to get into the CRO compound."

"Now, *that* idea *is* distasteful."

"Jake, no, I've been thinking about it." She rested her head against his shoulder, and when she spoke, he could feel her breath against his throat. "The best way for me to help you find the Trip X is for me to be in there." She lifted her head and looked into his eyes. "Remember our deal? Remember what you promised?"

"I didn't know what it would be like in there for a woman. Zoe, whatever you've heard about the CRO—"

"I knew exactly what I was getting myself into when I agreed to be a part of your team. I can handle it."

"But *I'm* the team leader, and I need you to try it my way first." And if his way didn't work… Jake wasn't sure how they'd handle the cameras in the bedroom. Maybe they could cover some, disable the others. Maybe they could pretend to make love, under the covers….

He changed the subject, trying to banish the image of Zoe in his bed, her body soft beneath his.

No. He refused to give up on the idea that they could

find the Triple X *and* keep Zoe safely out of harm's way. And out of his bed.

"I'm sorry it took me so long to get here," he said. "Christopher tends toward delusions of grandeur, and he imagined this terrible altercation the moment I stepped outside of the CRO gate. I think he was a little disappointed when I made it all the way into town without being chased by federal agents."

The song ended and they stopped for a moment, waiting for the next song to start. It had almost exactly the same slow, pulsating beat. He'd picked the songs well.

As they began dancing again, she shifted her body even closer and rested her head against his shoulder. How could she fit so perfectly in his arms?

"So how *did* you convince him to let you come to town?" she murmured.

"Well, I, um, I thanked him for his hospitality and sanctuary, but I told him that I wouldn't be able to stay with him any longer unless I at least had the opportunity to, um…" He laughed, embarrassed. "Well, to, you know…."

"Ah."

"And since there are no single women in the CRO over age thirteen…"

She lifted her head. "He didn't offer you one of his many wives?"

"Are you kidding? The man's almost obsessively possessive."

"Hmm. The sharing doesn't go both ways, huh?"

"Sharing?"

"Just more CRO unpleasantness. Women as chattel. You know, it's a good thing you made it into town today," Zoe interrupted herself. "The team was starting to make plans to liberate you. You had us all worried."

Jake swore softly. "Why can't they just sit tight and trust me?"

"They care about you."

"They think I'm too old."

"*You* think you're too old."

Jake pulled back slightly. "What the hell is *that* supposed to mean?"

Zoe shook her head. "Nothing. Look, Jake, I've been—"

"Nothing, my ass! You wouldn't've said it if it meant nothing."

"Okay, it meant something, but it's a personal something, and if we've got limited time to talk here, the personal stuff should be the last thing we get to."

He couldn't argue with that. Unfortunately it didn't make him wonder exactly what she'd meant any less. *He* thought he was too old. Jeez.

"I've been thinking about alternatives to this whole setup," she said. She pulled him close, breathing into his ear as if her words were seductive promises rather than a plan for an alternative operation.

God, he'd forgotten for a moment—he'd been standing there arguing with her. They were supposed to be just short of making out on the dance floor. He held her closer, and she moved toward him willingly, her breasts soft against him. He buried his face in her sweet-smelling hair. Oh, God.

"What's your take on the hierarchy of power inside the CRO?" she murmured, her breath hot against his ear. "I've always gotten the impression that Christopher Vincent's it. That without him, the organization would fall apart. And if that's the case, why don't we just grab Vincent on one of his trips outside of his compound? Hold him hostage in exchange for the Trip X?"

"I've thought about that, too," Jake admitted. He kissed

her neck, ran his hands down her back to cup her rear end. Oh, *God*. Bad mistake. But once his hands were there, it would've looked odd for him to move them right away, wouldn't it? What were they talking about? Hostage. Vincent. Right.

"It's not an option," he told her, hoping she wouldn't notice the huskiness of his voice. He cleared his throat. "Vincent's got contingency plans for all kinds of disaster scenarios. Everyone in the CRO compound has a battle station to go to if the Feds suddenly launch an attack. He's stockpiled enough food to withstand a two-year siege. He's got an escape route charted out of this bar, in case he suddenly finds himself a target while he's here."

She slipped her hands into the back pockets of his jeans, pressing his hips tightly against hers. "With or without an escape route, we could get him."

"I know that. But what I don't know is what his contingency plan is in regards to the Triple X. His lieutenants might not know what it is they've got. His orders might be for them to use it if he's taken. So, no, we're not going to grab him. Not without finding out more."

Jake tried to shift back, extremely aware of the fact that when she pulled him that close, there were no secrets between them—including the secret he'd been trying to keep about the enthusiastic way his body was responding to her nearness.

He tried to make his voice sound casual, conversational. As if he weren't affected by the sensation of her breasts against his chest, as if he couldn't feel her heat as she pressed herself against his thigh. "Hey, have you heard from Mitch?"

"Not since he's been arrested." Zoe smiled, her hands traveling up his back. "We almost didn't recognize him when we saw the news report on CNN."

"Yeah, he's good with disguises. I looked twice at that

little old man sitting at the bar just to be sure it wasn't him."

"It's not. Mitch is still in custody," Zoe told him. She ran her fingers through the hair at the nape of his neck and it felt impossibly, sinfully good. "He's being held at the same federal penitentiary where Christopher Vincent's stepbrother is doing ten to twenty for armed robbery."

Jake laughed. "Well, jeez, that's pure genius. I mean, I knew Christopher had a stepbrother who'd been in trouble with the law, but... Whose idea was it to send Mitch to the same prison?"

"I'm a fan of doing just that little extra bit of research," she told him modestly. "We lucked out that the stepbrother was in a federal jail and—"

"It was *your* idea. Good job, Lange. So you're the genius, huh?"

"Whoa," she said, laughing. Her eyes sparkled and danced with amusement. She was so pretty, so full of life. The longing that hit him was so strong, it took his breath away. "Don't go overboard. Yes, it was a good idea, but—"

She stopped short, her smile fading at the look he knew was in his eyes. He couldn't hide it, and he prayed she would think it was only part of the game they were playing.

They'd both stopped moving, and they stood on the dance floor just holding each other. She gazed at him, her beautiful lips slightly parted, and when he didn't move, she stood on her toes and kissed him.

It was the smallest of kisses, light and delicate, a feathery brushing of her lips across his. She searched his eyes again, then stood on her toes once more. This time she kissed him a little bit harder. This time she tasted him, gently touching the curve of his lips with the very tip of her tongue. And this time he kissed her, too, just as delicately, just as softly.

Jake's heart was pounding, and he was dizzy from wanting more. But he took his cues from her, letting her lead, refusing to push her into harder, deeper, longer kisses, no matter how badly he wanted just that.

She delicately swept her tongue into his mouth and he groaned aloud. She took him right to the point where he *knew* they were on the verge of crushing their mouths together and positively inhaling each other, but instead, she pulled back.

"We're both good actors," she whispered, "but we're not *this* good. Part of this is real, Jake, whether we want to believe it or not. That's what I was trying to say when I told you I'd make love to you. That I also *want* to make love to you."

Jake didn't know what to say.

She kissed him again, hot and sweet and long. "That's me kissing you, no games, no pretense. We can have it both ways, you know. We can do our jobs *and* get naked—if you can get past everything you need to get past, if you can come to the conclusion that you're not too old for this sort of thing."

"Ah," Jake said, finally finding his voice as she pulled free from his arms. "We've finally come to the personal stuff."

"I bet you look good naked," Zoe told him as she picked up her tray and headed to the bar.

Jake wanted both to laugh and cry. He'd never met anyone as completely in-your-face honest as Zoe Lange. She knew what she wanted, and she wasn't shy about asking for it.

She wanted him.

And his big problem was that he wanted her, too.

Even though he knew that wanting her was wrong.

CHAPTER EIGHT

"OH, HELL, HE'S NAKED!"

Bobby Taylor thrust his big hands in front of the video monitor. But because there was more than one camera, there was more than one screen to cover. Wes Skelly grabbed Zoe's chair and spun her so she was facing the other direction.

She just laughed at them. "Oh, come on, you guys. Like I haven't seen a naked man before? I grew up in a very small house with four brothers. I'm sorry to disappoint you, but the male anatomy has just never been a mystery to me."

"Yeah, but he's an admiral," the bigger SEAL told her. Bobby Taylor could have made a fortune playing professional football. At six feet seven inches, he weighed at least two-sixty, maybe even more. When he sat down, he took up two chairs, but very little of his bulk was fat. He was simply enormous. Yet despite that, he was one of the most graceful men Zoe had ever met. He was part Native American—part Navajo, he'd told her. He had the darkest, most serene brown eyes she'd ever seen. "He's earned the right to towel off after his shower without an audience."

"Besides," Wes added, "you don't want to be looking at him naked. He's an old man."

"He is *not*—"

"Okay," Bobby said. "He's got his shorts on. Although

it still seems a little disrespectful for us to be staring at an admiral when he's in his underwear."

Zoe spun her chair to face the row of video monitors. Jake stood, displayed from three different angles, combing his hair out of his face. One of the cameras must've been positioned directly behind the mirror, because he gazed straight into it, his eyes a vivid blue. His arms were over his head, his biceps and triceps flexing.

"I'm sorry, Skelly," Zoe said, tapping that screen. "But that is *not* an old man. I don't know where you get off calling him that. He's in better shape than you are."

His stomach was rock solid and his chest was muscular, despite being badly scarred.

"Wow," Bobby said, subdued by the sight of all those scars. "He's seen some action, huh?"

"Two years ago he was the target of an assassination attempt," Zoe said. God, if those scars were any indication, he'd been nearly mortally wounded. It was a miracle he was still alive. He'd miraculously escaped death many times while in Vietnam, too. Some people said he'd led a charmed life. Without a doubt, luck had always been his constant companion.

Zoe hoped that same good fortune was riding copilot with Jake right now. If Christopher Vincent even *suspected* Jake was there as a spy...

On the screen, Jake threw his comb on top of the dresser. He took his jeans from the closet. Too bad. He had very nice legs. As Zoe watched from three different angles, he pulled on his jeans and covered them up.

His bedroom was a former executive office for the old factory, the walls still covered with cheap, tacky paneling, ancient orange-shag carpeting on the floor, blessedly faded. The furniture was cream-colored, with gold ornamentation—directly from a low-rent motel liquidation sale. She'd have thought a group declaring themselves to be the chosen race would have a little more taste.

"Besides behind the mirror," Zoe mused, "the other cameras are, where? Over by this window..." She pointed to the screen. "And...here near the door?"

Wes spread the floor plan of the CRO compound—the former Belle Frosty Cakes factory—out on the counter behind her and she swiveled her chair to face him.

"In Admiral Robinson's quarters, the cameras are here, here and here." He highlighted the locations in pink.

"Any in Jake's bathroom?" she asked, leaning over for a closer look.

"At least one," he told her. "Here."

"Show me that one," she said, turning to the video screens.

Bobby keyed a command into the computer, and the image on the far left screen changed.

The camera in the white-tiled bathroom had a clear shot of the door, the sink and the toilet. But not the tub. The tub, with the shower, was off to the side, out of camera range. Interesting.

On the other two video screens, Jake buttoned up his shirt, pocketed his wallet and keys and left the room.

"Can you follow him?" Zoe asked.

"Yeah, as long as he doesn't go too fast." Bobby had fingers the size of hot dogs, yet they flew over the computer keyboard. "But even if we do lose him, it won't take long to find him again. As soon as he speaks, we can use the computer and trace him by his voice."

On screen, Jake walked purposefully along the corridor. He had a cocky walk, with a spring in his step more befitting a twenty-five-year-old. It was self-confidence, Zoe realized. Jake Robinson walked the way he did because he trusted himself completely. He liked himself, too.

It was powerfully attractive.

It had been two whole days since she'd seen him last, and Zoe felt a sharp tug of longing. She missed him.

They'd been together every evening at the bar for two and a half weeks before that. During that time Zoe had smuggled to Jake the equipment he'd needed to enable the SEALs to tap into the CRO security cameras. *And* during that time, they'd established a very hot, very high-visibility romance.

Zoe had made it clear to all the patrons of Mel's Bar that she was holding out for marriage. Despite the sparks she and Jake made on the dance floor, she publicly refused to bring him home with her. And Jake, he'd made it clear that he wasn't ready for any kind of commitment.

It was kind of funny, actually. In truth, the man was Mr. Commitment. He would still be married to his first wife right now if she hadn't died. And Zoe didn't doubt for one nanosecond that he'd still be *happily* married.

Conversely she, Zoe, had never even imagined herself married. She'd never seen the need, considering that she'd never truly been in love. She'd always purposely sought out and let herself fall halfway in love with men she knew would never be right for her. Halfway in love was all she'd wanted, though. It was safe. She knew exactly what she'd get, knew she'd never be in too deep, never out of control.

She was doing the exact same thing with Jake, too. Even if she could convince him to make their relationship more physical, more intimate, she knew damn well it would never go beyond that. He still loved his wife, and he wasn't looking to replace her.

Zoe could love Jake—just a little—and still be safe. So she did. And she used her feelings to bring a certain authenticity to her role. No, she would not sleep with him, not until they were married. Well, okay, pretending *that* was a stretch. A long stretch.

And at times, when Jake held her in his arms on the dance floor, or when she kissed him goodbye each night, she thought the sheer irony would drive her completely insane. Here Jake always pretended that he wanted to spend the night with her, and Zoe always pushed him away.

She could think of only one thing she wanted more than to spend these long, cold autumn nights with Jake Robinson in her bed. She wanted to find the Trip X. But that was the *only* thing she wanted more.

Still she sent Jake back to the CRO fort each night. And each night she slept alone.

Each day, she locked herself in the team's surveillance trailer, using the computers to access the CRO cameras, electronically searching for the missing canisters of Triple X.

She was exhausted, bleary-eyed and completely frustrated on many, *many* levels. She wasn't going to find anything this way. She had to get in there, inside that electric fence. She needed to search with more than just her eyes, restricted by the lens of a camera.

She had to get inside Christopher Vincent's private quarters, into those few rooms where there were no security cameras. The more she came into contact with Vincent, the more she was convinced that he was the type of man who'd get off on keeping a crate of deadly poison— enough to wipe out the capital city of this country—on the sideboard of his private dining room.

She'd had it. She'd played it Jake's way for long enough. She was going to get inside the CRO walls whether he liked it or not.

On the video monitor, Jake turned a corner, and with a flick of his fingers, Bobby made him appear on a different screen. The enormous SEAL didn't consult any list, didn't look at the factory schematic. He just somehow knew the camera codes.

"You've already memorized both the layout of this part of the factory and the location of the cameras?" she asked.

"I've got the whole factory up here." He tapped on his forehead. "I'm pretty good with maps."

Pretty good?

"Morning, John," Jake said in greeting to a man heading in the same direction. Bobby made another adjustment, and their conversation about the current dreary weather came in crisp and clear over the speakers, fading slightly as they moved away from one microphone, getting louder as they walked past another.

"Tell me about the audio signal," Zoe said. "Do all the cameras have microphones, or is there a different miking system?"

"There's a combination," Wes told her. "The dedicated mikes are higher quality, but they're also more expensive so there're fewer of 'em."

"Is it possible to speak quietly enough so's not to be heard?" Zoe asked. "I guess what I need to know is, once I'm in there, is there any way I'll be able to talk to Jake *without* the mikes picking up our conversation?"

"Mid to high-range frequency overload will block low-volume conversation," Bobby said. He typed in a new command, and on the right-hand screen, the CRO kitchen appeared. About a dozen women were in the big room, about half of them washing dishes. "See?"

"Run water," Wes interpreted. "And speak softly. But don't whisper. A whisper could cut through."

Sure enough, in the kitchen, water was running from the faucet, and Zoe could only make out the words of the women who raised their voices significantly when they spoke.

"We also found a spot where the security cameras were set up a little carelessly," Wes told her. He pointed to the floor plan again, and she stood to get a better look, stretching her legs. "Up here there's access to the roof. There must've been some kind of recreation deck there at some time. And the entire northwest corner of that area is completely out of camera range. It overlooks the millstream—an added bonus, running water. Again, speak softly, and your conversation will be covered by the sound of the water. You won't be overheard."

Bobby turned in his chair to face her, his dark eyes very serious. "Zoe, are you sure you want to go in there?"

"Yes."

"Don't take this the wrong way," he said, "but I'm not sure the admiral's got this under control."

"Admirals can lose touch," Wes agreed. Since Bobby was so tall and broad and always with him, Wes always seemed short and wiry in comparison. But Zoe had to lift her chin to look at him as he straightened up. He had a pack of cigarettes rolled up in his T-shirt sleeve, revealing a stylized barbed-wire tattoo that ran completely around an extremely well-developed bicep. He may have been wiry compared to Bobby, but only compared to Bobby. Wes Skelly was no lightweight, that was for sure.

"Since when did you start smoking again?" she asked him.

"Since I've been nervous as hell about this op," he countered. "Since we've been sitting here for weeks, relying *only* on Robinson, getting no closer to finding that Triple X crap."

"Human beings slow down," Bobby pointed out.

"After you hit a certain age, your reaction time really starts to suck," Wes agreed.

"It's a fact of life."

"Don't get me wrong," Wes said, "the admiral's a good guy—"

"For an admiral—" added Bobby.

"And we know he used to be a SEAL—"

"A long time ago—"

"But it *has* been about a million years and—"

"You know how on *Star Trek*," Bobby started earnestly.

"On *classic Trek*," Wes interjected with a grin.

"Whenever a commodore's on board the *Enterprise*—"

"And the intergalactic antimatter's about to hit the fan—"

"And this old, out-of-touch commodore takes command of the ship because he thinks he's got all the answers, and Captain Kirk's got to fight both the bad guys *and* the good guys to save the day?" Bobby continued.

"Bob and I are alarmed at the remarkable parallels we've found between those episodes and this current mission," Wes told her. "We're sitting out here in the woods with this old rusty commodore, and our captain's back in California. It doesn't bode well for the Federation."

Zoe started to laugh. "You guys are too much."

"Actually, Zoe…" Wes's grin faded. "We *were* kind of hoping you'd talk to the admiral, you know, convince him that it's time to try to get more of the team inside those walls."

They were kidding, but only halfway.

"You guys need to read a book called *Laughing in the Face of Fire* because you obviously have no idea who you're dealing with here," she told them. "You have no idea what Jake did in Vietnam, do you?" She knew they didn't. Their expressions were blank. "I can't believe you wouldn't at least try to find out *something* about your team leader." She laughed again, but this time in disbelief.

"Jake's not the commodore, boys. He's the captain. And if you're not careful, *you'll* be the good guys he's got to fight so he can save the day. He needs you standing beside him—not standing in his way."

"At the risk of annoying you," Wes said, "I have a theory that your loyalty to the admiral isn't really loyalty, but instead has something to do with the fact that you've been sucking face with him for the past few weeks. Sex confuses things. Particularly for women."

"*Excuse* me?"

"I think you annoyed her," Bobby commented, turning away to hide his smile.

"It's some kind of hormonal thing," Wes said, amusement dancing in his eyes. He *knew* he was completely pissing her off, damn him. "You *think* it's loyalty, but it's really just your hormones responding to the power of an alpha male, even if he is a little on the ancient side."

Zoe stood up. "Well, it's been fun, but it's time for me to leave this den of total ignorance. You know, I bet you could find the book-on-tape copy of *Laughing in the Face of Fire.* I realize now that reading might be too big of a challenge for someone as pea-brained as you, Skelly."

Bobby laughed. "What are the odds they've come out with a comic book edition? You might get him to read *that.*"

Wes pretended to be offended, but he couldn't keep a smile from slipping out.

"You know, if this was *Star Trek,* wiseass," Zoe heard him say to Bobby as she went out the door, "you'd be Lieutenant Uhura, sitting there in high heels, keeping hailing frequencies open. How does *that* make you feel?"

"Like I'm in damn good company," Bobby said.

Zoe wasn't in Mel's when Jake arrived.

He knew it was only a matter of time before she showed

up—she would've been paged as the surveillance team saw him leaving the CRO gates.

He nursed a beer as he stood by the jukebox, filled with the same sense of anticipation and dread he felt every night before he saw Zoe.

She would tell him hello—she always did—with a deep, searing, burning kiss. God, he loved kissing her. Loved *and* hated it.

Hated it because her kisses so completely overwhelmed him. When Zoe kissed him, nothing else existed. His world narrowed down to him and her, his mouth, her mouth, his arms around her, her body against him.

When Zoe kissed him, he could barely even remember his own name, let alone the taste of Daisy's kisses.

Zoe had completely invaded his dreams, as well. More than once he'd woken up reaching for her, so certain that his impossibly detailed, incredibly erotic dreams had been real.

Lately in his dreams, he only saw Daisy from a distance. He'd spot her from the bedroom window of his Washington apartment and go out the French doors onto the deck to call to her. Halfway there, he'd realize he was naked, that he'd just been in bed with Zoe. His voice would catch in his throat, and Daisy would disappear.

He didn't need Joseph and his dreamcoat to figure out what *that* meant.

He'd wake up, aching from guilt and need. It was not a good combination.

Jake glanced at his watch. Dammit, where *was* she?

Tonight he wasn't just anticipating her arrival because he wanted to kiss her. Tonight he had some vital information he needed to pass along.

"If you're looking for Zoe—" Carol, one of the other waitresses, the pretty, dark-haired, forty-something one, stood behind him, holding her tray "—she called in sick again tonight."

Sick. Again? Oh, damn, he'd purposely stayed away for a few days. What if she'd been sick all that time? What if she'd needed him? "Is she all right?"

Carol shrugged. "Gus thinks it's the flu. Personally, I just think she's pouting."

"Thanks for letting me know." Jake finished the rest of his beer and carried the empty bottle toward the bar.

"Before you go racing out to her place," Carol said, following him, "you should probably be ready for her to hand down an ultimatum. That girl wants some kind of commitment, Jake. She told Monica you've been dragging your feet so hard, she was starting to give second thoughts to becoming Christopher Vincent's fourth wife."

Jake nearly dropped the bottle. "What?"

Carol smiled. "Yeah, I figured you didn't know about that. Apparently your friend Christopher has been hitting on Zoe, too. He wants to add her to that sick little harem he's got going up there at the old Frosty Cakes place."

"She never said a word about that to me."

"I'm going to give you some unsolicited advice, Jake. Zoe's a little wild, a little out of control. That's her nature. But she wants a ring. This is probably the first time in her life she's held out for something like this, and I'm certain that she's serious. I know you haven't known her for that long, but she wants to get married before she turns thirty, and she's getting close to the point where she doesn't particularly give a damn *who* she marries. But she *is* in love with you. You should hear her talk about you—it'd make you blush."

"She *does* go on and on and *on* about you, Jake." Somehow the bartender had become a part of this conversation. The two old men who were permanent fixtures in the bar were also unabashedly listening in.

"If you feel anything for her at all, buy her a ring," Carol advised him. "Have Christopher Vincent do that mumbo-jumbo wedding ceremony that he does. It's not real, anyway. He has no more authority to officiate at a wedding than my pet poodle. But it'll make Zoe happy, you'll get what you want for as long as you want it, and it'll keep her away from Christopher. He's just a little too rough with women, if you ask me."

"You'd be a damn fool not to marry Zoe for real," one of the old men said. Roy. Zoe had told him that Roy was ninety-two years old. "If I were just twenty years younger, I'da asked her myself the first time she came in here."

ZOE'S TRAILER WAS PARKED just down the block, in the empty lot alongside Lonnie's gas station. The light was on as Jake approached.

She opened the door before he even reached the steps— she'd been watching and waiting for him.

She was wearing her jeans and that little flowered T-shirt she'd had on in Washington the first time they'd met. Her hair was down, long and silky around her shoulders. She wore almost no makeup, and her skin seemed to glow with good health.

"I guess you don't have the flu," he said as she closed the door behind him.

"Gee, you sound almost disappointed."

Her gym bag was packed, her backpack, too. They lay on the floor of the tiny hall that led to the trailer's single bedroom.

Dammit, she *was* actually trying to force his hand. She wanted him to marry her and bring her to the CRO compound.

"Going somewhere?" he asked. He tried to keep his voice and his smile pleasant, but he knew they were both a little too tight.

She met his gaze and didn't try to pretend either one of them didn't know exactly what was going on. "It's time, Jake."

"What if I say no, it's not time? What if I tell you no, you're not getting inside the CRO fort? Is that when you blatantly defy me—and sign on to be the fourth Mrs. Vincent?"

He was furious with her, but his anger wasn't entirely because she was attempting to override his authority. He was mad as hell that she could consider sex to be so insignificant, that she could hold her own self in such low esteem. He was livid at the idea of her giving herself to Christopher Vincent. Her motivation might be selfless, but dammit, it was *wrong*.

And it drove home the fact that she was willing to be with Jake, too, for the same wrong reasons.

And in a flash of insight that was a little too glaringly clear, Jake knew that he didn't want Zoe to want him, *too*—in addition to her desire to make this mission a success. He wanted Zoe to want him, period. In spite of the mission. Outside of the mission.

The way he wanted her.

She didn't blink. "You know that I'd prefer doing it this way. Going in there with you."

He let himself glare at her, let his words crackle with his displeasure. "Yeah, and *I'd* prefer doing it *my* way. I *am* the team leader, or have you forgotten?"

Zoe flinched at his high volume, but then lifted her chin in that way she had that could infuriate him and make him admire her, all at once. "*Are* you the team leader, Admiral? If so, why are you letting Jake the protective man interfere with what's best for this op? The plan was to get me inside that factory so I could help you find that Trip X. It was a good plan—until you stopped thinking like an admiral. You *promised* me that as far as my safety and comfort went, you'd let me draw the line. We had a deal—until you turned around and reneged."

"You want me to let *you* draw the line?" Jake couldn't believe it. "Where's your line, Zoe? As far as I can tell, it doesn't exist. You're not drawing any line at all, if you're willing to *marry* Christopher Vincent to get inside the CRO fence!"

CHAPTER NINE

JAKE WAS BEYOND UPSET.

For the first time since Zoe had met him, he didn't have a smile ready to pull out to help diffuse or relax the situation.

His eyes were cold and as hard as blue steel, and he looked at her as if she were a stranger, as if he didn't recognize her.

Zoe didn't know what to tell him. She opted for the truth. "I wouldn't really have married Christopher Vincent," she admitted. "I just thought… I don't know. Maybe it would give you the incentive you needed to get me in there this other…this *safer* way."

He clearly didn't believe her. Why should he? She'd worked hard to make him think she was tough and ruthless. "Things weren't progressing at a speed that satisfied you, so you decided to resort to emotional blackmail, is that what you're saying?"

She couldn't deny it, but she could try to justify it. "I'm the expert, Jake. I should be in there."

His eyes were as cold and as empty as the darkness of outer space, his voice flat. "I should send you home."

Her chin went up. "You could do that, Admiral, but you couldn't stop me from going to Pat Sullivan and getting reassigned right back here."

"And then you'd use the fact that Christopher Vincent wants to sleep with you to get through the CRO gates, right?" He laughed, but there wasn't any humor in it. "Funny, I thought I heard you just say you wouldn't do that."

Zoe felt like crying. She'd worked overtime to make Jake believe that she was blasé about sex. She'd pretended so hard that it was no big deal. She was not demure, she was not shy. She could use her looks and her body as just another tool of her trade.

She'd started out wanting to shock him, wanting to shake him up and, yes, wanting to impress him. She was a modern woman, a Gen X-er. She might be young, she might be a woman, but she was an expert in dealing with weapons of mass destruction, an authority in a field that was more frightening than the most terrifying horror movie. Yet despite that, she had the ability to remain detached and in control while sheer chaos raged around her. She was cool, she was tough, she could get the job done—sec, look? She could remain as emotionally un-attached as James Bond when it came to matters of the heart. That proved she had what it took to be good at her job, didn't it?

She *was* good at her job.

But none of the rest of it was true.

Except now he believed it was. And he was not impressed.

She'd painted herself into this unfortunate corner, there was no doubt about it.

Jake sat tiredly on the built-in sofa. "You know what the really stupid thing is, Zoe?"

She was. *She* was the stupid thing.

"I came into town tonight to tell you that we're out of time." Jake looked at her and gave her a crooked smile. "I came to find out if you still wanted to marry your way into the CRO compound."

Zoe sat across from him, suddenly sharply focused. "Out of time? How?"

"I found out when Christopher's planning to use the Triple X," Jake told her. "He's celebrating his fiftieth birthday in three weeks. He and his lieutenants have been talking about the big party they're having in New York City. How the big party's going to get covered by CNN. I figure we've only got about a week and a half before they'll try to move the T-X. We need to find it before then, for obvious reasons."

The CRO could carry it out of state in plastic baggies, in small amounts. And then the team would have a hell of a time tracking it down. They could recover most of the Triple X and thousands of people could *still* die.

They had to find it. Now.

"Yes," Zoe said. "Yes, I'll marry you."

SOMEONE HAD FOUND Zoe a white dress.

It wasn't a wedding dress, but with her hair up, she looked angelic.

Jake stood in the front of Mel's Bar, watching as she proceeded toward him, down an aisle they'd made by moving the tables and chairs. He didn't know the name of the song that was playing on the jukebox, but the melody was haunting.

Zoe was so beautiful, his throat ached.

But this wasn't real. None of this was real.

The CRO didn't believe in marriage licenses. They opposed state intervention in something as personal as marriage. And thus, according to their rules, Jake could propose marriage at 8:37 p.m. and be watching his bride walking down the aisle toward him by eleven that same night.

Beside him, Christopher Vincent cleared his throat. He smiled as Jake glanced at him. Jake smiled back. And felt a small surge of triumph. There was a lot that was really, *really* wrong about this mock wedding ceremony, but at least Jake knew one good thing that would come of it. After tonight, Christopher Vincent would have no chance of getting his hands on Zoe.

He could see apprehension in her eyes as she got closer. Her smile was tentative, and he knew he hadn't completely managed to hide his sense of dread.

Jake didn't want to marry her. He didn't want to pretend to marry her. And he *really* didn't want to bring her back to his bedroom at the CRO compound. It was hard enough resisting her here, in a public bar. How was he going to handle sharing quarters with her?

Somehow, he was going to do it. He was going to pretend to make love to her, and he was going to sleep in the same bed with her night after night. If anything could cool his body's eager response to her nearness, it would be those three security cameras positioned around his room.

Zoe handed the flowers she carried to Carol and took his hand. Her fingers were cold. Her dress was lovely, with no sleeves and a sweeping low neckline that exposed the tops of her full breasts, but it was a summer dress, and fall was cold and crisp and far more suited to turtlenecks here in Belle, Montana.

He took both of her hands in his, trying to warm them. She was wearing perfume—just the slightest, subtlest scent.

"Kneel," Christopher Vincent commanded.

Jake helped Zoe down onto the floor, then prepared to join her. But Chris stopped him.

"Just Zoe," he said.

She looked up at them, frowning slightly. "Just me?"

"You have to show the proper respect to your husband

and to the other men of the CRO," Christopher told her. "On your knees, head down, eyes averted."

This was it, Jake thought. This was where Zoe would stand up and laugh in Christopher's face.

But she didn't. She stayed there on the floor, and she bowed her head. And he knew again how high she thought these stakes were. If she would do this, she would do *anything* to find that missing T-X.

Anything.

The thought made his stomach hurt.

The ceremony was short, filled with words like "obey" and "submit," "abide by" and "yield." It was a step back toward the Dark Ages for women everywhere.

Yet throughout it all, Zoe murmured her acquiescence.

It was nothing like his wedding to Daisy, and yet Jake found himself hesitating as he reached down to take Zoe's hand. It was time to slip a plain gold ring on her finger, but the depth and meaning of the powerful symbolism was tarnished by the loss of equality. The ring seemed far more imprisoning as she knelt slightly behind him, as he tagged her as if she were some kind of pet or possession.

Taking a deep breath, he pushed the ring onto her finger. If she could kneel and bow her head, he could do this.

There was no ring for his finger—he was grateful at least for that.

Finally, at last, Zoe was allowed to rise.

It was time to kiss the bride.

She looked at him then, and there were tears in her eyes. And he knew that as hard as this had been for him, it had been a million times harder for Zoe—Zoe, who'd probably never knelt for anyone before in her entire life.

He kissed her softly, gently, trying to reassure himself as well as her that none of this was real.

She clung to him then, and he closed his eyes and held her close. Wishing...what? He didn't even know.

"I'm sorry," she breathed into his ear, barely loud enough for him to hear. "I'm so sorry, Jake. I know how hard this must be for you."

He pulled back to look at her in surprise as he realized that the tears in her eyes were for *him*.

The crowd in the bar was applauding. Carol and her friend Monica threw rice. And Jake stood there watching a tear escape from Zoe's eyes and slide down her cheek.

And he couldn't help himself.

He kissed her.

Not because he had to.

But because he wanted to.

Her lips were so soft, and she tasted impossibly sweet. How could someone as tough and strong as Zoe taste that sweet?

He gently coaxed her mouth open, taking his time, kissing her slowly, completely, deeply. Very, very deeply.

Time ground to a halt and the noise in the room faded to a dull roar. Nothing mattered, nothing existed but the woman in his arms.

He wanted to kiss her forever. He wanted this moment to go on and on, endlessly.

He felt her melt against him, felt heat pool in the pit of his stomach, felt his knees grow weak.

God, if a single kiss could be this good...

He pulled back, breathing hard.

Zoe's eyes were wide as she looked at him.

And then Chris and some of the other men from the CRO were slapping him on the back, shaking his hand, buying him a drink.

He looked at Zoe, surrounded now by Carol and Monica, old Roy and Lonnie, and she was still gazing at him, a question in her eyes.

He nodded. Yes. But she still didn't get it. Or maybe she didn't believe him.

"That was me kissing you," he told her silently, knowing she could read his lips.

She smiled, but her eyes welled with fresh tears. And this time he wasn't surprised.

CHAPTER TEN

IT WAS DEFINITELY WEIRD.

Walking into the CRO fort was like walking onto the set of her favorite television show.

Zoe had seen it, in complete detail, on the surveillance video screens many times before.

She'd studied the entire former factory while in the team trailer. She knew the layout nearly as well as Bobby Taylor now.

She could find the main kitchen in a blackout with her eyes closed if she had to. She knew where all the cameras and microphones were located in the compound yard. She knew the shortest route to Jake's quarters from any given point in the place.

But she hung back, letting Jake lead the way.

She would have to remember to let him walk several paces in front of her. A CRO rule.

He'd left his room unlocked—apparently everyone did. He opened the door, holding it politely, the way her father might have done for her mother, to let her go in first.

She knew this room well, too. The colors were slightly different than they'd appeared on the video monitors, though, the red-orange of the shag carpeting a little more brassy, the paneling a little more nicked and worn.

She looked into the mirror, wondering who was watching them right now. Were Bobby and Wes pulling a shift? Or Harvard? Or was it Luke O'Donlon? The entire team knew that everything said and done in this room was purely for the benefit of the cameras. They knew that nothing was real, but still...

She turned to face Jake. "Well. This is.... At least it's nicer than my trailer."

Jake set her bags down on the long, low dresser top. He forced a smile. "It'll do for now."

Holy Mike, could they sound any more uptight? They were supposed to be newlyweds, on their wedding night. They'd both been pretending they were eager to get back here, that they were hot to be alone, but now what?

Jake had definitely been right—this was not going to be any fun. Not while knowing three cameras and God knows how many people would be watching them.

He came toward her, slipping off the jacket he'd put over her shoulders during the ride to the factory. He carefully hung it on the back of a chair, then smiled at her again.

"Mind if I...?" He reached for her hairpins, starting to take them out without really waiting for her reply.

"No, I don't mind." She helped him, and her hair tumbled around her shoulders.

"I love your hair," he said.

Zoe closed her eyes as Jake ran his fingers through it.

"It's so soft," he murmured. "Like a baby's."

He was touching more than her hair, touching her neck, her throat, her shoulders, her arms.

She opened her eyes, and the sight of herself in the mirror caught her off guard. She looked completely enthralled, her eyes half closed, her lips slightly parted, each breath she took making her breasts press even farther out of this two-sizes-too-small dress Carol had pulled out of the back of her daughter's closet.

"Are you cold?" Jake whispered, his hands warm against her arms.

"No, I'm—"

"Yes, you are," he said, silently ordering her to agree. "Your arms feel a little cold."

What was he doing? "I am," she said. "A little."

He kissed her jaw, her throat, the tops of her breasts. The sensation nearly made her burst into flames. Cold was the complete last thing that she was.

"Why don't you climb into bed—under the covers?" He smiled. "We'll see what we can do to get you warmed up."

Ah. *That* was what he was doing. Once they were beneath the covers, no one would be able to tell if they were making love or simply trying on each other's underwear. Especially if they turned off the lights.

Zoe turned her back to him. "Will you unzip me?"

He hesitated slightly, and she knew that he'd been hoping she'd just keep the dress on. But that would seem odd—too odd. She glanced over her shoulder at him. "Please?"

He touched her then, fumbling slightly with the tiny zipper pull. She felt his fingers trail down the entire expanse of her back as she held the dress on in front.

He kissed her neck, his voice suddenly husky. "I'll be right out."

Jake turned out one of the lights as he went into the attached bathroom and closed the door behind him.

God, his heart was pounding. Without a doubt, this was going to be the longest night of his life. He washed his hands, stalling, trying to get his heart rate down to near normal, splashed water onto his face.

But when he closed his eyes, he could see only Zoe's

smooth, bare back. All that perfect skin beneath his fingers.

She wasn't wearing a bra.

He laughed aloud.

He was going to have to climb into that bed with her and pretend to make love to her—oh, and while he did that, she would be half-naked in his arms.

He gazed at his dripping-wet face in the bathroom mirror.

Maybe he could keep *his* clothes on.

Yeah, right. That would look very unsuspicious. After he'd been drooling after her for weeks, *he's* suddenly Mr. Shy?

God, maybe he should just give up and make love to her.

Jake looked hard into his own eyes, recognizing the truth, recognizing that *that* was what he really, *really* wanted tonight. Sex purely for the sake of sex. No strings. No responsibilities. Just Zoe's legs locked around him as he lost himself inside of her.

As he lost himself.

Lost. Himself.

And he *would* lose himself. He'd wake up in the morning, and everything he valued most would be gone. His integrity. His honor. His profound sense of what was good and right.

And how would he be able to look himself in this mirror then?

He wasn't ready for that. Not now. God, maybe not ever.

Jake took off his shirt, stepped out of his shoes and his pants and turned on the shower.

He knew what he had to do.

But he wasn't done stalling.

ZOE HEARD THE SHOWER go off as she lay in the dark, waiting for Jake.

She heard the rattle of the shower curtain being pulled back, and then silence.

God, her heart was pounding.

She waited and...

The bathroom door finally opened, flooding the room with light. And there was Jake, a dark silhouette with broad shoulders, a towel slung casually around his waist.

She couldn't tell if he was smiling. She kind of suspected he wasn't. But God, if there were ever a time she could have used one of his reassuring smiles, it was now.

He flipped the switch for the bathroom light, and the room again was dark. But not completely dark. The searchlights that illuminated the grounds of the compound shone in through the ancient blinds.

She could see Jake as he walked toward her, as he sat down on the edge of the bed.

"Sorry I took so long," he said. "It's been kind of a long day, and I thought you might appreciate it if I had a quick shower."

"I'm a little nervous," she whispered. Honestly. Not just for the benefit of the microphones.

Her eyes had adjusted to the dark, and she could see his face clearly. "I am, too, Zoe," he said quietly. Also honestly.

He smiled at her then. It was a smile that held an apology, a smile that was charmingly embarrassed, yet still self-assured enough to broadcast his awareness of the dark humor of this completely bizarre situation.

Zoe smiled back at him. "I think you're sitting out there because you want to hear me beg."

Something sparked in his eyes. "Begging usually works nicely for me. But tonight it's not necessary."

He dropped his towel on the floor as he slipped beneath the covers.

His skin was cool and smooth as he reached for her, as he kissed her. He pulled her close, his legs deliciously solid against hers as he intertwined them, his chest exquisitely solid against her breasts as his hands slid along the satiny back of her nightgown.

She could sense his surprise and then his relief. Oh, brother, had he really thought she would just be naked beneath these covers?

He had. He pulled back slightly to look at her, to check out the clingy black satin and lace that barely covered her breasts and swept all the way down to her thighs.

"Nice." His voice was husky; his eyes were warm. "Very nice. Very, very, *very* nice."

Zoe giggled. She couldn't help it.

Then Jake started laughing, too, and she laughed harder.

And once she started, she couldn't stop. This was just too absurd. She was finally in bed with this man that she wanted more than anyone in the world. She finally had him exactly where she wanted him, only she couldn't do anything about it because everyone and their right-wing, racist twin brothers were watching on their surveillance video screens.

Welcome to the Jake and Zoe Show.

It was completely insane. They were pretending to be lovers who'd waited to be married before making love, except they weren't really married, at least not in the eyes of the law, *and* they weren't really going to make love. Reality and pretense were all twisted in an enormously tangled, ridiculous knot.

Jake was fighting it. He was trying not to laugh, but that just made it worse.

Zoe clung to him giddily. Their sudden unexplained laughter would be considered extremely strange, but there was nothing either of them could do to stop.

Jake tried to kiss her, but couldn't do it. He buried his face in her hair, laughing so hard he was crying.

They had to do *something* to make it look as if they were getting it on. Zoe pulled him more completely on top of her, cradling him with her body, linking her legs around him and—

Jake tried to pull back, but he couldn't move quickly enough.

He was completely aroused. He'd been lying beside her in such a way that had kept her from knowing that, but now the hard truth—as it were—was unavoidable.

And just like that, they both froze, both stopped laughing.

"Oh, God, I'm sorry," he breathed. He was beyond embarrassed. He was mortified.

"No," she said. "No, Jake, because I want—"

"Don't," he rasped, and kissed her to keep her from saying it.

Zoe kissed him hungrily, telling him without words what he already knew.

I want you, too.

He groaned as she pressed herself up against him, groaned as she kissed him harder, sweeping her tongue more deeply into his mouth.

But then he pulled back. He stopped kissing her and started rocking the bed, his movements obvious from the squeaks of the springs, the way the mattress bumped the wall. But it so lacked finesse, Zoe struggled not to laugh again. Or cry. She was so overwhelmed with emotion and desire, she wasn't sure what would come out if she opened her mouth.

He collapsed on top of her with a shout, pretending it was over far too quickly, pretending he'd found release. They lay there, both breathing hard for many long seconds.

Jake was still rock solid against her thigh, and Zoe wondered if, like her, he was ready to weep from sheer frustration.

But then he rolled off her, swearing softly, and she turned to look at him.

He lay on his back, one arm thrown up and over his eyes. "I'm sorry," he said. His words were for the microphones—they were back in pretend mode. "It's been a long time for me and—"

"Sh." Zoe didn't dare reach for him, didn't dare touch him. "It's okay. We've got the entire rest of our lives to get it right."

"I'm just...embarrassed." He looked at her, lowering his voice. "I *am* sorry."

"It's okay." There was nothing else she could say, not without fear of blowing their cover, not without making Jake even more tense.

He'd kissed her this evening, for real, back in Mel's bar, but clearly he wasn't ready yet for anything more, despite his body's obvious betrayal.

She ached for him to hold her, ached for them to finish what they'd started, ached because she knew it wasn't going to happen. Maybe not ever.

She lay beside him, far too warm beneath the blanket, afraid to move for fear she might brush against him.

"Thank you for marrying me," she whispered, knowing how terribly hard all of this was for him.

Jake just laughed. "Yeah," he said. "Sure."

CHAPTER ELEVEN

JAKE STOOD IN THE SHOWER with his eyes closed, letting the water drum down onto his head.

He'd gotten maybe an hour of sleep last night.

He'd lain awake for hours, hyperaware of Zoe lying next to him in that bed.

It was only a double, not as big as the queen-size mattress he was used to, *and* it had a big, broken-down valley right in the center, to boot. Every time he tried to get comfortable, he sank toward the middle of the bed and ended up brushing against Zoe.

The smoothness of her legs.

The softness of her shoulder.

The cool satin of her barely there black nightgown.

Dear God. He'd been so glad at first that she'd put *something* on. But as the night had dragged on, he'd found himself thinking about the way that slinky texture had felt beneath his fingers, the warm firmness of her body beneath that, the black lace against the creamy fullness of her breasts....

Dear God.

Dear God.

She'd slept about as well as he had.

He'd sensed her, lying awake, tensely clinging to her side of the bed.

At one point, he'd heard her breathing deepen, heard her finally fall asleep. But as she'd relaxed, she'd turned toward him, nestling against him, her hand on his chest, her legs against his.

He'd tried gently to push her legs back, knowing he'd never sleep with her there like that, afraid of what might happen if he pushed his way between her thighs while they both slept. But as gentle as he'd tried to be, he'd woken her up. She'd stared at him, stared at her hand placed so possessively on him, and she'd retreated to her side of the bed with a murmured apology.

He'd finally slept fitfully, waking himself up every few minutes with a start, trying to police himself.

This last time, exhaustion had overtaken him. He'd slept for at least an hour.

And had woken up with Zoe wrapped tightly in his arms. Her soft rear end pressed against him, his face buried in her sweet-smelling hair, his right hand securely cupping her breast.

He'd extracted himself from her this time without waking her. Morning light was finally streaming in through the cracks in the blinds, and he'd gotten out of bed, aching in every way imaginable.

He'd gone for a run, pushing himself far beyond his usual five miles, and by the time he'd come back to the room, the bed was neatly made and Zoe was gone.

With luck, she was as good as Pat Sullivan had said she was, and she'd return to the room with the six missing canisters of Triple X in hand.

Jake laughed aloud, knowing how completely ridiculous it was to think Zoe could simply find the Trip X by walking the halls of the CRO compound on her first morning here, but irrationally hoping just the same. It was about time *something* in this op came easily.

"Hey," Zoe said, pulling back the shower curtain and stepping into the tub. "What are you laughing about in here all by yourself?"

Jake hit his head on the showerhead, quickly turning so that his back was to her. "Zoe! *Jeez!*"

He still had shampoo in his hair but he shut the water off, reaching for the towel that was hanging on the back of the bathroom door.

But she reached past him and turned the water back on.

Soap ran into his eyes and he swore sharply as he wrapped the towel around his waist despite the water streaming down on him. "What the *hell?*"

She leaned against him, close enough to speak directly into his ear, her voice low. "We can talk quietly in here. With the water running, our words won't be picked up by the microphones if we speak softly enough. And the camera is over the window. This is the only place in your entire suite where we can't be seen."

Jake nodded. "Well," he whispered, rinsing the soap out of his eyes. "Isn't this convenient?"

"Don't whisper," she warned him. "Use your regular voice—just keep it really low." She laughed softly. "You can open your eyes and turn around. I've got clothes on."

Thank God.

He turned around—and realized he'd offered up his prayer of thanks just a little too soon. Zoe was in her underwear—a running bra and an entirely too skimpy pair of panties.

"We have a little problem," she told him seriously, as if she always held important meetings in the shower, half naked.

Her running bra left little to the imagination to start with, but wet, it molded itself to her breasts. Breasts that he knew more than filled the palm of his hand. And he had big hands.

He focused on her eyes. Water beaded on her long

eyelashes, making her look even more freshly beautiful than ever.

"Problem?" he repeated stupidly.

"As a new member of the CRO through marriage," she said, her voice so low he had to lean closer to hear her, "I apparently only have probationary status here. I'm not allowed to leave this room unless you're with me."

Jake swore loudly, and she put her finger against his lips.

She pulled her hand back quickly, as if touching him had burned her, and he knew that despite her efforts to pretend otherwise, she was not unaffected by the fact they were standing together, barely dressed, in the shower.

I want you, too. The words he hadn't let her say out loud last night seemed to echo against the tile as the steam from the shower swirled around them.

Zoe cleared her throat. "The guard who escorted me back here wasn't completely up on the exact rules." She continued quietly, sounding far more businesslike and matter-of-fact than he could have managed given the circumstances. "But as far as I could gather, there's some sort of special vacation deal for newlyweds. As a woman, I'm supposed to work, but I'm not allowed to join a work party for at least four glorious days. Unfortunately, we don't *have* four glorious days to waste."

In order to hear her, Jake had to stand so close he could count the drops of water on her face. One of the drops ran down her cheek like a tear and landed on her collarbone. As he watched, it meandered down her chest, slowly gathering speed as it disappeared between her breasts.

Jake closed his eyes. The towel around his waist was completely soaked. It weighed about ten pounds and hung low on his hips. He had to hold it up with one hand as he kept the soap from his hair out of his eyes with the other.

"So now what?" he asked.

"So we temporarily ditch my intended plan to flit about, dodging cameras and guards like an invisible little ghost, and we march boldly—together, holding hands because, hell, it's our four-day honeymoon—into Christopher's private quarters."

She was starting to shiver, and he turned them both around so that she was standing directly under the stream of warm water. She tipped her head back, letting the water flow on her face and all the way down her smooth, flat stomach. She squeezed her hair back with her hands and smiled at him. "Thanks."

Jake hiked his towel up higher and moved closer so he could speak directly into her ear, careful not to touch her. "I know you think Christopher's keeping the Trip X somewhere in his suite, but I can't get past the fact that if the CRO's going to take out all of New York City in a matter of weeks, *someone, somewhere* has to be working on some kind of delivery system."

He slipped slightly on the slick bottom of the tub and caught himself on the tile wall, his other hand still firmly holding the towel. By some miracle, he'd managed not to touch her, but just barely. He held on to the wall, bracing himself, his arm extended past her head, about a quarter inch from her cheek.

"There's got to be a bomb or missile being made to carry the Triple X." He tried to continue as if nothing had happened, but his voice was raspy and he had to stop and clear his throat. "It's got to go off at the right altitude above the city, at a time when wind conditions are acceptable. The CRO's got to have a lab to—"

"It's not here," Zoe said definitely. She turned her head to speak into his ear, and her cheek grazed his.

Jake had never had to have his heart started again by

a jolt of electricity through paddles in a hospital's E.R., but he now knew what it would feel like.

"Sorry," she breathed. "God, this is…"

"Awkward," he said, trying to laugh. "Again."

"Maybe we should just…" She looked at him, and the flash of uncertainty in her eyes took his breath away. Zoe? Uncertain? But then she laughed, too, and whatever he had seen was gone. "If only we'd known, we could have packed our wet suits."

Zoe in a wet suit… "Do you scuba dive?" he asked.

"I'm learning. Or, rather, I was learning. It was mostly my friend Peter's idea, and when, well…" She shook her head and rolled her eyes. "Let's not go there."

Peter, huh?

"We've gone off track," she said briskly. "Where were we?"

"Discussing the lab," he said. Whoever Peter was, he was completely insane to have had Zoe and left her. "There's got to be a lab. Somewhere."

"Not here," she told him with complete confidence, instantly back on track. "Not in this facility. Just the quick look around I had this morning verified what I've seen from the surveillance cameras. And you said yourself you've been over this place with a fine-tooth comb. Maybe there's an outside source—"

"No. No way." Jake was just as convinced. "Vincent would *never* go outside of this little kingdom he's made."

Zoe released all the air in her lungs in a burst of exasperation. But then she froze, gazing into his eyes, ignoring the water that was hitting the back of her head. "Jake, what if…"

He could practically see her brain smoking, she was thinking so hard. She laughed aloud, the expression on her face morphing from disbelief to amazement to real excitement.

"Holy Mike, what if Chris doesn't know what he's got?" She gripped Jake's arm. "My God! He may think his birthday surprise will take out a few dozen racially inferior types in the New York subway system—kind of like that horrible incident in Japan a few years ago. He may not know he's got enough Triple X to turn the entire tristate area into a graveyard." She shook him slightly. "You've got to convince Chris that it's time to share secrets. Do whatever you have to do, Jake, but get him to tell you what the hell his plan is."

"Oh," Jake said. "Gee. Is that all?" He took her arm and shook *her* slightly. "What do you think I've been trying to do all this time, Zoe?"

She had the decency to look embarrassed. "I'm sorry."

Awareness dawned in her eyes the exact moment Jake realized it, too. They were holding on to each other, her hand on the taut muscles of his forearm, his palm against the smoothness of her shoulder.

Jake would only have to move his head about an inch and a half, and he would be able to kiss her.

She moved her hand. "Sorry. I'm...sorry."

He spun them both around so that he was standing once again under the force of the water. He released her so he could use that hand to rub the last of the shampoo from his hair. His other hand was still holding the towel for dear life. "Just let me rinse off," he said. "And then you can...do what you need to, and after, we can take a walk, see if Christopher's in."

"And after *that,* I have something I want to show you," she told him. "A place we can go to talk without being overheard. It's outside, though, so dress warmly."

Dress was the key word. It would be very nice to have

a private conversation in which they both had on all of their clothes.

Jake maneuvered his way to the other side of the narrow tub, reaching to open the curtain and step out.

But Zoe stopped him, holding on to the edge of his completely soaked towel. "Better leave this behind," she said. "And try to look happy."

Happy. Instead of impossibly, intensely, overwhelmingly, painfully, achingly frustrated and upset.

Jake laughed. No problem.

"THERE WERE AT LEAST three rooms he didn't show us." Zoe lay on her back in the warm autumn sun on what had probably at one time been the Frosty Cakes employees' recreation deck.

Christopher Vincent had welcomed them effusively into his private quarters. When Jake had told him Zoe was eager for a look around, the CRO leader had given her what could only be described as a significant glance when Jake's back was turned.

Zoe had given him a loaded smile in return, hoping that he'd give them a more thorough tour if he thought she was interested in whatever tawdriness he had in mind.

Whether he'd give them a more thorough tour or not, there was no way of knowing.

All Zoe knew was that the missing canisters of Trip X weren't anywhere in sight in his private dining room, his bedroom, his enormous private bath or the three suites his wives and their young children occupied.

Jake and Zoe hadn't been allowed into his private office. According to the layout of the factory that she'd studied in the SEALs surveillance trailer, she had to guess there were somewhere between two and four additional rooms in the area they hadn't seen. But a lab? She *still* didn't think so.

She turned to look at Jake, who was stretched out on his stomach, his arms folded underneath his head. His face was upside down from her perspective. He'd moved close enough to talk softly and still be heard beneath the rather bucolic sound of the nearby waterfall, but only their heads were together. His body and legs were a full one hundred and eighty degrees away from hers. Still, even that way, they were uncomfortably close. Too close.

She laughed. Two miles would've been too close, given the power of her attraction to him.

"What's so funny?" he murmured, his eyes half shut.

"You look tired," she said.

"You do, too."

"I didn't sleep much last night."

The half-lowered lids were only a ruse. His brilliant blue eyes were as sharp as ever. "Yeah," he finally said. "I know."

"May I say something that I feel needs to be said— even at the risk of embarrassing you?"

Jake closed his eyes. "No."

"Jake."

He opened his eyes and sighed as he looked at her. "What's the point?"

"For starters, we're going to be in bed again together tonight," she told him. "Have you thought about that?"

"The thought has crossed my mind one or two million times already today," he said drily.

"The fact that you had a—"

Jake closed his eyes. "Don't say it."

Zoe rolled onto her stomach, pushing herself onto her elbows, supporting her chin with the palm of her hand. "You know, I probably would've been offended if you *hadn't* been so turned on. The past few weeks have been *extremely* intense, and correct me if I'm wrong, but I've got to believe you haven't made love since—"

"No," he said, cutting her off. "You're not wrong."

Since Daisy died. Zoe swallowed, aware that Jake hadn't wanted her even to say Daisy's name. Her heart broke for him. And for herself. "You must miss her so much."

"She was irreplaceable," Jake said quietly.

Zoe had known that. She just hadn't thought it would sting quite so much hearing Jake speak the words aloud.

"You know I find you very attractive," Jake said. He laughed. "And if you didn't know that, well, after last night you certainly knew it, huh?"

"I knew," Zoe said. "Before last night."

"Forget about the part where I'm old enough to be your father, okay?"

"I have."

Jake laughed. "Yeah, well, I haven't. But let's pretend for the sake of argument that I have. This thing between us, babe, it's still going nowhere fast. I can't get past the fact that Daisy's still the woman I love. I just don't see myself—" He broke off, unable to continue.

Zoe nodded, gazing at the waterfall, trying to convince herself that the tears in her eyes were the result of the too-bright sun. She couldn't look at him. But she had to ask. "And those times when you really kissed me?"

He was silent for several long moments. "Contrary to what you believe, I don't always do the right thing."

She did turn to look at him then.

He smiled crookedly, tiredly. "I know you see me as that all-powerful hero from Scooter's book, but honey, in truth, I'm just a man. Lead me not into temptation and all that. Sometimes temptation is just a little too tempting, and then I make mistakes. And sometimes I just make mistakes—completely on my own. No help from any outside force. I don't want you—but I want you. Sometimes the part of me that wants you shouts down the other part."

Zoe studied his face. Jake. The man. He was right, in a way. For years he had been her hero. Invincible. Intrepid. Noble. Immortal. Yet beneath all that, he *was* just a man.

A very *good* man.

"So are you just planning to be celibate for the rest of your life?" she asked.

Her question caught him off guard. "I don't know," he said honestly.

"Well," Zoe said carefully. "When you do know, if the answer to that question is no, I hope you'll come and find me."

Jake put his head down on his arms and laughed. But when he lifted his head, propping himself up on his elbows the way she was, his eyes were filled with a curious mix of both sadness and heat. "See, now, like, right now is one of those times I really struggle with, because right now I have this completely overpowering urge to kiss you."

Zoe wanted to touch his beautiful face, to push back that unruly lock of hair that fell down over his forehead. But she didn't.

"You have to tell me the best way I can be your friend, Jake," she said. "Do I move closer when you say that to me? Or should I back away?"

He was close enough to kiss her, and his eyes dropped to her mouth before he looked into her eyes. "Are you strong enough to back away?"

Was she? "Right now, yes. Tomorrow? I don't know."

"Then back away," he breathed. "Please."

Zoe didn't move. "Tell me about Daisy."

Jake blinked. And laughed. And backed away himself. "Well," he said. "She was absolutely nothing like you."

Zoe quickly looked away, but apparently not quickly enough.

"Whoa," Jake said, catching her hand. "I didn't mean that the way it sounded. I mean, I meant it in a good way. You're so strong, so certain. You're a scientist, and Daisy…" He laughed. "She didn't have a lot of use for science or math."

Zoe gently pulled her hand free. Backing away. "She was an artist, right?"

"Yeah, mostly a painter, both oils and watercolor, although she did go through a charcoal phase, too. She was…" He forced a smile. "Pretty amazingly brilliant." He was quiet for a moment. "She never came out and said it, but she hated what I did—what I do—for a living. And when Billy decided he wanted to be a SEAL, too…" He shook his head. "She didn't like to talk about it. She just locked herself in her studio and painted." He rolled over onto his back and stared at the sky. "I think I managed to make her incredibly unhappy at times, but she loved me enough to pretend it was all right. And I loved her too much even to consider that she might be happier without me. And yet, you know, in our own way, we did okay. We had so much more than most couples I've known."

He turned his head and looked at her. "Okay, Lange. Your turn. 'Fess up. Who's this Peter?"

Zoe tried to smile, but she couldn't. "No one," she said quietly. "He was nothing. Not compared to what you had with Daisy."

"It's not fair to make comparisons."

"Yeah," Zoe said. "It is. You talk about love in a way that I can't even comprehend." She took a deep breath.

"You know, Jake, last night was the first time in my life I've ever slept all night in the same bed with a man."

He tried to hide his incredulousness and failed, sitting up to look at her. "Really?"

Zoe nodded and sat up, too, unable to meet his eyes. "I've had relationships—obviously—but it's always been, 'Well, gee, that was fun. See you in the morning.'" She braced herself and looked at him. "I've never lived with anybody. I've never gotten that close. I've never even wanted anyone to stay the night."

Jake had known a love the likes of which most people only dreamed. And she... She wasn't even one of the dreamers. She hadn't even dared to do that.

Jake sighed. His face was so serious without his usual hint of a smile lurking around his mouth. "This must be very hard for you. I'm so sorry. I've been thinking only of myself—"

"Look, it's no big deal. I just wish—" She broke off, unable to say it.

He touched her again, his fingers warm against the back of her hand. "What?"

She wanted to know what it would be like to sleep in Jake's arms, all night long, with his warmth and strength wrapped around her. But there was no way she could tell him that. Not after promising him she'd back away. She shook her head. "I wish a lot of things that are definitely better for you not to know."

Jake laughed as he stretched out on his back again, arms above his head.

He was silent for such a long time, Zoe turned to see if perhaps he'd fallen asleep.

But he was staring at the nearly painful blueness of the Montana sky. He met her gaze, though, as if he'd caught her movement out of the corner of his eyes, and he smiled.

It was a smile that echoed everything she was feeling. Longing. Sadness. The knowledge that the price they'd both pay for the sweetness of a temporary joining was a high one.

Too high for Jake.

CHAPTER TWELVE

"OH, YES," LUCKY O'DONLON said from his seat at the video monitors. "There *is* a god. Zoe's getting ready for bed."

On the other side of the trailer, Bobby and Wes didn't even glance up.

"Hey, Ren and Stimpy, didn't you hear what I said? Zoe. Moments. From being. Au naturel."

"Don't hold your breath," Wes said. "You're Lucky, but not *that* lucky. She knows exactly where the cameras are."

Sure enough, Zoe stood in the one place in the room where she had her back to all three cameras. And she undressed in segments, taking off her shirt and slipping on her nightgown while she still had on her jeans. She pulled both her jeans and her bra out from under the gown.

It was very disappointing.

On the other hand, the nightgown was black and short and very, *very* sexy. It highlighted her exceedingly generous upper body in a most pleasing way.

"Oh, man," Lucky murmured. "Imagine coming back to your quarters and finding *that* waiting for you."

Wes finally came to look over his shoulder. "Youch! Way to dress for bed, Dr. Lange!"

"Show a little respect," Bobby rumbled.

"I only said youch," Wes complained.

"Next time, say it with more respect." But even while

Bobby said the words, he pulled his chair closer to the video screens.

"Who was on duty last night?" Wes asked.

"I was," Bobby said.

"Am I correct in assuming that she put that on last night, and you didn't tell me?"

"It didn't seem to warrant a phone call to the other trailer," Bob said. "So, no, Skelly. I didn't. Besides, I happen to respect Zoe, so...I didn't."

"That is one beautiful woman." Lucky glanced at Bobby. "And I say that with the utmost respect."

"So where's the admiral?" Wes asked. "He is a seriously dedicated team leader if he opted for a sneak and peek instead of playing honeymoon for the cameras with a babe in a black negligee. Sheesh, can you imagine *having* to do that? For Uncle Sam, Mom and apple pie, yes, I *will* suffer and kiss the beautiful blonde. What kind of training do you think I should go for next, so that I'll be given this kind of assignment?"

"Yeah," Lucky said. "Talk about a silver bullet..."

"I think it must be very difficult," Bobby said. "For both of them. He cares a great deal for her. And Zoe..." He sighed. "She's falling in love with Jake."

Lucky and Wes both turned to look at him.

"You're nuts," Wes said. "He's way too old for her."

"She can't fall in love with him," Lucky said, turning to watch her on the screen. She was lying on the bed, on her stomach, as she read a book. "She's supposed to fall in love with *me*. Beautiful women always fall in love with me."

Wes shook his head. "You think you're kidding, but it's true. You're a babe magnet. When Zoe first walked into that meeting at the Pentagon, I cursed you out, Lieutenant, sir, because it seemed inevitable she would take one look at you and not even talk to the rest of us."

"As soon as this assignment's over," Lucky said with a sigh as he watched Zoe on the screen, "she's mine." He smiled. "Hey, it might be fun to actually have to chase a woman for a change."

"It's not going to happen," Bobby said. "She's got a jones for Jake."

"Since when are you on a first-name basis with an admiral?" Wes asked.

The enormous SEAL shrugged. "Since I found a copy of that book Zoe was talking about. It was in the library. Jake's pretty amazing. The things he did with explosives... The man's an artist. You should read it."

"Yeah," Wes said. "Right. Read. Maybe in my next lifetime. So where exactly *is* Admiral Amazing?"

Bobby took over the command keyboard and started to type, and on one of the screens a rapid-fire sequence of empty corridors began to appear.

"He just had a private meeting with Christopher Vincent," Lucky reported. "He endured the slimeball's company for more than two hours just to get a chance to ask him about this bogus birthday celebration. And when he finally did get down to business, Vincent tells him he's got to pledge all he's got to the CRO if he wants to be privy to CRO secrets. The admiral says, great. I'm ready to do that. Right now. Let's go. But Vincent says no. Not till after the honeymoon, essentially ordering the admiral to go back to his quarters and get busy with his new wife for the next three days."

"Perfect," Wes said, scoffing. "Zoe goes to all this trouble to get inside the compound, thinking it'll speed up the search, but what it really does is slow things down."

"Got him," Bobby said.

On screen, the admiral was heading down the corridor that led to his room. His pace slowed as he approached the door, and he paused for a moment outside, just staring at the knob.

"Oh, man," Lucky said. "I'd be knocking the door down, I'd be in such a hurry to get inside that room."

On the two screens that still showed two different angles inside the room, Zoe put down her book and looked toward the door.

It didn't open, and she slowly sat and then stood up, staring at it.

Outside the room, the admiral took a deep breath and finally reached for the doorknob.

Bobby keyed in the third of the bedroom cameras, and from the new angle, as the door opened, Lucky could see the man's face.

On screen, Zoe visibly relaxed. "I didn't realize it was you. I heard footsteps stop right outside the door and…"

The admiral turned to close and lock the door behind him. "Sorry I took so long. Chris can really keep a conversation going. I was a little afraid you might've gone out looking for me."

"Why would I do that?" she asked. "I knew where you were. Besides, you told me I had to stay here."

He turned to look at her, smiling slightly. "I guess I just—"

That was when he noticed what she was wearing.

"Boing!" Wes said. "Hel-lo, Mrs. Robinson. How *are* you this evening, dear?"

Lucky didn't know how he did it, but the admiral managed to keep his tongue securely in his mouth as he gazed at Zoe and her incredible nightgown.

The tension in the room was palpable, though. It carried through the airwaves all the miles across the valley, through the receiver, through the wires that led to the video monitors in the trailer.

Zoe spoke so softly, Lucky had to turn the volume up.

"I was just...reading. I was tired so I...got ready for bed a little while ago and..."

"Are you going to be..." The admiral cleared his throat. "Warm enough in that?"

"I don't have anything else."

"No flannel pajamas?"

Zoe laughed, a nervous burst that she tried to squelch. "It's pretty warm in here."

Well, that was the understatement of the year. Lucky could practically feel the heat rising from the screens.

Jake took his wallet and a set of keys from his pockets and put them on top of the long, low dresser. "You know if you're tired, and I'm not here, you don't have to wait up for me."

"The idea of waiting up for you isn't a particularly appealing one," Zoe said. "Is it going to happen frequently?"

"Well, you know, I hope not—" Jake moved toward her "—but if evening is the only time Christopher can schedule to meet with me—"

She moved out of his reach. "What's the deal with this place, Jake? When am I going to be able to leave this room?" She lifted her chin, made her voice louder, sharper. "What exactly do people do here for fun? Someone told me today that CRO women aren't allowed to go into Mel's. Don't get me wrong, it's not like I want my old job back, but I'd like a chance to go grab a beer if I want to. And if I'm not allowed to do that, when *am* I supposed to get a chance to kick back?"

"She's picking a fight," Bobby said. "Way to go, Zoe."

"And is it true what I've heard?" she added. "That in three days I'm supposed to join some sort of chain-gang work detail and *clean* all day long?"

The admiral gave her one of his let's-keep-this-in-perspective smiles. "I'm sure it's not *all* day lo—"

"While you do what? Stand around and be good-looking?"

Jake laughed aloud, and Zoe's expression got even more fierce.

"You think this is funny?" she said. "Then *you* go clean. I'll sit around with the guys."

"I'm sure I'll get to do my share of the cleaning. It's just they've found this place runs a little better if the women are organized in teams and—"

"So it *is* true," she said.

"It's just the nature of the commune, babe. Everybody's got to chip in."

"I'm sorry, I didn't quite hear what it is *you're* going to be doing? Sitting around burping all day with the rest of the men?"

Wes laughed out loud.

"And what about those three princesses and their ugly little babies?" Zoe continued. "*They* got served at dinner just like the men."

"Those are Christopher's wives and kids. You know, he's a little eccentric, he's got—"

"Three wives. I know. I saw their rooms. *They* don't have peeling paneling on *their* walls."

Jake reached for her again, pulling her into his arms. But she stood there stiffly, angrily. He kissed her shoulder, her neck, but she didn't move. She just stood there, straight as a rod. He tried to kiss her lips, but she moved her head and his mouth glanced off her ear.

"I'm really tired," she said tightly, pulling free from him. "I'm going to sleep."

"Oh," Lucky said, making a face. "The freeze-out. The temperature in the room just dropped to a frightening fifteen below."

As Jake watched, Zoe climbed into bed, turned on her side and clutched the blankets to her chin.

"Come on, Admiral," Wes said to the screen. "No self-respecting man would just stand there and watch his plans to get it on go up in smoke."

"Any self-respecting man caught in this situation would definitely drop to his knees and beg," Lucky agreed. "Honey, I'm so sorry. Of *course* I want to go to your crazy parents' house on the one weekend I have off this year...."

Wes nodded. "Of *course* I want to sell my racing boat and buy a washer and dryer."

"Of *course* I want to poke myself in the eye with this sharp stick. I don't know *what* I was thinking...."

"Zoe." On screen, the admiral sat down on the other side of the bed.

Zoe was absolutely silent.

"I'm sorry, babe. I thought you knew what this place was all about."

Nothing.

"Come on, Admiral Amazing. Down on your knees. Climb under the covers and get to work. Do *something* or this glacier's gonna freeze you to death."

Jake just sighed. "We can talk about this more in the morning." He stood up and tiredly went into the bathroom, closing the door behind him.

"He's just giving up," Lucky said.

"That's the point. He doesn't want to touch her," Bobby said.

"He's nuts. Why the hell doesn't he want to touch her?"

"He doesn't want to touch her because he *wants* to touch her," Bobby explained.

Lucky looked at Wes. "They're pretending to be married. So instead of pretending to get friendly, they pretend to have a fight, because *he* doesn't want to touch one of the ten most beautiful women in the world. That make any sense to you?"

"Nope." Wes shook his head. He looked at Bobby. "But you understand this, don't you? I am seriously worried about you, Robert Taylor."

ZOE CLUNG TO THE EDGE of the bed, listening to Jake breathe in the darkness, wondering if he'd fallen asleep yet.

She heard him draw in a deep breath and let it out in a sigh, and she knew he was as wide awake as she was.

She had a plan that she hoped would get her inside of Christopher Vincent's private office. As soon as the restrictions on her were lifted, she would go to him— alone—and request a private meeting. She would tell him she didn't realize the nature of the hard work involved in being a regular CRO wife. She would imply that she was much more suited to other tasks.

And if Jake knew she was planning to do this, he would have an absolute cow. No, not a cow, a full-grown stegosaurus.

Not that any of this would get that far. She would never put herself into a situation where she'd actually have to sleep with the CRO leader. She'd never compromise her sense of self that way, despite the fact she'd done everything but told Jake she would.

She sighed. This afternoon, she'd all but promised Jake she'd back away from him, and keep backing away. And she'd come up with that idea to stage a fight when he'd been out talking to Chris. Fight, and then go into a major pout. It had kept them from touching, kept him even from having to kiss her good-night.

Kept them from pretending to make love.

She'd seen the flare of intense relief in Jake's eyes

when he'd realized what she had been doing—and why. He wasn't the only one who had been relieved. She wasn't sure how much more close contact she could take.

"Zoe."

His voice was so quiet in the darkness, at first she thought she'd imagined it.

But then Jake touched her. Reaching across the grand canyon in the middle of the bed, he touched her, his fingers light against her arm.

Zoe's heart nearly stopped.

"I think we should stop fighting," he said.

Were his words purely for the microphones, or did he actually intend them to have double meaning?

"Come here," he whispered. "We'll both sleep much better if you let me hold you."

She turned to look at him. His face was dimly lit, his eyes colorless in the darkness.

"Come on," he said, pulling her toward him, meeting her in the middle.

His arms felt so good around her, tears stung her eyes. He wore no shirt, and his skin was so warm, his chest so solid. She could smell just a hint of his delicious cologne and the mint of his toothpaste.

She held on to him tightly, knowing she should push him away, knowing she'd virtually promised him she would.

She could feel his legs against her and—

Zoe looked at him. He was still wearing his jeans. Denim. The ultimate in protection.

He smiled that crooked smile she'd come to know so well. "This'll be nice," he breathed. "We both really need to sleep, and…"

And he'd not only remembered what she'd told him this afternoon on the roof, but he'd also read between the lines. He'd figured out one of the things that she'd wanted so badly was for him to hold her in his arms all night long.

Zoe kissed him. She couldn't help it.

He sighed as he met her lips in a kiss that was impossibly sweet. It was filled with desire, but coated in something else, something wonderfully warm, something so much stronger than mere passion.

"Good night," she whispered.

His voice was like velvet in the darkness. "Night, babe."

Zoe closed her eyes and, with her head tucked safely beneath his chin, she fell asleep listening to the steady beating of Jake Robinson's heart.

CHAPTER THIRTEEN

"Do you ever think about Vietnam?"

Jake leaned his head against the concrete block wall, lifting his face to catch the weak rays of the afternoon sunshine. "Nope. Never."

"Are you lying?"

Zoe was sitting next to him. They were sitting on the deck that overlooked the waterfall again. Killing time.

They'd spent the morning wandering around the CRO fort, searching for closed-off areas and locked doors that they might've missed. But they'd had to stop, afraid of being too conspicuous.

They'd then spent about an hour collecting as much information as they could about the CRO work teams—finding out what Zoe would have to do to be assigned to the team that cleaned Christopher Vincent's private rooms, including his office.

From what Jake could gather, the first thing she had to do was to be a part of the CRO for at least five years.

That meant they had to find another way in, another way to get the information they needed. And that way was going to be through Jake pledging his loyalty to the CRO and Christopher Vincent.

And that brought them here, to the roof of the factory, where they sat out of range of the cameras, their voices covered by the rush of the water. Killing time until their "honeymoon" officially ended.

Zoe had her hair pulled into a ponytail, and without any makeup on, she looked about eighteen years old. "You *are* lying," she said. "Aren't you?"

Jake opened his eyes and looked at her. "Yep."

"You probably never talk about Vietnam, right?" She had taken off her boots and socks and sat with her bare feet stretched out in front of her, legs crossed at the ankles. She had small, elegant feet—quite possibly the nicest feet he'd ever seen.

He went back to looking at the sky. It was much safer.

"A lot of the guys who were over there don't want to talk about it," he told her. "And people who weren't there, well... It's not something that's easy to explain. But you know what that's like. You probably never talk about the assignments you've been on."

"Most of my assignments have been top secret."

"Mine, too. But I meant the ones that weren't."

Zoe sighed. "Yeah, you're right. Peter could be pretty flip and, well, sarcastic. He was so jaded and cynical, I just never told him anything that really mattered." She glanced at him. "The bad stuff *or* the good stuff."

"I never wanted Daisy to get upset," Jake said. "I *did* talk to her about some of the really bad voodoo that went down in Nam. We both needed me to talk about that, just to get past it, you know? But it would really upset her when I talked about the reasons I'd kept going back—the reasons I stayed in the navy. She didn't understand why I needed it. She didn't understand what I got out of it."

"That sense that you're actually *doing* something, you're actually taking action, instead of just being a bystander." Zoe nodded. "There's so much hand-wringing that goes on in the world while nobody does a damn thing. I joined the Agency because I wanted to do more than compile frightening statistics about chemical and biological weapons. I wanted to track the suckers down and destroy them."

"And then there's the rush, too," Jake said. "She *really* didn't understand the adrenaline rush."

"I'm not sure I understand it myself." Zoe sat up, putting her socks and boots on as the late afternoon got colder. She pulled her legs underneath her to sit tailor style. "It's weird, isn't it? I was once…somewhere I shouldn't have been, in a country that would not have welcomed me with open arms under any circumstances. I was checking out reports that a pharmaceutical factory was cooking up anthrax. I went into the factory covertly, found what I needed to prove those reports were accurate and came back out—but not quite as covertly, after I nearly knocked over a security guard." She laughed, her eyes shining as she remembered. "It was insane. I was being chased by about twenty soldiers across the rooftops of the city in this amazing thunderstorm. Wind, lightning, hail—it should have been terrifying, but it wasn't. It was so exhilarating. So amazing. I can't explain it. I couldn't explain it then, either."

"You don't have to," Jake said, sitting up, too. "I know exactly what you mean. It's like, you're not just alive, you're *beyond* alive. It's…"

"Incredible," she finished for him, laughing. "It seems crazy. You look at a situation and there are all these risks, and you think, I should be running away from this as fast and as far as I can. You think, This time this could kill me."

"But then you think, But I bet I know how to beat this…"

"Yeah." She smiled. "I know how to win."

"So you do," Jake said. "You win, against all the odds, and it's so damn great."

"It's beyond great," she said.

She was sitting there, completely lit up, her eyes sparkling as she smiled at him.

Jake knew he was grinning at her, but he couldn't stop. "You must've been one of those kids who tried to parachute off the roof with a bedsheet."

"I had four brothers," she told him. "I had to learn to fight just so they'd let me tag along. And I had to prove—almost daily—that I was tough enough and daring enough to get inside the hallowed walls of their clubhouse. So, yeah, I did my share of roof walking. It drove my father nuts." She laughed. "I think I still drive my father nuts."

Her father had been in Nam. He was one of Jake's peers. A man whose life he'd helped save. A man who would definitely disapprove of the kind of thoughts Jake had been regularly having about his daughter.

Jake had woken up this morning with Zoe in his arms, and for about four very long seconds, his brain had played one hell of a trick on him. The extremely erotic dream he'd had about making love to her just moments before was still shockingly vivid in his mind, and he'd temporarily confused fantasy with reality, confused that dream with real memories. For a few endless seconds, he'd believed he truly had kissed her last night, her body arching eagerly up to meet his as he'd driven himself deeply inside of her.

But then reality intervened and he'd remembered what had really happened. Nothing. Nothing had happened.

Yet the thought of actually making love to Zoe had taken his breath away.

Yesterday, he'd told her that their relationship was going nowhere. He'd started to tell her that he couldn't imagine making love to any woman besides Daisy. He'd started to tell her he didn't see himself with anyone else—he just couldn't picture it.

But he hadn't been able to finish his sentence, because

it wasn't the truth. Not only could he imagine making love to Zoe, but he could see it in his mind's eye in shockingly intimate detail.

"What made you decide to join the navy?" she asked, pulling him back here, to the roof, where they both were fully dressed.

Her jacket was open and she was wearing a long-sleeved T-shirt tucked neatly into equally snug-fitting blue jeans. She seemed comfortable in her clothes, though, comfortable in her body. And why shouldn't she?

For most of his life, Jake had had the kind of good looks that most people made a big fuss over. But when he gazed into a mirror, he'd only seen himself. No big deal.

In the same way, Zoe had lived with *herself* all *her* life. She'd seen herself naked, washed that body every day in the shower, brushed her hair while looking into those liquid brown eyes in the mirror.

Like him, she was probably well aware that her package was wrapped in ultrahigh-quality paper, but—also like him—she had plenty of other, more important things to think about.

She was looking at him, waiting for him to answer her question about the navy. Why had he joined the SEALs?

"My father was a UDT man in the Second World War," he told her. "He was part of the underwater demolition teams, the precursors to the SEALs."

"Was he career navy, too?"

Jake had to laugh at that. "No. He was about as non-regular navy as anyone I've ever met. He was a diver before the war, spent most of his time doing salvage ops in the Gulf of Mexico, living on a boat down in Key West, pretty much being a beach bum. He was tapped to join the teams after the disaster at Tarawa, when the navy really started developing underwater navigation. He served in the Pacific until V-J day, and then he hunted down my mother in New York. He'd met her when she was a nurse in Hawaii. He went all the way to Peekskill and grabbed her out of the arms of her extremely boring fiancé, literally hours before the wedding, and pretty much immediately got her pregnant with me." He laughed again. "Frank, my father, was something of an underachiever, but when he finally decided to take action, he was extremely thorough."

"So you grew up in Peekskill, New York?"

Jake looked at her. "You planning to write up an article on me for *Navy Life* magazine?"

She laughed. Damn, she was pretty when she laughed. "Am I being too nosy?"

"Do I get to grill *you* after you're done with me?"

She smiled into his eyes. "You've read my Agency profile—probably the Top Secret-eyes-only version. So you know pretty much all there is to know about me."

"And you're telling me you didn't manage to get hold of *my* profile from the Agency?" he asked.

"Your Agency profile contains your full name, your date of birth and only a very brief sketch of your naval career, my mysterious friend. Most of what I know about you is from Scott Jennings's book. And he doesn't say anything at all about your childhood. I'm just…" She shrugged expansively. "Curious."

She was curious. But was it a professional or personal curiosity? Jake wasn't sure which alarmed him more.

He was silent so long, Zoe began to backpedal. "We don't have to talk about this," she said. "We don't have to talk at all. I just… I wanted…"

"We lived in New York until I was about three," Jake told her quietly. "I don't really remember it, but apparently we were poor but happy."

"Jake, you really don't have to—"

"I had an extremely unconventional—but incredibly happy—childhood," he said. "You want to hear about it or not?"

"Yes," she said. "I want to hear about it. Please."

"This is completely off the record," he said. "We're talking as Jake and Zoe. Not Admiral Robinson and Secret Agent Lange. Is that understood?"

"As Jake and Zoe," she said. "As friends. That's understood."

Friends. They *were* friends. That was why he felt so warm inside whenever she smiled at him. That was why he felt good just sitting here, next to her. It was why he could hold her in his arms all night long and wake up having slept better than he had in months. Years, even.

"Good," he said, letting himself get lost for a moment in her eyes. Friends. Yeah, they were friends.

"Are you waiting for a drumroll before you start?" she asked, eyebrows lifting slightly.

"Do you have a problem with me taking my time?" he countered.

Zoe smiled sheepishly. "Sorry. It's hard to break the habit of always being in a hurry. I'm not the most patient person in the world." She took a deep breath, letting it slowly out. "Please," she said. "Whenever you're ready."

Jake laughed. "I love it when impatient people think they can fool everyone and pretend that they're in control. Meanwhile, they're wound tighter than a yo-yo and ready to go off in twenty different directions from tension."

"I'm more than willing to discuss the causes of my tension—and potential ways to reduce a little of my stress. But something tells me you might want to stick to a safer topic right now."

Jake cleared his throat. "Yeah," he said. "Okay. Let's

see. Where was I? Peekskill. Right. I was about three, and Helen and Frank—my parents—both had jobs teaching at a private school, that is, until my great-uncle Arthur died."

Jake could think of three or four really powerfully excellent ways to relieve a little of his own stress, and he desperately tried to push them far, far from his mind. *Friends.*

"Artie had just a little less money than God, and he left it all to Frank. Frank being Frank, both he and Helen handed in their resignations on the spot. Helen being Helen, they stayed until the end of the school year. But in May, we all packed our things, put our furniture in storage and spent the next fifteen years traveling. We went *all* over the world—London, Paris, Africa, Australia, Hong Kong, Peru. If we found a city we liked, we stayed for a few weeks. But if it had a beach, we stayed much longer. We spent about two years in the Greek Islands. Another two in Southeast Asia, not too far from Vietnam. It wasn't always safe, the places we went, but it was *always* exciting. Frank taught me to dive and Helen homeschooled me. Instead of being poor and happy, we were rich and happy—not that you could tell we were loaded from looking at us."

Frank had been easygoing, almost to a fault, and Helen had been intensely driven, determined to completely finish every last little project she started. Jake had inherited her drive but had learned to disguise it with his father's laid-back attitude. He'd learned that in a command position, his men trusted him implicitly because of this—because of his relaxed air, his ability to exude the fact that everything was—or would be—okay.

"So you joined the SEAL units because you wanted to keep traveling?" Zoe asked.

"I joined for a lot of reasons. One of them was because

I had friends in Vietnam. I spoke the language, I…felt like I could make a difference, maybe help end the conflict." He smiled. "And of course, there's that age-old reason kids join the SEAL units—I had a fascination with explosives. I liked to blow stuff up. You know, SEALs can make a bomb from just about anything. Let me loose in a kitchen, and I can make a powerful explosive from the junk I can find under the sink." He grinned. "And I can have fun while I'm doing it."

Zoe laughed. "That's interesting," she said, "because in *my* line of work, I tend to try to *keep* things from blowing up."

"Maybe that's why we work well as a team," Jake said. "It's that yin and yang thing."

Yin and yang. Female and male. He shouldn't have said that, shouldn't have made the comparison. He held his breath, hoping she wouldn't go there again. Her last remark about stress had been about all he could take.

"I'm not used to working in a team," Zoe told him, neatly ignoring his potentially sexually loaded comment. "I'm used to going in someplace, completely on my own, and getting the job done without having to ask permission or wait for orders."

"Well, for someone who's not used to it, you're doing a damn fine job working on my team."

She chewed thoughtfully on her lower lip. "Does this mean you forgive me for trying to force your hand the other night?"

The night he'd gone to Mel's and had been told she was out sick. The night he showed up at her trailer to find her bags already packed, Zoe ready to go to the CRO compound one way or another. With Jake. Or with Christopher Vincent. The thought still made his stomach hurt.

"Zoe, I—"

She held up one hand. "No, don't answer that. I know

I was way out of line, and that's not something that can be fixed by only an apology."

Jake had to smile. "It would help at least a little if you actually *did* apologize."

"Oops." Zoe's answering smile faded as she gazed into his eyes. "I *am* sorry, Jake."

"But not sorry enough not to do it again if you had to."

Her eyes were completely subdued, level and sober as she looked at him. "Sitting out here like this, it's easy to forget why we're in the CRO fort. But if we don't find that Trip X soon…"

"I have an appointment with Christopher Vincent on Tuesday morning," Jake told her. "And if I can't convince him to appoint me as one of his lieutenants and let me in on the birthday party plans, I'll take a trip into town. On my way out of the gates, I'll give the rest of the team a signal. Cowboy and Lucky will go into Mel's while I'm there, and they'll 'recognize' me as former Admiral Robinson—wanted by FInCOM. I'll make it back to the compound, but within an hour, the place will be surrounded. We'll be in siege mode, but *I'll* be the catalyst, not the Trip X. The CRO still won't know the Finks know about the nerve gas—they'll think this is only about catching me. It'll buy us more time, because no one—and nothing—will leave the fort until the situation's resolved."

Zoe nodded. "And you don't think being surrounded by FInCOM agents might make Chris decide to try out the Trip X?"

"I'm willing to bet he won't. Of course that's something we'll have to monitor carefully from inside. And as the FInCOM target, I'd hope I'd be privy to any plans Christopher has to resolve the issue." Jake paused. "Again, this is the backup plan. First we wait and I go in and try to talk to Christopher."

"But not until Tuesday." Zoe sighed. "I feel as if this waiting is all my fault."

"It could be worse," Jake pointed out. "There could be a four-week honeymoon period instead of four days."

"I'm not very good at waiting," she admitted. "Sometimes even four minutes seems way too long."

"Back in Nam," he told her, "my team once got pinned down by these VC builders who came in and— It was the weirdest thing, Zoe. We were out in the middle of nowhere, and they started digging pits and building wooden flooring for tents literally feet from where we were hiding in the brush. We were pinned there until nightfall, and then, instead of getting the hell out of there and going back to civilization, we hung out for nearly four days. It drove the guys mad—we were just sitting there—but I had this hunch, and sure enough. The VC were building a POW camp. The tents were for their officers and guards. The pits were for the prisoners, mostly Americans. We just sat tight and watched as they brought in about seventy-five of our men.

"My SEALs started to hand-signal me." Jake moved his hands, making the signals that enabled a SEAL team to communicate without speaking. "Now? Attack now? And I just kept signaling wait. *Wait.* We were way outnumbered. There were too many VC, *and* there was no way we could've taken them all out without killing some of the POWs in the crossfire. Besides, I had another hunch."

Zoe nodded. "God bless those hunches, huh?"

It was the funniest thing. He was telling this story— one of his stories about a triumph in a war that had far too few triumphs, and he knew that Zoe understood everything he was saying. He knew she understood everything he'd felt. He'd helped to kill dozens of enemy soldiers that day, but in doing so, he'd saved over seventy Americans who otherwise would never have come out of that jungle alive.

It was crazy. In a way, this twenty-nine-year-old child understood him completely. He looked into her eyes, and he knew that she knew his anguish *and* his exhilaration. Even though she'd never been in quite that same situation, she *knew*. They were so alike in so many ways. And because of that, Jake had an intimacy with Zoe that he'd never had before, not with any other woman.

Not even Daisy.

Especially not Daisy.

Daisy had loved him, Jake knew that without a doubt. And he'd loved her, too, with all his heart. But despite that, there were parts of himself he'd purposely kept hidden from her. There were parts of his life that he'd simply never shared.

"So we sat there," he told Zoe, "and we watched while they ordered the POWs into those pits and into the cages they'd made—these little, cramped god-awful…" He exhaled his revulsion. "One of the prisoners, a Brit, he spoke in Vietnamese about prisoners' rights—and they hung him from his feet and tortured him to death."

He closed his eyes, remembering, hating the powerless feeling of knowing there was nothing he could do. He knew now as well as he'd known then that if he'd let his men attack, dozens of the other prisoners would be mowed down by the VC's automatic weapons. With those kinds of odds, in a direct firefight, the SEALs wouldn't necessarily win. And if they didn't win, they'd be dead—or worse. They'd be locked in those cages, too, thrown in those pits.

Zoe took his hand, linking their fingers together,

squeezing gently. "How many did you save?" she asked. "Seventy-four?"

He nodded, loving the sensation of their clasped hands far, *far* too much, hoping she'd pull her hand away, praying that she wouldn't.

"And still it's the one you couldn't save that you dream about, right?"

He forced a smile. "Funny you should know that."

"Tell me about the seventy-four," she said, still holding his hand.

Jake knew he should let go of her hand, maybe even move six inches or so away from her. Somehow they were now sitting close enough for their shoulders to touch, for their thighs to connect. How had that happened?

"How did you get them out?" she asked.

Jake drew in a deep breath. "Well, after they...did what they did to the Brit, they just left him hanging there. All the other prisoners went into the cages and pits without a fight, just completely beaten down both physically and psychologically." His voice shook. He couldn't help it, even now, all these years later. "God, Zoe, they were naked and starving—some of them skin and bones, some of them reduced to little more than animals and..."

He didn't know how it happened, but Zoe wasn't just holding his hand anymore. She was in his arms, holding him as tightly as he was holding her. Oh, dear God. He buried his face in her sweet-smelling hair, knowing for certain that if she kissed him, he'd be lost.

He had to keep talking, keep his mouth moving.

"After they were locked up, the camp commander sent a half a dozen men out to stand guard." His voice was raspy, but he couldn't stop to clear his throat. As it was, his lips were brushing the side of her face. "They'd built the camp in this sheltered area on the side of a mountain, and there was only one way in and out. So with the guards posted and the prisoners locked up tight—"

"Everyone else relaxed." She lifted her head to look into his eyes.

Her mouth was inches from his. Soft. Sweet. Paradise.

"We struck covertly after dark," he told her. "And we dispatched the VC soldiers silently, tent by tent."

She knew what that meant. Dispatched silently. She knew the price he'd paid for those seventy-four lives—he could see her complete awareness in her eyes.

"The six men standing guard went down just as easily. They never expected to be attacked from within their camp. We armed those POWs with the VC's weapons and walked down that mountain and out of that jungle."

Zoe pulled away from him slightly to narrow her eyes at him. "Why do I know it couldn't have been *that* easy?"

"We had a few firefights on the way back to our side of the line. But compared to some ops, it *was* very easy."

"I would've loved to see your captain's face when you came walking in with seventy-four POWs and MIAs."

He couldn't make himself let go of her. It felt too good holding her this way. She was so warm and soft against him.

"I didn't stick around to see anyone's face," Jake said. "We just dropped 'em and went back out there."

"Because you couldn't bear the fact that you'd only saved seventy-four instead of seventy-five?"

"We watched them cut him, Zoe. We watched the—" He shook his head, swearing softly. He pulled back and would have let her go, but she wouldn't release him. And he was glad of that. "Look, it wasn't something that I'm ever going to forget. But I swear, I played that scenario over and over and over in my mind—I still sometimes do. And there was no feasible way we could have saved him.

I made a choice to save the seventy-four." He laughed in disgust. "And in order to do that, I had to turn my back on that one very brave man."

"But that's the way life works," Zoe told him. Her fingers combed through his hair at the nape of his neck, both soothing *and* nerve-jangling. "Every time you face someone, you turn your back on someone else. Your team saved my father's life, Jake. His platoon was nearly wiped out, and he and about a dozen other marines were left for dead. You and your SEALs were the only ones brave enough to try to bring them out. You used explosives and with only seven men, you made the Vietcong believe we'd launched a counteroffensive. It provided enough of a diversion to get a chopper in there and get those men out."

"You know, I remember that," Jake said. "That was one of the long shots that actually paid off. Your dad was one of those men, huh?"

"Don't you realize, when you chose to go in after my father's platoon, you turned your back on dozens of other marines who also needed rescuing that day?"

Jake didn't know what to say. "I guess I never thought of it that way."

"It's all a crapshoot," she told him seriously, gazing at him with those impossibly beautiful brown eyes. "Every decision, every choice. You go with your gut, and you've got to trust yourself. But after it's all said and done, you've got to celebrate life. Seventy-four men went home to their wives and mothers because of you. Seventy-four lives that you directly touched, and hundreds and *hundreds* that you indirectly touched. Mothers who didn't spend twenty years flying an MIA flag on their porch. Wives who didn't have to raise their children alone. Children who didn't have to grow up without a father—or children like me who would never even have been born."

"I know all that. I just wish..." He sighed. "It just never seemed to be enough. I always found myself wanting to save just one more man. And then just one more, and one more. But the truth is, I could've been bringing five hundred men out of that jungle each day, and it still wouldn't have been enough."

"You told me you weren't that superhero from Scott Jennings's book, that you were just a man," Zoe said. "And if that's the case, you should try to keep your personal expectations down to the mere mortal level." She took a deep breath. "And as long as I'm criticizing, I've got to be honest and wonder why a man who's as alive as you would want to spend all his time keeping company with the dead."

She wasn't just talking about Vietnam anymore. She was talking about Daisy.

"Grieve and let her go, Jake," she whispered.

How was it possible that he could be thinking about Daisy while gazing into Zoe's face and wanting desperately to kiss her?

Grieve and let her go....

"We should go back," Jake whispered. "It's getting dark. You must be cold."

"I'm not cold," she told him, her gaze dropping to his mouth before she looked into his eyes. "Are you?"

He couldn't stand it anymore. "I really want to kiss you," he whispered. "It's killing me to sit here, holding you like this, and not kiss you."

"Then kiss me," she said fiercely. "You're not the one who died, dammit!"

Jake didn't move. He didn't have to move, because she kissed him.

What he should do and what he wanted fought the shortest battle in the history of the world, and what he wanted won.

He kissed her almost roughly, completely on fire, sweeping his tongue possessively into her mouth, pulling her on top of him so that she was straddling his legs. The heat between her thighs pressed against him, her breasts soft against his chest as he lost himself in the hungry sweetness of her mouth.

He heard himself groan as he touched the smoothness of her back, as his hands slipped beneath the edge of her shirt.

He might've gone along with it. Might've? He knew damn well he would have. If Zoe had tugged at his clothes, if she'd reached for the buckle on his belt, he wouldn't've been able to fight both her and himself any longer. He would've made love to her, right there on the roof.

But she pulled back, pushing herself off his lap, nearly throwing herself a solid five feet away from him, breathing hard, and swearing softly under her breath. "I'm sorry." She dropped her head onto arms that were tightly hugging her folded knees, unable to look at him. Her voice was muffled. "I promised you I'd back away, not attack you."

"Hey, it's not like we both didn't—"

"No?" she said, looking at him, her eyes a gleaming flash in the rapidly falling darkness. "Then what are you doing sitting over there? Why didn't you follow me over here?" She answered her own question. "Because just letting it happen is a whole lot different from making it happen."

He couldn't deny it.

"You know I want you," she said softly. "But I want you to want me, too, Jake. I don't want to make love to you thinking that this is only happening because of some temporary insanity on your part, or some chink in the armor of your code of ethics. I don't want to have to feel guilty for seducing you, or overwhelming you, or tempting you, or anything. I want you to look me in the eye and tell me you want to make love to me. I want to meet you as an equal. I respect myself too much to accept anything less."

Zoe pulled herself to her feet, brushing off the seat of her pants. "So," she said. "Unless you want to come over here and take my clothes off, I think I'll head back inside."

Jake didn't move. "Zoe, I'm—"

"Sorry," she finished for him. "Don't be. I know I'm asking for too much." She started for the stairs leading down off the roof. "Give me a few seconds before you follow. It can't hurt to give Chris the impression that we're still fighting."

A few seconds. Jake needed more than a few seconds to regain his equilibrium.

He stared at the sky and watched the first few stars of the evening begin to shine. The air had grown crisper, colder, and his breath hung in front of him in a cloud.

Indisputable proof that, as Zoe had pointed out, he was *not* the one who'd died.

CHAPTER FOURTEEN

ZOE HUMMED TO HERSELF as she got ready for bed. She hoped if she sounded calm and relaxed, she'd look calm and relaxed, as well—instead of completely, teeth-jarringly, heart-janglingly nervous.

Jake had watched her all through dinner. She'd sat at the table with the other women, and he'd sat next to Christopher Vincent. And every time she'd looked up, Jake was gazing at her.

She'd laid everything she was feeling out on the table this evening on the old recreation deck.

Well, nearly everything. She hadn't revealed this feeling of intense warmth she got every time the man smiled at her. She hadn't revealed the feeling of pulse-pounding, dizzying free fall she got from the desire she sometimes saw in his eyes.

She *had* told him how much she wanted him.

And Jake had turned her down. Again.

Yes, he was a man, and yes, he was attracted to her, but he didn't want her. Not really. Not desperately. Not the way she wanted him.

Normally, she didn't require being hit over the head with a hammer to receive a rejection. She didn't know why with Jake she insisted upon embarrassing herself again and again.

She put on her nightgown, wishing desperately that she'd brought something a little less revealing, wishing she'd brought her bathrobe. She'd purposely left it in the trailer, thinking it didn't quite seem like something Zoe the waitress would own. It was a little too demure, a little too classy for the part she was playing right now.

Jake sat on the edge of the bed, untying his boots, the muscles in his powerful arms and shoulders flexing beneath the cotton of his T-shirt and standing out in sharp relief in the low-watt light.

He'd told her no in every possible way. He wasn't ready for a physical relationship. He'd made that clear. He'd told her he wanted to be friends. And up on the deck, they'd been doing really fine as far as friendship went—or at least they had been before she'd gotten all stupid and started holding his hand.

She knew *that* was a mistake right from the moment her fingers had touched his, but she'd tried to convince herself that friends sometimes held friends' hands. Same thing when she suddenly found herself holding him in her arms.

But then she'd lost it. And she'd kissed him. Again.

And then, stupider and stupider, she'd had the gall to feel hurt when he'd let her know—again—that he truly wasn't interested in their relationship going in that direction.

Oh, if she hadn't stopped them, he might've let his good intentions slip. He might've let himself be carried over the line, bulldozed by the intensity of her passion.

She watched Jake's reflection as he pulled his T-shirt over his head and unfastened his jeans. He glanced over, and Zoe quickly looked away, but not before he'd met her eyes in the mirror. Great. Now he'd caught her watching him undress.

But instead of turning away, he moved toward her, toward the mirror. "If this bothers you, I can wear a shirt to bed."

It took Zoe a few long seconds to realize that he was talking about the latticework of scars on his chest.

"No," she said. Was he nuts? Was that *really* why he thought she'd been staring at him? It would have been hysterically funny if her sense of humor hadn't been stretched so thin. "Really, Jake, that doesn't bother me at all."

He was looking critically at himself in the mirror. "Funny, isn't it, that I survived Vietnam virtually unscathed, only to have this happen when I was supposedly safe at home?"

"I look at those scars," Zoe said softly, "and I can't believe you survived. It was some kind of assassination attempt, right?"

The killers had come into his own home, past his security guards. They'd gained entry by pretending to be part of a team of Navy SEALs sent to protect the admiral from death threats he'd been receiving. After he'd been shot, the navy had taken him to a hospital safe house and had publicly released news of his death, both to protect Jake and to catch the man who'd sent those killers.

Zoe had been in Kuwait when she'd heard the news on CNN, and she'd sat on the balcony of her hotel for hours that night, just looking at the lights of the city, deeply mourning the loss of a man she'd never met.

Jake met her eyes in the mirror. "It happened two years ago, Christmas. It took me a long time to get back to speed, physically." He turned and tossed his shirt into the laundry pile in the corner of the room, then took his wallet and keys and change from his jeans pockets, lining them neatly up on the dresser as he spoke. "You know, in a way getting shot wasn't so bad. I mean, with a physical injury, recovery goes in stages. It's all laid out for you. The doctors have done it before, there's no real mystery to the process.

"First the bullets are removed, and then the doctor

stitches you up. Then the wound is bandaged and drained, and you lie in a hospital bed, and you focus on surviving, one day at a time—one *hour* at a time if you have to. Then the bandages get changed, and the injury is cleaned, and you fight infection and sleep a lot so your body can heal. Then finally after you're out of the ICU, you stop merely surviving and start rebuilding your strength, still through bed rest. Then, even though it hurts like hell, you get mobile. You get out of bed and take first one step, and then two until you can make it over to the bathroom and back without falling down. Then there's physical therapy, more restrengthening.

"Sure, no two injuries are ever exactly alike," Jake continued, "and I had individual challenges each step of the way, but even getting around those challenges was pretty clear-cut. If I do A, then I'll improve. If I do B, I'll improve that much faster. If I do C, I'll hurt myself, so don't do C."

Zoe understood. He was talking about far more than his physical trauma. He was trying to explain himself, explain what he was feeling and why exactly he had turned her down again this afternoon.

"Emotional recovery isn't as easy." All his coins were in perfect little stacks on the dresser, and he knocked them over with a sweep of his fingers and went to sit on the bed.

He glanced at her, one hand on the back of his neck, as if it ached. "You're not dealing with muscles and bones. You're dealing with something far more fragile and far less identifiable. Something that doesn't have as clearly a defined list of steps to do, you know, to go about fixing the problem. See, like, if *you* do A, *you* might improve, but if *I* do A, I might end up in a worse place than where I started. Do you understand what I'm saying?"

Zoe nodded, holding his gaze. He was talking about

losing Daisy, about his dealing with his loss. "I do understand, and Jake, really, you don't have to—"

"On the other hand," he said with a crooked smile, "since it's all trial and error in terms of what works and what doesn't, it seems crazy to just never try A or B or even C, out of fear it's going to hurt worse. Because what if it doesn't hurt? What if it helps?"

What was he telling her?

"I'm tired of being afraid, and I'm tired of feeling so damn alone." His voice shook slightly, and he stood up swiftly, using both hands to push his hair from his face as he laughed in disbelief. "Jeez, this is perfect. Can I make myself sound any *more* pathetic?"

Zoe took a step toward him but stopped herself. Dammit, she wasn't going to do this again—offer comfort and then get horribly embarrassed and hurt when her deep-burning desire for this man overpowered her self-control.

But this time, Jake reached for her.

And as he drew her into his arms, she felt herself melt. Oh, God, she was the pathetic one.

His hands were against her back, her shoulders, her neck, running through her hair, the sensation enough to make her cling to him mindlessly. Dear God, what would happen if he kissed her?

He did, so sweetly, so gently, she had to close her eyes against the rush of tears that came. She knew she shouldn't, but she couldn't help it—she opened herself to him, and he kissed her harder, possessing her mouth with absolutely no uncertainty, completely and unquestionably in command.

This was all for the cameras. Zoe knew that their conversation must have been cryptic and confusing to anyone listening in, but this embrace was completely obvious. To anyone watching, anyone who didn't know better, it would look as if Jake wanted her. And as if she wanted him.

They'd be half right.

It was all she could do to stay on her feet, and she wasn't aware that he'd pulled her with him into the bathroom until he closed the door behind them.

He broke their kiss to lift her up as he stepped into the bathtub. Zoe was slightly off balance, and he held her with one arm as he yanked the curtain closed and turned on the water with a rush.

Jake still wore his jeans and she had on her black nightgown and they both were instantly soaked. The water was cold, it hadn't yet heated up, but maybe that was a good thing. God knows she was way too hot.

She tried to pull back from Jake but then stopped, extremely self-conscious about the fact that her silk gown was glued to her body, extremely aware that she was still touching him and he was still touching her.

But instead of letting her go, he pulled her close and kissed her again.

It was a kiss that meant business, a kiss loaded with passion and need and a wildly burning hunger.

It was a kiss no one but Zoe and Jake could possibly know about.

She looked at him in surprise, unable to believe what he was telling her.

"I want to make love to you, Zoe," he said softly, touching her hair, her face. "But there are four million reasons we shouldn't. The cameras—"

Her heart was pounding. He *wanted*. She was in his arms, her body pressed against the very solid length of his, her hands against the taut, slick muscles in his arms, his shoulders. It was finally okay to touch him. He *wanted* her to touch him. "No one can see or hear us in here."

"Our age difference—"

"I don't have a problem with that."

He smiled slightly at her vehemence, his fingers still in her hair. "How about the fact that I'm your team leader—"

"Technically, I'm here as a consultant for your team. You're not my boss. Pat Sullivan is. Believe me, I've already checked the rules. This isn't fraternizing. I'm a civilian."

He exhaled a short burst of laughter. "Well, it's good to know the shore patrol isn't going to rush in to arrest us."

"I can think of only one reason we shouldn't make love right this second," Zoe said, "and that's that all my condoms are in the other room, in my purse."

Jake took a small square of foil from his back pocket and tossed it into the soap dish that was attached to the tile wall. "I've got that part covered," he told her. He smiled crookedly, sweetly uncertain. "Or at least I will, if this is still what you want."

"It's what I want. Oh, God, it's what I want." Zoe pushed his wet hair from his face, her heart in her throat, completely aware of what he'd just told her by having that condom ready and in his pocket. He'd planned this. He'd come to terms with all of his reservations and he'd consciously made a choice. This wasn't accidental. It wasn't about reacting to high emotions and high passion. He wasn't being bulldozed. He truly wanted this to happen.

Still she had to be sure. "About those other three million, nine hundred and ninety-nine thousand reasons we shouldn't—"

"The hell with them. They don't hold up to the one very solid reason we should," Jake told her, kissing her hard but much too briefly on the mouth. His voice was husky, his eyes filled with heat. "Dammit, *I* want to, and *you* want to, and life's too bloody short. We're both grown-ups and—"

He kissed her again. Longer this time. Pulling her even closer and covering her breast with his hand. Touching, gently kneading, exploring the tautness of her nipple, his thumb rasping against the thin wet silk that covered her. The sensation was nearly unbearable, and she moaned aloud.

Jake did, too. "God," he gasped, pulling free from their kiss. "I've wanted to touch you like this since you walked into that meeting in the Pentagon."

Zoe had to smile. She had him beat. She'd clocked many, *many* fantasy miles with Jake Robinson—starting all the way back when she was a young teenager. He'd been her hero nearly half her life as she'd thrilled to stories of his bravery, his ability to command and his loyalty to those men who followed him.

But it was his soul, his very humanness—his confessed imperfections—that moved her in ways she'd never dreamed she could be moved.

Time seemed to slow as he looked at her, as he touched her, still gently, through the black silk of her gown. The fire in his eyes was incredible as he caught one finger in the slender strap and tugged it down her arm. The clinging triangle of fabric peeled away from her breast infinitesimally slowly, and Zoe felt her desire-tautened nipples tighten under the heat of his gaze.

Jake sighed his approval, smiling into her eyes before he lowered his head and kissed her breast. His lips and tongue were so soft against her, she felt herself sway.

The shower was drumming down on them both, steam swirling around them as Zoe helped Jake peel off her gown. He was no longer taking his time, and as he looked at her, standing naked before him, she felt nearly burned by the desire in his eyes. And then his hands were everywhere, his mouth—hungry now—everywhere else.

Dizzy with need, she reached for the waistband of his jeans, and he helped her, pushing down the zipper, tugging at his pants.

But the wet denim was plastered to him, and it stuck to his skin. Jake slipped on the slick surface of the tub and caught himself, laughing as he desperately tried to rid himself of his jeans. Zoe tried to help, but she suspected she was making the entire process even more difficult.

She was giddy with laughter, too, as they wrestled with this final barrier that lay between them. The irony was incredible. Jake had finally given in, yet he couldn't have made it more difficult for them to make love if he'd tried.

He sat on the edge of the tub and, with Zoe pulling and Jake pushing, they peeled his jeans off, one leg at a time.

Zoe pushed her wet hair from her face as she knelt on one knee in the tub, laughing at him. She was even more beautiful than Jake had imagined, and God knows he'd spent quite a bit of time imagining.

He wanted nothing more than to look at her, and as he did just that, her laughter faded, leaving behind only heat. The desire in Zoe's eyes was incredible, and Jake knew that he was looking right back at her in exactly the same way.

She moved toward him, slowly, still on her hands and knees.

His mouth was dry. He was sitting there, soaking wet, water drumming down upon him, yet his mouth had gone bone dry.

She reached for him, and he lunged for her, pulling her with him, tightly against him as he stood up.

This was the right thing. Despite all his reservations,

holding her like this, being with her like this felt so good, so *right*. His fears fell away, too. Silly fears like, that after three years, he might've forgotten how to do this, that after three years, he'd embarrass himself completely. More intensely complicated fears, like he wouldn't be able to go through with this, wouldn't be able to keep from thinking about—

But he could only think about Zoe. Zoe, who smiled into his eyes and made him feel hope again. Zoe, who held his hand and understood why he'd given his entire life to the navy, to the SEALs, because she'd been, perhaps not precisely there, but to very similar places.

Zoe, naked in his arms, soft and wet and smooth. It was beyond heaven. He ran his hands across her body, unable to get enough of touching her, her skin like silk beneath his fingers. He groaned aloud as he cupped her rear end, pulling her closer to him, feeling her so soft against his hardness, dying—just a little—as she reached between them and closed her fingers around him.

He kissed her, and she gasped into his mouth as he touched her just as intimately. She was so warm, so ready, and she opened herself to him, sliding her leg up and around his.

Jake reached for the condom in the soap dish, and his hand closed around Zoe's fingers.

He had to laugh. Zoe was many things, but reserved wasn't one of them. Beads of water sparkled on her eyelashes as she smiled at him and gave him the wrapped condom.

She slid down his body, kissing her way down his chest and his stomach and… Jake nearly crushed the little package in his hand.

God, he wanted a bed. He wanted to take Zoe into the other room and love her all night long. He wanted to take his time. He wanted her to lie back for him just to look at, her beautiful hair spread out on the pillows. He wanted to spend a solid hour just kissing her breasts. He wanted to explore every inch of her body with his mouth and the very tips of his fingers. And he wanted her to look into his eyes as he filled her completely.

He laughed aloud. The things she was doing to him were taking him dangerously close to the edge.

But this wasn't really what he wanted. He pulled her up, into his arms, and kissed her hard as he fumbled with the foil wrapper. He stepped slightly out of the stream of the shower and covered himself.

Zoe slipped behind him, and he could feel her breasts against his back, her stomach against his rear end as she rubbed herself against him. She wrapped her arms around him, her hands cool against the slickness of his chest and stomach. And lower.

"Am I helping?" she asked.

Jake laughed. "Oh, yeah."

"You know, you are," Zoe breathed into his ear, "without a doubt, the sexiest man I've ever met."

Jake turned toward her, that half-embarrassed, half-sheepish look in his gorgeous blue eyes, and she had to laugh. "You honestly don't think of yourself that way, do you?" she asked him.

"What way?" He pulled her hips against him as he lowered his head to touch the tip of her breast lightly with his tongue.

Zoe closed her eyes, pushing herself against him, farther into his mouth. He drew her in, harder, and then even harder, and she moaned her approval.

"As the complete hottie that you are," she told him when she finally could speak.

He lifted his head and laughed at her. "Wow, and all this time, I thought I was an admiral in the U.S. Navy."

"Admiral Hottie." Zoe laughed at the look he gave her.

His hands had taken up where his mouth left off. There was no doubt about it. Zoe knew he liked *her* body, too. She sighed as he caught her nipple between his thumb and fingers.

"I'm not even sure what that means," he said. "Hottie." He laughed. "Jeez."

"Check yourself out in the mirror sometime."

His eyes half closed as she pressed herself against him, as she started to move against him in a slow rhythm, and his hand tightened on her breast. "Is that all I am to you? A *hottie?*" His voice was still light, playful, but Zoe looked into his eyes and answered him honestly.

"The fact that you're a hottie is just a bonus," she told him, touching him, unable to keep herself from touching him. "I want you inside me, Jake, because I think that when I get you there, I'll have a little taste of everything really good and right that I've been missing all my life." She forced a smile. "Whoa. That was too intense, huh? I'm—"

"No," he said. "Don't apologize for being honest. I love the way you look, too, but we're also friends. *Good* friends. And that's what's making this so damn good already. Even though I'm still not inside you." He lowered his voice. "I'm dying to be inside you."

Zoe couldn't breathe, couldn't speak. She couldn't do more than let herself be kissed.

Jake's kiss was proprietary. It was completely possessive, controlling and commanding, but for the first time in her life, Zoe truly didn't mind.

He lifted her up, breaking their kiss so he could look into her face, into her eyes, as he slowly, *slowly*—screamingly slowly—entered her. He pushed her against the slick, wet tile wall, but there was nothing to hold on to, nothing to do but let him keep control.

With her legs around his waist and her back against

the slippery wall, her mobility was limited. But with Jake
still holding her gaze, with all the pleasure he was feeling
clearly written on his beautiful face, it was an incredible
turn-on.

And for the first time since Zoe could remember, she
placed the complete control of her immediate future into
another person's hands.

Into Jake's very capable hands.

He pushed himself a little bit farther inside of her,
smiling slightly as she moaned just a little too loudly.

"Sh," he breathed, still holding her gaze as he took his
sweet time.

His next thrust was just as slow but twice as deep, and
Zoe caught her lower lip between her teeth to keep from
crying out again.

Jake's smile widened. "That looks like something I
should be doing." He leaned forward and gently tugged
on her lip with his teeth. She moaned again—she couldn't
help it.

He laughed as he kissed her, filling her with his spirit
as well as his body. The pleasure was so intense, Zoe
couldn't do more than whisper his name.

With the shower raining down on her sensitized skin,
with his mouth doing things to her breasts that she'd never
imagined possible, with the cold tile against her back and
Jake, hot and heavy, moving so infuriatingly, wonderfully
slowly inside of her...

It was beyond perfect.

She breathed his name again, and even though she
didn't say it in so many words, he somehow knew she
was close to the edge.

"Come on, Zoe," he murmured, his lips on her ear, on
her face, on her throat, her breasts. "You're gonna take
me with you. I want to go right with you...."

Zoe kissed him. As wave upon wave of pleasure

exploded around her, she kissed Jake so she wouldn't cry out. He inhaled her in return, driving himself even harder, even more deeply inside of her. She felt him explode, felt him shake with his release, just as he'd promised.

And still Jake kissed her.

He kissed her and kissed her and kissed her, holding her there pinned against the shower wall, still buried deeply inside of her.

His mouth was so sweet, his lips so gentle, Zoe should have been in complete and unquestionable heaven. But she couldn't stop thinking. *Now what?* Jake had done it. He'd made love to another woman for the first time since his wife had died. What was he thinking? What was he feeling?

Was he kissing her because he was trying to avoid facing himself another few minutes longer? Was he overwhelmed with regret? Did he hate himself? Did he hate *her?*

But then, "I wish I could kiss you all night," he murmured, his breath warm against her ear. "I wish we could make love again, tonight, in a bed, no covers, lights on…."

Relief made her laugh. He sounded all right. That was a good sign, wasn't it? "As much as I'd like that, too, I think the fact that our entire SEAL team would be watching might be a little distracting."

Jake laughed, too, as he gently lowered her to the tub floor, as he turned away and efficiently cleaned himself up. "We're almost out of hot water," he said. "Want a shot at it before it's completely gone?"

"Thanks."

What had once been an awkward switching of positions in the crowded tub was now an opportunity for full body contact. Jake kissed her, and as she quickly lathered herself with the soap, he helped. He helped her rinse, too, his hands skimming her body, his touch so deliciously possessive. Who would've ever thought that would turn her on so completely?

He held her close, her back against his front, his arms wrapped around her, his hands caressing her breasts.

"I can't seem to get enough of you," he said softly. "I think I might need two solid weeks of leave, a hotel with room service, a heavy-duty lock on the door, a king-size bed and you."

Zoe closed her eyes as he weighed her breasts in the palms of his hands, as he kissed her neck, as she felt his body start to grow harder, already, against her rear end.

But then he caught her hand. Her fingers were water-logged, the tips starting to wrinkle. "Uh-oh, we've been in here too long."

The water was starting to run cold, and Zoe turned to look at Jake. "Are you ready to get out?"

"No." But he reached past her to turn off the water. And then he stepped back from her, reaching outside the shower curtain for a towel. He opened it as he handed it to her, wrapping it around her shoulders.

"Thanks."

He started to step out of the shower, to get a towel and dry himself off in the bathroom—he didn't care who saw him naked—but Zoe caught his arm.

"Really," she said quietly, looking into his eyes. "Thanks."

He laughed slightly, shaking his head as he looked away from her, at his feet, before he leaned forward to kiss her. "Thank *you*."

He stepped out of the shower, and Zoe realized he hadn't quite managed to look her completely in the eye.

He'd had no problem holding her gaze while they were making love, but afterward… She realized that after, he'd done everything possible to keep from having to let her look deeply into his eyes.

It was all an act. The sweet words, all of it. He wasn't okay with any of this—he was just pretending to be so as not to hurt her feelings. He was kissing her so he wouldn't really have to face the truth.

Zoe shook herself. That was absurd. Jake was quite possibly the most honest man she'd ever met. Why would he start hiding the truth from her now?

Unless maybe he was hiding that truth from himself, as well.

But now that the water was off, there was no way she could confront him.

The shower curtain opened slightly, and Jake leaned in. He held something out to her—one of his T-shirts. "I figured you wouldn't want to put that nightgown back on."

It was impossibly sweet and completely considerate, but Jake definitely didn't hold her gaze. He quickly backed away, letting the shower curtain drop.

"Thanks," Zoe whispered.

Okay, so he *wasn't* completely happy about this. She'd expected that, hadn't she? She had absolutely no right to feel upset, no cause for this sudden ridiculous rush of tears that pressed against her eyelids and threatened to escape.

What did she expect? That Jake would make love to her once and fall instantly in love with her? That he'd forget all about his life with Daisy?

Zoe scrubbed her face with her towel, fiercely willing her tears away.

But as she slipped Jake's T-shirt over her head, as she breathed in his familiar clean, warm scent, the tears returned.

And she knew with a clarity that was unquestionable that although Jake hadn't fallen head over heels for her, she was completely, indisputably, impossibly in love with him.

CHAPTER FIFTEEN

ZOE'S HEART BROKE INTO a thousand pieces as she stood in the doorway that led to the recreation deck, watching Jake as he sat alone in the cold morning air.

His back was against the concrete wall, his knees up and his head down on his folded arms.

It was entirely possible that he was crying.

Zoe had woken up this morning alone in their bed. It had been barely oh-six-hundred, and Jake was already gone.

She'd washed quickly, shutting her mind to the memories of all that she and Jake had done in that very shower just hours earlier. But after she'd dressed, Jake still hadn't returned.

She didn't need to be a rocket scientist to know where he'd gone. And even though she wasn't supposed to walk the halls of the former Frosty Cakes factory alone, she slipped out of their room and headed for the recreation deck.

"So are you just going to stand there, or are you going to come out here and talk to me?" Jake lifted his head to look at her.

How had he known she was here? She hadn't made a single sound as she'd approached. And she was positive that when her heart had broken, it had broken silently.

She moved toward him slowly, warily, certain that she

didn't want to see evidence of tears on his face. But his eyes were dry, and he managed to smile.

Zoe sat next to him, careful not to sit too close. "Are you all right?"

This morning he could meet her gaze. His eyes looked tired. "I expected to feel really bad." He didn't try to pretend her question applied to anything else. "I thought I'd feel, you know, as if I'd cheated on Daisy." He shook his head. "But I don't. I feel..."

He reached down and took her hand, lacing her fingers with his, squeezing her hand. Zoe just waited, praying he'd tell her how he felt. Praying he'd say the words she was dying to hear. It was ridiculous, really. In just a matter of seconds, she'd gone from brokenhearted to wildly hopeful. Holy Mike, if love could make a levelheaded person experience emotional shifts more often associated with mental illnesses, she wasn't sure she wanted to be in love.

Unfortunately, it wasn't something she could shut off.

She'd tried *that* this morning, too. It wasn't going to happen.

"I feel alive," Jake told her. "For the first time in years, I...honestly feel alive. It's..." He squinted at the overcast sky before glancing at her and smiling crookedly. "It's actually a little scary."

Alive. Alive was good.

Wasn't it?

"You're amazing, you know," Jake told her. He put his arm around her, pulling her close. "Last night was... amazing." He kissed her, and Zoe's hope grew about a mile and a half high, like that magic bean stalk in that fairy tale. "You're exactly what I needed." He kissed her again, longer this time, his fingers lightly tracing her collarbone at the open neckline of her shirt. *"Exactly."*

Zoe closed her eyes, dizzy from everything she was feeling. Desire—always desire, whenever Jake was concerned. He was, and would always be, the most desirable man in the world to her. Need, hope, she felt that, too, and pleasure—such sweet pleasure from his kisses and his touch.

Love. Oh, God, as terrifying as it was, she wanted him to love her, too. Just a little bit. She wouldn't need much to be satisfied—maybe just a tenth of the amount he'd given to Daisy....

He kissed her again, and she shifted closer to him, moving his hand so it covered her breast.

He sighed and laughed. "I guess it wasn't hard for you to figure out what I like, huh?"

Zoe kissed him, pushing herself more fully into his hand. "I'm glad I've got what you like."

"I like everything about you, Zoe," he said, pulling back to look into her eyes. "Not just your body."

Like. Not love. Still, his words were sweet.

"We're in tune," he told her, "you and me. I can be completely honest with you—about everything. You know as well as I do how important this mission is. You know exactly what the dangers and the risks are. I don't have to hold things back to keep you from being upset." He paused. "And I don't have to worry about hurting you when this op is over and we go our separate ways."

Oh, God. Zoe closed her eyes as she leaned against him. Now *she* was the one afraid to let him look into *her* eyes.

"Maybe that's why I'm so okay about this," he murmured, running his fingers through her hair. "I know you're not looking for anything permanent. I know you don't want anything more than sex—I mean, friendship, sure, but... What we did last night was intensely powerful, but…it was mostly physical. I mean…" He laughed. "You don't want to marry me, right?"

He didn't let her answer. She wasn't sure she *could* have answered. "But that's okay," he continued. "It's okay with me, and it's okay with you. And, see, that's what I think makes this work. I know that *you* know that I can't give you my heart."

Jake's heart.

In just a short amount of time, it had become the one thing in the world Zoe wanted more than anything. She wanted to walk out of the CRO compound in possession of the six missing canisters of Triple X, and Jake's heart.

Jake kissed her, and she sat there, with his arms around her, watching the first few flakes of snow drift from the overcast sky, praying he wouldn't see the truth when he looked into her eyes.

He was wrong.

Somehow she'd broken all of her rules. Somehow she'd let herself cross that line. She was crazy in love with him.

And she wanted his heart.

Desperately.

"He's NOT GETTING IT DONE," Lucky said. "We're almost out of time."

Harvard was giving him that stone-cold look that implied not only was Lucky a kindergartener, but he was a *misbehaving* kindergartener. "What do you suggest we do, Lieutenant? Mutiny?"

"No." Lucky took a deep breath. "Look. I just think it's been long enough. Let's try to get at least a few more men inside." He swore. "What we *should* do is get the entire *team* inside."

"That's not going to happen," Harvard said. "Because

even with my blond wig, my complexion is a little too far from fair."

"So let's get in whoever we *can* get in. Me and Cowboy. Wes. We can give him one of those skinhead haircuts—"

"Notice how he doesn't volunteer to shave his own head," Wes said.

Lucky was completely exasperated. "Dammit, what difference does it make?"

"If it didn't make a difference, you'd've volunteered to shave your own—"

"Fine, I'll shave my damn head! Let's just get the hell in there! I'm so damn tired of sitting here doing nothing!"

As soon as the words were out of his mouth, Lucky realized that the problem here wasn't necessarily with Admiral Robinson. The problem was *his*.

He swore again. And then he apologized. To all of them. Especially Wes Skelly and the senior chief. "I've got a little sister in San Diego. Ellen. She's still in college." He rubbed his forehead. God, his sinuses were killing him. "I keep thinking San Diego would be the perfect city for these clowns to test the Trip X, and it's making me crazy."

"I've got a little sister, too," Wes said.

"Yeah, I know that it's no excuse," Lucky said quietly. "We've all got family. I just… No offense, Crash, I know you're tight with the man, but admirals should stay behind desks."

"Even admirals who used to be SEALs who specialized in demolition?" Crash spoke so rarely that when he *did* open his mouth, the entire team paid attention. "Even admirals who became so proficient with C-4 explosives that they literally wrote the book we all trained from—as well as the book that might be just a little too advanced for a few of us here?"

"I didn't know that," Harvard admitted. "How come I didn't know that?"

"You wouldn't. As the leader of the Gray Group, Jake's worked hard to keep a low profile," Crash said. "That's why that book by Scooter Jennings irks him so much. I know some of you have read it."

"I have," Bobby said in his basso profundo. "It's good stuff."

Cowboy lifted the book out of his lap, flashing a sheepish grin. No wonder he'd been so quiet during all this. He was reading, and he was just a few pages from the end. "This reads better than fiction."

"I'm reading it after Junior," Harvard said.

"It's all true, you know," Crash said. "And it chronicles just one of Jake's tours in Vietnam. He's seen more action than all of us in this room combined."

Lucky couldn't keep his mouth shut. "But that was thirty years ago."

"He's been out from his desk and in the real world often enough since then," Crash told him. "You guys want to hear a story?"

"Oh, yeah," Wes said. "Uncle Crash, tell us kids a story."

"S squared, wiseass," Bobby intoned. "*I* want to hear."

Cowboy, even fewer pages from the end, put down his book.

Crash had their full attention. He smiled. "Jake was in Saudi Arabia during Desert Storm, and his team was assigned to take out this one Iraqi Scud missile launcher that kept evading us. The Iraqis would fire the Scud at our troops, then move that sucker to a new location. Jake's SEAL team was working off of satellite pictures and getting nowhere, so Jake—he wasn't an admiral yet, but he was close—he tells whatever commodore was in charge that he and his men were going to try to check things out a little closer to the source. What he *didn't* say was that a little closer turned out to be downtown Baghdad, deep inside enemy lines. When they got into the city, Jake and his team split up. They had the locations where the Scud launcher had been set and fired from over the past few weeks, so they searched those neighborhoods for a place where something that size might be hidden.

"Jake's team finds not one, but *two* Scud missile launchers, *and* they uncover the location of a chemical weapons storage facility. So there Jake is, in the middle of Baghdad, with more than enough explosives to take out a single Scud launcher but not quite enough to do all three targets. He knew he could try to stretch it thin, but that way he risked destroying nothing."

"Damn, what did he do?" Harvard asked.

"I'd've blown the Scud launchers and given the location of the chemical site to intelligence," Wes said. "Have them take out the place through air strike."

"Except those chemical sites were moved constantly," Lucky pointed out. "Even just a few hours later, it might've already been gone."

"*And* this one was in the middle of a residential neighborhood," Crash told them. "Not the most PC site for an air raid." He smiled again. "Jake managed to take out all three targets with no civilian casualties."

"How?" Lucky asked. "Did he find a munitions dump? Get his hands on more C-4?"

"No," Crash said. "He took his time. And he thought it through. And when he was ready, and *only* when he was ready, he placed the explosives he had very strategically. It was risky, but the man's a wizard when it comes to blowing things up. He trusted himself, and he got the job done." He was looking directly at Lucky. "I think we should do the same—trust our team leader to get the job done."

Lucky nodded. "Thank you, Lieutenant."

Message received.

On Tuesday, Zoe was assigned to clean bathrooms. She gave Jake a comically dark look as she headed down the hallway with Edith, a pale ghost of a woman who'd been assigned as her cleaning partner.

Edith looked as if she'd be a breeze to evade. With luck, their pairing would be ongoing.

Of course, it didn't really matter who Zoe was paired with. She would manage to get away from anyone. She was that good.

She was more than good.

She was...

Jake took several steps backward to watch her. Her hips swayed a little as she walked away. Just enough to advertise that the body inside those androgynous jeans was pure female.

They'd taken another late shower last night. Dear, *dear* God. Sex with Zoe was indescribable. It was...

Sex. It was purely physical. Two people having a damn good time with their bodies.

Zoe was so direct, so honest. She didn't play games, didn't try to make him guess what she wanted. She liked having sex the way he did—with her eyes wide open and the lights brightly lit.

He loved watching her eyes as he drove himself into her. He loved the way she seemed to look directly into his soul, the way the connection between them seemed an almost mystical thing. He loved the hunger of her kisses, the sheer intensity of her release. He loved the way she curled against him at night, touching as much of him as possible, as if despite all that they'd done, she still couldn't get enough of him. He loved the way, with just one look and smile this morning, she'd let him know she was anticipating making love to him again tonight.

He loved the way just watching her walk down the hall made him aware of the blood rushing through his veins, aware of his heart's steady rhythm.

Oh, yes, he was feeling very much alive.

Zoe turned to glance back at him, and he didn't look away. He let her know he was watching her. He let her see exactly what he was thinking.

She laughed, and an incredible surge of warmth seemed to detonate within him, radiating out, filling him with happiness.

She waved before she disappeared around the corner, and Jake stood there for several moments longer, struck by the realization that he was going to miss her today. For four days, they'd been together constantly. And as much as the waiting had frustrated him, he'd loved sitting with Zoe and talking for hours and hours and hours.

He'd loved learning about her, loved discovering the intricate ways her mind worked, loved her thoughtfulness and her quick sense of humor.

She'd filled more than the void in his life caused by his lack of a sexual partner. *Far* more.

And that realization shook him.

He'd been so certain of his feelings yesterday, as he'd sat by the waterfall in the early morning light. He'd been convinced that his relationship with Zoe felt so right because it didn't go beyond the physical. And yet his missing her today wasn't just about sex.

And then there was that annoying question he hadn't quite found a way to ask her. "So, babe. When you go undercover, playing husband and wife like this, does, uh, this sort of thing—you know, this intense physical attraction and mind-blowingly great sex—happen all the time?"

He shouldn't care about that, about who she'd been with in the past and why she'd been with them. He shouldn't care about the casualness that she assigned to sexual relationships. Why should he care about anything beyond these immediate moments and the fact that right now she wanted *him?*

He had absolutely no right to be jealous. Jealousy implied love, and…

Falling in love with Zoe Lange would be the mistake of his lifetime. What, did he honestly think she would ever agree to *marry* him? Yeah, right. Oh, she liked him, she desired him, and she probably wouldn't object to getting together and getting it on with him three or four or five times a year, whenever she rolled in to D.C. But marriage? Not a Twinkie's chance in a room full of eight-year-olds.

Get a grip, pal. Jake headed toward Christopher Vincent's office. *You're not looking to marry the woman. It's just the sex messing with your brain.*

Indescribable sex. With a woman whose smile and laughter made him feel truly happy for the first time in years.

Of course he was feeling happy—there was no big mystery to it. Sure, he liked her, sure she was smart and sharp and funny, but the bottom line was that in his mind, Zoe equaled sex. And sex equaled happy. After living like a monk for three very long years, sex definitely equaled very, *very* happy.

All of his warm, fuzzy feelings could be traced to the fact that Jake no longer had to imagine Zoe naked. He could pull her into the shower and see her naked anytime he wanted. See her and touch her and…

And that had nothing, *nothing* to do with love.

Love was what he'd had with Daisy. Slow and easy at times, hot and furious at others, ebbing and flowing like the tides. Love was years of understanding, the ability to communicate volumes with a single look or touch or smile. It was trust, it was faith, it was never to be doubted. It wasn't perfect, but it was the best thing he'd ever had.

There was no way a man could hope to find something so rare twice in one lifetime. And the thought of settling for something that didn't live up to what he'd once had...

No, he didn't love Zoe Lange.

But even if he did, he didn't have to worry. It would never work out.

Zoe would never expect anything long term, Mitch had told him. *Because she leaves, too. And she'll probably leave first.*

And Jake tried to convince himself that that thought made him feel so damned bad only because he would miss the indescribable sex.

"YOUR POSITION ON THE high council of the CRO can be secured immediately," Christopher Vincent said, eating a sticky bun as he sat behind his fancy oak desk in his private office, "through your willingness to share your personal wealth."

The room wasn't large. It didn't have one single window. But it did have three doors, all tightly shut, leading off the wall behind Vincent's desk. Jake was willing to bet that behind one of those doors was the CRO surveillance control room—and possibly the missing Triple X.

Jake held out his hands in a shrug. "Chris, you know as well as I do that all my funds are frozen. I've got over four million dollars in liquid assets—that I can't touch."

Christopher stood up and opened the door on the far left. It was only a bathroom. One down, two to go.

He turned on the light and rinsed his hands, raising his voice to be heard over the running water. "Personal wealth isn't limited to finances." He came out, drying his hands on a towel.

"Information," Jake said. "After thirty-five years in the U.S. Navy, I'm in possession of a great deal of information that might be useful to you." He sat forward. "Look, Chris, I've heard people talk about this birthday celebration you're planning. Let me sit in on the meetings, see if there's anything I can contribute—"

"Letting you sit in," Christopher interrupted, "would prove our trust in you. What are you going to give me that proves you're worthy of that trust? Something that proves your acceptance of me as leader of the CRO." He smiled tightly. "Let's be honest, Jake. I know you're a very ambitious man. You wouldn't have gotten where you did in the navy if you weren't. But if you've got any intentions of coming in here and taking over my show—"

"Whoa," Jake said. "Christopher. You *are* the CRO." He laughed. "Okay, I *am* ambitious, but my goal here is to sit at your right hand at the council table. Be your chief adviser. Your second in command. I'd never try to take you down or undermine your authority in any way." He lied smoothly. "Never."

Chris sat behind his desk. "Then prove it."

"I will," Jake said. "Like I said—through information. I can give you computer passwords. Back-door entrances to highly sensitive files. Information on security procedures in government buildings—"

"You have more to give than information," Chris said, "although I'll accept that as a sign of your loyalty—in part."

Jake shook his head. "Chris, I came to you empty-handed. As far as wealth goes, I don't have much. Even these clothes I'm wearing are yours and—"

"Zoe."

Jake sat back in his chair. "Excuse me?"

"You've got Zoe." Christopher smiled. "I'd say that makes you a very wealthy man."

Jake laughed, but then stopped when he realized that Christopher wasn't laughing, too. Holy God, the son of a bitch was serious.

Share his personal wealth. Share...*Zoe*. The CRO believed that a wife was a man's possession, but *God*...

"Why don't the two of you join me in my private dining room for dinner tonight?" Christopher said, standing up. "Seven o'clock. There's a high council meeting scheduled for noon on Friday, here in my inner chamber." He gestured to the door on the far right. "It would be nice—for all of us—if you could join us." He moved to the door that led out of his office, opening it for Jake, dismissing him.

Jake rose to his feet despite the fact that this conversation wasn't over. He had more to say, to protest, to explain, but the phone on Christopher's desk rang. And the guard outside the door gestured for Jake to follow him.

Jake didn't move. "Look, Chris—"

"I'll see you at dinner tonight." Christopher nodded to the guard, who stepped forward and took Jake's arm.

There was nothing he could do short of creating a scene. Christopher's door shut behind him as the guard ushered him into the corridor, closing that door behind him, as well.

And Jake stood in the hallway, certain of what had just been implied and sickened by it.

If Zoe slept with Christopher Vincent, Jake would be in.

If Zoe slept with Chris...

Jake laughed aloud, a sharp burst of disbelieving air, as he headed briskly down the hallway toward his room. No way! He wasn't going to let Zoe anywhere *near* Christopher the scumball Vincent. She was *his,* dammit, and he wasn't about to share.

Except she wasn't really his. Their marriage wasn't really a marriage. It wasn't legal. And even if it were, Zoe wasn't the kind of woman any man could ever completely possess.

He took the stairs down two at a time, moving faster, almost running.

But there was no way he could outrun the truth.

Jake had found a way to get the information they needed. If Zoe slept with Chris, he'd find out at noon, Friday, exactly what the CRO intended to do with the stolen Triple X. And he'd probably even locate the missing canisters.

If Zoe slept with Chris.

He stopped short, gripping the handrail tightly, sitting down right there in the stairwell between the second and third floor, directly in the blind spot between two surveillance cameras.

Oh, God. She would want to do it. Sex just wasn't that big a deal to Zoe. She'd made that more than clear to him many times over. She'd as much as told him she was willing to do anything for this mission. *Anything.*

Except it wasn't knowing that that made his stomach hurt so badly he had to sit down. It was the knowledge that it mattered so much to him. Here he'd been pretending that what he shared with Zoe was only sex.

But it wasn't.

The thought of her with Christopher Vincent—the thought of her with *anyone* else—made him completely crazy. He didn't want to share her, not her body, not her

smile, not her laughter, not *any* of her. He wanted her
for his own.

Because he was completely in love with her.

God, no, how could he be? He still loved Daisy.

None of this made any sense.

Maybe he just wouldn't tell Zoe. Maybe he wouldn't
even give her the option.

Jake pushed himself to his feet.

And maybe the canisters of Triple X would be waiting
for him back in their room. Maybe this mission would
just take care of itself.

But even if it did, even if Christopher Vincent surrendered the missing nerve gas to them this afternoon, Jake
was going to lose because—mission accomplished—Zoe
would be off to Saudi Arabia. Or Amsterdam. Or Soma-
lia. Only God would know when she would be back again.
Or even *if* she would be back.

The irony was intense. For all those years he'd been a
SEAL, *he* had been the one who'd always left.

And Jake had to laugh—it was either that or cry—
because only now, by falling in love with Dr. Zoe Lange,
did he fully understand just how much Daisy had loved
him.

CHAPTER SIXTEEN

"I NEED TO SEE MY WIFE."

Zoe looked up from what seemed like the four hundredth toilet bowl she'd cleaned in the span of three hours.

"I don't care if lunchtime is in thirty minutes." It *was* Jake's voice. "I need her right now. *Zoe!*"

"In here." She pushed herself to her feet as Jake steamrolled over poor pale Edith and came right into the ladies' room.

"Hey." His smile was unnaturally tight and the look in his eyes completely wild. Something was really wrong. "Nice rubber gloves. Yellow looks good on you, babe."

"You all right?" she asked quietly.

He shook his head infinitesimally. No. "Yeah, sure. I'm just breaking you out of here a little early, that's all." He looked behind him. "Do you have a problem with that, Edith?"

Zoe peeled off the gloves and quickly washed up in the sink.

"Well," Edith said. "Technically, we're not—"

"Sorry for any inconvenience," Jake said, grabbing Zoe's hand and pulling her with him into the hallway.

He had her jacket in his other hand and was already wearing his.

Her first thought was that something had gone very wrong and they were evacuating—getting out of there fast. But as Jake punched open the door to the stairwell, he went up instead of down toward the main floor.

Up. Toward the recreation deck.

She had to run to keep up with him, he was moving so fast.

But finally they were there. Jake burst into the open air as if he'd been holding his breath all that time.

She followed. "Jake, what's going—"

He kissed her. He dropped her jacket on the deck, dragged her into his arms and covered her mouth with his in a kiss of pure possession, pure need.

It was electrifying, mesmerizing—his mouth so demanding, his hands slightly rough and very proprietary. The sheer power of his desire sent her instantly aflame.

Was *this* why he'd come searching for her? Because he needed her? Because he finally realized just how very much he needed and—please God—even *loved* her?

He fumbled with the buttons on her shirt, growling in frustration, finally pulling, buttons flying everywhere. The front clasp of her bra gave just as easily, and the shockingly cold morning air hit her naked breasts. But Jake's hands were warm and his mouth was hot as he touched her, kissed her, the rasp of his chin delicious against her skin as he buried his face against her.

"Oh, Zoe," he breathed. "I need—"

He kissed her again, his fingers at the waistband of her jeans, unfastening the button, releasing the zipper.

"Yes," she said. She needed, too.

He stopped kissing her only long enough to shake his jacket off his arms, to throw it onto the deck with hers. Then he pulled her down with him onto the soft cushion those jackets made. His muscular body was so wonderfully solid, so deliciously heavy on top of her, cradled between her legs. She could feel his hardness and she reached for his belt buckle, wishing the layers of thick denim that kept him from her would just instantly be gone.

He pulled back onto his knees, easily ridding her of her jeans as she kicked off her sneakers. He lowered his pants, covered himself and then, God, he drove himself hard inside of her.

She cried out, she couldn't help it—and he swallowed her cry of pleasure with the fiercest of kisses as he filled her again and again with hard, deep, demanding thrusts.

He didn't try to pretend that his need for her didn't completely control him. He didn't hold back, his kisses feverish, his hands and body deliciously possessive.

And Zoe abandoned all pretense, too. She let herself love him—wildly, furiously, passionately—body, heart and soul.

He was everything she'd ever wanted and everything she hadn't known it was possible to want. The hero was just a shadow compared to the humanness, compassion and honest reality of the man.

This incredible man who burned for her with the same urgent fire that consumed her very soul.

She felt his body tighten and tense, felt him shake, heard him rasp her name, and the sheer power of his release made her explode. Pleasure pulsed through her, so intense, so scorchingly wild. She opened her eyes, and the brilliant blue of the sky seemed close enough to touch. Her senses were almost painfully heightened as she smelled the subtle scent of Jake's cologne and felt the warmth of his breath against her neck, the slick heat of his body against hers, the sharply cold air against her legs, the indescribable sensation of him, still hard inside of her as he thrust just one more time, as the fierce waves of her release finally slowed, finally subsided.

Zoe closed her eyes, holding tightly to him, afraid that she might cry from the exquisite wonder of it all. But then she had to laugh. She would never have believed that she could have had the absolute best sex of her entire life in the so-very-submissive missionary position.

"Jeez," Jake breathed without moving, his mouth against her neck. "What a gentleman. I didn't even wait for you."

"You didn't have to," she told him. "I was right there, with you." Her voice shook. "God, Jake…"

He was still breathing hard as he lifted his head to look at her, acknowledgment in his eyes. What they'd just shared had been as powerful and as intense for him, too.

"When you came looking for me like that, I thought we were in some kind of trouble." She made her voice even lighter. "I had no idea the trouble was physiological."

"Zoe, I…"

She held her breath. This was it. He was going to tell her that he loved her. Please, God, let him love her, too….

But the expression in his eyes was completely unreadable. His ready smile was nowhere to be found. "I've found out how I can gain access to Vincent's high council."

Not the words she wanted to hear. Still, she managed to hide her disappointment. "But that's *great!*" She searched his eyes. Wasn't it? "How?"

"I need to prove my loyalty to the CRO and to Christopher Vincent," Jake said. "He's got this little share-the-wealth program. I think it's some kind of power trip for him. Whatever his followers have got, he wants a share of. Money. Information." He briefly closed his eyes. "Wives."

Wife sharing. Oh, God.

"Of course the bastard probably wouldn't be as interested in a guy's wife if she didn't happen to look like you, and…" Jake broke off, looking at her more closely, incredulousness in his eyes. "You know about this, don't you?"

She couldn't lie to him. "Chris mentioned something about it to me. I guess he sees himself as the equivalent of some kind of feudal lord and…" She shook her head. "I just didn't expect him to approach *you* about it."

"What, did you expect him to approach *you* about it?" Jake's eyes were nearly as cold as the freezing air that slapped her skin as he pulled himself away from her. "And what the hell were you going to do when he did?" He swore sharply. "Don't tell me. I don't want to know."

He had been mostly dressed, and it didn't take him long to pull himself together. Zoe had to search for her underpants, turn her jeans right-side out, find her sneakers. Her shirt had no buttons, and the plastic clasp of her bra was broken. She shivered, clutching the front of her shirt together, uncertain what to say, how to explain.

Jake wrapped her jacket around her. "Dammit, Zoe." His voice shook. "You could've at least let me in on the plan."

"It wasn't a plan," she told him. "It was…just an option I thought I should keep open. Jake, the man was dogging me for weeks. I thought I could go in there and talk to him. Tell him I was thinking about accepting his offer. I would have told you before I did anything. I thought at least it would be a way into his private office."

"Well, I've been in his office now," Jake said tightly. "It's small, no windows, one desk, three chairs. Three doors on the wall behind Vincent's desk. The left is the bathroom. The right a room he referred to as his inner chambers. There was no sign of the missing canisters. I'm betting they're in that inner chamber."

Which he would have access to—provided he share Zoe with the CRO leader.

Zoe's hand shook only slightly as she pushed her hair from her face. "So what did he say to you about…?" She managed to make her voice sound remarkably calm, but she couldn't say the words aloud.

"It was all implied," Jake told her. "He spoke of sharing my wealth. Mentioned you. Invited us both to his private dining room tonight at nineteen hundred—seven o'clock."

"Both of us?"

"I asked one of his lieutenants." Jake's voice was raspy. "Apparently the way it's done is, he invites us both, and I send you alone, along with my regrets, pleading I'm feeling slightly under the weather." He laughed, a short bark of disbelief. "Believe it or not, it's considered an honor for Christopher Vincent to mess with your wife." He dropped his head into the palms of his hands. "Crazy-assed, twisted sons of bitches."

Zoe took a deep breath, filled with a sense of dread. "So. Did you tell him yes or did you tell him no? That we'd—*I'd* be there for dinner?"

He looked at her, his eyes nearly as blue as the sky overhead. "We can cancel."

"That's a yes," she said. "You told him *yes.*"

Jake shook his head. "I didn't say yes."

"But you didn't say no."

"I didn't answer him one way or the other."

"Silence generally implies an affirmative," she said tightly.

"Yeah," Jake said, the muscle flexing in the side of his jaw. "I know."

He put his head into his hands, unable to hold her gaze.

Zoe closed her eyes against the rush of tears. Did he actually think… Could he honestly expect… "Are you asking me to have sex with Christopher Vincent?" God, what he must think of her, if he could ask such a thing.

"No." Jake lifted his head. His eyes were rimmed with red, as if he, too, were fighting tears. "I'm not asking you, Zoe. I could never ask that of someone under my command. Except you're not really under my command, are you? And you haven't been completely honest with me about this other *option* you had standing ready. Maybe you've got a better plan in mind to get me into the inner council?"

She shook her head. "I don't," she whispered.

"I'm not going to ask you do this," Jake told her. "But I'm also not going to tell you *not* to do it. I'm giving you the choice." He cleared his throat. "I know this… this sort of thing doesn't particularly bother you, so…" He shrugged as he forced a smile. "It's your choice."

Zoe was dying. She wanted him to tell her not to do it. She wanted him to refuse to let her do it. She wanted him to hold her tightly and tell her that he was never going to let her go, that he honestly didn't believe her capable of such coldhearted self-exploitation.

"Do you…" She had to stop and clear her throat. Amazingly, her voice came out even and clear. "Do you want me to do it?" She had to know.

He looked her squarely in the eye. "This doesn't have anything to do with me."

The last of her hope died, and she turned to look out over the valley. "I see."

She'd done such a good job bluffing. She'd convinced him so completely that she was tough and strong—emotionally made of Teflon. He obviously thought she wouldn't think twice about prostituting herself this way in the name of their mission. He clearly didn't approve, and despite the fact that he'd made incredibly powerful, passionate love to her just moments ago, he didn't think that her buying their way onto the inner council through sex had anything to do with him.

Zoe felt like throwing up. Or bursting into tears.

Instead, she nodded. "What am I supposed to wear?"

CHAPTER SEVENTEEN

LUCKY POURED BOBBY a cup of coffee and set it down near the video screens in the surveillance trailer.

"Thanks," Bobby said.

"Any change?"

"Zoe got assigned to a two-woman work detail cleaning bathrooms," Bobby stated. "Jake came in a little while ago and pulled her out. They headed toward the roof and have been out of contact for the past hour and a half. I've been cruising around, following Vincent's two top lieutenants—neither one of 'em win any prizes, except maybe Dullest Human Beings on Earth."

Lucky pointed to the screen that showed the CRO mess hall. "Isn't that Jake?"

"Jake." Bobby glanced at him. "Finish reading the book?"

Lucky smiled. "Yeah."

"Like him better now, huh?"

"I'm still working on the like part, considering he's spending all his time kissing my woman."

"You never had a chance with Zoe, and you know it." Bobby keyed in some numbers, and the screen showed the camera on the other side of the room, closer to Jake, who was sitting alone at a table, lunch tray in front of him. "Yep. It's definitely the admiral."

Lucky leaned closer. "Is it my imagination or... Does he look okay to you?"

"Looks wound pretty tight. I wonder where Zoe is." Bobby typed in a steady stream of numbers, and lightning-quick pictures flashed on the other two screens. "Whoops, there she was."

"Wait a minute," Lucky said. "You saw her? How could you see *anything* in that?"

Bobby shrugged, calling back the image he'd spotted. "I'm pretty good with visuals." On the center screen, Zoe walked briskly down the hallway, heading toward the room she shared with Jake. She smiled brightly as someone passed her.

Bobby hit the commands to show the cameras inside the room as Zoe went inside.

But no sooner was she inside the door than she leaned against it, her smile vanishing. It was as if her legs suddenly failed to support her, because she slid down, back against the door, so that she was sitting on the floor.

She hugged her legs and bent her head and...

Zoe was crying.

She was shaking, sobbing as if her heart were breaking.

Bobby looked at Lucky and Lucky looked at Bobby.

On the other video screen, Jake toyed unenthusiastically with his food. He tossed his fork onto the tray and rested his forehead in the palm of his hand, a picture of total despair.

But then Jake sat up. And with both hands on the table in front of him, he made a gesture, a hand signal that the SEALs used. It was brief but unmistakable.

Get ready.

"Did you see that?" Lucky asked, nearly jumping out of his seat. "Was that what I thought it was?"

"Yes, sir. That was definitely a message for us."

Jake had only made the signal once, but they had it down on tape.

Lucky reached for the phone. "Yeah, Skelly, it's O'Donlon. Is the senior chief there? Bob and I have something we want him and the rest of you guys to see," he said. "Oh, and on your way over? You might want to run."

ZOE PULLED HER BASEBALL CAP down over her eyes as she pushed the cleaning cart into Christopher Vincent's private quarters.

No one had noticed yet that she wasn't a part of the regular cleaning crew. Or if they had, they'd been downtrodden and beaten into submission too often to care.

Melissa, Amy, Ivy, Karen, Beth and Joan. Zoe had had to learn their names from the color of their hair. Their faces were too similar—they looked exhausted and as if they'd lost all hope.

Zoe moved like them, as if she, too, ached both physically and emotionally, as she took the supplies for cleaning the bathroom toward the door to Vincent's private office.

The door was ajar, and she went in without switching on the light.

It was exactly as Jake had described it. Big desk. No windows. Three doors. No sign of the canisters of Trip X anywhere.

The bathroom was on the left. Zoe tried the knob of the far right door as she went past. Locked. So was the center door. The bathroom was half open, and she turned on the light. It was tiny. One toilet and a sink. According to the Frosty Cakes factory layout she'd looked at with Bobby and Wes, there was enough unaccounted-for room in this part of the building for a good-size security headquarters, as well as a conference room–size inner chamber.

She didn't have her lock pick, but she had a paper clip

from Vincent's desk. In the light of the bathroom, she unbent the piece of metal and—

The office light went on. "Who are you? What are you doing in here?"

"Cleaning the bathroom?" Zoe blinked owlishly as she unobtrusively tried to slip the paper clip into the back pocket of her jeans. She only got it in halfway before the long-bearded man got too close.

He was Vincent's second lieutenant. "You're the new girl. This couldn't possibly be your assignment."

Zoe made her bottom lip start to quiver. "I was told to clean bathrooms. But I…I got lost, and I didn't know what to do, so I followed a cleaning crew in here and—"

"Get out." Lieutenant Beard held open the door. *"Now."*

Zoe grabbed her cleaning supplies and sprinted for the door. On her way out, the second lieutenant hit her so hard on the back of the head that her ears rang and she stumbled to her knees. It was all she could do to keep herself from spinning and giving the bastard a roundhouse kick to the bearded jaw.

But she didn't. She kept her eyes lowered, her head down. If she was going to make it out of here without *completely* blowing her and Jake's cover, she wasn't going to do it by advertising her black belt in karate.

Beth, the leader of the cleaning team, smacked her, too, as Zoe pushed herself onto her feet. "What are you, stupid? You just can't go wherever you want. You were given an assignment."

Zoe let her eyes fill with tears. It was amazing that she had any left after the way she'd cried just an hour ago. But apparently, she still had plenty to spare. All she had to do was think about Jake, and her tears came in force.

"I'm sorry," she murmured. "I lost Edith, my partner, and I got scared and I saw you and…"

"Go back to the kitchen," Beth said sharply. "Edith will probably be waiting for you there."

Zoe stared at her stupidly. This was it? No being dragged in front of Christopher Vincent? No questions about what she'd been doing in his private office?

"Go," Beth said.

Zoe turned and ran.

THE COMPUTER'S ALARM sounded, piercingly loud, and Lucky turned to see Harvard leaning over Crash's shoulder, looking at the screen.

"What've we got?" H asked.

"A key word match," Crash told him grimly. "Three words came up. *Zoe. Spy.* And *birthday.*"

Harvard swore.

The computer was programmed to listen to and record every conversation that came in from the heavily wired CRO fort. Harvard had written a program to search for groups of key words that, when used in a single conversation, might signal trouble.

Cowboy joined them. "Play it back," he said.

"We've got video, too," Crash told them as he cued up the digital recording. Lucky rolled his chair closer. "Here we go. Looks like we're in Christopher Vincent's outer office. This can't be good."

A man on the tape spoke. "What's this?" It was Christopher Vincent's now too-familiar voice. On the video screen, the CRO leader straightened and came into camera range. He'd been bending over, picking something off the floor, but now his face was directly in front of the camera. Yeesh.

Lucky had one word for Christopher Vincent. Tweezers. It was his only real hope. Because, damn, that single eyebrow wasn't going to get him a *GQ* cover anytime in the near future.

"I don't know, sir." Another man stepped into the frame. It was Ian Hindcrest, Vincent's second lieutenant—another beauty pageant contestant from hell, what with the six-inch-long ZZ Top beard. He took whatever Vincent had been holding. "It looks like… Yes, it's a paper clip, sir."

"Who's been in here today?" One thing about having a unibrow, when Vincent glowered, he *glowered*.

Hindcrest took a step backward. "You had a series of morning appointments, but the cleaning crew was here after lunch, so I'd guess—"

"The cleaning crew." Vincent's glower became downright scary. "There was a memo on my desk from the crew leader, but she's a moron, I couldn't read her writing. Something about some incident today? Your name was on the page."

"Of course." Hindcrest brightened. "I was intending to type up my report about the event this evening. That rather dim new girl, the blonde, wandered in here by mistake."

"Zoe," Vincent said.

"That's the one."

"Wandered where exactly?"

"I found her in your office." Hindcrest gestured to the door behind him. "Preparing to clean the bathroom."

"In my office." Vincent nodded, his voice getting louder. "And it didn't occur to you that this new girl—who's still only a probationary member of the CRO—might have gone into my *private* office because she's a *spy?*" He was flat-out shouting, and Hindcrest's eyes had glazed over.

"Spy?" the bearded man said weakly.

Wes swore pungently, voicing what they all were thinking. "She's made. She's in trouble now."

"This isn't a paper clip." Vincent snatched the piece

of metal from Hindcrest's hand. "It's a makeshift lock pick, dammit! I have no doubt she was trying to break into the inner chamber. Or maybe she'd already been in there, already seen what she needed to see! I knew it. There was something about her."

"The chemical—" Hindcrest cut himself off, aware he'd said too much. He cleared his throat. "The birthday surprise. Is it…?"

"Jackpot," Harvard murmured.

"It's still there," Vincent said, "but we've got to assume she's after it." He swore. "Robinson's probably in on this, too. The son of a bitch!"

"I'll call the guards to bring them in," Hindcrest said.

"We've got to warn them," Bobby rumbled.

"How?" Wes asked. "Send up signal flares?"

"No," Vincent said on the tape. "Not yet. He's got information I need. Let's let them think their cover's intact. In the meantime, let's get my birthday surprise started on its journey. Call Herzog and Jansen. Tell them they're leaving for New York a few days early."

"Yes, sir."

"That's all of the tape," Crash said grimly. "At least it's all that the computer flagged."

Harvard was already on the phone. "We need immediate stepped-up satellite surveillance. We need code-red intercept teams stopping anyone and anything that so much as pokes a nose outside that CRO gate, and we need…" He looked at Lucky and covered the mouthpiece of the telephone. "We need help. Get on the other secured line, Lieutenant. Call in the rest of Alpha Squad. We need 'em here *now*."

JAKE COULDN'T WATCH as Zoe wove her beautiful golden hair into an intricate, elegant style. But he couldn't not watch, either. A French braid, he remembered it was called. Daisy's hair had been too curly and wild and thick to wear in that particular fashion. So this was a first for him, watching Zoe's long fingers complete the transformation from jeans-clad tomboy to elegant, graceful, coolly formal beauty.

It was another first for him, too.

Jake had never watched Daisy get dressed up to go have sex with another man.

The thought made him sick.

How can you do this? He had to clench his teeth to keep the words from escaping. *Don't go.*

She wore a black skirt that redefined the word *short* and a black tank top that hugged her body and framed the tops of her breasts as if they were some kind of work of art. Her long, shapely legs were clad in the sheerest of stockings, her black heels at least three inches high.

She leaned closer to the mirror to apply a final touch of lipstick and then stepped back to survey herself as she closed her makeup bag with a snap.

She met his gaze only briefly in the glass.

"Well," she said.

Jake couldn't speak.

"I guess it's time," she said.

He found his voice, but he had to clear his throat about four times before his words could be understood. "It's still a little early."

Don't go.

"I can't walk very fast in these shoes."

"Ah."

She turned to face him, squaring her shoulders and lifting her chin slightly. She finally met his eyes, but she somehow kept her *own* gaze cool, distant. "So. I guess I'm out of here."

Don't go.

He couldn't believe she was actually going to do this.

"I guess I'll see you later," she said, heading for the door.

Don't go.

She reached for the doorknob, opened the door. And she closed it behind her, leaving without even looking back.

CHAPTER EIGHTEEN

ZOE HAD TO STOP AND sit down, drop her head between her legs to keep herself from fainting.

God, she was going to throw up.

Jake hadn't stopped her.

He'd just watched her get ready, watched her walk away.

This didn't have anything to do with him. He'd told her that himself.

She couldn't keep her breathing steady, couldn't stop herself from being buffeted by the raggedness of each breath she took in and out, couldn't stop her hands from shaking and her stomach from churning.

Ask not what your country can do for you. Ask what you can do for your country. Whoever would've guessed it could be *this?*

WHEN JAKE STOOD BY the mirror, he could still smell Zoe's perfume. It was a subtle fragrance, mysterious and light. He'd watched her put it on—just two short spritzes into the air that she'd then walked through.

She usually didn't wear any scent at all, but she'd worn this on their wedding day. Their *mock* wedding day.

He closed his eyes against the memory of Zoe standing in her trailer, bags already packed, chin held high as she'd prepared to confront him, tough and strong and ready to do whatever she had to do to get inside the CRO gates.

Whatever she had to.

She'd looked at him that same way tonight. Right before she'd walked out the door.

She was cool, she was calm, she was completely in control. She was prepared to do whatever needed to be done, regardless of the sacrifice to herself. She was strong enough and tough enough.

But Jake wasn't, dammit. He *wasn't* strong enough. And even though love didn't seem to be part of Zoe's working vocabulary, the fact remained that he loved her.

Whether he liked it or not, whether he wanted to or not, he *loved* her.

And despite telling her otherwise, despite her matter-of-fact indifference to this entire situation, he was *not* going to allow her to do this.

He was the team leader, dammit. He had every right to tell her what she could and could not do.

And she *could not* do this.

Jake burst out of the door and headed down the hallway at a dead run.

Please, God, let him catch her….

ZOE STOOD UP.

Holy Mike, she hated wearing heels. Sure, she'd taught herself to run in them—for those times when she had to. But despite the hours of practice, she never quite felt as confident when she was wearing heels as when she had on her sneakers.

She smoothed her skirt and took a deep breath. She'd made up her mind and she knew beyond the shadow of a doubt exactly what it was she had to do.

Resolutely, she started walking carefully on those high heels, her heart firmly in her throat.

This wasn't going to be easy.

As a matter of fact, it was, quite possibly, going to be the hardest thing she'd ever done in her entire life.

DICK EDGERS STOPPED him in the stairwell.

"Hey, Jake! I understand you're joining us in the inner council Friday. Congrats."

"Sorry, Dick, no time to talk." But when Jake moved right, to go around the man, Dick moved to his left, blocking him. And when Jake moved left, Dick moved right.

"Whoops," Dick said, laughing. "Sorry!" Jake all but lifted him up and moved him out of his way.

Jake cursed the delay, cursed the fact that he'd waited so long to go after Zoe, cursed the entire situation, cursed himself for letting the charade go this far.

And when he was done cursing, he started to pray. Please, God, let him catch her. Please, God...

He took the stairs three at a time and hit the door onto the floor that led to Vincent's quarters at a full run.

And nearly knocked Zoe onto her rear end.

He caught them both, holding her tightly, relief flooding through him. He hadn't been too late. Thank God. Thank *God.*

"What are you doing here?" she asked as he pulled back to look at her.

"You're going the wrong way," he said. Vincent's quarters were to the right, all the way down at the end of the hall, but she'd been heading toward the stairwell.

He realized that her eyes were filled with tears and she was shaking. Still, she lifted her chin as she met his gaze. "I'm drawing the line," she told him.

He realized instantly what she meant. He'd told her once before that he didn't trust her to draw a line marking what was and was not comfortable for her on this mission.

But she was telling him, right now, that she was not going to go through with this farce. *She* was telling *him*.

He kissed her—hard—right there in the hallway. He didn't care who could see them, he simply didn't give a damn anymore. She kissed him just as fiercely, clinging to him as if she were never going to let him go. But a kiss wasn't enough. He had far too much to say.

Jake pulled her with him into the stairwell and down the stairs. There was a men's room on the next floor.

She could move pretty fast in those heels when she wanted to, and he led her down the other hallway. Still holding her hand, he pushed open the men's room door, pulled her inside and locked the door behind them.

Releasing her hand, he turned the water on in all three sinks. As the roar from the faucets filled the room, he knew they could be seen but not heard. Zoe knew it, too.

She stood hugging herself as if she were cold.

"You were coming after me," she said.

"I was," he admitted. "I couldn't let you do this. It was crazy of me even to pretend that something this insane would be all right, because it's *not*." He swore. "I was ready to order you to back down, to forbid you from going further. And if that didn't work, hell, I was ready to get on my knees and beg you if I had to."

She was in his arms then, holding him as if he were her salvation. And she was crying. Brave, strong, tough Zoe had dissolved into tears.

"I didn't want to do it," she told him. "I wanted you to tell me not to. I kept hoping you'd stop me, but you just seemed to think it was something I'd do, something you expected of me. And when you said it had nothing to do with you…"

Her face crumpled, and she clung to him.

"I'm sorry," he murmured. "Jeez, Zo, I'm so sorry."

"I wasn't completely honest with you, Jake." She drew in a deep breath as she pulled back to look into his eyes, wiping her face with her hands. "I wanted to impress you, make you think I was like, I don't know, James Bond or something."

He had to laugh at that.

"And you *believed* me, even when I tried to tell you it wasn't true. And then it got even worse because I…" She lifted her chin a little higher. "I fell in love with you."

Jake stopped laughing.

"That's what I was coming back to tell you." Fresh tears brimmed in her eyes. "I've never used sex to get information or…or anything. Not ever. I've never slept with anyone I didn't love at least a little, only with you I…I don't know what happened. I thought it would be safe to fall a little bit in love with you because I know you can't love me, but somehow a little bit became a little bit more and then more and… And it's good, it's a *good* thing because I didn't think I'd ever feel this way about anyone, but now I know, and it's wonderful and… and tragic, too, because now I also know what you lost when Daisy died, and I'm so, *so* sorry." Her tears again escaped.

Jake held her tightly, bemused, amazed, a lump in his throat. Zoe was crying for *him*. Her tears now were for his loss. She was, without a doubt, one of the most remarkable human beings he'd ever met.

"I know you still love her," she said softly, her face wet against his neck. "I'm not asking you to stop loving her. And I know I can't replace her. But maybe, if you don't mind, we can keep seeing each other for…I don't know, a while, after this mission is over?"

Jake tried to clear the lump from his throat, but it

wouldn't budge. "A while," he repeated. "About how long is a while?"

He could feel her breath warm against his throat. He could sense her weighing her responses, wondering the best way to answer his question.

"Honestly," he told her. "Tell me honestly, babe. How long—honestly—would you want that while to last?"

"I guess," she said carefully, "I was hoping for anything between, say, thirty years and forever. Leaning heavily toward forever."

Forever. Jake closed his eyes as he held her even closer. "Oh, Zoe, your forever's a whole lot longer than mine. My life's half over—yours is just starting and, jeez, I'm—"

She covered his mouth with her hand. "It's okay," she said. "You asked me to be honest, so I was. I know you're not ready for anything like this. And I know now's not the best time for another installment of the you're-too-old-for-me debate. Right now we've got a different problem to deal with."

"Vincent's expecting you in his dining room," Jake agreed. "You're already five minutes late."

"What are we going to do?"

"I signaled the team this afternoon," Jake told her. "They're on standby, waiting for my next command."

"I keep coming back to our theory that Vincent doesn't truly know what he's got—that he doesn't know what the Trip X is capable of," Zoe said. She wiped the last of her tears from her face. "We haven't found any kind of delivery method, no missiles lying around. No bombs—unless they're already locked up tight with the Triple X and—"

"I'm ready to gamble," Jake said. Hell, Zoe loved him. He was feeling pretty damn lucky tonight. "Are you?"

She could read his mind. "Gamble that the Trip X is

somewhere in Vincent's private office behind one of those two locked doors?"

"It's either there or it's somewhere outside this facility," Jake said. "I'm convinced of that."

She nodded. "I am, too."

"Okay," Jake said, thinking fast. "Here's our plan. We take control of Christopher's private quarters. You and me. Between the two of us, we can hold off the entire CRO until the SEALs arrive."

Zoe looked skeptical. "Without a weapon?"

"I'm sure Christopher has something in there we can liberate. And have you seen the door to his office? You would need a serious explosive to get that open after it's been locked. The trick is in getting it locked *behind* us instead of in front of us." He started to pace. "Look, here's what we do. You go to Christopher's dining room. Make a big deal over the fact that you've heard his chef is a four-star gourmet, that you've been really looking forward to this meal. Don't let him skip right to the dessert—which I've got to assume is you."

"I won't."

He stopped pacing to look searchingly into her eyes. "Are you really okay with this, because if not—"

"I'm okay with this." Zoe's smile was tremulous. "I'm *really* okay that you trust me to be able to handle Vincent."

"While you're doing that," Jake told her, "I'm going to rig the main power supply and the backup generator to blow. I'll try to take out the main computer while I'm at it."

"Are you telling me you can make a bomb from cleaning supplies—things that are just lying around—that will do *that* much damage?" she asked.

"Well, I probably could, but I don't have to." Jake

smiled. "I brought two bricks of C-4 plastique into the fort, inside your duffel bag."

She stared at him. "Holy Mike! What if my bag had been searched?"

"It was," he said. "I hid the C-4 in with a couple slabs of modeling clay and some other art supplies. No one knew."

"Including *me*."

"I thought it would be better if you didn't know."

"That's what *I* thought about Vincent's proposition."

"No more secrets," Jake said. "Okay?"

Zoe smiled weakly. "Then I guess I better tell you that this afternoon I snuck into Vincent's quarters with a cleaning team."

Jake closed his eyes. "Zoe. God."

"It was all right. Ian Hindcrest found me in there, but I played dumb, and all he did was send me back to the kitchen."

"Why would you risk everything to—"

"Because I thought if I found the Trip X I wouldn't have to have sex with Christopher Vincent!"

There was absolutely nothing Jake could say in response to that. Nothing but, "I'm sorry."

"It was okay, Jake. I got shoved around a little, but Hindcrest bought my story."

Shoved around a little. Coming from the queen of the understatement, that could mean anything. It helped a lot that she was standing in front of him, looking to be in one piece.

"What are the odds he didn't tell Vincent about the incident?" he asked.

"I'll take care of that," Zoe promised. "When I go in there, I'll confess to Chris I was so eager to have dinner with him, I snuck into his office this afternoon, hoping to get a chance to talk to him." She turned his wrist, looked at his watch. "Meanwhile, I'm now *ten* minutes late."

"I'm not sure I want you to go at all now."

"Just tell me your plan," Zoe said. "*Please.* You just rigged the power and computers with a bomb. Then what?"

"I'll set a delayed fuse and go up to Christopher's quarters. I'll make a stink, play the part of the jealous husband, make like I've reconsidered this whole sordid deal, push my way into the room. Once I'm there, the bomb will go off, power will go down and in the confusion, we'll overpower Vincent—"

"With what? The salad fork?"

"That could get messy. I was intending to just use my hands. Get a grip on him, threaten to snap his neck. Hopefully there'll be a guard or two in the room. Once they drop their guns, we'll be armed."

Zoe nodded. She didn't say a word about the fact that Christopher Vincent had at least fifty pounds and several inches on Jake. She didn't doubt his ability to do precisely what he'd said. She didn't make a single comment about his age, about the fact that it had probably been years since he'd threatened to snap another man's neck. She had complete and total faith in him. He couldn't keep himself from kissing her.

"We'll lock ourselves into Vincent's private office," he continued, "and we'll sit tight until the rest of the team arrives. Your job is to not let the scumbag touch you and to be ready for me, you got it?"

"I do."

"Good," Jake said. "Now go. And make it look as if you're going even though I don't want you to. Let's get that jealous-husband thing happening starting now."

She pulled away from him, twisting free from his arms,

her words contradicting her body language. "Be safe, Jake."

It wasn't hard for him to look as if he didn't want her to leave. "You, too, babe."

Zoe hesitated at the door, looking at him. "I love you."

How could three little words make him feel both so damn good *and* so damn bad? "Zoe—"

She was gone.

LUCKY HAD BEEN LEFT behind to man communications.

He wasn't completely certain how it had happened. One minute he'd been ready to move out with the rest of the team and the next he was waving goodbye from the window of the trailer.

Somebody had to stay behind. Somebody had to watch those video screens, hoping for another communication from Admiral Jake Robinson. Somebody had to be ready to relay that information to the team.

Lucky had hoped that that somebody was going to be Bobby or Wes. Or Cowboy.

He had his headset and lip mike on, connecting himself to the rest of the team, now split into two groups, one led by Cowboy, the other led by Crash and Harvard. He could hear the second group's chatter over his phones as they circled the sky in a plane above the Frosty Cakes factory.

Jake and Zoe had split up, and Lucky was following them both, keeping them both on screen—no easy task for anyone besides Bobby.

Zoe was in the stairwell, looking as if she'd stepped out of his own personal sexual fantasy. He liked women dressed in what he thought of as contradictions. And Zoe's breathtakingly short skirt and low-cut top combined with the rather formal, opera-bound debutant-style of her hair really worked for him.

He forced his attention away from Zoe and onto Jake. The admiral left the men's room on the fourth floor and went into the same stairwell, heading down, though. But then he stopped, looking up, and Lucky realized Zoe had run into trouble.

She'd left the stairwell. He could hear raised voices from the other side of the door on the stairwell camera, and he quickly adjusted, keying in the numbers to pull in the picture from the security cam in the hallway.

It jumped onto the video screen. Ian Hindcrest and a half a dozen armed guards had surrounded Zoe.

Lucky swore, and over his headset, Harvard's voice responded. "What's happening, O'Donlon?"

"We've got six zealots with Uzis, aiming them at Zoe."

"I don't know what you're talking about." Zoe didn't look frightened, only amused.

Jake had moved silently up the stairs, and he stood, right outside the door, listening and looking out, the door open infinitesimally.

"So you deny you were in the leader's office today as a spy."

Zoe laughed. "Spy? Me? Do I look like a spy?"

"She's definitely made," Lucky reported. "We've got some serious trouble here, Senior Chief."

He knew exactly what Jake had to be thinking. Every instinct the man had was screaming for him to go out there and start kicking butt, to rescue Zoe.

Except one unarmed man against six men with automatic weapons... There was no way in hell he could possibly succeed. Three seconds after he leaped out from behind the door, Zoe would still be in trouble, but he'd be too dead to help her. One of those grim-faced cleaning crews would be mopping what was left of him off the floor.

No, it was definitely neither the time nor place to attack.

"Take her to General Vincent's office," Hindcrest ordered the guards.

General. Talk about a sudden promotion. Of course, when you run your own little fantasy world behind a high electric fence and walk around with security guards with Uzis, you can call yourself Lord God Almighty if you want.

"Does Jake know about Zoe?" Harvard asked over his headphones.

"Yeah. He's on it, Senior. But there's only one of him and he's not armed."

As Zoe was led away, Jake turned and went down the stairs, moving fast.

Lucky followed him via camera down the stairwell, down the hall to his room. The admiral grabbed what looked to be—hot damn!—two solid bricks of C-4 explosive and a bunch of fuses and was back out in the hall, moving fast.

It wasn't until then, until Jake hit the stairwell going down again, that Lucky realized the man was sending him a steady stream of hand signals.

Now, Jake was signaling. *Now. Over and out.*

God, Lucky had missed it all. Do *what* now?

He quickly rewound the tape. "Got a message incoming from the admiral," he announced as he watched it. "He says he's taking out security, power and computers, *and* he'll blow a hole in the electric fence, as well." He snorted. "Well, sure, why not? One guy doing the job of ten men. Who does he think he is, one of the X-Men?"

"No, just Jake Robinson," Harvard responded.

"He says five minutes—oh, is that all? Or maybe even

less till it blows. He says he needs support. He says come in as covertly as you can, as quickly as you can. He says he's ready to guess where the package—meaning the Trip X—is, but it's just a guess. Wear gas masks, be ready for anything, don't forget there are women and children here. He says come now. *Now.*"

On the other video screen, Zoe had arrived in Christopher Vincent's outer office.

She looked so small, so fragile compared to the CRO leader's bulk. She was looking at something Vincent held in his hand.

"That's a paper clip," she said. "You're all worked up over a *paper* clip?" She laughed. "Chris, I'm a *waitress*. I'm not a *spy*. That's crazy!"

Christopher hit her with his fist, like a club against the side of her head, and as Lucky watched, Zoe went down, hard.

"Move fast, team," he said, his heart in his throat. "Zoe's in serious trouble."

THE ROOM SPUN, AND ZOE clung to the floor, trying desperately to regain her senses, fighting the waves of nausea and dizziness that made her want to retch.

That was her fault. Her fault. Crazy. She should have remembered that Crazy Christopher went ballistic when he was called crazy.

Her head pounded and her vision blurred as two of the guards dragged her to her feet. She fought to focus her eyes. Christopher stood in front of the open door to his private office. That door was heavy duty, as Jake had pointed out, with dead bolts that would withstand anything short of explosives. If she could get in there and lock that door behind her…

"Here in the CRO fort, like most countries, treason is a capital offense." Vincent was holding a gun on her.

Zoe blinked, but the gun was real, not a result of the problems she was having with her eyes.

It was a German-made Walther PPK twenty-two caliber. The kind of gun any inbred militia leader with Hitler aspirations would take pride in owning. "Is Jake Robinson also here to spy on us?" he asked her.

Zoe let herself start to cry. "Chris, I don't know *what* you're talking about—"

"Yes," he said. "He is, isn't he? He's here because of the anthrax."

Every now and then, there came a mission in which it was necessary to accept that her cover had been blown. And if Christopher Vincent thought that the poison he'd appropriated from the Arches test lab was merely anthrax...

It was definitely time to lay all of her truth cards out on the table.

Zoe stopped crying, stopped pretending. "Chris, you don't have anthrax. What you have is called Triple X. It's a nerve agent. A chemical weapon that's deadlier than even *you* can imagine."

"So you *are* a spy."

"I'm here to try to help you," Zoe told him. "If you give me the missing canisters of Triple X now, I'll make sure it's known that you cooperated fully—"

"Guilty," Christopher said. "I find Jake and Zoe Robinson guilty as charged. Their sentence is death, to be carried out immediately." He looked at his guards. "Find Robinson. *Now.*"

Zoe kept talking. "Chris, this is the dead-last thing you want to do. If you kill me, if you harm *anyone,* if you even attempt to use the Triple X, the CRO will be crushed."

Christopher Vincent lifted his gun, and as Zoe stared into the deadly blackness of its barrel, she prayed. God, please don't let Jake come bursting in the door right now. Please, God, keep him far, *far* away from here.

"OH, GOD," LUCKY SAID. "Oh, God, he's going to kill her!"

There was nothing he could do. He could only watch on the video monitors, completely unable to stop the murder that was about to happen miles away in the CRO compound. It was the most awful, completely impotent moment of his entire life.

He was going to watch this woman he admired so much, his *friend,* die while he sat here, unable to lift a finger to save her.

Zoe could barely stand after that blow Vincent had given her to her head, but the guards moved back from her, out of their leader's range.

Zoe was still talking, telling Vincent about the Triple X, trying to make him understand that the United States government would not rest until they recovered it.

Vincent smiled, and...

"No!" Lucky shouted. *"No!"*

The bastard fired the gun, the roar deafening over his headphones.

And the screens all went black.

"Sit-rep, O'Donlon." Harvard's voice came in. "What are you shouting about?"

Lucky worked frantically to get some sort of signal. But there was nothing. There was no signal to receive.

Jake, true to his word, had taken out the security system.

"Security's down," Lucky rasped. "But, God, H! Vincent shot Zoe. Point-blank. The bastard executed her." His voice shook, and he couldn't stop the tears that came to his eyes. "I've got it all on tape."

"Oh, God."

"Cowboy's team intercepted all six canisters of the Triple X about ten minutes ago." Zoe would've been so glad to hear that. Lucky pushed his lip mike away from his mouth so the senior chief wouldn't know he was sitting here crying like a baby. But, dammit, this operation wasn't over yet. He didn't have time to lose it this way. He took a deep breath and repositioned his mike. "As far as I know, Jake's still alive. But they're looking for him, Senior. Let's make sure we find him first."

"We will. But we're still about two minutes from contact." Harvard's voice was grim, cold.

"If you come face to face with Christopher Vincent," Lucky said, doing what he knew Harvard was doing—turning his grief into frozen hard anger, "hurt him bad for me."

JAKE COVERED HIS HEAD as his fourth and final bomb took out a big piece of the fence surrounding the CRO fort. It was hard to blow a fence like that, and he'd used a little too much of the C-4. Bits and pieces of what once had been trees and underbrush rained down on him.

He shouldered the Uzi he'd appropriated from a careless guard. A guard who'd have one hell of a headache when he finally woke up.

Jake moved silently through the darkness toward the factory—toward Zoe.

She was still in there. He prayed she was able to take advantage of the sudden explosions, of the power going out. But even if she wasn't, it didn't matter. Because he was going in after her.

Smoke alarms were wailing, and he could hear shouting, sounds of confusion from inside.

He hadn't used enough of the explosive to start a real fire, but the smoke and dust were thick. And the complete darkness had to be daunting to a group of people used to living under the constant scrutiny of bright spotlights.

Jake was nearly to the door of the building when he looked at the velvety blackness of the night sky.

It wasn't so much that he'd heard them or seen them. It was more that he'd sensed them.

And sure enough, it was his SEAL team, parachuting in, dropping out of the sky.

So much for blowing the hole in the fence to let them in.

The SEALs gathered their chutes as they landed, unhooking themselves, instantly armed, weapons locked and loaded.

Senior Chief Harvard Becker recognized Jake almost as quickly as Jake recognized Harvard.

"Sir. Are you all right?"

"I'm fine." Jake had smeared himself with dirt in an attempt to cover the reflective paleness of his face as he'd crossed to the fence in the brightly lit yard. "But Zoe's still in there. I could use some help getting her out—and finding that damned Trip X, as well."

"Sir, the Trip X was intercepted by Lieutenant Jones and his men. Christopher Vincent tried to send it to New York tonight." The door to the building opened with a crash, and they all stepped farther into the shadows. Bobby and Wes had joined them, as well as Billy, and two other men Jake recognized but didn't know—Joe Catalanotto and Blue McCoy, the Captain and XO of SEAL Team Ten's Alpha Squad. Harvard apparently didn't call just anyone for backup. And despite their higher rank, they were standing back and letting Billy and Harvard run this show.

"Jake, I think it would be really smart if we got you out of here right now," Billy said.

"You better think again, kid, because I'm not leaving without Zoe."

Billy looked at Harvard, who shook his head very slightly. Bobby looked at his feet.

"You guys gonna help me help Zoe, or what?" Jake asked.

Silence. Complete, total silence.

Then Harvard put his hand on Jake's shoulder. And Jake realized Bobby Taylor was crying.

"Jake," Harvard said, his voice thick with emotion. "Zoe doesn't need our help anymore."

No. Jake knew what they were telling him, but he couldn't believe it. He looked at Billy and saw the awful truth echoed in the kid's eyes.

"She's dead," Billy said. "I'm sorry, Jake."

CHAPTER NINETEEN

ZOE WAS DEAD.

Jake stood there. Somehow he managed to stand there, to keep his knees from crumbling, to keep himself from folding into a ball of pain and anguish. "No," he said.

"Lucky saw that prick Vincent kill her. He shot her right before the power went down." Wes sounded strangled.

Zoe was dead.

Pain screamed through Jake, growing louder, stronger with every beat of his heart, with every ragged breath that he took. And as it grew, it changed. It boiled and churned and hardened and blackened, and it numbed him. It deadened him, and all the joy and the life that Zoe had breathed back into him with her laughter and brightness over the past few weeks dried up and skittered away like leaves in the cold winter wind.

Zoe was dead.

"Please, Jake," Harvard said again. "We've got what we came for. The Triple X has been recovered. It's time to move you to safety, sir."

ZOE'S ARM WAS ON FIRE.

She sat on the floor of Christopher Vincent's inner office in the dim emergency light, bleeding onto the carpet, listening to the sound of the CRO guards pounding on the steel-reinforced door.

She'd surprised Vincent by rushing toward him rather than away right before he'd discharged his weapon. She'd dived for his feet, and he'd tried to compensate, but his bullet had only skimmed her.

It was just enough to make her bleed like crazy and hurt like hell.

But at least she wasn't dead.

And the pain was a good thing. She could use it to keep her focus—to keep herself from blacking out from that blow to the head he'd given her.

She crawled toward Christopher's desk on her hands and knees, afraid if she stood up, she'd fall over.

She searched the desks, hoping for some kind of weapon—a handgun, a switchblade, anything.

She found a book of matches and... She had no pockets. Damn, not wearing her jeans was so inconvenient. She tucked it into her bra, hoping she wouldn't inadvertently light herself on fire.

The door to the fabled inner chamber was still tightly locked, and she searched for a paper clip. She unfolded it and set to work on the lock.

JAKE LOOKED AT THE UZI in his hands. "Does somebody have an M16 for me, or am I going to have to use this piece of crap?"

The captain finally cleared his throat and spoke. "Begging your pardon, Admiral—"

He looked into the man's compassionate brown eyes. "No," he said. "No, Captain, I'm not ready to be taken to safety. I suggest if you have further support available, you talk to them via radio and tell them about the hole I just blew in the fence. Remind them that there are women and children here. I need eyes open and brains working. No autopilot. The same goes for the rest of you. Because we're going in there. Our goals are twofold, gentlemen.

We're going to apprehend Christopher Vincent. And we're going to recover Zoe's body. She was a member of this team, and SEALs don't leave teammates behind. Even when they're KIA."

Killed in action. Jake's voice shook. Even the numbness spreading through him couldn't keep him from hurting as he spoke the acronym he'd hated so passionately for so many years.

Zoe had loved him. A miracle had happened, and he'd been given a second chance to find happiness. She hadn't been Daisy, but no one was. No one could have replaced all that he'd had with Daisy. But in the exact same way, Daisy hadn't been Zoe. Zoe had touched parts of Jake's soul that Daisy would never have been able to reach even if their life together had lasted another thirty years.

There was no way really to compare, no contest as to which woman he had loved most, because although he had loved them both, he'd loved them differently.

And yet, when Zoe had offered him forever, he'd been too obsessed with doing the math. He was too old for her. When she turned fifty, he'd be seventy-four—if he even lived that long. It had seemed so absurd, and he couldn't understand why she would want that, why she would want him.

But he understood now. Because love didn't always make mathematical sense. And forever was completely relative. Zoe wasn't ever going to turn fifty now. Not ever. Her forever had been obscenely short.

And Jake had forsaken every opportunity in the far-too-briefness of their time together and hadn't even told her that he loved her.

He felt ancient as he looked into the still-young faces of his SEAL team. "I loved her," he said, his words far too little, far too late. "Who's going to help me bring her out?"

Bobby stepped forward, pulling a twelve-gauge shotgun from a holster he wore on his back. "Since you're taking the point, Admiral, you might want to carry this."

Admiral. When Bobby said it like that, it wasn't a title, it wasn't a rank. It was his old nickname from Nam.

Harvard nodded, his dark brown eyes deadly. "We're right behind you, Admiral. Lead the way."

ZOE FOUND IT.

The Triple X.

Behind the locked door to Vincent's inner chamber, inside a cheaply made safe.

It was no longer stored in the testing lab's metal canisters. Instead, someone had put the powder in old coffee cans. Here at the CRO compound, they'd replaced the Folgers crystals with the dried ingredients of a deadly nerve gas.

In the office, the door strained against the battering it was receiving from Vincent and his guards.

Zoe closed and locked the door to the inner chamber, and using all her Girl Scout training, she set about building a campfire in a small metal trash can right on top of Christopher Vincent's conference table.

She could only destroy half of the chemicals. There was no sprinkler system in this part of the factory, but the possibility of someone bursting in and spraying the fire with water and creating a massive amount of potent Trip X was not worth the risk.

She used single sheets of paper as kindling and twisted chunks of computer reports in place of wood.

She took the matchbook from her bra and lit the fire, waiting for it to really start burning before she added the A component of the Triple X.

She knew that the chemical would burn clean. The

smoke would be nontoxic. But smoke didn't have to be toxic to kill.

This room had no windows and only the one door.

Already the smoke was chokingly thick.

She added the first coffee can of chemicals to the fire, then stayed low to the floor. She stayed as far away as she could from the flames, praying she'd have time to destroy all the chemicals before the smoke overcame her.

THE FIRE ALARM WENT OFF.

Jake and his team had just moved out of the stairwell and onto the fifth floor.

The noise was deafening—it came from one of those old-fashioned bells attached to the concrete block wall. It was good. It would mask their approach. No one would hear them coming.

There was one emergency light at the end of the hallway. It was old, with a bulb that sputtered and flickered, giving the impression that they were lit by leaping flames.

Welcome to hell.

Jake slowed as they moved closer to the door that led to Christopher Vincent's private suite of rooms. And when the door opened, he moved against the wall into the shadows. He didn't need to look behind him to know that Harvard and the rest of the team had disappeared, as well.

Christopher came striding out.

He was followed by his entourage of guards and lieutenants.

"Get the car, Reilly," he ordered. "Bring it to the front and—"

Jake stepped into the light, shotgun held high, finger heavy on the trigger. "I think you can probably leave the car in the garage for now, Reilly," he said, shouting over the noise of the alarm.

Christopher Vincent froze, but behind him, a half a dozen guards shouldered their weapons.

Jake didn't have to turn around to know that his SEALs were standing behind him, their weapons already locked and loaded. He could see them in the eyes of Vincent and his men.

"What do you think, Chris?" Jake shouted over the alarm. "My guess is we could have it out right here. Maybe some of your guys will get away, but *you* sure as hell won't. Do you know what a twelve-gauge can do to a man at ten feet?" Jake turned his head slightly without ever letting his eyes leave Vincent. "Hey, Bob, what you got in here? Double-ought buckshot?"

"Five rounds of it." Bobby's deep bass voice had no problem cutting through the racket.

"One round'll do," Jake told the CRO leader. "Think of it as the equivalent of me firing, oh, about six or seven regular bullets all at the same place at the same time. It'll put a big hole in you, Chris. And while I'm looking forward to doing that, you may not be, in which case it would be really smart of you to tell your men to drop their weapons. *Now.*"

Jake had played mind-game poker plenty in his career, but this was no bluff. He suspected Chris recognized the edge of insanity he saw in Jake's eyes.

"Do as they say," Christopher ordered his men.

Harvard took over, collecting their weapons, pushing the men onto the ground and searching them none too gently for anything they might be carrying concealed.

"Can someone shut that damn thing off?" Jake asked. His head was aching and his stomach hurt. Part of him wished Christopher Vincent hadn't given in. It didn't seem fair that he was still alive while Zoe...

He was going to have to go in there, into Vincent's quarters, and carry Zoe's lifeless body out of here.

Bobby raised his MP-4, and, firing a single burst, shot the alarm bell right off the wall. The silence seemed only to emphasize Zoe's absence.

"McCoy and I'll hold Bozo and his clowns here," Captain Joe Catalanotto of Alpha Squad volunteered. "We've got another team already inside the gate coming up to meet us, but it might be a good idea to use Vincent as a hostage, guaranteeing our safety out of here."

"I've got a sit-rep if you want one, Admiral," Harvard said.

Jake didn't have a headset, but the other men did. "Any casualties?"

"None so far." Harvard corrected himself. "Besides Zoe." He cleared his throat. "The other teams have run into some opposition, but not a lot. A couple of men have locked themselves in one of the storage sheds. And we had a sniper on the roof with the lousiest aim in the Western Hemisphere. He's been taken care of."

Jake looked at the captain. "These dirtwads are going to be charged with treason, conspiracy and murder. If they so much as look at you funny," he ordered, "shoot them."

"With pleasure."

Wes stepped forward. "Admiral, I want to bring to your attention the fact that there's a raftload of smoke coming from Vincent's quarters."

Smoke.

It was rolling out the door, already thick against the high ceiling of the hallway.

Holding his shotgun at the ready, Jake pushed through the door into Christopher's outer office. The smoke was even thicker in there.

He braced himself as he made a quick visual sweep of

the room, but there was no sign of Zoe, no broken body bleeding on the floor.

The door to Christopher's private office was hanging on its hinges. The smoke seemed to be coming from there. Covering his face with one arm, Jake again took the point.

Zoe wasn't in Christopher's private office, either.

The smoke was coming from behind the door to Christopher's inner chamber.

Hope hit Jake hard in the chest, taking his breath away. Somehow Zoe had survived. Somehow she'd gotten in here, found the Triple X and was now...burning it?

But Harvard had told him they'd recovered the missing canisters, and Lucky had seen Zoe....

Die? Or fall? And what exactly had been inside those canisters Lieutenant Jones had recovered? No one besides Zoe would be able to identify whether or not it actually was the Trip X.

The door to the inner chamber was locked, and Jake pounded on it. "Zoe! It's me! It's Jake—open up!"

Harvard was beside him, compassion in his eyes. "Sir, I don't—"

"She's in there!" Jake was sure of it. But the smoke was in there, as well. And just standing out *here* was making him choke and cough.

This door was as heavily reinforced as the other. The lock was a piece of junk, but it would take too many precious minutes to pick it. If Zoe *was* in there, she'd been breathing in the smoke for quite some time. If she *was* in there, she was dying.

Jake hadn't been able to do a damn thing when Daisy had died. He hadn't been able to fight her cancer, to wrestle it to the ground and even *try* to save her life.

But he sure as hell could try to save Zoe.

"Stand back," Jake ordered, tossing the shotgun to Bob

and taking the last of his C-4 from his pocket. It wouldn't take much, just a little around the lock. He lit the fuse, moved behind Vincent's desk and...

Boom.

The door swung open, and smoke billowed out, chokingly thick, coming from a garbage can that flamed atop a huge conference table.

Jake was the only man without a gas mask but the first one inside. He couldn't see a damned thing, but if Zoe *were* in here, she'd be on the ground.

He found her in the corner. She'd torn nearly half the carpeting off the floor, yanking and pulling it on top of her to create a small pocket of air for herself.

She was unconscious and streaked with blood from a bullet wound on her arm and soot from the fire. But she was still breathing.

She was still alive.

Jake didn't pretend that he wasn't crying as he carried her out of there.

"She's alive!" Wes was practically running in circles around him.

Harvard followed him, too, taking off his gas mask as they hit the fresher air in the hallway. "Sir, we intercepted six canisters of what we thought was the Triple X outside the gates. But it sure looks as if Zoe thinks she's found the chemicals right here. There are six coffee cans in there, three empty. I think that's what she was burning."

"Stay with the rest of it, Senior," Jake ordered him. "Don't let it out of your sight." He raised his voice. "I need to get Zoe down to the medics *now*. Let's get this sideshow moving!"

With Vincent and his men in handcuffs, Bobby's shotgun aimed at the CRO leader's head, and with the rest of the SEALs surrounding Jake and Zoe, they went down the stairs and into the yard without mishap.

FInCOM had arrived, and as the dark-suited agents read Christopher Vincent his rights, Jake carried Zoe through the hole he'd blown in the fence to a waiting ambulance.

The medic gestured to a cot inside the vehicle. "You can put her there, sir."

"No," Jake said.

The medic looked at him in surprise.

Jake smiled to soften his words. "No, you see, I'm... I'm not going to let her go."

"Ever?"

He looked down to see Zoe's eyes had opened. Her voice was whispery from a throat that must've been raw from all the smoke she'd inhaled. Her hair hung in strings from her French braid, and her face was streaked with soot and blood. He was certain he'd never seen her look more beautiful.

"No," he told her. "Not ever."

The medic was about twenty years old and trying as hard as he could not to listen as he gently slipped several thin tubes from an oxygen tank into Zoe's nose.

"Give us a minute," Jake said to him. "Will you, pal?"

The medic faded back. Or maybe he didn't. Maybe Jake just stopped seeing him as he lost himself in the depths of Zoe's eyes.

He touched her then, her face, her hair, her throat, unable to keep his eyes from filling again with tears. "I thought you died," he told her quietly. "Lieutenant O'Donlon saw Vincent shoot you, and...we all thought he'd killed you, Zo."

"Oh, Jake," she whispered.

"But then you really could've died," he said. "What the hell were you doing, starting a fire in a room without ventilation?"

"I was doing my job," she said quietly. "And I trusted that you'd do yours and come get me out of there. I took a gamble that this teamwork thing would pay off." She smiled. "I won."

"Yeah," Jake said. "I did, too."

"I think this would be a really great time for you to kiss me," she said.

Jake laughed and kissed her. "I love you, Zoe."

She shook her head. "Oh, Jake, I don't need you to say that."

"Yeah, but I need to say it," he said. "I thought I would never get a chance to. I thought…" He had to clear his throat before he could go on. "Zoe, I would be honored if you would agree to make this craziness legal and stay Zoe Robinson. You see, I'm too old to—"

"Jake, how can you ask me to marry you—in a completely half-assed way, might I add—and then in the same breath claim to be too old—"

"You want to let me finish? I *am* too old. I'm too old not to learn from the past. I didn't expect to outlive Daisy," Jake told her. "And let's face it, babe, your job being what it is, it's entirely possible that I could outlive you, too. I had a taste of that today, and it was pretty damn sobering. The truth is, neither of us can possibly know how much time we'll have together. And we're both of us too old to waste another precious second of it."

Tears were leaving clean tracks in the soot on her face. For a tough operator, Zoe cried more than just about anyone he'd ever met. He kissed her. "Marry me." He kissed her again, longer this time. "I want you to be my friend and my lover and my wife for however long forever lasts." He smiled at her. "How was that? Not quite so half-assed that time?"

She was smiling through her tears. "That was…inspirational. And very persuasive." She laughed. "Not that I particularly needed persuading."

"If that's a yes," Jake said, "it's very half-assed."

Zoe laughed. "Yes," she said. "It's a yes."

Jake lost himself in the sweetness of her lips. He'd thought she'd been taken from him. He'd lived an entire wretched lifetime in that endless fifteen minutes in which he'd believed she was dead. He loved this woman completely. But there would be people who looked at them and wondered, people who wouldn't understand.

"I have to be really honest with you," he said, looking into her dark brown eyes. "There's a big difference in our ages, and nothing we do or say is going to change that. I know you don't care, and I don't care anymore, either. But people—my colleagues—are going to look at me and look at you and think I'm getting away with something here."

Zoe reached up and touched his face. "Your colleagues and friends are going to look at me and think I'm a poor substitute for Daisy."

"You are," Jake told her. "But then again, Daisy would be a tremendously poor substitute for you." He kissed her hand. "I'm not looking for a replacement for Daisy. There's no such thing. I'll always love her—it's important you know that because she's part of my past. But there's room in my heart for both the past and the future. And babe, you're my future."

There was so much love in her eyes as she looked at him he nearly started crying again.

"I love you," she said.

Jake smiled. "I know."

EPILOGUE

"YOU ALL RIGHT?" Billy Hawken asked.

"Yeah," Jake said as the limousine pulled up to the church.

He looked at the kid. *Kid.* Jeez. The kid was a Navy SEAL with the somewhat dangerous-sounding nickname of Crash. The kid was also older than Zoe. The kid hadn't been a kid in fifteen years. Heck, even back when Billy was ten, he hadn't really been a kid. He was still far too serious, far too intense—except when he was with Nell, his wife.

Jake had heard the two of them giggling together until nearly two last night, up in the guest bedroom. Crash Hawken—giggling. Whoever would've thought it possible?

"Are *you* okay with this, kid?" he asked as they got out of the car. *Kid.* Jeez. Old habits died hard.

Billy didn't hesitate. "I am. Completely," he said. He smiled. "Zoe looks at you the way Nell looks at me. I'm happy for you, Jake."

"I love her," Jake told the young man who was the closest thing to a son he'd ever had, the young man to whom Daisy was the closest thing to a mother *he'd* ever had.

"I know," Billy said. "I've seen the way you look at her, too."

"This isn't just a…a second-best kind of thing." Jake

felt the need to explain. "Zoe and me, I mean. But that doesn't mean that Daisy wasn't—and isn't—first, too. God, does that make any sense at all?"

Billy hugged him. "Yeah, Jake," he said. "You know, I had a dream about Daisy last night. She was having lunch with William Shakespeare. It was weird, but nice. One of those dreams where you wake up and feel really good."

"Shakespeare, huh?" Jake laughed. "Cool."

"Yeah." Billy motioned toward the church. "You want to go in?"

"Yeah," Jake said. "Come on, kid. Let's go get me married." He put his arm around Billy's shoulders, and together they walked up the stairs.

Zoe was a vision.

Walking toward him, down the aisle of the church, on her father's arm.

Sergeant Matthew Lange, USMC, Retired.

Matt seemed like a really nice guy, a straightforward, honest guy. He seemed genuinely pleased that Zoe was marrying Jake. Lisa Lange, Zoe's mother, was also honestly happy for her daughter. They were good people, solid people.

It was kind of cool, actually. He'd never had in-laws before.

His children had a chance of knowing at least one set of their grandparents.

His children.

Zoe smiled into his eyes as she took her place beside him, and he couldn't help but think about last night. While Billy and Nell had been giggling in the guest bedroom, Jake and Zoe had been sharing their own secrets.

Such as the fact that Zoe wanted his baby. Enough to retire from her job as a field agent—at least temporarily.

It hadn't been an easy decision to make. She was good at what she did. And the Agency would miss her, badly.

Jake suspected her decision was at least partly based on the fact that she knew how badly *he* wanted children. Daisy had been unable, and found the adoption process too painful, and…

He'd tried to convince Zoe that he would be okay with whatever decision she came to, but the truth was, *his* biological clock was ticking. Sure, he could father a baby when he was sixty-five, but how long would he be around to take care of that child?

Last night, she'd come to him with the ultimate wedding gift. And last night, they just may have created a small miracle.

Jake took her hand.

And as he promised Zoe all that he could promise her, he smiled.

"I love you," he whispered as he bent to kiss his bride.

Zoe smiled, too. She knew.

* * * * *

IDENTITY: UNKNOWN

For Lee Brockmann

CHAPTER ONE

"Hey, hey, hey there, Mission Man! How ya doin', baby? Rise and shine! *That's* my man—open those eyes. It's *defi*nitely the a.m. and in the a.m. here at the First Church Shelter, we go from horizontal to vertical."

Pain. His entire world had turned into a trinity of pain, bright lights and an incredibly persistent voice. He tried to turn away, tried to burrow down into the hard mattress of the cot, but hands shook him—gently at first, then harder.

"Yo, Mish. I know it's early, man, but we've got to get these beds cleaned up and put away. We're serving up a nice warm breakfast along with an A.A. meeting in just a few minutes. Why don't you give it a try? Sit and listen, even if your stomach can't handle the chow."

A.A. Alcoholics Anonymous. Could it possibly be a hangover that was making him feel as if he'd been hit by a tank? He tried to identify the sour taste in his mouth but couldn't. It was only bitter. He opened his eyes again, and again his head felt split in two. But this time he clenched his teeth, forcing his eyes to focus on a smiling, cheerful, weather-beaten African-American face.

"I knew you could do it, Mish." The voice belonged to the face. "How you doin', man? Remember me? Remember your good friend Jarell? That's right, I tucked you into this bed last night. Come on, let's get you up and headed toward the men's room. You could use a serious washing up, my man."

"Where am I?" His own voice was low, rough and oddly unfamiliar to his ears.

"The First Church Homeless Shelter, on First Avenue."

The pain was relentless, but now it was mixed with confusion as he slowly, achingly sat up. "First Avenue...?"

"Hmm." The man named Jarell made a face. "Looks like you had yourself a bigger binge than I thought. You're in Wyatt City, friend. In New Mexico. Ring any bells?"

He started to shake his head, but the hellish pain intensified. He held himself very still instead, supporting his forehead with his hands. "No." He spoke very softly, hoping Jarell would do the same. "How did I get here?"

"A couple of Good Sams brought you in last night." Jarell hadn't gotten the hint, and continued as loud as ever. "Said they found you taking a little nap with your nose in a puddle, a few blocks over in the alley. I checked your pockets for your wallet, but it was gone. Seems you'd already been rolled. I'm surprised they didn't take those pretty cowboy boots of yours. From the looks of things, though, they *did* take the time to kick you while you were down."

He brought his hand to the side of his head. His hair was filthy, and it felt crusty, as if it were caked with blood and muck.

"Come on and wash up, Mission Man. We'll get you back on track. Today's a brand-new day, and here at the shelter, the past does *not* equal the future. From here on in, you can start your life anew. Whatever's come before can just be swept away." Jarell laughed, a rich, joyful sound. "Hey, you've been here more than six hours, Mish. You can get your six-hour chip. You know that saying,

One Day at a Time? Well, here on First Avenue, we say one *hour* at a time."

He let Jarell help him to his feet. The world spun, and he closed his eyes for a moment.

"You got those feet working yet, Mish? That's my man. One foot in front of the other. Bathroom's dead ahead. Can you make it on your own?"

"Yes." He wasn't sure that he could, but he would have said nearly anything to get away from Jarell's too-loud, too-cheerful, too-friendly voice. Right now the only friend he wanted near him was the blessed, healing silence of unconsciousness.

"You come on out after you get cleaned up," the old man called after him. "I'll help you get some food for both your belly and your soul."

He left Jarell's echoing laughter behind and pushed the men's-room door open with a shaking hand. All of the sinks were occupied, so he leaned against the cool tile of the wall, waiting for a turn to wash.

The large room was filled with men, but none of them spoke. They moved quietly, gingerly, apologetically, careful not to meet anyone's eyes. They were careful not to trespass into one another's personal space even with a glance.

He caught a glimpse of himself in the mirror. He was just another one of them—disheveled and unkempt, hair uncombed, clothes ragged and dirty. He had the bonus of a darkening patch of blood on his dirt-stained T-shirt, the bright red turning as dingy as the rest of him as it dried.

A sink opened up, and he moved toward it, picking up a bar of plain white soap to scrub the grime from his hands and upper arms before he tackled his face. What he truly needed was a shower. Or a hosing down. His head

still throbbed, and he moved it carefully, leaning toward
the mirror, trying to catch a look at the gash above his
right ear.

The wound was mostly covered by his dark shaggy
hair and...

He froze, staring at the face in front of him. He turned
his head to the right and then to the left. The face in the
mirror moved when he moved. It definitely belonged to
him.

But it was the face of a stranger.

It was a lean face, with high cheekbones. It had a strong
chin that badly needed a shave, except for a barren spot
marked by a jagged white scar. A thin-lipped mouth cut
a grim line, and two feverish-looking eyes that weren't
quite brown and weren't quite green stared back at him.
Tiny squint lines surrounded the edges of those eyes, as
if this face had spent a good share of its time in the hot
sun.

He filled his hands with water, splashing it up and
onto his face. When he looked into the mirror again, the
same stranger looked back at him. He hadn't managed to
wash that face away and reveal...what? A more familiar
visage?

He closed his eyes, trying to recall features that
would've been more recognizable.

He came up blank.

A wave of dizziness hit him hard and he grabbed at
the sink, lowering his head and closing his eyes until the
worst of it passed.

How did he get here? Wyatt City, New Mexico. It was
a small city, a town really, in the southern part of the
state. It wasn't his home...was it? He must've been here
working on...working on...

He couldn't remember.

Maybe he was still drunk. He'd heard about people who'd had so much to drink they went into a blackout. Maybe that was what this was. Maybe all he'd have to do was sleep this off and everything he was having trouble remembering would come back to him.

Except he couldn't remember drinking.

His head hurt like the devil. Heaven knew all he wanted to do was curl up in a ball and sleep until the pounding in his brain stopped.

He leaned down into the sink and tried to rinse the cut on the side of his head. The lukewarm water stung, but he closed his eyes and persisted until he was sure it was clean. Long hair dripping, he blotted himself dry with some paper towels, gritting his teeth as the rough paper scraped against his abraded skin.

It was too late to get stitches. The wound had already started to scab. He was going to have a scar from this one, but maybe some butterfly bandages would help. He'd need his first-aid kit and... And... He stared at himself in the mirror. First-aid kit. He wasn't a doctor. How could he be a doctor? And yet...

The men's room door opened with a bang, and he spun around, reaching beneath his jacket for... Reaching for...

Dizzy, he staggered back against the sink. He wasn't wearing a jacket, just this sorry T-shirt. And sweet Lord help him, but he had to remember not to move fast or he'd end up falling on his face.

"The Ladies' Auxiliary is having a clothing drive," one of the shelter workers announced in a too-loud voice that made many of the men in the room cringe. "We've got a box of clean T-shirts, and another one full of blue jeans. Please take only what you need and save some for the next guy."

He looked up into the mirror at the stained and grimy T-shirt he wore. It had been white at one time—probably just last night, although he still couldn't remember back that far. He pulled it up and over his head, gingerly avoiding the wound above his right ear.

"Dirty laundry goes into this basket over here," the shelter worker trumpeted. "If it's labeled, you'll get it back. If it's torn, throw it out and take two." The worker looked up at him. "What size do you need?"

"Medium." It was something of a relief to finally know the answer to a question.

"You in need of jeans?"

He looked down. The black pants he was wearing were badly torn. "I could use some, yeah. Thirty-two waist, thirty-four inseam, if you've got 'em." He knew *that*, too.

"You're the one Jarell called the Mission Man," the shelter worker remarked as he searched through the box. "He's a good guy—Jarell. A little too religious for my taste, but that wouldn't bother you, would it? He's always giving everyone nicknames. Mission Man. Mish. What kind of name is Mish anyway?"

His name. It was…*his* name? It was, but it wasn't. He shook his head, trying to clear it, trying to remember his *name*.

Dammit, he couldn't even remember his *name*.

"Here's a pair what's got a thirty-three-inch waist," the shelter worker told him. "That's the best I can do for you, Mish."

Mish. He took the jeans, briefly closing his eyes so that the room would stop spinning around him, calming himself. So what if he couldn't remember his name? It would come back to him. With a good night's sleep, it would *all* come back to him.

He told himself that again and again, using it like a mantra. He was going to be fine. Everything was going to be fine. All he needed was a chance to close his eyes.

He went into the corner of the room, out of the line of traffic around the sinks and stalls, and started to pull off one of his boots.

He quickly pulled it back on again.

He was carrying a side arm. A .22-caliber.

In his boot.

It was slightly larger than palm-sized, black and deadly looking. There was something else in his boot, too. He could feel it now, pressing against his ankle.

He took his jeans into one of the stalls, locking the door behind him. Slipping off the boot, he looked inside. The .22 was still there, along with an enormous fold of cash—all big bills. There was nothing smaller than a hundred in the thick rubber-banded wad.

He flipped through it quickly. He was carrying more than five thousand dollars in his boot.

There was something else there, too. A piece of paper. There was writing on it, but his vision swam, blurring the letters.

He took off the other boot, but there was nothing in that one. He searched the pockets of his pants, but came up empty there, too.

He stripped off his pants and pulled on the clean jeans, careful to brace himself against the metal wall the entire time. His world was tilting, and he was in constant danger of losing his balance.

He slipped his boots back on, somehow knowing how to position the weapon so that it wouldn't bother him. How could he know that, know what size jeans he wore, yet not know his own name? He put most of the money and the piece of paper back in his boot as well, leaving several hundred dollars in the front pocket of his jeans.

He came face-to-face with his reflection in the mirror when he opened the door of the stall.

Even dressed in clean clothes, even washed up, long, dark hair slicked back with water, even pale and gray from the pain that still pounded through his battered body, he looked like a man most folks would take a wide detour around. His chin had a heavy growth of stubble, accentuating his already sun-darkened complexion. His black T-shirt had been washed more than once and had shrunk slightly. It hugged his upper body, outlining the muscles of his chest and arms. He looked like a fighter, hard and lean.

Whatever he really did for a living, he *still* couldn't remember. But considering that .22 he had hidden in his boot, he could probably cross kindergarten teacher off the list of possibilities.

Rolling up his torn pants, he tucked them under his arms. He pushed open the men's-room door and skirted the room where breakfast and temperance were being served. Instead, he headed directly for the door that led to the street.

On his way out, as he passed the shelter's donation box, he dropped a hundred-dollar bill inside.

"MR. WHITLOW! Wait!"

Rebecca Keyes headed for Silver at a dead run, swinging herself up into the saddle and digging her boots into the big gelding's sides. Silver surged forward, in hot pursuit of the gleaming white limousine that was pulling down the dude ranch's dirt driveway.

"Mr. Whitlow!" She put two fingers in her mouth and whistled piercingly, and finally the vehicle slowed.

Silver blew out a loud burst of air as she reined him in next to the almost absurdly stretched-out body of the car. With a faint mechanical whine, the window came down and Justin Whitlow's ruddy face appeared. He didn't look happy.

"I'm sorry, sir," Becca said breathlessly from her perch atop Silver. "Hazel told me you were leaving, that you were going to be gone a *month* and I… I wish you had informed me earlier, sir. We have several things to discuss that can't wait an entire month."

"If this is more of your wages garbage—"

"No, sir—"

"Thank God."

"—because it's *not* garbage. It's a very real problem we're having here at the Lazy Eight. We're not paying the ranch hands enough money, so they're not sticking around. Did you know we've just lost Rafe McKinnon, Mr. Whitlow?"

Whitlow stuck a cigarette between his lips, squinting up at her as he lit it. "Hire someone new."

"That's what I've been doing with staff turnovers," she said with barely concealed frustration. "Hiring someone new. And someone else new. And…" She drew in a deep breath and tried her best to sound reasonable. "If we'd simply paid someone solid and responsible like Rafe another two or three dollars an hour—"

"Then he would've asked for another raise next year."

"Which he would have deserved. Frankly, Mr. Whitlow, I don't know where I'm going to find another stable hand like Rafe. He was a good man. He was reliable and intelligent and—"

"He was obviously overqualified. I wish him luck at his next endeavor. We don't need to hire rocket scientists, for God's sake. And how reliable do you need a man to be, to shovel—"

"Mucking out the stalls is only a small part of the job description," Becca countered hotly. She took a deep breath, forcing herself to calm down again. She'd never won a shouting match with her boss, and she wasn't likely to start winning that way now. "Mr. Whitlow, I don't know how you expect the Lazy Eight to gain the reputation of being a high-class dude ranch if you insist on paying your staff slave wages."

"Slave wages for slave labor," Whitlow commented.

"My point exactly," Becca said, but he just blew cigarette smoke out the window.

"Don't forget about that opera thing in Santa Fe next week," he commanded as, with a soft buzz, his window began to shut. "I'm counting on you to be there. And for heaven's sake, dress like a woman. None of those pantsuits that you wore last time."

"Mr. Whitlow—"

But the window closed tightly. She had been dismissed. Silver sidled to the right as the limo pulled away and Becca swore pungently.

Slave wages for slave labor, indeed. Except Whitlow had it wrong. He believed he was paying his staff low wages for low-priority, bottom-of-the-barrel, physical-labor jobs. But the truth was, without those jobs done and done well, the entire ranch suffered. And if the owner insisted on paying low, the quality of work he'd get in return would also be low. Or the workers would leave—like Rafe McKinnon had, and Tom Morgan last week, and Bob Sharp earlier in the month.

It seemed all Becca did these days was office work. Far too often, she found herself sitting inside, behind her desk, doing phone interviews to fill all-too-frequently-vacated staff positions.

She'd taken this job at the Lazy Eight Ranch because it was an opportunity to use her management skills *and* put in most of her hours out-of-doors.

She loved riding, loved the hot New Mexico sun, loved the way the storm clouds raced across the plains, loved the reds and browns and muted greens of the mountains. She loved the Lazy Eight Ranch.

But working for Justin Whitlow was the pits. And who said a woman couldn't look feminine in a pair of pants, anyway? What did he expect her to wear to schmooze with *his* friends and business associates? Something extremely low-cut, with sequins? As if she could even afford such a thing on her pitiful salary.

Yes, she loved it here, but if things didn't change, it was only a matter of time before *she* walked, too.

THE NIGHT WAS MOONLESS, but he lay quietly on his stomach, taking the time for his eyes to get fully used to the dark again, and in particular the dark here, just inside of the high-security fence.

He breathed with the sounds of the night—crickets and bullfrogs and the trees whispering overhead in the gentle wind.

He could see the house on the hill, and he silently crept closer on his knees and elbows, staying low, staying invisible.

He stopped, smelling the cigarette before he saw the red glow of light. The man was alone. Far enough away from the house.

He silently lifted his rifle, double-checking it before he sighted along the sniper's scope. He brought the night-vision setting up a notch so he could really look at the target. And the man with the cigarette *was* the target. Not the gardener out for a late-night stroll. Not the chef hunting for the perfect variety of wild mushrooms. No, he recognized this man's face from the photos he'd seen. He gently squeezed the trigger and...

Boom.

The muffled sound of the gunshot still managed to pierce his eardrums, set his teeth on edge, stab through his brain.

Eyes wide open, he sat up, instantly aware that he'd been dreaming. The only noise in the dimly lit room was his ragged breathing.

But the room was unfamiliar, and he felt a new wave of panic. Where in hell was he now?

Wherever it was, it was a far cry from the church shelter he'd woken up in yesterday morning.

His gaze swept across the impersonal furnishings, the cheesy oil paintings on the wall, and it came to him. Motel room. Yes, he'd checked in to this place yesterday morning, after leaving the shelter. His head had been pounding, and he'd wanted only to fall into bed and sleep.

He'd paid in cash and signed the registration M. Man.

Heavy curtains were pulled across the windows, letting in only a tiny sliver of bright morning light. Hands still shaking from his dream, he pushed the covers off, aware that the sheets were soaked with his own sweat. His head still felt tender, but no longer as if the slightest movement would make him want to scream.

He could remember, almost word for word, the brief conversation he'd had with the man at the motel's front desk. He remembered the aromatic smell of coffee in the motel lobby. He remembered the clerk's name—Ron—worn on a badge on his chest. He remembered how endlessly long it had taken Ron to find the key to room 246. He remembered pulling himself up the stairs, one step at a time, driven by the knowledge that soothing darkness and a soft bed were within reach.

He could remember that dream he'd just had, too, and he didn't want to think about what it might mean.

He stood up, aware that the movement jarred him only slightly, and crossed to the air conditioner, turning it to a higher setting. The fan motor kicked in with a louder hum, and coolness hit him in a wave of canned air.

Slowly, deliberately, he sat back down on the edge of the bed.

He could remember the shelter. He could see Jarell's smiling face, hear the sound of his cheerful voice. *Hey, Mission Man. Hey, Mish!*

He closed his eyes and relaxed his shoulders, waiting for memories of being brought into the shelter, waiting for memories of what had happened that night.

But there was nothing there.

There was only…emptiness. Nothingness. As if before he'd been brought to the First Avenue shelter, he hadn't existed.

He could feel a new sheen of perspiration covering his body despite the cooler setting of the air conditioner. He'd slept off whatever had ailed him—whether it was the result of alcohol or some other controlled substance or simply the blow he'd received to his head. In fact, he'd slept solidly for more than twenty-four hours.

So why the hell couldn't he remember his own damned name?

Hey, Mission Man. Hey, Mish!

He stood up, staggering slightly in his haste to get to the mirror that covered the wall in front of a double set of sinks. He flipped on the light and…

He remembered the face that looked back at him. He remembered it—but only from the bathroom mirror at the shelter. Before that, there was...

Nothing.

"Mish." He spoke aloud the nickname Jarell had given him. The word sent a small ripple of recognition through him again, as it had yesterday morning. But what kind of name was Mish? Was it possible that he remembered— very faintly—Jarell calling him that when he was first brought into the shelter?

Mish. He gazed into the unfamiliar swirl of green and brown that were his own eyes. What kind of name was Mish? Well, right now, it was the only name he'd got.

Mish splashed cold water on his face, then cupped his hand under the faucet and drank deeply.

What was he supposed to do now? Go to the police?

No, that was out of the question. He couldn't do that. He wouldn't be able to explain the .22 and that huge wad of money he was carrying in his boot. He knew—he didn't know how he knew, but he did—that he couldn't tell the police, couldn't tell *anyone* anything. He couldn't let anyone know why he was here.

Not that he could have, even if he'd wanted to. *He* didn't know why he was here.

So what was he supposed to do?

Check himself into a hospital? He turned his head, gingerly parting his hair to look at the gash on his head. Without yesterday's fog of pain clouding his eyes, he knew with a chilling certainty that the wound on his head had been the result of a bullet's glancing blow. He'd been shot, nearly killed.

No, he couldn't go to a hospital, either—they'd be forced to report his injury to the police.

He dried his face and hands on a small white towel and went back into the main part of the motel room. His boots were on the floor near the bed, where he'd left them last night. He picked up the right one, dumping its contents onto the rumpled sheets. He turned on the light and sat down, picking up the .22.

It fit perfectly, familiarly into his hand. He couldn't remember his own name, but somehow he knew he'd be able to use this weapon with deadly accuracy if the need ever arose. This weapon, and any other, as well. He remembered his dream, and he set it back down on the bed.

He pulled the rubber band off the fold of money, and the piece of white paper that was fastened along with it slipped free. It was fax paper; the slippery, shiny kind that was hard to read. He picked it up and angled it toward the light.

"Lazy Eight Ranch," he read. Again, the name was totally unfamiliar to him. There was an address and directions to some kind of spread up in the northern part of the state. From what he could tell from the directions, it was about four hours outside of Santa Fe. The words were all typed, except for a note scrawled across the bottom in big round handwriting. "Looking forward to meeting you." It was signed, "Rebecca Keyes."

Mish opened the bedside-table drawer, looking for a telephone book. But the only thing inside was a Gideons Bible. He picked up the phone and dialed the front desk.

"Yeah, is there a train station or a bus depot in town?" he asked when the desk clerk came on the line.

"Greyhound's just down the street."

"Can you give me the phone number?"

He silently repeated the number the clerk gave him, hung up, then dialed the phone.

He was going to Santa Fe.

CHAPTER TWO

BECCA WAS OUT FRONT, helping Belinda and Dwayne welcome a van load of guests, when she first spotted him.

He would have been very easy to miss—the solitary figure of a man walking slowly along the road. Yet even from this distance, she could tell that he was different. He didn't have the nonchalant swagger of the cowboys that worked the nearby ranches. He didn't carry the bags and sacks of crafts and jewelry that many of the local Native Americans took into Santa Fe to sell. He had only one small bag, efficiently tucked under one arm.

He turned into the Lazy Eight's long drive, as somehow Becca had known he would.

As he drew closer, she could see he wasn't wearing the Western gear that was the standard outfit of the Southwest. He had on the blue jeans, but he wore a new-looking T-shirt instead of a long-sleeved Western-cut button-down shirt. His arms were deeply tanned, as if he spent quite a bit of time outside.

His black boots weren't the kind a real cowboy would wear, and he wore a baseball cap instead of a Stetson on his head.

From a distance, he'd looked tall and imposing. Up close, he merely looked imposing. It was odd, really. He had to be at least an inch or so shorter than six feet, and he was slender, almost slight. Yet there was a power about him, a quiet strength that seemed to radiate from him.

It may have been in the set of his shoulders or the angle of his chin. Or it may have been something in his dark eyes that made her want to step back a bit and keep her distance. His gaze swept across the drive, over the van and the luggage and the guests, over the ranch house, over the corral where Silver was waiting impatiently for another chance to stretch his legs, over Belinda and Dwayne, over *her*. With one quick flick of his eyes, he seemed to take her in, to memorize, appraise, and then dismiss.

Becca tried to look away, but she couldn't.

He was impossibly, harshly handsome—provided, of course, that a woman went for the dark and dangerous type. His face was slightly weathered, with high cheek-bones that even Johnny Depp would've been jealous of. His lips were gracefully shaped, if perhaps a shade too thin, too grimly set. His dark hair was longer than she'd first thought, worn fastened back at the nape of his neck. His face was smooth-shaven, but he had a scar on his chin that added to his aura of danger. And those eyes…

Becca watched as he approached Belinda. He spoke softly—too softly for Becca to hear his words—as he drew a piece of paper from his pocket.

Belinda turned and pointed directly at Becca. He turned, too, and once again those eyes were on her, coolly appraising.

He started toward her.

Becca came down the ranch office steps, meeting him halfway, pushing her beat-up Stetson further back on her short brown curls. "Can I help you?"

"You're Rebecca Keyes." His voice was soft and accentless. His words weren't a question, but she answered him anyway.

"That's right." His eyes weren't dark brown as she'd first thought. They were hazel—an almost otherworldly mix of green and brown and yellow and blue. She was staring. She knew she was staring, but she couldn't seem to stop.

"You sent me this fax?"

This time it *was* a question. Becca forced her gaze away from his face and looked down at the paper he held in his hands. It was indeed fax paper. She recognized the standard directions to the ranch, caught sight of the messy scribble of her handwriting at the bottom. "You must be Casey Parker."

He repeated the name slowly. "Casey Parker."

He didn't look the way he'd sounded during their telephone interview. She'd pictured a larger, older, beefier man. But no matter. She needed a hired hand, and all of his references had checked out.

"Do you have any ID?" Becca asked. She smiled to soften her words and explained. "It has more to do with filling out employee tax forms than verifying that you're who you say you are."

He shook his head. "I'm sorry, I don't. My wallet was stolen night before last. I got into some kind of fight and…"

As if to prove his story, he took off his hat and she could see a long scrape above his right temple, disappearing into his wavy dark hair. He had a bruise on his cheekbone, too. She hadn't noticed it at first—it was barely discernible underneath the suntanned darkness of his skin.

"I hope you don't make a habit of getting into fights."

He smiled. It was just a slight upward curve of his lips, yet it managed to soften his harsh features. "I hope not, too."

"You're a week early," Becca told him, hoping her briskness would counteract the effect his quiet smile and strange words had had on her, "but that's good, because another hand quit on me yesterday."

He was silent, just standing there watching her with those eyes that seemed to see everything. For a moment, she was almost convinced he could see back in time, to yesterday morning's disastrous conversation with Justin Whitlow, and back even further to Rafe McKinnon's quiet resignation. For a moment, she was almost convinced he could see her anger and her frustration and her defeat.

"You *do* still want the job…?" she asked, suddenly afraid that he didn't like what he saw. After all, bad things always came in threes.

He turned, squinting slightly at the blinding blueness of the summer sky. His gaze swept across the valley, and Becca was certain that unlike most people, this man saw, really *saw* the stark New Mexico countryside. She was sure that with his intense hazel eyes, he could see the terrible, almost painful beauty of the land.

"You own this place?" he asked in his quiet voice.

"I wish." The words came out automatically and all too heartfelt. As his eyes flicked in her direction, she felt exposed—as if, with those two little words, she'd given too much of herself away.

But he just nodded, his lips curving very slightly in the beginnings of a smile.

"Who *does* own it?" he asked. "I like to know the name of the man I'm working for."

"The owner's name is Justin Whitlow," Becca told him. "He's the one who pays your wages. But I'm the boss. You'll be working for *me*."

He nodded again, turning back to gaze out at the vista, but not before she saw a glimmer of amusement in his dark eyes. "I don't have a problem with that," he said quietly.

"Some men do."

"I'm not some men." He looked back at her again, and Becca knew without a doubt that his words were true. This quiet, slender man with the watchful hazel eyes wasn't just "some men."

But exactly what kind of man he was, she didn't know for sure.

"HEY, BABE, LONG TIME no see." Lt. Lucky O'Donlon of U.S. Navy SEAL Team Ten's Alpha Squad pulled Veronica Catalanotto into his arms and kissed her hello as he came into the kitchen of his captain's house.

"Luke. Hi. Did Frankie let you in?" Ronnie's smile was warm and she seemed genuinely glad to see him. And since she was one of the top ten most beautiful, nicest, smartest women he'd ever met, that welcoming smile was going to be good for quite a number of fantasy miles. But then she went and ruined it by smiling exactly the same way at Bobby and Wes, who had come in behind him. "How was your trip, boys?" she asked in her extremely classy British accent.

Captain Joe Catalanotto's wife always called the intensely dangerous and highly covert operations that Alpha Squad was sent out on "trips." As if they'd been away sightseeing or visiting museums.

Wes rolled his eyes. "Oh, man, Ron, we came really close to being cluster—"

Bobby's size extra-extra-large elbow went solidly into his swim buddy's side.

"Fine," Wes said quickly. "It was fine, Ronnie. As always. Thanks for asking, though."

Veronica wasn't fooled. Her smile had faded, making her eyes look enormous in her face. "Is everyone all right?

I mean, of course I've already asked Joe, but I'm not sure he'd even tell me if someone *had* been hurt."

Ever since a year and a half ago, when the captain had nearly been killed by terrorists on what should have been a routine training mission, Veronica looked even more fragile than she had before when the squad went out on an op. She'd never found it easy to deal with the fact that her husband regularly left—sometimes without any warning—on highly dangerous missions. And now, after seeing Joe in a hospital bed, fighting for his life, it was even more difficult for her.

"Everyone's fine," Lucky said quietly, taking her hand. *"Really."* Hotshot Cowboy Jones had jammed his ankle coming in too hard from a HALO jump, but aside from that, they'd all made it back to California in one piece.

Veronica smiled, but it was a little too bright and a touch too brittle. "Well," she said. "Joe's expecting you. He's down on the beach."

"Thanks." Lucky squeezed her hand before he released it.

"Should I set extra plates for dinner?" Veronica asked evenly.

Lucky exchanged a look with Bobby. The captain had called them to this meeting on their pagers, sending them an urgent code. Whatever was up was important. Despite the fact that they'd only been home a day and a half, chances were they'd be going wheels-up again within the next few hours. And knowing the way Joe Catalanotto liked to lead from the front, it was more than likely he'd be shipping out with them. It seemed, however, that he hadn't mentioned anything about that to his wife.

"I don't think so, Ronnie," Bobby told her gently. "Probably not this time. It really smells great, though. Those cooking lessons are paying off, huh?"

"I was working all day," she told him ruefully. "Joe made the stew."

Damn. The captain's wife may have been beautiful, smart and sexy as hell, but the woman was a menace in the kitchen.

"Are you sure you can't stay?" she added. "There's plenty and it's quite good. There's no way Joe and Frankie and I can possibly eat all of it."

"Something's come up. I think the captain's planning to take us kids out on another field trip," Wes told her before either Bobby or Lucky could muzzle him. Mr. Insensitive and Completely Oblivious. "So, yeah, we're sure we can't stay."

"Well," Veronica said tightly. "Off for another month, are you? Thanks for letting me know, although that's something that would've been nice to hear from Joe."

Double damn. Lucky cringed. "Ron, honest, I don't know what's up. If he didn't mention anything to you, well, maybe we're *not* going anywhere."

Veronica visibly composed herself. And sighed as she looked up into their somewhat panicked faces. "Don't look at me like that," she chided them. "I'm stronger than you think. I knew what I was getting before I married him. I don't have to like it when Joe leaves—isn't that what you SEALs always say? I don't have to like it, I just have to do it. Just take care of him for me, all right?"

She was pretending to hang tough, but her lower lip trembled an infinitesimal amount, giving her away. "Go," she said. "He's waiting. And you can tell him he doesn't have to worry about breaking the terrible news to me anymore."

Lucky followed Bobby and Wes out the kitchen door but hesitated on the deck, looking in through the window to watch her set only two places at the kitchen table—

for herself and Frankie, her toddler son—still trying not to cry.

Lucky knew by the time Joe came back to the house, she'd be perfectly composed and probably even smiling.

Veronica's acceptance of Joe's career was a rare thing. SEALs had a divorce rate that was off the scale, in part because many of their wives simply couldn't take the strain of being left behind again and again and again, waiting and worrying.

"I'm never getting married," Lucky murmured to Wes as they went down the steps that led to the beach.

"You and me, Luck," Wes agreed. "Unless Ronnie decides to leave the captain. Or am I already too late? Have you already started marking your territory in a big circle around her? No offense, Lieutenant, sir, but that kiss was just a little too friendly."

Lucky was stung. "I was just saying hello. I'd never—"

"You'd never what, O'Donlon?" All six feet and four dangerous inches of Joe Cat materialized from the mist that was blowing in off the Pacific. One second they were alone and the next he was breathing down their necks. How the hell could a man built like a professional football player *do* that?

"I'd never hit on your wife," Lucky told his captain bluntly. There was no point in trying to hide the truth from Joe Cat. Somehow he'd find out—if he didn't already know. That's why he was the captain. "I'd never, ever, *ever* hit on Ronnie." Lucky shot Wes a disbelieving look. "I can't believe you think I'd do something that low, Skelly. My feelings are seriously hurt—"

"What's happening, Captain?" Bobby interrupted.

Joe Cat motioned toward the ocean. "We need to walk," he told them. "We really should be talking in a secured room, but getting one would raise too many eyebrows, and that's the last thing I want to do."

Whatever this was, it was bigger than Lucky had imagined. He stopped giving Wes dirty looks and focused on what the captain was saying.

But Joe was silent until they were next to the breaking surf. The beach was deserted and misty, the setting sun hidden behind clouds.

"I've been doing some work for Admiral Robinson," Joe Cat finally told them, his voice low. "Acting as a liaison for one of his longhairs who's out on a black op for the admiral's Gray Group."

Longhair was the name given to any SEAL who might need to blend in with a dangerous and motley crowd of terrorists and mercenaries at any given moment. He had to go on top secret, extremely covert "black" operations, where a man with a military haircut would stick out like a sore thumb. And once that man stuck out, he would be one very dead sore thumb.

So these covert op SEALs got tattoos. They pierced their ears. They didn't shave for weeks on end. They dressed in what would have been known as "grunge" in the early nineties. And they grew their hair very, very long.

Of course, when it came to longhairs, the captain should talk. He wore his own hair in a thick, dark braid down his back. When he shook his hair out, he looked like a pirate or maybe a really wild rock star—and absolutely nothing like a highly decorated, extremely well-respected captain in Uncle Sam's Navy.

"The admiral's off doing diplo-duty in a place where it's impossible to get a secured telephone line," Joe Cat told them curtly. "I can't even report to him that as of twenty-four hours ago, his SEAL missed his weekly check-in. And frankly, I'm concerned. Apparently this guy's better than a clock when it comes to check-ins. So I've got to go out to New Mexico to try and track him down, and I need a team to watch my six."

New *Mexico?* What the...?

The captain looked at Bob, then Wes, then Lucky. "I'm looking for volunteers here. This will be a black op as well—completely off the record, no paperwork, no acknowledgment of the situation by any of the top brass. If you choose to come along, you'll be paid, but not in the usual way. In fact, you'll have to take leave so your whereabouts can't be traced."

It sounded like some serious fun. "Count me in, Skipper," Lucky said, and Bobby and Wes were only nanoseconds behind him.

Their captain nodded. "Thanks," he said quietly.

"Who's the little lost SEAL we're tracking down?" Wes asked. "Anyone we know?"

"Yeah," Joe said. "You worked with him six months ago. Lt. Mitchell Shaw."

"Oh, man," Bobby said in his basso profundo, voicing exactly what Lucky was thinking. "He's gonna be hard to find if he doesn't want to be found, Cat. He's a chameleon—good with disguises. The admiral once told me that he nearly pulled the hair off a little old lady, thinking she was Mitch under cover."

"What's a Gray Group operative doing in New Mexico?" Lucky asked.

"This is top secret information I'm about to give you," Joe told them seriously. "It goes no further than the four of us, understood?"

"Yes, sir."

Joe sighed, turning to squint out at the ocean for a moment. "Remember that break-in at Arches?"

Last year, the security at Arches Military Testing Lab in Colorado had been breached and six canisters of Triple X had been stolen. Lucky, Bobby, Wes and Mitch Shaw had all been part of the team that located and destroyed the deadly nerve gas. Yeah, they remembered that break-in all too clearly.

"The Trip X nerve agent wasn't the only thing taken," Joe Cat continued grimly.

Wes ran his hand down his face. "I don't think I want to hear this."

"Plutonium," Joe said. "Enough was taken to make a small nuclear weapon."

A small nuke. Great.

"Shaw was working to track it down," Joe Cat continued. "He was following a lead both he and Admiral Robinson thought was probably empty. That's why he was out there alone. The bulk of the Gray Group's manpower is working from the other end—finding the potential buyer seemed easier than finding the plutonium in the haystack. But now that Shaw's gone missing, I'm not sure what's going on."

"New Mexico's a big state," Bobby commented.

He was right. And if Mitch was working a black op, he wouldn't have broadcast his whereabouts to anyone. "How the hell are we gonna find him?"

"Shaw was carrying ten counterfeit hundred-dollar bills," Joe answered Lucky. "Admiral Robinson implemented a technique used by the spooks at the Agency— apparently his wife's a former agent. See, how it works is if some bad voodoo goes down and the agent—or SEAL in this case—is eliminated by the opposition, that funny money tends to go into circulation. It makes sense, right? An agent is hit and his or her body disappears. But if you're the guy who did the hit, you check pockets for weapons or cash. No point in sinking *that* in the quarry with your victim's earthly remains, right? So the money changes hands, so to speak. In the past, this method has occasionally been effective enough to track all the way to the killers. Once they start spending the money—as soon as it's ID'd as fake—it's like a big red flag gets dropped."

"Are you saying you think Lieutenant Shaw is dead, sir?" Wes swore sharply. "I liked the guy."

"I don't know what's up with Shaw," Joe told them. "But one—and only one—of his counterfeit hundred-dollar bills showed up in Wyatt City, New Mexico. In the donation box of the First Church Homeless Shelter, of all places."

"When do we leave?" Bobby asked.

"We've got a flight out to Las Cruces in three hours," Joe said. He smiled crookedly. "I, um, need a little time. I haven't exactly told Ronnie yet that I'm leaving."

"Well, sir, we, uh…" Wes braced himself. "*I* kind of took care of that for you, Cat."

Joe closed his eyes and swore.

"I'm really sorry, Captain," Wes said.

"Skipper, you know… Me and Ren and Stimpy here can handle this. You don't have to come along—it'd be overkill anyway," Lucky earnestly told the captain. "We've worked with Mitch, we know what he looks like—at least when he's not in disguise. And like you said, the rest of the Gray Group's covering the other end. Give yourself—and Veronica—a break." He paused. "And give me a chance to practice those leadership skills they worked so hard to teach me at the academy, sir. Let me take care of this."

Joe looked up at the hillside above the beach, at the warm lights of his home cutting through the thickening fog.

He made up his mind. "Go," he said. "The paperwork giving you leave is already at the base. But I want sit-reps over a secured line every twelve hours."

"Thanks, Captain." Lucky held out his hand.

Joe clasped it and shook. "Find him. Fast."

"ARE YOU CASEY?"

Casey. Casey Parker. If that *was* his name, why couldn't he remember it? "Yeah, that's me."

A ten-year-old kid had come into the barn. He stood in front of Mish now, his eyes magnified by a crooked pair of wire-framed glasses. "I'm supposed to tell you to saddle up a pair of horses for me and Ashley. Ashley's my sister. She's a pain in the butt."

Saddle up some horses...

"What's your name?" he asked the boy.

"My real name's Reagan. Reagan Thomas Alden. But people call me Chip."

Mish turned back to the stall he was shoveling out. "Rumor has it, Chip, guests under age eighteen aren't allowed to ride out on their own."

"Yes, but...I'm not signed up for a ride until after *four o'clock*. What am I supposed to do until then?"

"Read a book?" Mish suggested, getting back into the easy rhythm of his work.

"Hey!" Chip brightened. "*You* could ride out with me and Ash. There's this place, about a half a mile east of here where there's these big, creepy-looking rocks, kind of like some giant's fingers sticking out of the ground. I could show 'em to you."

"I don't think so."

"Come on, Casey. You're not doing anything important right now."

Mish kept right on shoveling. "The way I figure it, I've got one of the most important jobs here—making sure the horses you ride have a clean place to sleep at night."

"Yes, but…wouldn't you rather be riding?"

Mish answered honestly. "No." The truth was, he could remember nothing about horses. If he'd at one time known how to ride, that knowledge had slipped away with his memories of his name and his past. But somehow he doubted that. Somehow, he got the sense that horseback riding was a subject he'd never bothered to learn much about.

It was troublesome. If he *was* Casey Parker, then he'd lied to get this job. And if he *wasn't* Casey Parker, then who in heaven's name *was* he?

Casey Parker or not, he couldn't shake the feeling that he wasn't going to like finding out who he really was.

The handgun in his boot. The wad of money. The bullet wound. It all added up to the same grim conclusion: he was not on the side of the angels.

If his dream had held just one ounce of truth, he was a killer. He was someone who shot and killed other people for a living. And, if that was the case, he didn't want to remember who he was.

He—and the world—would be better off if he simply stayed here for the rest of his days, shoveling manure and—

Mish lifted his head, listening intently to a low rumble. Was it thunder? Or an approaching truck?

"That sounds like Travis Brown," Chip told him. "Doing what Becca calls his first-rate imitation of a damn fool."

It was the sound of pounding hoofbeats—faint, but growing louder until it became a clatter of noise directly outside of the barn. It was accompanied by a high-pitched whinny of fear and pain from the horse. *That* sound was echoed almost identically—except this second scream came from a human throat. Mish dropped his shovel.

"That's Ashley!" Chip bolted for the door, but Mish swung himself over the wall of the stall and beat him there.

A riderless horse stood on its hind legs, pawing the air as a man dressed in fringed leggings and a leather vest lay sprawled behind him. A young girl crouched in the dust in front of the enraged horse, covering her head with her arms.

Mish didn't stop. He started toward the girl at a sprint.

He could see Rebecca Keyes running just as quickly toward them from the direction of the ranch office. Her hat fell into the dust, and she reached the horse's bridle just as Mish grabbed the girl and pulled her out of harm's way.

The horse's slashing hooves came within inches of Rebecca's face, but she didn't flinch.

Mish shoved the girl into Chip's arms and stood ready to come to Becca's aid. But she simply and slowly backed away, letting the animal have some space.

The horse's sides were torn, as if slashed with too-sharp spurs. His mouth was frothing and flecked with blood. His dark body was slick with sweat and trembling.

The man who'd been thrown scrambled out of range of the beast's powerful back hooves. "Did you see that?" he said as he pulled himself to his feet. "That damned horse nearly killed me!"

"Quiet!" Becca didn't even look in the man's direction.

All of her attention was focused on the horse. Although she didn't speak loudly, there was stern authority in her voice.

The rider wisely shut up.

As Mish watched, the horse returned to all fours. He twitched nervously, though, sidling and still trembling. Becca moved closer again, crooning softly to the frightened animal, her hands and body language nonthreatening.

She could have been a lion tamer. Mish felt his own tension start to drain from his shoulders and neck just from the sound of her soothing, hypnotic voice. As she gazed at the horse steadily, Mish could see none of the anger that he knew she must be feeling toward the abusive rider.

He knew that her eyes were an unremarkable shade of brown, but as she looked at the horse, they reflected a serenity that was almost angelic. And for a moment, as he gazed at her, Mish couldn't breathe.

Rebecca Keyes wasn't what most folks would consider to be beautiful. Oh, her face was pretty enough—cute, actually. It was maybe a touch too round, though, making her look younger than she really was. Or maybe she *was* just plain young, he didn't know for sure. Her nose was small and couldn't be described as anything other than childlike. It was dotted with freckles that added to that effect. Her mouth was generously wide, her lips gracefully shaped. The only makeup she wore was a light coat of gloss on those lips—and Mish suspected she wore it as protection from the harsh sun rather than for cosmetic effect.

But as she reached for that shuddering horse, soothing, peaceful comfort seemed to radiate from her every movement, her every word, her every glance, and Mish could not breathe.

He wanted her to turn to him, to look at him that way, to lay her gentle hands on him, to bring to *him* the peace he so desperately needed.

Instead, he watched as she touched the horse.

The animal snorted, nervously sidestepping, but Becca moved with him. "It's okay, baby," she murmured. "Everything's going to be okay… Shhh…" She ran her hands down the horse's neck. "Yeah, everything's all right now. Let's get you cleaned up." She looped the reins over the animal's head, leading him gently toward the barn. "Casey here will take care of you," she added, still talking in that sweet, soothing voice, "while I take care of the idiot who hurt you."

She looked up at Mish, reaching out to hand him the reins, and just like that, the warm calm in her eyes flickered and changed—replaced by sheer, cold, nearly murderous anger. She was going to "take care" of the rider, indeed.

But first she turned toward the young girl who'd nearly been run down in the driveway. "Are you all right, Ash?"

Ashley and Chip were standing alongside the barn, arms still around each other. The girl nodded, but she was clearly shaken.

"Chip, run to the office," Becca crisply ordered the little boy. "Have Hazel crank up the cellular phone and locate your parents." She turned back to Mish. "Get that horse inside the barn."

Mish gently tugged on the reins, leading the huge animal into the quiet coolness of the barn. He looked up into the beast's big brown eyes, and could see mistrust. He tried to gaze back confidently, but knew he was failing. Truth was, he didn't have a clue what to do.

He wrapped the reins around one of the bars on the nearest stall, keeping one ear tuned to what was going on outside of the barn.

"Mr. Brown, you have exactly fifteen minutes to pack your bags and get down here to the ranch office," he could hear Becca tell the man who'd been riding the horse, her tone leaving no room for any dissent.

There was a buckle that seemed to hold the saddle on and Mish tried to unfasten it, but the animal shifted away, snorting. He was no Dr. Doolittle, but he couldn't miss the horse's message. *Don't touch me.*

Outside, Brown sputtered. "*I'm* the one who was thrown—"

"You've had your warnings," Becca cut him off, her voice tight with anger. "You've been told again and again that you may *not* wear spurs with *any* of our horses. You've been told again and again not to yank the reins, to treat the horse the way *you'd* want to be treated if *you* had a bit in your mouth."

Mish put his hand on the horse's neck. He just rested it there, steady and firm, trying to push all of his uncertainty far away, knowing the animal could sense it. He *could* do this. He'd seen enough Westerns. He had to get the saddle off, and the blanket underneath, then somehow cool the horse down.

"You've been told again and again that horses *must* be kept to a slow walk around the ranch buildings," Becca's voice continued. "This time you might've badly injured Ashley Alden. And this time, I'm done giving you warnings. This time, I'm telling you to pack your bags and get off this ranch."

"I want the sheriff! I want an ambulance—I hurt my back in that fall! I'm going to sue—"

Mish reached for the buckle again, this time his movements steady and sure. The horse twitched and blew air out of his nose, hard, but Mitch got the job done. He lifted off the saddle and set it on top of a rail. And then he couldn't resist sneaking a look out of the barn door. A crowd had gathered—guests and ranch hands silently watching.

Becca had Travis Brown backed against the split wood railings of the corral, her eyes shooting fire. When she spoke, her voice was soft but it carried in the stillness.

"Go ahead and call the sheriff, Hazel," she said to the gray-haired woman on the ranch office steps, her eyes never leaving Brown. "It's entirely likely that Ted and Janice Alden will want to press charges against Mr. Brown for nearly killing their daughter. Reckless endangerment—isn't that what it's called?"

"You can't kick me out. I'm a shareholder."

"You're an *idiot*," Becca said sharply. "Get the *hell* off this ranch."

He moved toward her, threateningly. "You little bitch! When Justin Whitlow finds out about this—"

"Fifteen minutes, Brown." He towered over her, but Becca didn't back down. She stood her ground, chin raised, as if daring the man to raise a hand to her.

The man pushed past her, exaggerating his limp as he headed toward the guest cabins.

Becca turned, looking first at Hazel. "Did you reach the Aldens?"

The plump older woman nodded. "They're on their way."

"Call the sheriff, too—in case they want to register a complaint."

"Already done."

Becca's gaze swept across the crowd and landed on Mish. He realized suddenly that he'd come all the way out of the barn, toward her, ready to jump in if Brown had tried to strike her.

"How's Stormchaser?" she asked, heading directly toward him. "The poor baby's going to have to go into therapy after this."

"He doesn't seem to want me to touch him," Mish admitted, following her back into the barn.

She gave him an odd look over her shoulder. "*She* doesn't know you. *She's* bound to be a little spooked."

She. The horse was female. He hadn't even thought to look. He'd simply assumed that since the animal was so big and powerful… Thou shalt not assume. He'd broken one of the biggest rules, and he'd given himself away.

Rules. Rules of *what?* God Almighty, it was back there, just out of his line of sight. All of the answers, dancing at the edge of his mental peripheral vision. He wanted to close his eyes, to somehow grab hold of the truth, of his identity. But Becca Keyes was talking to him.

"Why don't you get her cooled down," Becca said, obviously repeating herself as she gazed at him with her seemingly average brown eyes.

She was challenging him. Her words were a test—she wanted to know if he could do it.

But he couldn't.

Mish met her gaze levelly, honestly. "I'm afraid that's a little out of my league. But if you tell me exactly what needs to be done, I can—"

She'd already turned away from him. "Perfect," she was muttering. "Incredibly, amazingly, stupendously *perfect*." She spun back to face him. "You're telling me you don't know how to cool down a horse, aren't you?"

"I'm a quick study," he said quietly. "And you're short of hands—"

"Short of brains, too, obviously." There was a flare of that hot-burning anger in her eyes, but the heat was weakened by her frustration and disappointment. "Dammit. *Dammit!*"

The disappointment was hard to take. He would have far preferred her anger. "I didn't intend to deceive you." He couldn't explain. How could he?

She just laughed as she took the saddle blanket from Stormchaser's back. "Right. Go and make sure Brown's packing his bags. He's in cabin number twelve. Walk him back to the office, finish up the stalls, then stay out of my sight for the rest of evening. I can't handle this right now—we'll talk in the morning."

Mish may not have known a thing about horses, but he knew when a situation called for silence.

He turned and left the barn. He'd awakened again this morning with no past, no name, no sense of self. Yet somehow he now felt even emptier inside.

CHAPTER THREE

IT WAS AFTER TWO O'CLOCK in the morning, and someone was pounding on her apartment door.

Becca sat up, groping for her flashlight in the darkness and coming up empty. The pounding continued—a frantic tattoo accompanied by a high-pitched voice calling her name. She flung herself out of bed and nearly stumbled as she made her way to the light switch on the wall.

Grabbing her robe from the hook next to her closet, she moved toward the noise and opened the door.

Fourteen-year-old Ashley Alden stood on the other side of the screen, her face streaked with tears. "Chip's gone," she said.

Becca pulled the girl inside and shut the screen before the entire mosquito population of New Mexico came into the kitchen with her. "Gone where?"

"I don't know! I was in charge, and I fell asleep, and when Mom and Dad came home, Chip was *gone!* He took the blanket off his bed—I think he's playing cowboy and sleeping outside somewhere." Ashley was trying her best to hold back her tears, but a fresh flood brimmed in her eyes. "And now *they're* fighting, and a storm's coming and *some*one's got to go find Chip before he's struck by lightning!"

The girl was right. A storm *was* coming. Becca could hear the ominous rumble of thunder in the distance. Although dangerous, lightning was the least of their worries.

If Chip had set up his bedroll in one of the arroyos, or on the gentle valley of the dry riverbed... It didn't have to be raining here for the arroyos and river suddenly to flood. It only had to be raining upstream.

She looked at the kitchen clock. Two-fifteen. No doubt the Aldens had stayed at the local roadhouse, drinking until the two o'clock last call. And if that was the case, they weren't going to be a whole hell of a lot of help in finding their son.

Thunder crackled again, closer this time.

Still, she was going to need all the bodies she could get.

"Go get your mom and dad," she commanded Ashley, already on the cordless phone to Hazel. "And wake up as many of the other guests as you can. We'll meet in front of the ranch office."

Ashley disappeared out the door.

Hazel sounded dazed as she answered her phone, but she rallied quickly.

Becca pulled a pair of jeans on over her nightshirt as she rattled out a stream of orders to her assistant. "Wake up Dwayne and Belinda—tell them to saddle up the horses. The search'll be easier on horseback." She yanked on her boots and jammed her hat on her head. "I'll wake the hands in the bunkhouse."

THE BUS RIDE WAS INTERMINABLE, but as the driver pulled up to the checkpoint at the first of the fences, Mish didn't want it to end. He closed his eyes, not wanting to see the gate shutting behind them, locking him in. He kept his eyes closed. There was no point looking at the security. No point studying the watchtowers and the fences. He was here. And he'd stay here until Jake got him out.

The bus jolted to a stop, but Mish didn't move until

one of the guards approached and unlocked him. He had been wearing both arm and leg shackles.

Mish stood up, and the guard roughly pulled his arms behind him, cuffing his hands behind his back. He still wore a tether, a short length of chain that connected his two ankles. It was hard navigating the steps down from the bus, and he jumped the last two, landing lightly in the dusty prison yard.

Prison. He was in prison. He felt sick to his stomach as he looked up at the harsh gray buildings towering above him.

"Move it," one of the guards barked. "Inside. Let's go."

Mish started to sweat. Out here was bad enough, but at least out here he still had the sky, open and free above him. Inside would be only walls, only bars, only these chains that marked him as a very, *very* dangerous man.

The guard shoved him and he stumbled, but he forced himself not to react, to find serenity from deep inside, that same serenity that had saved him so many times before. He was here. He didn't have to like it. He just had to endure it. Jake was counting on him. Jake needed him to…to…

The answers were there—who Jake was, and what he needed Mish to do there in prison—but they were just beyond his grasp.

Everything shifted then, the way dreams often do. And then Mish was in an alley, thunder rolling as the first huge drops of rain began to fall. In an instant, he was soaked.

He pushed his wet hair back, out of his face, wishing he had a ponytail holder. Dim light gleamed on the barrel of his side arm and he ducked into the shadows, waiting for the footsteps to come closer. Closer…

"Casey! Come on, Casey, wake up!" Rough hands shook him, and Mish opened his eyes, instantly awake,

Rebecca Keyes leaned over him, her hair tousled from sleep.

He was shocked. What was she doing in his bed? Not that he didn't want her there, because he did. Badly. But he couldn't remember how she'd gotten there. And he couldn't imagine acting on his attraction for this woman. It would be flat-out wrong to become intimately involved with *any*one until he'd reintroduced himself to himself.

He couldn't imagine Becca allowing herself to be seduced, either. She'd been so frostily angry with him. How had that happened? He couldn't remember how he'd convinced her to warm up and sleep with him. And maybe worst of all, he couldn't even remember the sex. And that was shockingly alarming.

Was this more amnesia? It didn't make sense. He could remember going to bed—alone—and turning off the light. He could remember the way Becca had looked straight through him during dinner. He could remember waking up in the shelter, his head pounding. He could remember Jarell, the motel, the bus ride to…

Prison.

He'd dreamt about *prison*. Being cuffed and chained. Remembered someone named Jake…

She shook him again. "Snap to, dammit! I need you to help."

Reality crashed in. Mish was lying in a cot barely large enough to sleep one, let alone two. And Becca wasn't dressed for a night of one-on-one—unless her idea of one-on-one was a cattle-roping contest. She was wearing jeans and boots and a wide-brimmed cowboy hat on her head.

He sat up, the blanket sliding off of his bare chest, and

Becca took a step back, as if afraid he wasn't wearing anything at all beneath those covers.

He was. Boxers. He also remembered keeping them on last night.

"Chip Alden's gone AWOL," she told him bluntly, "and we've got a storm moving in. I need all the manpower I can get—searching for the kid before the riverbed floods."

Mish nodded, clearly reading her silent message. She needed all the help she could get—even from a low-down, good-for-nothing, lying snake such as himself.

He swung his legs out of bed and pulled on his jeans and the T-shirt he'd worn yesterday, slipping into his boots as she turned and sprinted away. He followed her, quickly catching up. Thunder continued to rumble as the crowd of guests and employees gathering outside the ranch office glanced worriedly up at the dark sky.

Becca quickly split them into groups, sending them off in different directions, some on horseback, some on foot.

"Check the barn and public buildings," she ordered Mish before easily swinging herself up onto a horse and riding out.

He could hear the echoing voices of the search parties as they headed into the darkness, calling loudly, hoping to awaken the sleeping boy.

His was a throwaway job. He knew Becca didn't think they'd find Chip in the barn or the dining hall or even the arcade room. But someone had to look there, and he was that someone.

He went into the barn.

Stormchaser was the only horse left in the stables, and she cocked her ears curiously at him, as if amazed by all of the predawn activity.

It had been Stormchaser's stall that Mish had been cleaning when Chip had come into the barn just that afternoon, to try to con him into saddling up a pair of horses.

Mish froze, suddenly hearing an echo of Chip's pre-pubescent voice. *There's this place, about a half a mile east of here where there's these big, creepy-looking rocks, kind of like some giant's fingers sticking out of the ground....*

There was a relief map of the ranch on the barn wall, and Mish quickly measured the scale with his fingers, trying to find those rock formations Chip had mentioned. He knew how to read maps, and he easily found something six-tenths of a mile east-northeast that might've been those rocks. It was right next to a low-lying area—the dry riverbed.

Thunder cracked, closer this time, and the first plump drops of rain began to fall, hissing on the dry barn roof.

If Chip had set up camp in that riverbed...

Mish ran out toward the corral, but everyone was gone. He could hear their voices in the distance. Most of them had headed south.

He went back into the barn, where a huge flashlight hung by the door. But even using that, it would be impossible for him to achieve any real speed running more than a half a mile over the rough terrain.

He turned and looked Stormchaser directly in the eye.

She whinnied nervously as another bolt of lightning flashed, the boom of thunder close behind.

"Yeah, I don't like this weather, either," Mish said to the horse, opening the stall door, "but I know where this kid is, and I've got to get out there, so what do you say we make this a team effort?"

Stormchaser didn't disagree. Of course, she didn't exactly agree, either.

"I've never done this before in my life." Mish took a bridle down from the wall, speaking in a low, soft, soothing voice, the way he'd heard Becca talk to the horse. "But I spent most of yesterday watching the procedure, so let's just give it a try, okay?"

As Mish drew closer, the mare clenched her teeth.

"I think this bit thing is supposed to go *behind* your teeth, not in front of them," Mish told her, still in that low voice. "And I think I saw the other guys touch you back here a bit, and just kind of wait until you're maybe not paying quite so much attention and then...*slip* it in. There we go. Good horse. Atta girl. Way to go."

Stormchaser snorted, chomping disgruntledly on the bit.

"I can't imagine that feels very pleasant," Mish continued, slipping a saddle blanket onto her strong chestnut-colored back. "I can't imagine any of this is a whole lot of fun for you, especially after the way that idiot treated you this afternoon."

He took a saddle off the wall, gently placing it in the center of the blanket, and secured the belt around the horse's belly. As he'd seen the other ranch hands do, he waited until Stormchaser relaxed, and then tightened it several notches.

The stirrups seemed to be about the right length for his legs, so he looped the reins over the horse's head and led her out into the night, tucking the flashlight under one arm.

The rain was falling heavier now, and Stormchaser tried to back away, into the barn.

"No, you don't," he murmured to the horse, pointing her in the direction he wanted to go. "What kind of tough-as-nails Western cow horse are you, anyway?" He put his left foot into the stirrup and held on to the pommel. "I'm probably doing this all wrong and backwards, so I appreciate your patience," he said as he tried to imitate the move Becca had made, and swing himself into the saddle. He landed with a thud, nearly going over the other side. "Whoa!"

Stormchaser snorted, pricking up her ears as Mish took gentle hold of the reins. He had to remember that these things were attached to the horse's tender mouth.

Now, what was the opposite of whoa? "Giddyap!" he said.

Lightning flashed, thunder crashed, and Stormchaser bolted.

BECCA COULDN'T BELIEVE her eyes. Lightning flashed again, and again she saw Stormchaser, running like a bat out of hell with Casey Parker lying low and flat along the mare's neck, riding like a seasoned rodeo cowboy. She felt a flash of annoyance—the guy had led her to believe he didn't know the least little thing about horses—including riding.

She moved to cut them off just as Casey reined Stormchaser in.

"I know where Chip is," he called out, seemingly unaware of the rain that was now falling steadily, streaming down his face.

He nudged Stormchaser's sides, and the horse took off again. Becca followed, pressing Silver hard to keep up.

She had her flashlight on, and in its bright beam, she could see that Casey wasn't riding like a professional cowboy—he was holding on for dear life.

"I talked to him this afternoon," the man shouted to

her, "and he wanted to go out to this place where there were some rock formations."

Finger Rocks. God, that was right on the edge of the dry riverbed. Only, with all this rain, it wasn't going to stay dry for long—if it wasn't already flooded from the rain up in the mountains.

Becca gave Silver his head, letting him fly across the ground, praying they weren't too late. Please, God, let them find this little boy still alive....

She heard it before she saw it.

The river was running.

Lightning flared, and Finger Rocks appeared out of the darkness, looming crazily over them. The water in the riverbed was dark and frothy, and filled with bobbing logs and debris being washed downstream.

There was no sign of Chip.

Becca slid down off Silver, using her flashlight to illuminate the banks of the river.

Casey was still atop Stormchaser, and he pointed out into the rushing water. "There!"

She saw it, too.

She saw what might have been the top of a small head near a branch that had been snagged on an outcropping of rocks.

"Chip!" she shouted over the roar of the river and the bursts of thunder. "Chip!"

The head moved and became a small, pale face that reflected the light from her torch.

It was Chip. He was clinging for dear life to the end of a weathered old branch.

As Casey slid down off Stormchaser, Becca saw him take in the situation with a glance. The branch Chip was holding on to was wedged between two rocks at the river's edge, right before the water took a hard loop to the left and swept even faster down the hill. The white water down there told of rapids—rocks that could crush the life out of a ten-year-old flung against them with the water's raging force.

It was only a matter of time before the debris knocked Chip free from his perch and swept him downstream.

The tumble of rocks at the side of the river made it treacherous going. Casey slipped and slid over them, turning back to give Becca a hand.

She didn't need or want his help. "I'm fine," she shouted at him. "Keep going!"

Finally, they were both there.

"Hang on, kid," she heard Casey call to Chip. "We'll get you out of there!"

"I want my mom!" The little boy was weeping. "Please, I want my mom!"

"Just let us pull you out of there, and we'll find her right away," Casey told him, his voice reassuring. They *would* get the boy out of the river. And if he was feeling any doubt about it, he wasn't letting it show. He tugged at the thick end of the branch Chip was clinging to, but it wouldn't give. Becca set down her flashlight and helped. It didn't take long to realize that the damned thing wasn't going to budge. They weren't going to be able to free the branch to pull the kid out of there.

The rain was falling unmercifully now, streaming off the brim of her hat in a solid sheet.

"I'll have to climb out after him," she shouted to Casey.

He used one hand to wipe the water from his face, little good that it did. He shook his head. "No. I'll do it."

"Are you kidding? That branch won't hold your weight!"

"It might not hold yours."

"Hold on to my legs," Becca told him. "If the branch breaks, I'll hang onto it, and you can haul us both out of the water."

He didn't like it, but she didn't give him a chance to argue. She just started inching her way out along that branch.

She could feel his hands on her legs, his fingers hooking around the bottom edges of her jeans. She could see Chip's pale, frightened face as lightning flashed again.

The boy was edging toward her, even as she was moving closer to him.

She was so close. Another foot and a half, and—

It happened so fast.

A piece of wood barreling downstream caught Chip full in the chest, and with a shriek, his handhold on the branch was broken.

Becca heard herself scream as the boy, eyes wide with terror, fingers reaching for her, was swept underneath the water.

She felt herself hauled upward and nearly thrown onto the shore and sensed more than saw Casey scrambling back up and over the rocks. She grabbed for her flashlight, holding it high, illuminating the river, praying for a glimpse of Chip's brown hair, praying he'd manage to grab hold of another branch.

She saw him!

Dear God, no! The boy was being swept downriver. Another few seconds, and he'd hit those rapids.

But then she saw Casey, running along the riverbank, heading directly for the place where the river turned. She saw him dive, a graceful, athletic movement.

And then he was out of range of her light, and she saw nothing more.

MISH KNEW WITHOUT A DOUBT in the stretched-out seconds that he hung suspended over the raging water that he knew how to swim.

And he didn't just know how to do the dog paddle. He *knew* how to *swim*. As uncomfortable as he'd been while riding Stormchaser, here in the river he was completely in his element. He was at home in the water unlike anywhere else in the world.

He hit the river with a splash and it grabbed him, tugging, pulling, yanking him downstream. He went with it, using its power to push him up back toward the surface. Only when his head was above water again did he fight the current, searching for any sign of Chip.

He saw the debris coming—it looked like a solid chunk of a telephone pole—but he didn't have time to get completely out of the way. It hit him solidly in his left side, pushing him under and spinning him around, the white blaze of pain made worse by the water burning his lungs.

He kicked and stroked against the pain, surfacing with a rush, coughing out the water he'd inhaled and gasping in a blessed flood of air.

And the kid was swept right into his arms.

If he hadn't believed in the workings of some kind of higher power before, he did now.

Mish let the force of the water take him again, using his strength as a swimmer merely to steer them toward the rocky shore.

And then he was crawling out, his side on fire, Chip still clinging to his neck, both of them sobbing for air. And Becca was there, helping pull the kid to even higher ground. She then reached for him.

Lightning flashed, and he saw that she'd lost her hat. Her dark curls were plastered to her head and beneath her jacket, her shirt was glued to her breasts. It wasn't a shirt, he realized. She was wearing a white nightgown. And absolutely nothing underneath. She had an incredibly gorgeous body, but it was her eyes he found himself wanting to see again. Brimming with the warmth of emotion and relief, her eyes were impossibly beautiful.

He could have sat there in the rain all night, just waiting for the lightning, so he could get another glimpse of her face.

But Becca scooped Chip into her arms and pushed herself to her feet. "Let's get back to the ranch."

TED ALDEN, CHIP'S FATHER, came out of their cabin. "The doctor says he's got a few broken ribs, but his lungs are clear and his blood pressure's strong. We'll monitor that through the rest of the night—make sure there've been no internal injuries we don't know about."

The rain had stopped, and the clouds were breaking up. Becca could see the first faint stars shining hazily in the sky. She nodded. "Do you need help? You look as if once you fall asleep, you're going to stay asleep for a day or two."

Alden ran his hands down his face. "No, we've got the alarm clock set. And Ashley's set hers, too. Just in case."

"Well, I'm here if you need me."

"Thanks."

Becca turned to go, but he stopped her.

"We've caused nothing but trouble this trip. Are you going to ask us to leave tomorrow?"

She had to laugh. "You mean, like the way I asked Travis Brown to leave?" She shook her head. "No, I'm trying not to make a habit of running paying guests off with a shotgun. It's bad for business."

"Thank that cowboy again for me," Alden said. "If the two of you hadn't been there, Chip might've…"

Chip *would* have died.

Becca knew what Ted Alden couldn't bring himself to say aloud. His son would have died. The hell with her—she'd had very little to do with saving the boy's life. The truth was, if it weren't for Casey Parker, they would be dragging that river right this very moment, searching for Chip's crushed and lifeless little body.

Becca swallowed a sudden rush of intense emotion. She had to blink hard to push back a surge of moisture in her eyes. "I'll thank him," she said quietly. "Kiss Chip good-night for me, all right?"

Alden nodded, easing the screen door shut behind him.

It must have been the fatigue bringing all these waves of emotion to the surface. Becca couldn't remember the last time she'd cried, yet here she was, ready to curl up into a soggy ball and weep like a baby.

Everything was all right. The boy was safe. But she couldn't keep herself from thinking about what might have been. She couldn't help remembering that look of pure fear on the little boy's face as he was swept out of her reach, *Why didn't you save me?* echoing in his eyes. If Chip had died, his face would have haunted her for the rest of her life.

If Chip had died…

What if Casey hadn't been there with his amazing ability to swim like some kind of sea animal? What if the river had swept Chip past him? What if…?

Her insides churned and bile rose in her throat. She had to sit down, right there on the edge of the muddy road, and try her damnedest not to retch. She clung to her wet jacket, wrapping it tightly around her, praying for the nausea to pass.

"Are you all right?" The voice came out of the darkness, soft and gentle.

"Yeah," she lied, not wanting to look up and into the bottomless depths of Casey's eyes, not wanting him to see that she was shaking. "I'm just... I'm..."

She felt him sit down next to her, felt his closeness and warmth. He didn't say anything. He just sat there as she tried to breathe, as she desperately tried to regain her equilibrium and stop this damned shaking that was rattling her very brain.

When he finally did start to speak, Becca thought she might've been imagining it. His voice was so soft and perfectly woven into the velvet tapestry of the predawn.

"You know, I don't think I've ever ridden a horse before," he told her. "At least not since I was a kid. I don't know why I haven't tried it—it was great. Exhilarating. Kind of like flying. But you already know that, right? I can picture you as the kind of kid who was born astride a horse." He paused, but only briefly. "When I was riding Stormchaser, I remember thinking it was kind of like being on a motorcycle, except this thing I was riding had a brain and a *soul*..."

Becca knew exactly what he was doing. He was gentling her, soothing her with the softness of his voice, the way someone might talk to a frightened animal. The way she'd spoken to Stormchaser just that morning. And as Stormchaser had, she clung to the sound of that gentle voice. It was the only thing solid and steady in a night that was spinning and shaking.

No, it wasn't the night that was shaking. *She* was shaking. And crying, she realized. Although there was nothing she could do to stop her tears. Nothing at all.

He was still talking, describing his ride, describing the way he'd put the bridle and saddle on Stormchaser. His words were unimportant and she stopped listening, focusing only on the rise and fall of his voice. And when he reached out and touched her, gently, lightly running one hand across her shoulders and down her back, she didn't pull away. She didn't want to pull away. Instead she leaned toward him, letting him enfold her in his arms.

He held her as she trembled, rocking her slightly back and forth, infusing her with his warmth, encircling her with his solid strength. "It's okay now," he murmured over and over. "Everything's okay."

It was working. She could feel her nausea begin to fade, felt herself relax into his strong arms.

And he *was* strong. His slenderness was only an illusion. His arms and chest were solid muscle. She hadn't missed that fact when she'd gone in to wake him up and found him half-naked in bed. He had no extra fat or weight on his body, none at all. Yet his arms were soft, too. Gentle.

He continued to stroke her back, then ran his fingers gently through her hair, murmuring words of reassurance. He held her close without being threatening, offering only comfort, falling into silence as her trembling finally stopped.

She let her head rest on his still-damp shoulder, let her eyes close, let all of the awful what-ifs float away.

Except for one. What if this man whose arms felt so good around her turned his head and kissed her?

Becca opened her eyes. That was a completely crazy thought. She pulled herself away from him, pushing herself to her feet.

She shivered slightly, cold without Casey's arms

around her, as the first glimmer of dawn started to light the eastern sky.

He was still a shadow, sitting in the grayness. Becca backed away quickly, both afraid that he might break the silence, and afraid that he might not.

"There's no way I could ever pay you enough for what you did tonight," she said softly. Oh, she could think of one way she could certainly *try* to repay him, but she firmly pushed that wayward thought away.

"I didn't pull the kid out of the river for money," he said.

"Oh, no," she said, afraid she might've offended him. "I didn't mean that. I just meant... I wish there was some way I could thank you for what you did." Her voice shook slightly. "And for sitting here with me just now."

"Sometimes the hardest part of the battle comes after it's over," he said quietly, "when the adrenaline level drops and there's nothing left to do but think about what went down."

Becca lingered as the sky continuously grew lighter, knowing she should say good-night and put a healthy distance between herself and this man. She was drawn to his gentle voice and quiet smile more than she wanted to admit. And as for his arms...

"Were you in the army?" she asked, instead of taking her leave.

He was silent for several long moments, then he pushed himself to his feet in one easy, fluid motion. "Are you sure you want to start a conversation right now? You look as if you could use about twelve hours in bed."

With him? The thought popped into her head and she tried her hardest to pop it right back out again. What was wrong with her tonight? "You're right," she said. "I'm just... I'm still..."

He held out his hand. He had big hands, strong, capable-looking hands that were calloused from hard work. Attractive hands that were attached to attractive arms.

"Come on," he said. "I'll walk you back to your cabin."

Becca shook her head. "I'm okay." She was afraid to touch him again. Even just his hand. "Thank you again, Casey."

He nodded, dropping his hand. "I have a nickname," he told her, "that I prefer to answer to. It's Mish. I know it's…unusual, but it's how I think of myself."

"Mish," she repeated. "Is it Russian?"

"No. It's short for…" He laughed almost self-consciously. "It's short for 'Mission Man.'"

Mission Man? "What does that mean?"

She saw another flash of his straight white teeth in the growing dawn. "I'm not sure I know myself. It's just a handle I was given by a…a friend."

Becca backed farther away. "Well, thank you. Mish." She paused. "We should… probably set up a time to talk in the morning," she told him awkwardly.

"Whenever you like," he answered simply. "You know where to find me."

CHAPTER FOUR

Lt. Lucky O'Donlon sat alone in the back corner booth, in a deserted section of the Denny's on Water Street in Wyatt City, New Mexico, finishing his breakfast.

Water Street. Yeah, right. The entire street—the entire *town*—was dry as a bone. He'd woken up after a ten-minute combat nap this morning, yawned, and his lip had split. God, he missed the ocean.

He and his team had arrived in Las Cruces later than he'd anticipated. By the time they'd gotten their hands on an inconspicuous-looking car and driven all the way through the desert to Wyatt City, it had been well after midnight. Lucky had grimed himself up, said goodbye to Bob and Wes, gotten out of the car nearly a mile away from the First Church, and had walked over to the homeless shelter there.

As he now watched, Bobby and Wes sauntered out of the shiny new motel across the street from the Denny's, clearly in no huge hurry to meet him for their scheduled sit-rep. In fact, Wes stopped to light a cigarette in the parking lot, cupping his hands to shield his match from the wind.

Bobby nimbly plucked the cigarette from Wes's lips and tossed it to the gravel, grinding it out under his size-seventeen-and-a-half boots. And, as Lucky watched, they argued for the nine-thousandth time about Wes's inability to quit smoking.

Or rather Wes argued, and Bobby ignored him.

Bobby headed for the restaurant, and Wes followed, still arguing. They were showered and shaved and looking far fresher than Lucky. They were both wearing jeans and T-shirts, and Wes actually had a weather-beaten cowboy hat jammed onto his short brown hair.

Bobby, with his darkly handsome, Native American features, looked like he could be one of the locals in Wyatt City. Wes looked exactly like what he was—Popeye the Sailor man in a cowboy hat.

"I'm gonna quit," Wes was saying as they came into the restaurant and headed back toward Lucky's table. "I swear I am. I'm just not ready to quit right now."

Bobby finally spoke. "When we're out on an op and we're buddied up, I can smell the smoke on your breath from yards away. And if *I* can smell you, so can the opposition. You want to kill yourself by smoking, that's your business, Skelly. Just don't kill *me*."

For once in his life, Wes didn't have anything to say.

Bobby sat down next to Lucky, clearly preferring, like the lieutenant, to keep his back to the rear wall. Wes slid all the way over on the other side of the booth, sitting half-turned, his back against the mirrored side wall, so that he, too, could see the rest of the restaurant. Good habits died hard.

Too bad *bad* habits died hard, too. Bobby was dead right about Wes's smoking. When they were out in a group, the scent of a cigarette smoked six hours earlier could conceivably put them all in jeopardy.

Bobby gazed at Lucky. "Whoa, you smell ripe. Sir."

"And you both look as if you had ample opportunity to shower after a great night's sleep."

"The room was very nice, thanks."

"Yeah, I'm looking forward to seeing it from a prone

position with my eyes closed," Lucky told them. Unfortunately that wasn't going to be soon.

He hadn't gone to the church to sleep. He'd been there to check the place out thoroughly—to sneak and peek and find out as much about the shelter as he possibly could. He'd spent most of the night chatting up the volunteer workers, finding out how the system worked.

"The shelter's purely a church-run organization," he told Bob and Wes. "The only rules are no drugs, alcohol, weapons or women on the premises. And the men have to be out of both the building *and* the neighborhood before 8:00 a.m. because the facility's used as a preschool starting at 8:45."

"Anyone remember seeing Mitch?" Wes asked.

Lucky shook his head. "No. And they don't keep records of the men who use the shelter. But they *do* have records in the church office of the volunteers who work the different shifts. One of you is going to have to go into that office and charm a list out of the church ladies who work there. We've got to find out who was on duty the nights we think Mitch might've been there."

Wes pointed to Bobby. "He'll do that. Church ladies give me a rash."

Bobby shrugged. "I'll do it—if you quit smoking."

"Oh, God." Wes slumped forward so his head was on the table. "Fine," he said, his voice muffled by his arms. "I'll quit smoking. You just keep any church ladies away from me."

Bobby turned to Lucky. "Luke, I've been thinking. If Mitch came into the shelter in disguise…"

"Yeah, I've been thinking that, too." Lucky signalled the waitress to freshen his cup of coffee. She poured cups for Bob and Wes, too, and told them she'd be back in a minute to take their order. He waited until she was gone to continue. "If he doesn't want us to, we're probably not going to find him."

"Provided he's still alive," Wes said darkly.

Lucky took a sip of his now-hot coffee, feeling it burn all the way to his stomach. "How well did you guys get to know Mitch Shaw last year when we were working with Admiral Robinson?"

Bobby looked at Wes, and Wes looked at Bobby. Guys who had been swim buddies for years, the way these two had, could have entire conversations with a single glance.

"Not very well," Bobby admitted. "He pretty much kept to himself."

Wes looked at Bob again. "Or hung out with Zoe Lange."

"Zoe *Robinson,* now." Bobby sighed from the memory. "I always kind of figured Mitch had a thing for her."

"She have her baby yet?" Wes asked. "I never knew a pregnant woman could be so sexy until Zoe got knocked up."

"She's not due for another few weeks," Lucky said, looking at Bobby and rolling his eyes in exasperation. Only Wes could refer to the pregnancy of a highly decorated and respected admiral's wife as "knocked up." "Can we stay on track here? Let's focus on Mitch Shaw. I didn't get to know Mitch very well either."

"He was one spooky dude," Wes said.

"Jake Robinson trusts him," Bobby pointed out. He frowned slightly at Wes. "And don't talk about him in the past tense, please."

"Okay." Lucky pointed at Bobby. "You go make friends with the office staff at the church." He pointed at Wes. "You get on the computer and search out whatever personnel records and files you can about Mitchell Shaw. I want to know where he grew up, what his nickname was during BUD/S training, what medals he's won, his favorite vegetable, his favorite color. I want to know everything there is to know about this guy."

Bobby stood up. "I'll grab a doughnut on my way out." He pulled the motel room key out of his pocket and put it on the table in front of Lucky. "You'll be wanting that."

"I want it but I'm not going to use it. I'm going to go check out the neighborhood around the church shelter. See if anyone in the grocery shops remember seeing Mitch. And as soon as the bars open, I'll check them out, too."

"Forgive me for singing the same old refrain, but you look worse than you smell, Lieutenant," Bobby said. "Maybe you should crash for a few hours."

"We've got another check-in with the captain coming up in twelve hours," Lucky reminded them. "I'm not looking forward to giving him a repeat of this morning's sitrep—that we're here but we're still clueless." Lucky slid out of the booth's bench seat and threw enough money onto the table to cover his breakfast. "I'll take a quick shower, but that's all I have time for. Let's meet back at the motel at 1300 hours."

"God, I wanted a real breakfast." Wes gazed longingly at the scrambled eggs and ham pictured on the menu, then pushed himself out of the booth.

"I'll buy you a super-deluxe breakfast special to go," Bobby said, "if you'll trade assignments with me."

"Searching computer records versus duking it out with the church ladies?" Wes shook his head. "I don't want breakfast *that* bad."

THE ALDENS WERE LEAVING.

Mish waved goodbye to Chip as the van pulled away, down the long driveway.

Last night's events had been too much for them. Their vacation was over, Ted Alden had told him as he'd thanked Mish again. Besides, they wanted to get Chip checked out by their personal physician back in New York.

"Are you completely insane?"

Mish turned to see Becca standing slightly behind him. She was holding a piece of paper in her hand and...

He turned away, recognizing it as the exorbitant check—a thank-you gift, the man had called it—Ted Alden had tried to press into his hand as he said goodbye.

"How could you refuse to accept this?" Becca asked, moving in front of him, holding the damned thing up.

There was no way he could explain that the thought of taking money for saving a kid's life made him squirm— especially since the nightmarish dreams that continued to haunt him made him wonder if maybe he'd earned that big wad of money he carried by *taking* people's lives.

"I didn't go into the river after Chip because I wanted a reward," he told her. "I did it because I liked the kid." He shook his head. No, that wasn't exactly true. "Look, I would've done it even if I *didn't* like the kid. I just...I did it, okay? I don't want Alden's money. He thanked me—that was enough."

Mish headed back toward the barn. There were stalls to shovel out and other chores that needed doing. He'd gotten a late start today, *and* he was moving more slowly than usual, thanks to that piece of telephone pole that had smashed into him in the river. He didn't think his rib was broken, but it probably had been cracked. Either way, there wasn't much he could've done about it. He'd grabbed an Ace bandage from the first-aid kit in the barn, and he'd wrapped himself up—not that it really helped. It hurt, but that would fade in time.

Becca followed him, a sudden brisk breeze making

her clutch her cowboy hat to her head. "Casey—*Mish*. God, this check is for a *hundred* thousand dollars! That kind of money is nothing to Ted Alden—he's got bushels of it back on Wall Street. But for someone like me or you... You can't just say 'no thanks' to an opportunity like this."

He stopped short, and she nearly ran into him. "Funny, I thought I already did."

She was completely bemused and almost entirely confused as well as she stood there gazing up at him, as if she were trying to see into his head. "I promised Ted I'd talk you into accepting this."

"You're going to have to break your promise, because I don't want it," Mish said again. He reached for it, intending to tear it up, but she pulled it away from him, safely out of reach, as if she *had* been able to read his mind.

"Don't you dare! I'm going to hold on to this for you while you think about accepting it. Take all the time you need."

Exasperated, he turned back to the barn. "I don't need time. I've already thought about it. You'll just have to send it back to him."

Again, she followed, all the way inside. "With this kind of money, you wouldn't have to work here, shoveling horse manure for most of the day."

He glanced back at her as he picked up his shovel and started doing just that, trying to ignore the flare of pain in his side. "Are you firing me?"

"No!" Her answer came quickly. "That's not why I said that. I *need* you to stay, I'm shorthanded already, but actually I'd..." She cleared her throat. "I'd like it if you stayed."

Mish didn't stop his work cleaning out the stall, but he couldn't keep himself from glancing up at her again.

She was wearing jeans and a long-sleeved shirt open and untucked over a T-shirt. It hid the soft curves he didn't need to see to know were there. She'd fit perfectly in his arms last night. Maybe a little *too* perfectly. As she gazed back at him, her eyes were dark brown, bottomless pits that he knew he could fall into and lose himself in far too easily.

She was looking at him as if he were some kind of hero. And he knew with a flash that his refusal to accept that money had only made her like him more. *Damn.*

"That is, if you want to stay," she added, embarrassment tingeing her cheeks with pink. "You know, just... for a while."

Mish forced himself to look away, forced himself not to think about the fact that he couldn't remember the last time he'd had sex. Of course he couldn't remember. Everything before Monday was a total blank. Yet still, somehow he knew—as he'd known the waist and inseam measurements of his jeans—that it had been a long time since he'd been with a woman. A very long time.

And he found this woman to be incredibly appealing.

She'd turned down his offer to walk her back to her cabin as the sun was starting to creep over the horizon early this morning. That had been a good call on her part—Mish didn't know what he'd been thinking at the time. She'd just been through an emotional wringer and surely had been vulnerable.

He himself had been running what-if scenarios all morning. It had been sheer luck that Chip had been swept directly into his arms in the river. Sheer luck the kid hadn't been killed. The line between what was and what might have been was a very thin one. Tragedy had been averted by mere inches. And afterward, Mish had been a little too close to an emotional edge himself, and he knew now what he'd only suspected last night.

It wouldn't have taken much for that friendly comfort he'd given Becca to turn into comfort of an entirely different kind. If he'd walked her home and she'd invited him in, he would've kissed her sweet mouth. And if he had kissed her...

He focused on the job at hand, attempting to banish the too-vivid thoughts of just where kissing Becca might've led. He couldn't let himself think that way. It wouldn't be fair to her. It wouldn't be right.

Mish couldn't tell her the truth, although, Lord, there were times when he longed to confide in her. But he couldn't. Just the thought of it filled him with an overpowering sense of unease. Somehow he knew he wasn't supposed to talk about any of this—why he was here. He couldn't risk revealing too much, couldn't give anything away. Why? He didn't remember. But the need for secrecy had obviously been ingrained in him. He couldn't tell her.

And he'd already deceived Becca once—by convincing her he was capable of this job as a ranch hand, during that phone interview he couldn't remember. There was no way he was going to deceive her again by becoming physically intimate with her. At least not until he knew for sure exactly who he was. And maybe not even after that.

This was not a woman who'd want to have anything to do with a criminal. And he was probably an ex-con at best, if his dreams of handcuffs and prison walls were based on any kind of truth.

Although, when she looked at him the way she'd been looking at him just a few seconds ago, it was easy to imagine his resolve to keep his distance flying right out the window. It was easy to imagine her melting willingly in his arms as he pulled her down with him, right here on the sweet-smelling, fresh hay he'd just spread on the floor of the stall and…

Lord have mercy. Yes, it had been far, far too long since he'd been intimate with a woman.

But Becca wanted him to be a hero, so he was going to do just that—by not letting himself get too close to her.

She looked down at the check she still held in her hands, her cheeks still slightly pink, as if she'd been able to follow his wayward thoughts. "I just can't imagine why you would want to work for slave wages, with somebody willing and ready to hand you this much money."

Mish shrugged as he set the shovel down. "Money's not everything." He picked up the handles of the nearly full wheelbarrow and pushed it out of the stall. He passed closely enough to Becca to catch a whiff of the same fresh perfume he'd breathed in last night when he'd wrapped her in his arms. Lord, but she smelled good. He moved away from her quickly, leaning closer to the overpowering contents of his wheelbarrow to exorcise her scent as he headed toward the back entrance of the barn.

"It may not be everything, but it's damn close," Becca countered, following him out. "If *I* had this kind of money—" She broke off. "Mish, please, you should at least *think* about accepting this check. This could be the break you need."

He squinted against the bright morning sunshine as he pushed his pungent load out to a manure pile well back from the barn, his side smarting with every step he took. "Your giving me this job was the break I need," he said. "Of course, that assumes I need a break in the first place."

"You walked in here with one change of clothes under

your arm, no wallet and no ID," she pointed out. "You accepted a job at an embarrassingly low hourly rate. This isn't the movies. I've pretty much rejected the idea that you're some kind of eccentric millionaire in disguise."

He glanced back at her. "Yeah? What if I am?"

Becca laughed, her eyes sparkling with amusement. She really had beautiful eyes. "If you are, why the heck are we having this conversation while you lug a load of manure in this heat? Let's call for a break and reconvene for dinner at your favorite restaurant in Paris. Because as long as you can afford it, I've always wanted to fly on the Concorde."

She was teasing, but there was some truth in her words. She wanted to have dinner with him. He could see it in her eyes. Mish dumped the wheelbarrow, feeling glad—and very stupid. He didn't *want* her to like him. He *couldn't* want her to like him. Yet he was happy that she did. "Sorry, I seem to have misplaced my bank card."

"Aha," she said with another smile. "Proof that even if you *are* a millionaire in disguise, you need a break."

She had such a beautiful smile, it was impossible not to smile back at her. And as he did, Mish felt himself start to slip.

She more than merely liked him. He may not have been able to remember his own name, but he knew how to read a woman. And this woman was Interested, with a capital *I*. If he pulled her into his arms and lowered his head, she would lift her mouth to meet his. And while getting it on with her on the floor of the barn in the middle of the day was stretching the edges of the fantasy envelope, the idea of spending the night in her bed in the very near future was not so far-fetched.

But she wanted a hero, he reminded himself. So instead of moving closer, Mish took a step back.

"I *do* need a break," he told her, willing her not to move any closer. "And the fact that you're letting me stay despite knowing that I lied to you is—"

"But you didn't," she told him, moving closer despite his attempt to control her through telekinesis. She moved close enough for him to see the individual freckles that swept across her nose and cheeks. Close enough to see the flecks of green and gold mixed in with the darker brown of her eyes. "Not really. I looked in your personnel file, at the notes I made when we spoke on the phone. You definitely omitted some information, but I didn't ask, so it wasn't a lie. You told me you were mainly a handyman and that you'd worked on ranches before. I made the mistake of assuming you'd be able to handle the horses, too."

Personnel file. There was a personnel file with his name on it, somewhere in Becca's office. It was entirely possible that file would contain his last known address and phone number. He had to have some clothes, some belongings *some*where, didn't he? If he could find those, he might start to remember who and what he was.

"I wasn't completely honest with you, either," Becca continued. "I didn't mention the fact that your starting salary isn't going to increase any time in the near future. The owner of the Lazy Eight doesn't believe in raises."

"The money you're paying me is good enough for now." Mish pushed the wheelbarrow back toward the barn. He was far from done with the stalls, yet it was nearly time for lunch. He was simply going to have to grit his teeth against the pain and pick up his pace.

Becca's pager went off and she looked down at it, turning it off. "Shoot, I've got to go take this call." She started toward the office, walking backward. "What do you say you let me treat you to a drink after dinner tonight? As a sort of a thank-you? There's a roadhouse about twelve miles down the road—it's not too far away. They have a really great band on Thursday nights."

She'd asked him out.

Mish had thought he was safe as long as he kept his distance and didn't do something crazy like invite her to have dinner or a drink with him. But he should've known that Rebecca Keyes wasn't the kind of woman who'd sit back and wait for something she wanted.

"Um," he said, but she didn't give him a chance to figure out how he could turn her down without hurting her feelings.

"I've got to run," she told him with another of those killer smiles that made his insides tangle. "I'll talk to you later."

And she was gone, leaving Mish with an entirely new set of what-if questions.

What if he let himself go out with her? She only wanted to have a drink. It wasn't as if she'd invited him over to her place to spend the night, was it?

So what if he went? He'd have a chance to sit across the table from her in some dimly lit bar. He'd have a chance to gaze into her eyes as they talked.

As she asked him questions about himself.

Where he came from. Where he'd worked before this. Questions about his family. His childhood. His hobbies. Former girlfriends. *Present* girlfriends.

Lord God, what if he was married? What if he had a wife and children somewhere, but he simply couldn't remember them?

Of course, it was entirely likely that if he *had* been married, his wife had left him while he was in *prison*.

Mish shook his head as he began shoveling out the next stall in the barn, almost welcoming the punishing pain in his side.

Yeah, he was one hell of a hero.

CHAPTER FIVE

MISH CLEARED HIS THROAT. "Excuse me. Is Becca here?"

Hazel, the gray-haired woman who worked part-time in the Lazy Eight's office, looked up from her computer and smiled at him. "Oh, hi, Casey. Yeah, she's in the back. You want me to call her for you?"

"No," he said. Somewhere in this office was a personnel file with his name on it. Was it in the file cabinet underneath the far window, or the one next to the computer? "Thanks, but if she's busy, it's not necessary."

"She's not busy. *Becca!*" Hazel called, then turned back to Mish. "A package came for you today," she told him.

That drew his attention away from the file cabinets. A package. For *him?*

"It says Hold For Arrival," she continued, pushing her chair back and pulling herself to her feet, "but since you arrived early, I can just give it to you now, can't I?"

Hazel pulled a small brown padded mailing envelope from a set of mail cubbyholes and slid it across the counter to Mish.

A *package.*

There didn't feel as if there could be much inside as he picked it up and turned it over. There was no return address, not even on the back. "Casey Parker" and the address at the ranch was written in a large, faintly childish hand. The handwriting—messy block letters—was completely unfamiliar to Mish. But then again, just a few days ago, his own face had been unfamiliar.

The post-office cancellation stamp on the package read "Las Cruces." That was the closest large town to Wyatt City, where he'd woken up in a homeless shelter. Coincidental? Maybe.

Maybe not.

"Hey, Mish, hi. Did you get mail?" Becca came out from the back, her eyes and smile warm, clearly glad to see him.

"Yeah, I, uh, did." Mish nodded to Hazel. "Thank you."

"Anything good?" Becca leaned over the counter, smiling up at him.

"Nah." He shrugged as he tucked the package under his arm. "Just, you know, tax information from my accountant—about my stock portfolio."

She laughed. "Oh, of course."

Mish's heart rate had accelerated at the thought of what he might find inside that innocuous brown envelope, but he'd wait for the semi-privacy of the bunkhouse to open it. He couldn't imagine what might be in there that he'd need to keep private, but then again, he hadn't suspected he'd find a huge wad of money and a .22-caliber handgun in his boot, either.

"It's going to be slow around here tonight," Becca told him, her chin in her hands, her eyes warm as she looked up at him. "If you'd like, we could leave as early as six, grab some dinner while we're out…?"

At least he'd *thought* it was the package that had made his pulse kick into double time. But maybe it had been the sight of Becca's smile.

It would be so easy to tell her *yes*. It was what he

wanted to do, *and* it would keep him from disappointing and possibly even embarrassing her. Rejection was never fun, even when it was done as gently as possible, with the best of intentions.

He glanced over at Hazel who was working on the computer again.

"Actually…" He lowered his voice, and Becca leaned closer to hear what he had to say, close enough for him to catch a whiff of her subtle, sweet scent. But it wasn't perfume, he realized. That was her hair he could smell— her shampoo. And that made so much more sense than perfume. Becca didn't seem like the type of woman who would get dressed in worn-out jeans and a T-shirt, apply only sunblock to her face, and then spritz herself with designer perfume for a hard, hot day of work on a ranch.

"Actually what?" Her voice was husky, and he realized he'd been staring at her for many long seconds, just breathing in her sweetness.

Their two heads were close together. Almost close enough to kiss. Thank heavens the counter was between them or he might well have pulled her into his arms, both Hazel and his good intentions be damned.

Even if he hadn't already completely lost his train of thought, he would have done so as Becca's gaze dropped to his mouth. She quickly jerked her gaze back up, but she'd given herself away. Her body language may have been inadvertent, but it was unmistakable. She wanted him to kiss her.

And he wanted…

He wanted to bury himself in the serenity of her beautiful eyes. He wanted to hide from whomever and whatever he'd been in his probably lurid past. He wanted…

"It's funny, isn't it?" she said softly. "When an attraction is as strong as this." She laughed in disbelief. "I mean, where did it come from? Why does it feel so *right?* Mike Harris—he was a cowboy who worked here up until a few weeks ago—he asked me out maybe five different times. He was good-looking, too, like you, but…" She shook her head. "We had a lot in common, but there was no chemistry. I thought it was the bad timing—I was trying to figure out whether to keep working here or to start sending out résumés, but that hasn't changed. I'm *still* trying to figure out what to do with my life. The timing's *still* lousy. And yet…" She forced a nervous smile, as clearly as shaken by his proximity as he was by hers. "Here I am, asking you to dinner. Go figure, huh?"

Mish found his voice. "The timing's bad for me, too, Becca. *Really* bad."

Becca glanced at Hazel, who seemed completely absorbed by the information on her computer screen. "I have four million things I need to take care of before I'm done for the evening. What do you say we pick up this conversation in a few hours and—"

Mish forced himself to straighten up, to back away. "I think it would be better if I just stayed here at the ranch tonight."

He looked down at the floor so he wouldn't have to see her face. She straightened up, too.

"Oh," she said quietly. "The timing's *that* bad, huh?"

"Yeah. I'm sorry." He truly was. He knew it was time for him to take his sorry ass and make a quick exit, but instead, he made the mistake of looking up. And when he saw the mixture of embarrassment, disappointment and chagrin in Becca's eyes, he couldn't seem to make himself go anywhere. Instead he opened his mouth again. "I'm also… I could really stand to get to sleep early tonight," he told her. "I got a little banged up in the river and…"

Wrong. That was the dead wrong thing to say, and he knew it as soon as the words were out of his mouth. Someone like Becca wouldn't respond to news that he'd been hurt by casually waving and saying "Oh, too bad. Hope you feel better—see you in the morning."

"It's nothing, really," he added hastily. "Just, you know, a cracked rib."

"Just?" Becca looked at him as if he'd just announced his intention to cross the Pacific Ocean in a leaky canoe. "Oh, my God, Mish, why didn't you tell me last night you were hurt? You didn't say anything at all!"

"I'm fine," he said, silently cursing himself even while a completely twisted part of him enjoyed her wide-eyed concern. "A piece of wood—nothing big—hit me while I was in the water. Like I said, it's only a—"

"Cracked rib," she finished for him, her gracefully shaped lips tight with disbelief. "I know what a cracked rib feels like, my friend, and I'm sorry, it's not an *only*." She opened the hinged part of the counter that allowed access to both the front and the back of the room with a bang. "Get in the truck, I'm taking you to the hospital."

"No!" He *couldn't* go to the hospital. If one of the doctors or nurses looked a little too closely at the healing wound on his head…

She looked surprised at his vehemence—even Hazel glanced up. Mish forced himself to smile. "You know that all they'll do is wrap it, and I've already done that." *Let's be grown-ups about this,* he told her with his tone.

But Becca was upset. "How do you know it's not broken? I've heard of people with broken ribs actually puncturing their lungs—"

"It's not broken." Mish raised his voice to speak over her. "I know it's not broken because I've had medical training."

He was as surprised by his words as she was. *Medical training.* He hadn't been thinking, and the words had just spilled out. Dear Lord, was it possible he really was a doctor? Or was he just an accomplished liar?

Whichever it was, he'd managed to distract her from her mission of getting him into the truck and to the hospital.

"Look, I'm just a little bruised," he told her, pushing for a win while he was ahead. "Nothing a good night's sleep won't go a long way toward healing."

Becca still didn't look convinced. "I wish you'd told me about it last night."

"I should have," he agreed. "You're right. I just... I knew it wasn't that big a deal. You had enough to think about, and..." He had to put his hands in the back pockets of his jeans to keep himself from reaching out to touch her reassuringly. "Don't make me go to the hospital, Bec. I'm too tired to handle their red tape and...and to sit in the waiting room for hours, and..." He shook his head. "Come on. Please?"

She exhaled a burst of air, as if giving in to a tough decision. "Let me see it."

He blinked at her in surprise. "Let you...?"

"You heard me," she said brusquely, motioning toward the open counter and the door behind it. "Step into the back room if you're modest. Do it right here if you're not. Take off your shirt and let me see."

She wasn't kidding.

"It looks worse than it is," he told her. "It's pretty badly bruised—doing the ugly rainbow thing, you know. Yellow and green and purple?"

"Now it's *badly* bruised? I thought it was just a 'little' bruise."

"Well, yeah, it is. I meant compared to other bruises

I've had. You know. I mean, I've had worse." Lord help him, he was babbling.

Becca crossed her arms. "Then what's the big deal, Parker?"

The big deal was that he'd managed to wrestle his T-shirt on this morning, but taking it off—especially now, after he'd tightened up a whole lot during the day—was going to be next to impossible. Or screamingly painful. Or both.

"I don't think I can get my T-shirt off," he admitted. "I'm okay, you understand? I just have a little bit of...of discomfort when I lift my arms above my shoulders."

It was the understatement of the century, and Becca knew it, too.

She shook her head in exasperation. "You should've worn a shirt that buttons in the front."

"Yeah, well, the butler must've sent them all to the dry cleaner." He was able to make a joke, but he was ashamed to admit he didn't have a shirt that buttoned down the front. He felt his face heat with embarrassment. What kind of man didn't have more than a few T-shirts, four pairs of boxer shorts and two pairs of jeans to his name? He'd hoped he'd regain his memory and find his closet, but clearly that wasn't going to happen any time soon. And whoever had sent him this package clearly hadn't included his wardrobe.

He had to go into town, spend some more of that money he'd found in his boot. He just hoped it was his to spend.

Becca put her hand on his arm. Her fingers felt cool against his skin. "I'm sorry," she said quietly, squeezing him slightly before she pulled her hand away. "I didn't mean to sound—"

"No," he interrupted her, wishing he'd covered her hand with his, glad that he hadn't. "It's all right."

"I have a few shirts you can borrow. Castoffs from old boyfriends," she explained with a rueful smile. She raised her voice, turning toward the back of the room. "Hazel, excuse me. Do you still have that big pair of scissors in your desk?"

Hazel opened her top drawer. "Miracle of miracles, I actually do."

"May I borrow it, please?"

"Sure thing." Hazel approached them with the scissors, her eyes betraying her curiosity. "What's up? You going to give the hero of the hour here a haircut?"

"Nope. I like his hair long." Becca smiled up at him a little too grimly. "Hold still please, Mish."

She reached out and as she pulled the bottom edge of his T-shirt from his jeans, her cool fingers brushed his stomach. Mish nearly went through the roof. What the...?

"Hold still, dammit," she said again, making it an order as she brandished the scissors.

"What—" he started.

"I'm cutting this off of you." She grabbed hold of his T-shirt again and started to do just that. She had to saw at the bottom hem, the scissors were so ridiculously dull.

Hazel laughed aloud. "Rebecca, honey, there's a time and place for everything, but—"

"He was hurt last night," Becca told her assistant flatly. "He was hit by a big chunk of wood running down the river when he jumped in after Chip."

"It wasn't a *big* chunk—"

"And now he's having some *discomfort*." she glowered up at him. "He thinks he cracked a rib, and he just told me about it now. *Now*. Hours and hours and *hours* later.

He can't get out of his shirt without it giving him more *discomfort,* so I'm cutting it off so I can see how bad it really is, okay?"

"I guess that makes sense, but if someone walks in here—"

"Do me a favor, Hazel," Becca said, "and run to my cabin. There're a couple of large, button-down shirts hanging in my closet, toward the back. One of 'em's red. Go and get it for me, please."

"Are you kidding? And miss *this?*"

"Go. Please?" Becca finally managed to cut through the hem, and she put the scissors down on the counter. She took the package Mish was still holding and set it down as well.

"You want me to lock the door behind me?" Hazel was having way too much fun. She winked at Mish. "You know, it's been a *real* long time since Becca's cut off a cowboy's T-shirt. You should be honored. She doesn't do this to just anyone."

"Hazel." Becca closed her eyes. *"Go."* She shook her head as the door closed behind Hazel, purposely not meeting his gaze. "I'm sorry—I didn't mean to embarrass you. Which side is it on?"

Which side...?

"I'm afraid of nicking you with the scissors, so I'm going to tear your shirt—at least up to the collar. But I don't want to bump your broken rib."

"Cracked," Mish corrected her. "Left side." He reached for the cut in the T-shirt. "I can do this."

But her hands were already there. And she tore the cotton upward, swiftly but carefully.

The sound of the fabric tearing seemed impossibly loud in the stillness of the room. It was a dangerously erotic sound, one that implied impatience and hinted at an intense passion.

They were alone, and this woman he wanted so badly was literally tearing off his clothes. Heat coursed through him, flames licking the desire he'd so carefully concealed, and bringing it to life. Amusement followed instantly, but it wasn't enough to extinguish the heat.

It was hard to swallow, hard to breathe. Her fingers brushed his bare chest as she gave another pull and tore his shirt all the way to his collar. It was that second time that completely finished him off. He desperately tried to fight his growing arousal even as he laughed softly at the absurdity of it all, but it was a losing battle.

Becca was standing close enough to kiss, and Lord, he wanted to kiss her. He wanted to pull her tightly against him, so she could feel just what she did to him. He wanted to wrap her legs around him, cracked rib be damned.

But he didn't. He stood perfectly still, his hands down at his sides, all amusement completely gone as he forced himself not to reach for her. The effort of doing so, however, made him start to sweat.

She made a soft sound of dismay when she saw the colors of his bruise spreading beyond his Ace bandage. Reaching again for the scissors, she began to saw through the heavier cotton of his crewneck collar.

She had to move even closer to do it, her thigh pressed against his, her breasts brushing his chest. Mish closed his eyes, feeling a bead of perspiration trickle down the side of his face, praying she'd be done soon. He was trying to be good, but he wasn't a saint.

Finally, she cut through. He opened his eyes only when she stepped back, when he heard the clatter of the scissors on the counter. But he was premature—the torture wasn't over yet. Becca moved closer again, and began to peel his shirt off his shoulders.

"Don't lift your arms or try to help," she instructed him softly, her hands cool against the heat of his skin. She worked his sleeve down his right arm, touching him every inch of the way, and then gently pulled the rest of the shirt from his left.

Mish unfastened the bandage himself, stepping slightly back from her, bracing himself for the words he knew were coming.

"God, you call that a *little* bruise...?" Her words were laced with a tough disbelief, but she actually had tears in her eyes.

"I told you, it looks worse than it is." Please God, don't let her start to cry. If she did, he'd never be able to keep from reaching for her.

She blinked them back forcefully, grimly. "That must've hurt like hell. It hurts you right now—even just to stand there, doesn't it?"

She was angry at him, and while anger was better than empathic tears, it could get him taken to the hospital if he wasn't careful.

"Becca, I swear," he said calmly, as matter-of-factly as he could manage, considering the way his heart was still pounding from her touch. "It's really not that bad."

"Bad enough for you to break out in a cold sweat." With one finger, she caught a bead of perspiration that was dripping down his face, holding it out somewhat triumphantly to show him.

That wasn't cold sweat. It was very, very hot, very steamy sweat. But it was probably better that she didn't know that.

"I can't believe you put in a full day of work," she continued, refusing to be calm or matter-of-fact in response.

"I can't believe I stood there and watched you mucking out the stalls, and I didn't have a clue you were hurt!" She was so angry her voice was shaking. She crossed to the back of the office, her movements jerky as she opened one of the drawers and took out a key. "As of right now, you're out of the bunkhouse and staying in cabin twelve. I'm marking it unavailable on the books—it's all yours until the end of next week. After that, be ready to clear out if we get any walk-ins, but I doubt we will. We're not full up with guest reservations for another month and a half." She slapped the key onto the counter in front of him. "I'm also giving you a week off."

He opened his mouth, and she held up her hand. "At full pay," she added as ferociously as if she'd just informed him he was getting twenty lashes. "And if it doesn't heal enough for you to move without pain by then, I'll give you another week, but you'll have to let the doctor in town check you out first. Does that sound fair?"

"I appreciate your generosity," Mish told her. "But it's *not* fair. Not for you. You're already short-staffed."

She looked startled, as if she'd never expected him to consider that. "I'll take care of your chores."

"Along with your regular job?"

It was insane, and she knew it. "I'll...call Rafe McKinnon. He told me he was going to his brothers' for a few days before he started looking for work up north. I'll give him that raise he wanted. He'll come back in a flash. He had a major thing for Belinda."

"I thought you said the owner didn't want to—"

"To hell with what Justin Whitlow wants," she said fiercely, coming back out from behind the counter. "If he doesn't like the way I manage his ranch, he can just fire me."

With her eyes sparking and her chin held high, she

looked unstoppable. If he weren't careful, she would bull-doze straight over him. "You say that as if it would be a good thing." He tried to smile, keep things a little more light.

She glared back at him. "Maybe it would be. If I'm too damned chicken to quit, then I have to make him fire me, don't I?"

"There's a difference between being chicken and being cautious."

Mish didn't know what was happening. Becca was standing still, but she just kept getting closer and closer to him. And then he realized that he was the one who was moving toward her, pinning her back against the counter. He was drawn toward her as absolutely as if he were a magnet and she were true north. He could smell her hair, see every individual freckle on her nose, watch the irises of her beautiful, warm eyes widen as he leaned closer and closer.

He forced himself to stop, just a whisper away from the softness of her lips, and he felt a rush of relief. Another second, and he would have kissed her. Another fraction of an inch and...

She still didn't move, yet her lips brushed against his. He heard her sigh, saw her eyelids flutter closed as he kissed her again.

As *he* kissed *her*. What was he doing? Was he completely insane?

This was wrong. This was crazy. This was...

Incredible.

She tasted as sweet as he'd imagined, her lips introducing him to a whole new definition for the word *soft*.

Three kisses was enough. Lord, it had to be, it was three kisses too many. And he surely—well, *probably*—

would've pulled away from her after three, if only she hadn't touched him.

But the sensation of her hands on the bare skin of his arms was one he couldn't deny himself the pleasure of knowing. And when she slid her hands up to his shoulders, and then to the hair at the nape of his neck…

Three kisses became four and five and more and he lost count, lost all sense of up and down, lost himself in the dizzying sweetness of her mouth.

He pulled her close, dying to cup the softness of her breasts in his hands, but settling for the feel of her against his chest. He kissed her longer, deeper, but still slowly, claiming complete ownership of her mouth.

She'd worked his hair free from the rubber band he'd used to hold it back, and as she ran her fingers through it, he knew the truth.

Three *hundred* wouldn't be enough.

He had to stop kissing her. This could have been the rightest wrong he'd ever done, but it *was* wrong.

Her hands trailed down his back, cool against the heat of his skin, and he groaned.

And Becca nearly jumped back, away from him. "Oh, God." She brought her hand up to her mouth, her eyes enormous. "I'm so sorry—did I hurt you?"

He stared back at her. *Hurt* him…? And he realized she wouldn't have pulled away if she hadn't thought she'd somehow hurt his bruised side. If he hadn't made that strangled sound, she'd be kissing him still. He didn't know whether to laugh or cry.

"There's a Jacuzzi up by the swimming pool," she told him. "Just inside the main cabana. It might help if you spent some time soaking."

"I'm okay." Mish had to clear his throat. "It's not that bad, really."

How was it possible that mere moments ago his tongue had been inside of her mouth, yet now they were talking to each other as if they were strangers?

They *were* strangers.

And he shouldn't have kissed her. "Becca, I really have to—"

The office door opened with a squeak. And Mish quickly turned toward the counter, suddenly extremely aware that he was standing there not only without a shirt, but still nearly fully aroused as well.

"Oh, yikes," Hazel said. "That must really hurt."

He could only hope she was referring to the bruise on his side.

She turned to Becca. "Sorry that took so long. Going into your closet should merit hazardous-duty pay."

"Ha, ha." Becca took the shirt from her assistant. "I've assigned cabin twelve to Mish, at least until the end of the week. He's got some sick days coming to him, as well."

She moved behind Mish, holding the shirt open, so that he could slip his arms into it with relative ease. The soft cotton smelled like Becca. It was like being enveloped by her hair.

As if she'd been touching him forever, she gently turned him to face her. "Need help with the Ace bandage, too?"

Mish glanced at Hazel, who was back at her computer, across the room.

"I need…" What? To take off Becca's clothes? Undeniably. He lowered his voice, leaned closer to her. "To talk to you. Come outside with me for a sec."

It would be private, but not as private as pulling her with him into the back room where he could shut the door and…

Becca glanced at Hazel, too. And she scooped the key

to his cabin, his package and his bandage off the counter. "I'll walk you over to number twelve."

"Thanks, Hazel," Mish called, letting Becca open the door for him. Without the bandage, every step he took seemed to jar his side. Of course, it jarred with the bandage on, too.

"Feel better, sweetie. And don't keep Becca out too late tonight."

"Ignore her," Becca said. "You have permission to keep me out as late as you want."

Oh, Lord. Mish waited until they were both several yards away from the office. "Becca, look, I let myself get carried away back there, and I want to apologize."

She stopped short, right there in the driveway. "Are you apologizing for…kissing me?"

"No, I'm…" He briefly closed his eyes. "Yes. Yeah, I am."

Becca started walking again, quickly enough so that he had to work to keep up with her. "That's funny. I didn't seem to think any of those kisses warranted an apology. I mean, jeez. If you're sorry about *those,* well, the ones you *aren't* sorry about must be out of this world."

"Becca, I—"

"That was a joke, Parker. You're supposed to laugh." She turned, slowing her pace as she walked backward. "I don't suppose you'd want to discuss this over dinner." One look at his face and she turned around again. "Yeah, I didn't think so."

"I meant what I said about the timing being bad for me," he told her quietly. "I'm sorry if I confused things back there by finding you completely irresistible."

Becca laughed as she glanced at him, shaking her head. "Well, there's the prettiest rejection I've ever heard."

"I *am* sorry," he said again. "I don't know what happened."

She handed him the key, the package and the Ace bandage. "The cabin's down to the left," she told him. "I'll have dinner brought to you on a tray tonight."

"That's not—"

"Don't worry," she said. "It won't be me carrying the tray. I can take a hint—particularly after it's hammered home."

Mish watched her walk away. "Becca."

She turned back, her eyes subdued.

"If it were purely a matter of what I wanted... If there was nothing else to consider..."

She smiled crookedly. "Get some rest," she said. "It's got to be tiring being so damn nice."

"IT'S DEFINITELY MITCH'S case," Lucky said to Wes over the phone. "Remember that old leather thing he always carried? Called it his bag of tricks? Well, it's here. In bus locker number 101."

Lucky had lucked out and found Mitch's bag on his fifth try. The locks had been ridiculously easy to pop open—the luck had come from the lack of bus station security guards to question why he was opening locker after locked locker.

"We're going to set up twenty-four-hour surveillance," Lucky decided. "If he's anywhere in this part of the state, sooner or later he's going to come back for his bag. And when he does, we're going to be watching."

"Sitting in a bus station for hours on end," Wes contemplated. "Bob's gonna hate that almost as much as I do."

"You don't have to like it, you just have to—"

"Do it. I know, I know," Wes interrupted. "You've gotta stop reading those Rogue Warrior books."

"Look, since I'm already here," Lucky said, "I'll take the shift till 0100 hours. I'd offer to stay later but—"

"You've only slept an hour in the past forty-eight. Don't be a hero, Lieutenant. I'll be there at 2000."

"Make it midnight, Cinderella, and I'll take you up on that offer," Lucky countered, looking out the grimy windows at the street. "But first trade in the Batmobile for something with tinted windows. This place is a ghost town. We're going to get looked at if we're sitting in here, watching the lockers. We'll need to sit out on the street." They'd have a clear shot of almost the entire bus station if they parked a vehicle in the right place. "You and Stimpy can duke it out over who plays watchdog for the rest of the night. Any word from our beamish, churchgoing boy, by the way?"

Wes laughed. "Believe it or not, he's taking one of the church ladies to dinner. He left a message saying that we need to talk to a guy named Jarell Haymore. He was on duty the night we think Mitch might've been at the shelter."

"So if Bob's already found that out, what's he doing taking this lady to dinner?"

"Beats me. He gets weird sometimes."

"What'd *you* find?" Lucky asked, his gaze sweeping the bus station. Even when he wasn't looking directly at it, he kept the row of battered lockers in his peripheral vision. Nothing moved. Anywhere. The bus station was as empty now as it had been an hour ago.

"Well," Wes said, "let's see. Mitch Shaw's nickname during BUD/S training? The Priest."

Lucky laughed. "You're kidding."

"Yeah, and you're going to love this. There are still

rumors floating around that Shaw either was or *is* some kind of, ahem, shall we say…man of God?"

"A SEAL who's really a priest?" Lucky shook his head in disbelief. "No way, Skelly. That reeks of BUD/S legend. Kind of like the story about the boat team that got so hungry they barbecued the instructor—and were secured two days early, and given shore leave in Hawaii for their ingenuity. I just don't buy it."

"*I've* never seen him with a woman," Wes said. "Have you ever seen him with a woman?"

"Yeah," Lucky said. God, he was tired. "I saw him with his tongue dragging in the dust as he followed Zoe around out in Montana. And you did, too."

"Yeah, yeah," Wes said impatiently. "Zoe Robinson could make a dead man stand up and dance. But Bob and I went drinking with Shaw a few times after we got back to Coronado. He never went home with anyone—not that I ever knew about. And it wasn't a case of no opportunity, if you know what I mean."

"He *is* a covert operative," Lucky pointed out. "He probably knows a thing or two about how to be discreet. Let's keep this conversation moving forward, Skelly. What else did you find out about him?"

"Medal, medal, medal. Every time the guy turned around, he was being awarded another damn medal," Wes said. "Eighteen, to date."

Eighteen. Lucky swore in admiration.

"Yeah. Won his first medal when he was—get this— fifteen years old."

What? "Are you serious?"

"Why would I make this up?"

"Maybe it was a typo, or—"

"It's too unreal, Luke. It's got to be true. Combine that with Shaw having gone into the SEAL program his first year in the navy. In fact, I think he went from the recruiter's office to BUD/S training. How often does that happen?"

"Never?"

"No, it happened at least once. With Mitch Shaw. The man won two more medals straight out of BUD/S. Since then, it's been kind of a yearly thing for him. 'Oh, it's April. Time for another trip to the White House to add to this collection on my chest.'"

Lucky exhaled a burst of air. "Well, if that's the case, I think we can pretty much assume he hasn't sold the plutonium to the first third-world country ready to hand him a suitcase filled with a million dollars in small bills."

"I don't know about that, Luck-meister. It's these superheroes you've really got to watch out for. When they turn, they turn *bad*. Guys like Shaw are lugging around a ton of resentment. You know, 'The United States made fifteen billion dollars because I saved the world, and all I got were these eighteen lousy medals…'"

Lucky laughed. "Yeah, Skelly, right. You keep on thinking that way. This is a man Admiral Robinson trusted with his life."

"That's true," Wes admitted. "Apparently Robinson tapped Mitch Shaw to join his Gray Group at its inception. In other words, Shaw was Gray Group's agent double-oh-*one*. You know, I'm glad I didn't know all this last year. This guy scares me."

"Anything else?" Lucky asked, rolling his eyes. *Wes* was the scary one.

"I've got some feelers out," Wes said. "You know, asking around, looking for anyone who might've gone through BUD/S with him. But apparently not too many people survived and… Oh, my *God!*"

Lucky nearly dropped the phone. "What? Skelly—sit-rep! What's happening?"

"Bobby just walked by with…"

"What?! Who?"

"Oh, baby! Bobby's church lady looks like a super-model! She's got long hair and a miniskirt and lo-o-ong legs and…" Wes started to laugh hysterically. "I gotta go—maybe she has a sister."

Wes hung up, and the silence in the bus station was even more complete than it had been before.

Bobby just walked by with a church lady who looked like a supermodel. Go figure.

Lucky and Wes had both made the mistake of making an assumption, while the truth was, there were no real givens in this world.

Bobby had ended up lucky, in the company of a beautiful woman for dinner, while Lucky had wound up alone in a urine-scented bus station.

Lucky would have assumed the odds of that ever happening were impossibly low.

Kind of like the odds of Admiral Robinson's top covert operative selling out his country by selling stolen pluto-nium to the highest bidder.

God, what if it was true? What if Mitch Shaw *had* turned?

CHAPTER SIX

MISH SAT ON THE PORCH of his cabin, waiting for the sun to set.

He'd slept fitfully all day, his dreams haunted by violence. He'd awakened countless times, his heart pounding and his side throbbing. He sat quietly now and tried to pull apart the visions into his past that his subconscious had belched up, like malodorous bubbles from a tar pit. Because dreams, although sometimes imagined events, were often based on things the dreamer had seen or done, weren't they?

There had been a man in religious robes, standing bravely in front of a group of men with assault weapons. Terrorists. It had happened in a heartbeat. One of them had raised his sidearm and fired a double burst into the man's head. And as Mish had watched, helpless as a child, so filled with fear and horror that he didn't even dare to cry out, the man had slumped, a lifeless rag, to the floor.

The image still made him feel sick.

He'd dreamed of gazing through a sniper scope, dreamed of sighting a target and squeezing the trigger. He'd dreamed of more personal violence as well. Hand-to-hand combat, a martial-arts free-for-all with the only rule being survival.

And he'd dreamed of a woman—his mother? It was hard to say; her face was turned away, and it kept changing.

She sat, her head bowed in grief, weeping. When she *did* look up at him, her tear-bruised eyes silently accusing, he realized she was Becca, and he sat up, instantly awake.

It didn't take much to figure *that* dream out. He was trouble. He'd always been trouble, and the only thing he could bring Becca was pain.

A party of riders approached, heading out for a late-afternoon trail ride. Becca led the way, giving him no more than a brief glance, lifting a hand in a vague greeting as she passed.

True to her word, she'd kept her distance all day—except for that one brief appearance in his dreams.

Hazel had brought him both breakfast and lunch on a tray.

Dinner was going to be served in just an hour, but Becca would be out on the ride for most of that time. Mish could go sit with the guests and...

He didn't want to sit with anyone. He didn't want to do anything except get into the ranch office and look at that personnel file. He needed to find out his former address, and then he had to go there—wherever "there" was—to see if anything was familiar to him.

Frustratingly, the package that had come in the mail yesterday had held no answers—only more questions. It had contained only a key.

It was a bank key—the kind that unlocked a safe-deposit box. But there were no markings on it, no note stuck in with it, nothing. It could have belonged to any of hundreds of safe-deposit boxes in any thousands of banks in New Mexico. Or the world. Why keep it only to New Mexico? This key could well have come from anywhere.

It was driving him mad, his complete lack of a past.

Mish had spent some time today gritting his teeth and

trying to force himself to remember. Who was he? *What* was he? But the answers continued to elude him.

All he knew for absolute certain was this relentless sense of unease. Don't tell anyone. Don't talk about why he was here. Don't reveal his weaknesses...

The sound of Becca's laughter drifted back to him through the lengthening shadows, and he had to wonder—not for the first time—if maybe, just maybe he'd be better off not knowing.

"OH, MY GOD, WHAT ARE you doing in here?" Becca jumped back from the office screen door when she realized someone—Mish—was inside. She grabbed hold of the porch railing to keep herself from falling backward down the stairs.

"I'm sorry, I didn't mean to scare you." Mish stepped outside. "I was..." He cleared his throat. "I was actually looking for you."

She stared at him. "In the *dark?*"

"Well, no," he said mildly. "Of course not. There was a light on in the back. I knocked, but no one answered, so I went in."

Becca moved past him, trying not to notice how good he looked standing there in the soft moonlight, wearing the red shirt, sleeves rolled up to his elbows. Her heart was pounding, but only because he'd startled her. She refused to let it be for any other reason.

"The door was unlocked?" she asked. Inside, she turned on the lights. *All* of the overhead lights, not just the pleasantly dim one on her desk.

Mish squinted slightly in the glare as he followed her. "I had no problem getting in."

"I'll have to talk to Hazel. This door needs to be locked at night." She shuffled through the papers on her desk, aware that he was standing there watching her, aware that she was wearing her bathing suit under a very short pair of cutoffs, aware that she had virtually thrown herself at him and he had pushed her away.

But he'd just said that he'd come there looking for her. She glanced over at him. "So what's up?"

He had the kind of dark hair and complexion that had helped coin the phrase "five o'clock shadow." It was now after eight, and he had stubble worthy of the cover of *GQ* magazine. He rubbed his chin in a spot where he had a small white scar as he shrugged. "I just, um… I don't know, really. I was feeling a little better, and I wanted to…" He shrugged again.

"I'm glad you're feeling better. You look…" Delicious. "As if you're…feeling better." Oh, God, why didn't she just go over and drool on his boots?

"I'll definitely be back before the week's out," he told her. "Helping in the barn, I mean."

"What are you, nuts?"

He smiled. It was ludicrous. When he smiled he was even more good-looking. "No, just…bored."

"Ah," she said. "Bored." Becca found what she was looking for—tomorrow's sign-up sheet for the tennis court—and she breezed past him toward the door. She held it open and gazed at him pointedly. He got the message and went out. She flicked off the lights, and shut the door behind her, making sure it was securely locked. "Is that why you came looking for me? Because you were bored?"

"Oh, Lord," he said. "*No.* Absolutely not. I just… I…"

"Forget it." Becca was embarrassed for herself all over again. And angry at herself, as well. She'd practically invited him to kiss her yesterday, and then when he had, she'd stupidly assumed that he'd been as affected by those kisses as she was. They had been nuclear-powered kisses, kisses that completely bulldozed over any of *her* doubts about bad timing. Hey, for the promise of more kisses like that, she would have invented a whole new calendar. It had been well over twenty-four hours since his lips had last touched hers, and her knees were *still* weak.

Yet Mish had said *no thanks* and walked away. It was a new twist on an old story—a man who was in such a hurry to leave he didn't even bother to start the love affair first.

But right now he was blocking her path. "I was just thinking that even though the timing's bad…" He couldn't quite hold her gaze. "I don't know," he admitted. "It feels kind of like playing with C-4…" He broke off, shaking his head slightly. "I mean, like playing with explosives," he continued. "But…"

"You want to go get a drink?" she asked him. "Or are you thinking we should skip the formalities and just go straight to bed?"

Oops, her anger was showing. But at least she'd managed to get him to meet her eyes. "I'm sorry," she said. "That was rude of me, and uncalled-for, and—"

"This was a really bad idea," he said quietly. "You're still upset with me, and you have every right to be. I'm really sorry." He turned to leave, and this time she blocked *his* path.

She knew he would eventually leave. Call it whatever you like, self-sabotage, a built-in defense mechanism, lowered expectations, whatever, but she simply didn't hook up with guys who were viable candidates for anything long-term. She knew that about herself. She was okay with Mish leaving. In fact, she was practically planning for it to happen.

That was because she was a realist. That was because she faced the truth and was honest with herself.

But there was a very, very small fragment of time in every relationship, right at the very start, where magic *could* conceivably happen. There was a small moment, maybe an hour or a day or maybe even as long as a week, where hope reigned, and possibilities seemed as limitless and wide as the vast New Mexico sky.

And during that moment, happily-ever-after didn't seem as much like a myth. And true love didn't sound quite so much like some con artist's clever lie.

Becca knew, she *knew,* that Casey "Mission Man" Parker's vocabulary didn't contain the word *forever.* But when she'd looked into his eyes as he'd slowly lowered his mouth to hers, something had shifted, and in that instant she'd been filled with enough hope to cloud her 20/20 vision.

She could have squeezed an entire month of hope out of just one kiss.

"How can you just ignore this?" she asked, gesturing between them. Once again she was throwing herself in front of the rejection train, heaven help her. But she *had* to know. "How can you walk away from something that has such incredible promise?"

He smiled, a beautiful, regretful, slightly crooked smile. "Well, that's just it. For someone who's walking away, I seem to be back where I started, don't I?"

"So where on earth did you learn to swim like that?"

Mish looked down into his glass of beer. He drank imported Canadian beer, he'd somehow known that without really having to think about it. The light from the pool area lit the amber liquid in a way that was completely familiar. Yes, he'd sat in the shadows and stared into many a glass of imported beer and—he tried to make it completely effortless—he'd learned to swim back when he'd...

Nothing. Nothing came.

"I don't know," he told her. "I've been able to swim since before I can remember."

He had to toss the focus back to Becca, but gently. He was treading a conversational tightrope here. If he asked her the obvious questions about herself—where are you from, how long have you worked here—she'd take that as an invitation to simply turn around and throw similar questions back at him.

He didn't want to lie to her, didn't want to make up a fictional past. Yet at the same time, he knew he couldn't tell *anyone* about his amnesia. Not even Becca with her beautiful eyes.

"I bet you can't remember the first time you rode a horse," he said.

She smiled, and he was glad she'd caught him breaking in to the ranch office. If she'd come along two minutes later, he'd have slipped out undetected, and he'd be sitting alone in his cabin, frustrated by the lack of information in his personnel file.

That file had contained a previous address and a phone number in Albuquerque. There was a fax number jotted on the margin that had a Wyatt City exchange. Other than that, his so-called file was absurdly thin. Still, an address and phone number was more than he'd had to go on an hour ago.

And, unlike an hour ago, he was no longer sitting in his cabin, alone.

"Actually," Becca said, "I can remember in complete detail the first time I rode a horse. I was ten, and it was

May. It was warm for New York—I can still feel the sun on my face."

She closed her eyes, lifting her face slightly, as if toward the sun, and just like that, everything Mish was feeling flip-flopped. This was a mistake. Yes, he enjoyed Becca's company. He enjoyed it too much.

He knew he should stand up, plead sudden intense fatigue—which would go over better than insanity—and walk, very, very quickly, back to cabin 12.

Alone.

What was he doing, sitting here this way? Letting himself dream about kissing the graceful length of her neck? Letting himself imagine burying his face in the soft, sweet-smelling cloud of her hair? Letting himself remember how it had felt to kiss her, the giddy, breathless sensation of her mouth and body pressed against him? Letting himself fantasize about waking up early, in bed next to her, and watching her sleep?

He was a killer.

Okay, maybe he didn't know that with absolute certainty, but he was pretty close to positive. He'd certainly spent some time in jail—and if he had to guess what for, the carnage that splattered his dreams provided a heavy-duty hint.

"I sat there in a saddle for the first time," Becca continued, opening her eyes and giving him a smile that would have melted a glacier, "with all this power and grace beneath me. I was so awed, so completely overwhelmed, I nearly cried. The horse was a mare named Teacup, and she must've encountered a dozen little girls just like me every day. She was patient and dignified, and whenever she looked back at me, she seemed to smile. And I fell completely in love. From that moment on, my goal in life was to spend as much time riding as I possibly could. Which wasn't easy, considering I lived in New York."

He couldn't keep himself from asking. "In the city itself?"

"No, about forty-five minutes north of Manhattan. Mount Kisco." She paused, and he braced himself. Here it came. "How about you? Where are you from?"

He'd actually prepared for this one. "I never know what to say when people ask me that," he told her. "I've lived in a lot of different places. I'm not really sure which one I'd call home."

Thankfully, she didn't seem to think his evasive answer was odd, and he turned the focus back on her. "But I don't think I've ever been to Mount Kisco, New York. It's hard to imagine a town with riding stables and horses only a few minutes north of New York City."

"The really good stables were in Bedford," she told him. "I used to ride my bike ten miles…" She laughed. "So I could work in the stables for free. In exchange for riding time, you know? Funny, I still work for close to nothing, only these days I don't have a lot of extra time to ride." She rolled her eyes. "Of course, when Whitlow gets back and fires me, I'll have a *lot* of free time, but nowhere to stable Silver."

"Silver's your horse?"

Becca nodded. "Yeah. This summer we're celebrating our seventh anniversary."

"Silver," he said. "Named after…?"

"Yes, the Lone Ranger's horse. Hi, ho Silver, away. Yeah, I know what you're thinking—not very original. But I didn't name him. And I didn't geld him, either. He was already cut when I bought him."

She laughed then. "That's one way to identify a man

who's a greenhorn," she continued. "Talk about geldings.
He'll wince every time."

Mish laughed self-consciously. "Did I?"

Her smile was so sincere and contagious. "Oh,
yeah."

"It seems…so barbaric."

"Stallions can be pretty wild," she told him. "And too
much testosterone in one stable can create chaos. They
fight, sometimes pretty viciously. And they get…shall we
say *amorous* at the most inopportune moments. Like the
time that the Mortensons—four kids under age eight—
were staying here at the ranch. I swear, every time we
turned around, Valiant had broken through his fence
again and was mounting one of the mares."

How had this happened? They were sitting here talking
about sex. True, it was only about horses having sex, but
still…

Mish cleared his throat and grabbed hold of the conversation with both hands. "You know, I just can't believe
Justin Whitlow would fire you." He took another sip of
cold beer. "This place can't run itself. And from what
Hazel's told me, she's not interested in your job."

Becca drew lines of moisture on the plastic table with
the bottom of her glass. "I don't blame her—the way
things've been going, *I'm* not interested in my job." She
looked up at him. "I don't suppose any of the places
you've worked recently were looking for a manager?"

Mish forced himself not to shift in his seat. "Not that
I know of, no." He finished his beer, knowing that it was
time for him to stand up and say good-night. He had to
get out of here before her questions got more personal.
Or before he did something completely idiotic, like hold
her hand. If he held her hand, he would kiss her again.
And if he kissed her again…

"Yeah, I didn't think so." She sighed, her chin resting dejectedly in her palm. "God, I despise the whole job-hunting, résumé thing. And the thought of going into a new position, in a new place, expending all that energy, hoping that this time it'll be better or at least *different*, and then…" She sighed again. "It's depressing. Finding out it's all exactly the same. Same struggles, same old boss-induced problems."

"You need to work for yourself," Mish told her. "Buy your own spread."

Becca laughed. "Yes, thank you very much, I should, but last time I looked, the millionaires weren't exactly lining up with marriage proposals. And the bank's not likely to give me a three-million-dollar mortgage with only a beat-up pickup truck as collateral."

He couldn't seem to force himself to stand up. "Is that really what it would cost?"

"I don't know," she admitted. "It's so outside of the realm of possibility, I haven't even checked to see if any local properties are for sale."

"Maybe you should."

"Why torture myself?" she challenged.

"It's only torture if you think in terms of what you don't have. If you look at it as something to strive for, it's a dream. And it's amazing what people can achieve with just a little bit of hope and a dream."

She was looking at him the same way she had back in the barn, the same way she'd looked at him right before he'd kissed her in the office. Her eyes were soft and so impossibly warm.

"What's your dream, Mish?" she whispered.

"Peace," he said. He didn't have to hesitate. "My dream is to find some peace."

Oh, Lord, he was doing it again. He was leaning toward

her, closer and closer and... He pushed himself back in his seat and somehow managed to smile. "Peace, and a ride into Santa Fe tomorrow morning."

"Santa Fe?" She shifted slightly back in her own chair. "Are you leaving already?"

She'd moved just slightly, barely noticeably. That and the shade of disappointment in her eyes were almost imperceptible. Yet there was something about her words, something about her resignation that sucker punched him with a double dose of emotion. Frustration. And anger. Anger at himself. Anger at her for guilting him out every time he...

Every time he...

Left...?

What the *hell...?*

"Mish, are you all right?" Across the table, Becca's eyes were wide as she gazed at him.

He took a deep breath, blowing it out hard. "Sorry," he said. "I was... That was...déjà vu or something, I don't know. Weird." He ran his hand down his face. "I'm just... I'm going to Santa Fe—Albuquerque, actually—for a few days. I have something that needs to be taken care of. I figured as long as you're giving me this time off, I might as well put it to good use. I'll be back by Monday at the latest."

She was still watching him closely, concern in her eyes. "Anything I can help with?"

Becca wasn't being nosy. She actually meant it. She wanted to help.

But what would she do if he told her, "Yeah. See, I have complete and total amnesia. I have absolutely no idea who I am—oh, except for the little clues I've picked up here and there, which lead me to believe I'm a hired assassin and an ex-con. While I go visit the previous address that was listed in my personnel file and try to stir up any suppressed memories, why don't you check out the faces on the most-wanted list in the post office, and see if you can find me there?"

Mish cleared his throat. "No," he said instead. "Thanks, though."

She poured the rest of her beer into her glass. "Well," she said. "I'm actually driving into Santa Fe day after tomorrow, if you want to wait until then to go. I've got to put in an appearance for the Whitlows at a fund-\raising dinner for the Santa Fe Opera."

"Thanks," Mish said again. "But the sooner I get there, the better. I really should go tomorrow."

"Maybe," Becca said, then stopped. She laughed. "God, this is insane, but… I have an extra ticket to the dinner. The food's great…and I'm just *so pathetic*--I can't believe I'm asking you out *again*." She laughed again as she slumped over the table, head buried in her arms.

Mish didn't know what to say.

She lifted her head and looked him in the eye. "I don't do this with everyone. In fact, I've never done this with anyone. I just…really like you."

Her words warmed him. She *liked* him. "I don't know why. You don't know me, Bec. I could be someone awful."

"No, you couldn't. You're too nice. You have this basic goodness at the core of your being—"

He let loose a pungent curse he rarely said aloud. "You don't know that. So I pulled a kid out of a river. That doesn't make me a saint."

"Maybe not, but it makes you someone I want to know better." She leaned toward him. "Come to this dinner with me—as a friend. We can set some boundaries right now, if you want. No sex. Okay? We meet at the dinner, we leave separately. No pressure, no temptation, even."

Mish had to laugh at that. "You know, I think this is a first for me. Being enticed to go out to dinner by the promise of *no* sex."

Her eyes sparked. "If you want, we can set different boundaries—"

"No," he said hastily.

"I'll leave the ticket at the door for you," Becca told him. She stood up, and he rose to his feet, too. "The party's being held at the Sidewinder Café—it's a restaurant near the center of town. Doors open at six. I'll probably arrive at six forty-five."

He had nothing to wear to a formal party. And even if he did, he had no business deceiving this woman any further. She thought he was *nice*. He knew—for both of their sakes—he should stay far away from her.

But when he opened his mouth, he said, "All right. I'll see you on Saturday. At six forty-five."

He was completely insane.

"Well," Becca said. "Good."

And she smiled. And when she smiled, her entire face lit up, and as Mish watched her walk away, being completely insane suddenly didn't seem so terrible.

BOBBY AND WES CLIMBED into the van, carrying two paper bags from which there escaped an incredibly delicious aroma.

"Hey," Lucky said, glancing up from the less-than-inspiring view he had of the bus station lockers. From where he was parked, he could see locker number 101 through the tinted van windshield and through the bus station window. It wasn't the most inconspicuous surveillance setup, but it was better than sitting on the grimy plastic bus-station chairs, in full view of anyone driving by. "I didn't expect you guys for another few hours."

"Man cannot live on M&Ms from the candy machine alone," Wes said, digging through the bags. "So we brought you this celebratory meal from Texas Stan's."

With a flourish, Wes handed Lucky a large container of Texas Stan's four-alarm chili and a plastic fork.

"Bless you, Ren. Bless you, Stimpy. What are we celebrating?" Lucky asked, taking the lid off the container. God, it smelled good.

"Joe Cat called," Wes reported, his mouth already filled with one of Texas Stan's spicy beef enchiladas.

Lucky nearly dropped the chili. "Did Shaw turn up?"

"No," Bob said from the backseat. "The news is good, but not *that* good. The captain had a message for you from your sister."

"Ellen?"

"Yeah." Wes grabbed for one of the sodas, using it to hose down the inside of his mouth. Lucky knew from experience that Texas Stan's spicy enchiladas were only slightly less hot than the chili. "She called to tell you she's getting married."

Lucky laughed at that. "Yeah, right, Skelly. Very funny. What did she really want?"

"We're serious," Bobby said. "Ellie's engaged. I called her from the motel. She sounds really happy."

"The guy's some college geek," Wes reported.

They weren't kidding. Lucky carefully put down his container of food. "Ellen's not old enough to get married. She's only...what?" He had to do the math. "Hell, she's barely twenty-two."

"My little sister, Colleen, is twenty-two." Wes took

another bite of his enchilada. "Ann frr's hrr errrurr mmrrr."

"Colleen *is* old enough to get married," Bobby countered, completely able to understand him even with his mouth full. "You guys look at your little sisters and see ten-year-olds. It's like you're stuck in a time warp. Other guys look and see two very hot, very full-grown women."

Wes swallowed and turned to face the backseat. "Colleen? *Hot?* No way. Last time I was home, she skinned her knee skateboarding. She's the world's oldest living tomboy—she doesn't even know she's a girl. Thank God."

"Oh, come on, Skelly." Bobby shifted so that he was sitting forward and the entire van shook. "Remember when we visited her at college? Guys like her. A *lot*. They were always dropping in to her dorm room, remember?"

"Yeah, she's a great mechanic and they came asking her to fix their cars," Wes countered. "That's not the same thing."

"There's no way I'm letting Ellen get married," Lucky said grimly.

"Maybe she's pregnant," Wes said helpfully. "Maybe the geek knocked her up."

Lucky glared at him. "You should consider a new career writing greeting cards, Skelly. You always know *exactly* the right thing to say." He glowered at Bobby in the rearview mirror. "Why aren't *you* eating?"

"He's having dinner again with the supermodel."

Bobby smiled serenely. "Her name is Kyra."

"I hate you," Wes said. "First you make me stop smoking, now this."

"Trade you Kyra for Colleen."

Wes snorted. "Yeah, sure you would." He turned to

Lucky. "I got email today from a SEAL went through BUD/S training with the Priest."

Ellen was getting married. Lucky shook his head in disbelief.

"Actually," Wes expounded, "this guy—Ruben is his name—he went through BUD/S, but the Priest—Mitch—didn't."

That caught Lucky's attention. "Come again?"

"Apparently, Mitch didn't make it through BUD/S his first time around. It took him two tries." Wes paused and noisily sucked down half of a milk shake. "It's a great story, Lieutenant. You're going to love this."

Lucky just looked at him. Waiting.

Wes was unperturbed as he searched for a napkin and delicately wiped his mouth. "Ruben told me in this email that the Priest made it nearly all the way through BUD/S—no complaints, not a lot of talking at all. Just silently getting the job done."

"Unlike those of us sitting here who talked nonstop through basic training," Bobby interjected.

"I'm not talking to you anymore," Wes said. "I hate you, remember? You've let a supermodel come between us."

Lucky closed his eyes. "Skelly."

"Yeah. So it's the morning before Hell Week starts, right? And the Priest wakes up, and he's got the flu. Raging fever, intense intestinal distress. I mean, he's sick as a dog. Sicker. He knows if any of the instructors find out, he'll get pulled and stuck in the hospital."

Wes finished the rest of his milk shake. "So," he continued. "He keeps his mouth shut. At least he tries to. But he gets pulled when he starts vomiting blood. Dead giveaway he's got some medical problem. They try to talk him in to ringing out, but he refuses. They drag him to the hospital, but as soon as they leave him alone, he breaks out of his room. He goes out the window—and this is with a hundred-and-four-degree fever—and rappels to the ground from the fifteenth floor.

"Ruben told me the Priest just showed up back in Coronado. Middle of the night. He just rejoins his boat team as if he's never been gone. He can barely stand, but there he is. 'Ready for duty, sir!' This time, the instructors figure they'll just wait for him to keel over, but when he falls, he crawls. The tough little sonuvabitch doesn't stay down. So they promise him he can start over again with the candidates from the next cycle, but that's not good enough for the Priest. He won't quit. They end up having to knock him out with a shot of Valium. And when he wakes up, Hell Week's over."

"Oh, man." Lucky couldn't imagine going through Hell Week, that awful endurance test while stricken with the flu.

"He came through the next cycle," Wes said, "head of the class."

For several long moments, they sat quietly.

"Wherever he is," Bobby said, breaking the silence, "I hope he's okay."

Then Wes spoke, voicing aloud the question running through Lucky's mind. "Is it possible for a guy like that to sell out?"

"No way," Bobby said.

Lucky wasn't so sure.

CHAPTER SEVEN

BECCA TOOK A GLASS of champagne from the waiter's tray, smiling her thanks, trying her hardest to pay attention to Harry Cook as he talked about his granddaughter's first ballet recital.

Harry was a sweet man—generous with his millions, too—and Becca had met four-year-old Lila during last year's Children's Hospital fundraising picnic. The story Harry was telling was amusing, but Becca was finding it hard to focus.

She turned her back on the arched entrance that led into the restaurant from the lobby, determined not to spend the evening waiting for Mish to show.

Or not to show.

That was tonight's question.

She took a sip of champagne, forcing herself to slow down, to breathe. She usually didn't drink during these parties. After all, she was being paid to attend, to schmooze, to reinforce Justin Whitlow's contacts with the well-to-do population of northern New Mexico.

But tonight, she needed the champagne.

She laughed with everyone else as Harry finished his story, as he did what had to be a rather accurate imitation of Lila's final bow, but then she broke away from the group, heading toward the door to the Sidewinder's central outdoor plaza.

The night air was much warmer than the relentless

chill of the restaurant's air-conditioning. And since the long dress she was wearing exposed all of her arms and most of her back, she welcomed the heat.

There were only a few people outside, and Becca was glad to take a breather from the crowd. She sipped her champagne, gazing up at the strings of festive lights that decorated the plaza, dancing in the gentle breeze.

Mish wasn't going to come.

Even if he *did,* he would probably be too embarrassed to enter the high-class restaurant in his jeans and T-shirt.

The moon was a sliver in the sky—far more beautiful than the strings of lights. And the breeze carried the scent of flowers—proof that nature could provide far more enticing decorations for a party than even the chic Sidewinder.

Becca looked up at the moon, refusing to wonder if she would ever see Mish again.

If she didn't, so be it. He'd been around when it had been most important—to save Chip's life. If she had to choose between that and his appearance tonight at this party, well, that was a no-brainer. As much as she liked Mish, she'd take Chip, alive and well, any day. And even though Mish wasn't going to show, well, at least the possibility of his appearance had inspired her to wear this dress.

It had been hanging in the back of her closet for years, hanging in the back of her *mother's* closet since before Becca had been born. Her great-grandmother had made it during the 1930s. It was elegant and graceful and undeniably sexy. Blatantly sexy.

Definitely not something she wore every day.

She heard the door to the restaurant open, like a portal to a different world. The music and laughter was momentarily louder before it closed again, shutting out all but the heartiest laughter and the faint kitchen sounds of dishes clinking together.

Becca glanced up to see a man in a dark suit stop to get his bearings, still standing by the door. He wasn't Mish—his hair was too short, and besides, the suit looked expensive. She looked away. But she could see him from the corner of her eye as he took in the bar on the far side of the plaza, the couples talking quietly in the shadows, the strings of lights, the flowers, the trees, the moon.

He looked at the moon for a long time.

She turned her back to him before he could glance at her a second time.

One thing about this dress, it made men take long second glances. And some men even were bold enough to approach her.

Sure enough, she could hear his footsteps on the bricks, coming closer. He'd started walking toward her.

Becca turned toward the door, ready to nod politely on her way back into the restaurant and...

"Sorry I'm a little late. The bus from Albuquerque had a flat."

Mish?

It was. He'd gotten a haircut. And a new suit. And he was so clean-shaven, he must've stopped for a touch-up in the men's room before coming outside.

"You look incredible," he told her, his voice nearly as velvety-soft as the night.

"You do, too." Her own voice was husky as well.

He smiled crookedly, his eyes crinkling slightly at the edges. "Yeah, I cleaned up pretty well, huh?"

She touched the lightweight wool of his jacket sleeve. "Where on earth did you get the money for this?"

He stepped back slightly, pulling free from her grasp,

putting both of his hands into his pockets. A gentle reminder. No sex. No touching. "I called my man Jeeves, had him wire me some funds from my Swiss account."

Becca laughed. "I'm sorry, I shouldn't have asked. It's none of my business."

"Truth is, I had some cash," Mish told her. He'd been hoping he'd find the rest of his clothes and his other belongings—books, at least, because *surely* he had books—at the address listed in his personnel file. But he'd gone all the way to Albuquerque only to find that the address had been a fake. The street existed, but not the number. It had been a business district, filled with run-down pawnshops and seedy topless bars. Everything about it was completely unfamiliar.

The phone number Mish had found in the file had been disconnected, as well.

He'd spent nearly two days wandering around Albuquerque, looking for something, *anything* that triggered any kind of recognition.

The closest he'd come to a flicker of memory had been when he'd gone to the mall and tried on this suit. As he slipped on the jacket and looked at himself in the mirror, he'd gotten the sense that something was wrong. He'd worn suits before, but the jacket had been different. There was something about the neckline or the collar or… He'd stared at himself in the three-way mirror until the fitting-room clerk had gotten nervous, but the answer hadn't come to him. How could a suit jacket be different? Men's jackets had been virtually the same for nearly a hundred years. It didn't make any sense at all.

"How are you feeling?" Becca asked.

"Much better," he told her. "Although I'd appreciate it if you could refrain from elbowing me in the side for another day or two."

She laughed. "I'll try."

She really did look amazingly beautiful. Her dress was a killer, with narrow straps that were barely there, but necessary to hold up the front, like some kind of feat of engineering. The fabric was shimmery—not quite white, not quite gold, but a color somewhere in between that set off her golden-brown curls almost perfectly. She'd actually tried to comb her hair into some semblance of a style, using clips to hold it in place, but it was rebelling. He had to smile.

"You decided to leave your cowboy hat home, huh?"

"No, just out in the truck," she countered.

Mish kept his eyes on her face, away from all that smooth skin, away from the golden-white material that clung enticingly to her breasts and stomach and fell in a smooth sheet all the way to the floor. But he couldn't resist taking a peek at her feet.

"No," she said, "I'm not wearing boots." She lifted her skirt slightly to show him.

Her shoes looked like something Cinderella might wear. Delicate and barely there. As sexy as the dress.

She was smiling at him, and despite the fact that he was playing with fire here tonight, he felt himself start to relax. Albuquerque had held no answers. Maybe he'd never find out where he'd come from, what he'd done. And maybe that was okay.

"Are we allowed to dance?" he asked her.

She knew he was referring to the no-sex rule, and she thought about it. "I think it's probably okay. I mean, as long as we're in public, sure. We can dance. But only after dinner."

Mish had to laugh, and he couldn't begin to guess. "Why only after dinner?"

She finished her glass of champagne and set it down

on a nearby table, giving him a smile that warmed him to his very soul. "Because I'm starving."

She headed for the door, and Mish followed her inside.

He probably would have followed her anywhere.

"SHE MOVED NEXT DOOR when I was in second grade," Becca told Mish.

They'd found a table in a quiet corner of the restaurant, and had talked about books and movies while they'd had dinner. Or rather, she'd talked. Mish had listened.

He was listening still, watching her across the small table, giving her every ounce of his attention. He listened with his eyes as well as his ears, his face lit by the flickering light from a single candle. It was a little disconcerting to be the focus of all that intensity. But it was extremely nice, too—as if everything she had to say mattered. As if he didn't want to miss a single word.

"We were inseparable right through high school," she continued. "And when we went to college, we stayed tight. Peg was going to be a kindergarten teacher, and I was going to be a veterinarian." She had to smile. "Only I hated it. I don't know what I expected—probably a few years of classes and then an internship spent cavorting across the countryside with the doctor from *All Things Bright and Beautiful,* helping birth lambs and foals and bunnies. Instead, I was stuck in a city animal hospital, tending to dogs that had been hit by cars. House pets that had been abused. We had one woman bring in her cat—someone had sprayed him with lighter fluid and set him on fire. It was..." She shook her head. "It was really awful. But I was determined not to quit. Being a vet had been my dream for so long. I couldn't just abandon it."

Mish had been watching her, his eyes the most perfect

blend of green and blue and brown, but now he looked down, into his coffee cup. "It's hard to admit you've made a mistake, particularly on that scale."

"I think I was afraid of my parents' disapproval," she admitted.

He looked up again, into her eyes, and Becca felt the room tilt. "So what happened?"

"Peg was diagnosed with cancer."

Mish nodded, as if he'd been expecting her to tell him that awful news about her lifelong best friend. "I'm sorry."

"It was Hodgkin's disease. In an advanced stage. She did chemo and radiation, and…" God, it had been ten years, and Becca *still* had to blink back tears. Of course, she never talked about it, never talked about Peg. She couldn't remember the last time she'd given so much of her soul away for free. But she truly wanted Mish to understand. Because maybe then he'd know why she'd been pursuing him so relentlessly.

"She died eight months later," Becca told him.

Silently, Mish reached across the table and took her hand.

Becca felt fresh tears well as she gazed down at their intertwined fingers. His hands were warm, his fingers broad and work roughened. She wanted him to hold her hand, but she didn't want him to do it out of pity.

Gently, she pulled her hand free. "She knew she was dying," Becca said. "And even though I'd stopped complaining about school—how could I bitch about something as trivial as boring classes and dull teachers when she was going through this real-life hell?—she knew I was unhappy. And she made me talk about it. Yes, I hated school, but I wouldn't quit. I felt trapped by my expectations and my sense of responsibility. And she asked me what I loved doing best, more than anything else in the world. Of course, she knew—I loved riding. I told her, great, who was going to pay me money to ride all day? And she told me to go be a cowboy, work on a ranch, to do whatever I had to do—just make damn sure that I was happy. Life was too short to waste."

Mish's eyes were beautiful but inscrutable. He surely understood what she was telling him, but he didn't acknowledge that her words applied to him—to the two of them and the attraction that simmered between them. And when he spoke, he surprised her. "So why are you still working at the Lazy Eight?"

She didn't answer right away. "I love New Mexico." It sounded exactly like what it was—an excuse for wimping out.

Mish nodded.

Becca briefly closed her eyes. "Yes, okay, so I'd be much happier working for myself. I bought a lottery ticket tonight. Maybe I'll get lucky and win enough money to buy my own ranch." And maybe Silver would grow wings and fly. Or—even more unlikely—maybe she'd wake up tomorrow morning with Mish in her bed.

She looked away, suddenly aware she'd been eyeing him as if he were the dessert cart. "I should really go schmooze."

"You know, sometimes it works better if you make your own luck," he told her as she pushed her chair back from the table. "If you seek it out rather than waiting for it to come to you."

Becca touched him then, just lightly, the tips of her fingers sliding down his cheek in the softest caress. "Haven't you noticed me trying?"

She walked away, her heart pounding, before she could see his reaction.

She'd taken the first step across those boundaries they'd set between them and the next move was Mish's. Would he stay or would he run?

BECCA KNEW EVERYONE who was anyone in Santa Fe.

She worked the room like a pro, shaking hands, remembering names, introducing Mish with a brief anecdote about the people he was meeting. "This is James Sims. Don't ever put money on the game if you golf with him. He's good enough to go pro," and "Mish Parker, Frank and Althea Winters. Their granddaughter was just accepted at Yale University. Biochemistry major."

It wasn't an act. She was really good with people. And they all liked her, too. Who wouldn't, with her warm, inclusive smile?

She hadn't expected him to stick around after dinner. Mish had seen the surprise in her eyes as he'd approached her by the bar after he'd had a second cup of coffee—and let his pulse return to normal.

He wasn't sure himself why he hadn't left. Her message had been all too clear as she'd told him the story of her friend's death. Life was too short. Cut to the chase. Take the plunge. Just do it.

And, in case he'd been completely dense, she'd driven the message home by touching him lightly, provocatively. *Come home with me tonight.*

Mish wanted to. He wanted to give in. The temptation was so strong, it seemed to buzz and crackle around him. He knew he *should* run for the door.

As he watched, Becca let herself be waltzed out onto the dance floor with a man in his eighties.

She sparkled as she laughed with him, and since she was at a safe distance, Mish allowed himself the luxury of aching for her. He longed to lose himself in the sweetness of her body, the warmth of her mouth. It was more than sex, although it was certainly about sex, too—he couldn't pretend otherwise. He burned for her, but he also wanted to lie down with her in his arms, to fall asleep and dream not about the past, but of the future.

A clear, bright future, unshadowed by mistakes and regrets and hidden doubts.

Mish stood there watching Becca, not running anywhere. He couldn't run. He was completely glued in place.

The song ended, and the old man led her back to him.

And then, for the first time in what had seemed like hours, they were alone. The room was clearing out, the party almost over.

"The band's getting ready to pack up," she said, attempting to refasten one of the clips in her hair.

They still hadn't shared a dance. It was probably just as well.

"Where are you staying?" he asked, not touching her for the nine-thousandth time that night. He had to find the strength to stay away from her. She deserved someone better than him.

"I'm down the street at the old Santa Fe Inn. They've just restored it—it's beautiful." She smiled. "Don't worry, I won't ask if you want to come see it." She held out her hand for him to shake. "Thank you for a lovely evening."

Mish gazed at her hand in disbelief. Did she honestly think he would briskly shake her hand and let her walk out into the night, wearing a dress that would draw the attention of every human male within a ten-mile radius?

"I'll walk you to your car," he told her.

"I'm parked over at the inn."

Damn. "Then I'll walk you to the inn." Walking her to her hotel would be a mistake. He knew that for a fact before the words even left his mouth.

"You really don't have to," she said as if she could read his mind.

"I won't come inside," he told her. Told himself.

"Well," Becca said as she headed toward the door, "I won't force you to, so you don't have to look so tense."

Mish rolled his head slightly. "I'm not tense."

Becca just smiled at him.

The night air was cooler now, and she took a deep breath as they stepped out onto the street.

A group of men had just come out of a bar named Ricky's across the street, and were heading back toward the center of town. There were four of them, and as Mish watched, they noticed Becca. First two, then three and four. Heads turned, body language changed. Their stares weren't disrespectful, just very, very interested.

And he resisted the urge to put his arm—or at least his jacket—around her shoulders.

She took another deep breath, and her dress clung to her in a way that was hard to ignore. And now he was staring, too.

"It's a beautiful night." She hugged herself, rubbing her upper arms. "I love it when it cools off like this."

"Are you warm enough? I can give you my jacket..."

Becca smiled at him. "Considering we're about twelve more steps from the inn, and considering it's probably all of seventy degrees, I think I'll survive without danger of frostbite, thanks."

Mish could see the sign out in front of the inn. The place was, literally, just a few dozen yards away. In just a few moments, Becca would go inside and he'd be alone.

"Why did Justin Whitlow want you to come to this

party tonight?" he asked, hoping maybe she'd linger, praying that she wouldn't. "I mean, was the point just to keep his name on the tip of everyone's tongue, or was there something else you were trying to do?"

She gazed up toward the moon. "Whitlow's actually trying to arrange a fundraising event for the opera at the Lazy Eight. He gets to be the big generous benefactor that way, because he'd donate the facility. Except, of course, people would have to stay over. And then there would be the publicity he'd get for hosting the event. Not to mention the bonus of showing off the ranch to all those Santa Fe Opera supporters who have money to burn."

"Money to burn."

She turned to glance at him, amusement in her eyes, a small smile playing about the corners of her lips. "Yeah. Amazing concept, isn't it? But nearly everyone I introduced you to tonight has more money than they know what to do with."

Mish touched her. For the second time that evening, he couldn't help himself. He just stopped short and took her arm. "There's your answer, Becca."

She didn't know what on earth he was talking about. But she didn't pull away. Her skin was so soft beneath his fingers, he was momentarily distracted, temporarily thrown.

She was standing close enough to kiss, and the way she was looking up at him—eyes wide, lips slightly parted— he nearly gave in to the temptation to cover her mouth with his own.

But he didn't kiss her, though he didn't release her, either. "You just spent four hours tightening your relationship with dozens of men and women who have—in your words—'money to burn.' Come on, Bec, don't you get it? These people *like* you. If you went to them with a plan to buy a spread and turn it into a vacation ranch, you could very well find yourself all the financial backing you'd need right here in Santa Fe."

She was wary, keeping her natural enthusiasm buried, at least for the moment. "I'd need to work it all out— down to the last detail—before I started asking anyone for money. I'd have to find a piece of property…" She shook her head. "God, I don't have time to go driving halfway across the state to—"

"Use the internet," Mish interrupted. "The computer back at the Lazy Eight office has internet access, doesn't it?"

"Actually, it doesn't," Becca told him. "But I just got access on my laptop. I'm trying to create a website for the Lazy Eight. In my spare time." She laughed. "I hear myself say that, and I sound completely insane. *What* spare time?"

He finally let go of her, and took a step back. When she laughed, he found her irresistible, but kissing her now would only complicate things beyond belief. "When we get back to the ranch tomorrow, we can use your laptop to search for properties listed for sale."

"My laptop's upstairs in my hotel room," Becca told him.

Upstairs. In her room. Mish didn't say anything, didn't move. He just looked at her, imagining the hushed quiet of this four-star hotel's rooms, imagining one that smelled faintly of her unique brand of shampoo, imagining dim lights, a king-size bed, Becca turning her back to him, his fingers finding the tiny zipper pull at the back of her dress and…

"I've only been online a few times," she continued. "Is it really possible to do that kind of a property search?"

Mish nodded. "Yeah, I think so. We'd just need to use

a search engine. Plug in the information we're looking for and…"

She was looking at him curiously. "Where did you learn about the internet?"

Um. Good question. It was just one of those things he knew, like the waist size of his jeans. He shrugged. "I don't know. I just…picked it up here and there, I guess."

"Would you mind coming up and…" She broke off. "I'm sorry. This can wait for tomorrow." She looked chagrined. "I didn't mean to make you uncomfortable."

"If you like," Mish said, "I can come up for a few minutes—help you get signed on and started." But then he would leave.

"This isn't just a ploy to get you up to my room," she told him earnestly.

Mish laughed. "I know." He—and she—would be safe as long as he didn't kiss her. And he *wasn't* going to kiss her. "I won't stay long."

CHAPTER EIGHT

"Okay," Mish said, "here we go. This looks more like the kind of place you're looking for."

Becca inched her chair even closer to the computer screen. She'd long since kicked off her shoes, and she curled her feet and legs underneath her long skirt.

Mish had thrown his jacket onto the bed at least forty-five minutes ago, and had loosened his tie and rolled up his sleeves to his elbows.

It was amazing. He worked the keyboard and mouse of her computer the way Becca handled horses. It was as if the computer were a part of him, a permanent attachment.

She had to laugh. Her new ranch hand was a secret computer nerd.

"Look," he said, doing something with the mouse and making new pictures flash on the screen. "This one looks really great. The price seems right. It doesn't have a *whole* lot of acreage, but it borders a state park, so—"

"It's in California," Becca realized as she leaned even closer. "Down near San Diego."

"It's beautiful down there," Mish told her, doing something with the mouse and the computer to mark the site so that she could find it again.

"God, but California…?" Becca shook her head. "Everyone I know is here in New Mexico. I don't know anyone who lives in California."

"I live in California," he said. His hands suddenly stilled on the keyboard and he looked up at her. "I'm from California." He laughed.

What was he telling her? That he wanted her to move to California to be near him? It didn't make sense. He didn't even want to kiss her. Why would he want her to live near him?

"San Diego," he told her. "I lived there when I was a kid. We had a beach house. It was…" He laughed again. "I actually remember this. The ocean's so beautiful and…"

He was gazing at her, but he quickly looked away, returning his attention to the computer screen as if he'd just realized how close together they were sitting.

"I should go," he said quietly. "I've already stayed too long."

"You know, I think that was the first time I've ever heard you volunteer information about yourself," Becca mused.

He shrugged, forced a smile. "I don't have a whole lot to tell." He rubbed his forehead as if he suddenly had a headache.

"I've been trying to guess," she said, resting her chin in her hand. "What exactly did you do, Mish? Something you're still paying penance for? Is that why you turned down Ted Alden's check? You don't drink—at least not heavily. I've never seen you drink more than a single beer. Tonight you only had soda even though there was an open bar. And you've made no attempt at all to replace your stolen driver's license. I don't know a single man who wouldn't have put a priority on getting his license back. Unless he didn't have one. Unless it had been revoked. Maybe for D.U.I. Am I getting warm?"

Mish sighed. "Becca—"

She touched him. She put her hand on the taut muscle of his suntanned forearm, wanting to touch him despite the fact that he'd pushed her away every other time she'd reached out for him.

"It doesn't matter to me," she told him quietly. "Wherever you've been, whatever you've done, it's irrelevant. Whatever mistakes you've made, they're in the past. I like who you are right now, Mish. I don't care where you went to college, or if you dropped out of high school, or got left back in second grade. I'd love to know those things about you, sure, but only if you want to share them with me. If not, that's okay, too."

She slid her hand down to his, and Mish turned his arm over so that their fingers could interlock. He stared down at their two hands, knowing the inevitable. He and Becca had been barreling toward this moment from the instant he'd agreed to attend the fundraising dinner with her. Despite everything he'd told himself, he'd known it from the start. He was here, in Becca's room, because he couldn't stay away.

"I don't know many men—or women—who would've jumped into that river after that boy. It was dangerous as hell, and you didn't even hesitate."

"I'm a strong swimmer."

"You're a good man."

He levelly met her gaze. "If I were a good man, I'd say good-night right now and leave."

"I said you were good. I didn't say you were a saint."

She was close enough to kiss, and he knew, unless he did or said something soon, that she was going to kiss him.

"I can't give you what you deserve," he whispered. And then he kissed her, because he couldn't wait for her to kiss him, not one second longer.

Her lips were as sweet as he remembered, her mouth eager, hungry. She melted against him, her arms slipping up around his neck, pulling him closer.

He'd meant to kiss her softly, sweetly. Instead he almost inhaled her, his hands sliding against the smooth fabric of her dress, against the soft warmth of her body beneath.

Her bed was three steps away. All he had to do was lift her up and...

He pulled free, breathing hard. "Becca..."

Her brown eyes held a clear echo of that powerful kiss's molten heat. "Stay with me tonight."

"Just tonight?" His voice sounded husky to his own ears. "Is that really what you want—a one-night stand?"

"I'm looking for a lover—and a friend—who'll stick around only until it's time to leave," she admitted. "But it's impossible to know when that time will be, especially when a relationship is just starting. Still, I would hope it wouldn't be after only one night."

"So you want a...relationship."

Becca laughed at that. "You say it as if it has a capital *R*. As if it's something enormous and terrifying."

He couldn't joke about it. "Isn't it?"

"No! I hate to break it to you," she said, "but we've already *got* a relationship. We've had one from the moment you walked onto the Lazy Eight and asked for Becca Keyes." She shifted impatiently in his arms, tightening her grip on him, moving closer when he would have set her aside. "All I want is to change the parameters of that relationship to include long stretches of time that we can spend naked together. But that time's not infinite. Frankly, I don't believe in forever."

She held his gaze as if she were trying to convince him of the truth she spoke by letting him see into her soul.

"Honest, I'm not looking for true love, Mish. I promise you, when the time comes, I'll let you walk away." Her eyes were gentle then as she pushed his hair back from his face. "You don't have to worry about hurting me."

She kissed him. Softly, then harder and deeper, and he kissed her back until the room spun, until he couldn't breathe, until he thought his heart might explode in his chest. He should make a break for the door and not stop running until he hit the other side of town. Because he could taste forever in her kiss. Despite everything she'd said, it was back there. A hint of promise that made him want... Made him want...

It couldn't be... Was the bittersweet longing that he could practically taste his *own?* He nearly laughed aloud.

Wouldn't *that* be the ultimate in irony? Here was this fabulous woman giving him everything he could possibly want from a lover—including the serenity of knowing she had no expectations—and *he* was the fool who was falling hard.

Becca broke their kiss and pulled back to gaze searchingly into his eyes. She shook her head at all the doubt and confusion he knew was swimming there.

"How can you possibly kiss me that way and still resist this?" she asked. She laughed in disbelief. "Maybe you *are* a saint."

He *wasn't* in love with her. He was infatuated, sure. He was wildly attracted, without a doubt. But *love...?* He barely knew her. No, this was about sex, about chemistry, about attraction. It had to be.

So why *was* he resisting?

"There's a lot I can't tell you, Bec," Mish confessed, torn between wanting to open up about his inability to remember his past, and that intense conviction deep in his gut that he shouldn't breathe a word about it to anyone. "About myself, I mean, but…I do know I'm no saint."

"Then stay," she whispered. "Please." Her gaze dropped to his lips, and for a fraction of a second, time hung.

Anticipation surrounded Mish breathlessly, heart-poundingly. She'd told him she didn't need to know more about him than she already knew. She'd told him she wasn't looking for more than a short-term lover. She'd given him permission to keep his secrets to himself, guilt-free.

And then she leaned forward and kissed him again.

And it was all over.

Even back when he'd first walked into the inn, there had probably only been a six-percent chance that he would walk back out of this hotel before dawn. But that chance just dropped to zero.

His willpower had been completely shattered.

He wasn't going anywhere.

Except maybe to heaven.

He pulled her hard against him, filling his hands with her softness, sliding his palms along the bare skin of her arms and back, breathing in the familiar, sweet scent of her hair as he kissed her again and again and again— deep, ravenous, soul-reaching kisses that shook him to his very core. He felt her hands at his throat, unfastening his tie, pulling it free, then worrying the buttons of his shirt.

She seemed determined to get his clothes off him, and as far as brilliant ideas went, he was right there with her, one hundred percent. He found the zipper at the back of her dress and unfastened it, then pulled back to yank his unbuttoned shirt free from his arms.

She gasped as her hands touched his Ace bandage. "Oh, no, I forgot all about… I didn't hurt you, did I?"

He had to laugh. "You're killing me," he told her, "but not the way you mean. I'm fine."

"Honest?"

This was one thing he *could* be honest about. "Yes."

"And you'll tell me if it hurts?"

He laughed again. "It hurts, but—"

"Not the way you mean," she finished with him, laughing, too.

Her smile grew slightly wicked, and he watched, spellbound, as she rose to her feet and pushed the thin straps from her shoulders. Her dress fell off her in a sheet, pooling at her feet, leaving her naked save for a pair of shimmering silk panties.

She was beyond beautiful, and he reached for her, needing to touch the smoothness of her skin, the soft fullness of her perfect breasts, needing to hold her close, to feel her naked against him.

She touched him, too, with her hands, with her mouth, slowly running her fingers up his arms, across his shoulders, down the muscles of his bare chest, gently across his bruised side, driving him half-mad from the sensation.

How could something that felt so right be so wrong?

And it *was* wrong. Despite all that she'd told him, he knew it was wrong to make love to her without telling her the truth, without admitting that he didn't know what that truth was. Who was he? He honestly didn't know. Becca thought he was a good man. He strongly suspected otherwise.

Mish had reason to believe he'd done terrible things in his past, and here he was, right on schedule—giving in to temptation again.

Except when Becca kissed him, it didn't feel wrong. When Becca kissed him, when she touched him, it felt right in a way he'd never experienced *right* before.

And dammit, he wanted more.

He pulled her down with him onto the bed, kissing her, touching her as she cradled him between her legs. He could feel her heat as she pressed herself up against his arousal, and the sensation was dizzying and so perfect, he wanted to weep.

He felt her reach between them, felt her unfasten his belt, his pants, and then she was touching him, her fingers against his skin. It felt impossibly, paralyzingly, mind-blowingly good.

This woman wasn't looking for forever. She expected this fire they were fanning to life between them to burn hot and white, and then burn out. She had no misconceptions where this love affair was concerned, and she wouldn't be hurt when he left. She wasn't in love with him—at least not really. She didn't believe in true love.

Becca tugged at his pants, and he rolled off her to help her push them down his legs. Together they pulled off his boots, took off her panties. And then, finally, they were both naked. Mish pulled her on top of him, kissing her, desperate to be inside her, surrounded by her slick heat. He could feel her against him. All he had to do was shift his hips and...

But she moved when he moved, lifting herself away from him. "Whoa," she said, laughing. "Wait a sec—safe sex, birth control! I've got condoms in my bag. Don't move, okay?"

Mish was staggered. He couldn't have moved if he'd wanted to. A condom—he'd completely forgotten about using one. He'd been more than ready to make love to Becca, despite being totally without protection. If she hadn't stopped him...

She pulled a foil-wrapped package from her purse, and came back to the bed, tearing it open.

"I'm sorry," he said, his voice hoarse as he pushed himself up on his elbows. "It's been a while for me, and I wasn't thinking."

"I hope you don't mind wearing this," she told him, kneeling beside him. "Because I'm afraid it's non-negotiable."

"No." He pulled her toward him, unable to keep from touching all that smooth, soft skin. "I never mind being forced to do something intelligent. I seriously don't know how I could have—"

She smiled at him, amusement dancing in her eyes—she was so beautiful. "Considering I was trying to drive you to distraction, I can't really complain when it worked."

"Distraction, huh?" Her thighs were smooth against him, her breasts so soft in his hands. He bent to kiss her, to draw her into his mouth. She moaned, and just like that the pulsating fire was back, heat flickering white-hot through his veins. "I'm just glad you had a condom," he murmured.

She handed it to him. "I always keep them on hand," she breathed, "in case Brad Pitt comes to town."

Mish lifted his head, and Becca laughed. "Just checking to see if you were still paying attention," she told him. "If you want to know the truth, I bought a box because despite all my promises to be good, despite all the times you told me *no,* I still had designs on you."

She'd spoken the words lightly, but he touched her face gently, his eyes almost soft beneath the heat of his desire. "I didn't tell you no because I didn't want you. You *do* know that, Becca, don't you?"

She knew it now and she was glad—so glad—that she hadn't given up.

She kissed him, tasting his hunger for her, feeling

his need in the way that he held her, the weight of his desire.

Becca reached between them—he was taking too long—and helped him cover himself. She straddled him then, rolling him over onto his back as she kissed him, his arousal sinfully hard against her stomach.

He explored her body with his hands and mouth as if he were a starving man at a banquet, as if he would never be able to get enough of her.

It was an incredible turn-on—the way he looked at her as if she were the sexiest woman he'd ever seen, the way he touched her as if she were some kind of goddess or angel or…

"Becca," he breathed, and she loved the way her name sounded in the midnight velvet of his voice. He reached between them to touch her intimately, lightly first, then harder. "Please, may I—"

She would have agreed to anything, promised him everything else. *"Yes."*

He lifted her up then, turning them both over so that he was on top of her, his weight between her legs. She raised her hips to meet him and, oh, the look in his eyes was nearly as incredible as the sensation of him, thrust hard and deep, inside of her.

He held her gaze as he began to move, and the connection between them was so profound, her heart was completely in her throat. How could this be? This was supposed to be…well, if not casual, then at least *ordinary*. She hadn't anticipated feeling as if her entire soul were exposed to the elements. She hadn't dreamt that this man's kisses might resurrect all of her long-buried hopes of happily-ever-after.

That was crazy. This was sex. It was *great* sex, but it *was* only sex.

But as Becca looked into the eyes of this man who was making such wonderful, exquisite love to her, she saw possibilities that made her breath catch in her throat. She saw her future stretching out before her, and for the first time since forever, her journey was not a solitary one.

She laughed aloud. They *were* crazy, these thoughts that were invading her.

But when Mish smiled, too—his eyes crinkling at the edges with his pleasure and joy—she knew she was in trouble.

Big trouble.

He somehow knew just how to move to please her most—long, slow strokes that stole the air from her lungs, that left her dying for more.

And when her release ripped through her, it tore her open, scorching her very soul. She closed her eyes and clung to him, feeling him explode as well.

And when he lowered his head and kissed her, she closed her eyes and let him claim her mouth as thoroughly as he'd just claimed her heart.

CHAPTER NINE

MISH COULD SMELL THE FEAR.

It hung, sharp and unmistakable, in the small room. He'd been trapped there for hours with the others. There were twenty-four of them—mostly women and young girls. Some had been weeping continuously. When one of them left off, another started in.

He was numb.

The man in the religious robes lay on the floor where he'd fallen, half of his head blown away, his hands outstretched, wide and reaching, surprised by his own death.

He'd died trying to negotiate the release of the women and children. But the terrorists would not negotiate. They all knew that now.

And so Mish waited. He sat with his back against the far wall, and he waited, trying not to shake. He looked at the walls, at the ceiling—anywhere but at that pool of darkening blood on the floor.

But then the door opened, and everything moved too fast. A black man, an American, scrambled up from the hostages—launching himself at the men with guns. Shots were fired as Mish lunged to his feet. The American staggered back, but not before wrenching an assault weapon from one of the terrorist's arms.

More gunshots. The American went down hard, the weapon skittering across the floor.

Toward Mish.

He didn't think. He reacted, picking it up, his finger squeezing the trigger before he'd even got it aimed. The force pushed the barrel up as he fired, and he fought to push it down, sweeping the entrance to the room, spraying the terrorists with bullets, splattering the back wall and doorway with their blood and brains.

Someone was screaming, the voice raw and guttural with rage, but barely loud enough to be heard over the deafening machine-gun fire.

But then it was over. The men on the floor before him were undeniably dead. He'd killed them. He stopped shooting and realized that the voice—and the rage—were his own.

The American was bleeding badly, but he grabbed another assault weapon and kicked the door shut.

"Good job," he told Mish through the blood that bubbled on his lips. "Way to send them straight to hell, Mish."

Mish stared at the bodies, stared at what he'd done.

He'd killed them. God help him, he'd pointed the weapon, and taken the lives of three human beings. He may have sent them straight to hell, but what had he done to his own soul?

And he turned, because over on the other side of the room, the dead man in the robe was pushing himself up and off of the floor. The half of his face that was left was frowning, and he raised his hand, pointing accusingly at Mish. "Thou shalt not kill," he intoned. "Thou shalt not kill."

He took a step toward Mish, and then another step. And Mish realized with a jolt of shock that the man wore a liturgical collar, streaked bright red with blood.

And what was left of the dead man's face might as well have been his own.

Mish sat up in bed, his heart pounding, gasping for air.

Someone stirred in the bed beside him. Becca. It was Becca. She sat up, too, hesitantly touching his back. "Mish, are you all right?"

The hotel room came into focus, dimly lit by the first light of dawn that streaked in through the tops of the heavy window curtains.

Mish fought to control his ragged breathing, fought to bring his pulse back down to normal. "Nightmare," he managed to say.

"A bad one, huh? Want to talk about it?"

He pushed his sweat-soaked hair back from his face with hands that were still shaking. "No," he said. "Thanks."

She put her arms around him and lightly kissed his shoulder, and he turned toward her, grabbing her and holding her far more tightly than he had a right to, kissing her far more proprietarily than he should have. But he desperately needed grounding, desperately needed her.

"Mmm." She smiled up at him in the slowly growing light as she ran her fingers through his hair. She didn't seem to mind the dampness. "I'm sorry you had a nightmare, but I'm not sorry you woke me up, especially when you kiss me like that."

She was naked. They both were. And as Mish gazed into her eyes, detailed memories of the power and passion of last night came crashing back, full force.

He had made love to this woman, and she to him, in a way that had been beyond description, beyond comparison.

And she deserved to know the truth about who he was—or who he wasn't.

He'd stared at the ceiling for a good portion of the night, struggling with wanting to tell her of his missing past, and this overpowering sense of knowing—this absolute *conviction*—that he would not be allowed to tell her anything about himself, even if he knew.

She kissed him, pulling him back with her against the pillows, intertwining their legs. "I've got a few days off coming to me," she murmured. "What do you say we order a steady supply of room service, tell them to hold all my calls, and just stay here until Tuesday morning?"

Mish wanted to do it. He wanted to hold the world at bay for two days straight. And why couldn't he? As far as he was aware, he was the only one searching for himself.

And who could know? Maybe he'd find himself here in the safety and warmth of Becca's eyes.

And if not, maybe he'd have figured out a way by then to tell her who he feared he was.

"'Til Tuesday sounds great," he whispered between kisses. In truth, it sounded about a lifetime too short, but that wasn't something he'd ever dare admit, either to her or to himself.

He kissed her longer, deeper, willing himself to stop thinking, to just *be*.

With Becca's eager help, that wasn't hard to do.

THE CALL FROM JOE CAT came in just after dawn.

Lucky had only been asleep for about twenty minutes, but he snapped instantly awake—especially after he heard the Captain's familiar New Yawk accent.

"More of Shaw's funny money turned up," Joe Cat said

without ceremony. "This time in a men's clothing store in Albuquerque. Two bills."

Lucky turned on the light next to the motel-room bed. "We'll go check it out, but I'm not going to leave that bag in the bus station locker without a babysitter. I got a gut about this one, Cat. Mitch Shaw has had that bag for a long time. If he's alive, he's coming back for it. I've buddied up the surveillance—Bobby and Wes are watching the station right now." He started pulling on his pants. "But I could head north in about five minutes."

"No, stay in Wyatt City," the captain commanded. "Crash and Blue are already on their way to Albuquerque." He gave a disparaging laugh. "I'd be with 'em, but the admiral's allegedly flying in today. I need to be on hand to give him a sit-rep. I just thought it'd be smart for you to know Shaw's still fairly local. In state, at least."

Lucky kicked his pants back off and settled back on the bed, phone tucked under his chin. "Unless he's dead and someone else is spending his money."

"Yeah, I think we've got to consider that possibility," the captain said seriously.

"But what if he's not dead?" Lucky asked. "Is there a chance he's trying to send some kind of message to us by circulating those bills?" Surely Mitch knew which of the bills he carried were fake and which weren't.

"That's what I keep coming back to," Joe Cat said. "What if Mitch Shaw located the...missing material?" Even though it was a secured line, he was careful not to use the word *plutonium*. "What if he's in deep with the people who have control over that material, and can't check in? Using the money might be his way of flagging us down, getting backup into the area."

"Except we spoke to a guy named Jarell at the homeless

shelter," Lucky reported. "He remembers seeing Mitch. He was brought in late at night, barely conscious, apparently falling-down drunk, with the fight kicked out of him. Jarell only saw him that one night, said he left before breakfast, said as far as he could tell, Mitch was alone. He also said Mitch left a jacket behind, but Jarell wouldn't give it to us—he wouldn't even let us look at it."

"Get it," the captain said.

"Yeah," Lucky told him. "I'm working on that. But that church has something going on 24/7. There's always someone there, so we're going to have to get creative. But don't get your hopes up, Skipper. Even after we *do* get it, chances are that jacket's not going to tell us jack."

Joe Cat sighed. "I don't know this guy Shaw at all. Is he a heavy drinker? Is he into drugs at all? Is it possible he's gone on some kind of binge?"

"I've never seen him have more than a single beer," Lucky said.

"Which could fit into the pattern of a problem drinker," the captain pointed out. "He keeps it under control, until suddenly he can't anymore. And then it's not one beer, it's a dozen, and he's off and running."

"Jarell said he was so skunked, he couldn't even remember his own name." Lucky shook his head. That was hard to imagine. Quiet Mitchell Shaw completely out of control.

"There's a question I haven't been able to stop thinking, Luke. Do you think he might've turned—you know, embraced the dark side of the force?"

Lucky closed his eyes. "I don't know, Obi-Wan," he said. "The admiral's not going to like this, but I don't think we can rule out that possibility at this point."

THE PHONE RANG.

Becca opened her eyes and found that she'd fallen asleep draped half on top of Mish. It should have been uncomfortable to sleep like that, her leg thrown across his thighs, her head resting on his shoulder, but it wasn't. She fit against him perfectly.

His eyes were open, and he gave her the sexiest, sleepiest good-morning smile as she reached across him for the telephone.

She couldn't resist and she stopped to kiss him, hoping that whoever was calling would just give up and go away. But they were persistent and the phone kept ringing.

"I knew I should have told the desk to hold my calls," she complained with an exaggerated sigh as she picked up the phone. "'Lo?" she said into the receiver, pulling the cord back with her, settling into the warmth of Mish's arms.

She could feel his arousal, heavy against her thigh, feel his fingers trailing lightly, deliciously down her back from her shoulder to her rear end and back again.

"Becca? This is Hazel. I'm sorry, did I wake you?"

Becca sighed, but even the thought that her assistant wouldn't have called unless there was a real problem at the Lazy Eight wasn't enough to detract from the pleasure of Mish's touch.

"It's nearly eight, and I thought you'd be up," Hazel continued apologetically. "I'd offer to call back later, but this really can't wait."

"What's the problem?" Becca had to work to keep her voice even and controlled as Mish lowered his head to her breast. He kissed her lightly at first, then slowly drew her nipple into his mouth. She bit back an exclamation, and he lifted his head, smiling at her like the devil incarnate.

Like an outrageously handsome devil incarnate.

"We seem to have something of a mystery on our hands," Hazel told her.

Mish lowered his head and kissed his way down her stomach, stopping to explore her belly button with his tongue.

"Oh, God," Becca said. "Hazel, are you sure I can't call you back in just a few minutes—an hour tops—I promise?" Mish kissed the inside of her thigh, and she closed her eyes. "Please?"

"Becca, it's about that Casey Parker. That Mish character. Did you know that he's gone? He cleared out of cabin twelve the day before yesterday, and I've seen neither hide nor hair of him since."

Becca laughed. Hazel's big mystery was no mystery. Becca knew exactly where Casey Parker was—*and* exactly what he was doing.

And, oh, she liked what he was doing, but she pulled back from him, shaking her head, widening her eyes. No way could she talk on the phone while he did that.

He grinned at her and her laughter bubbled over again. "Hazel, I'm sorry. I thought I mentioned it to you. Mish had some business to take care of in Albuquerque. He should be back at the ranch on Tuesday."

"Well, it's going to be interesting when he returns," Hazel said, "especially if the man who was just here at the office decides to come back, too. Because then we'll have *two* Casey Parkers on our hands."

Becca could see the promise of paradise in Mish's eyes. He was behaving himself, lying down at the end of the bed, lightly stroking her foot. But despite his distance, he was obviously distracting her, because Hazel's words just didn't make any damn sense. "I'm sorry. *What* did you say?"

"Two," Hazel repeated. "Casey Parkers. Pretty bizarre

mystery, huh? A second Casey Parker just showed up at the Lazy Eight, claiming you'd hired him on as a ranch hand. He was looking for a package that was supposedly waiting for him here at the office. He was pretty bent out of shape when I told him we'd filled our quota of Casey Parkers for the month and I'd given that package to the first one. I even had to call Rafe McKinnon down to the office to flex his muscles."

Becca sat up, her full attention on Hazel's words. "Is he still there?" she asked. "Call the sheriff and—"

"He's gone. He drove off in a wild hurry after he found out there'd been a Casey Parker here before him. I don't know *what's* going on."

"He's an imposter." Even as she said the words, Becca knew they made no sense. Why would someone show up at the ranch pretending to be Casey Parker?

"*Some*one's an imposter," Hazel said. "And that's why this phone call couldn't wait. Becca, I know there was something brewing between you and this Mish. Promise me you'll be careful if you see him again today?"

"Hazel—"

"Because Casey Parker Number Two had picture ID. He had a driver's license," Hazel told her. "He was a big guy with a gray beard and a beer belly, and it was *definitely* his picture on that license."

And Mish had had no ID at all.

He was sitting on the end of the bed, watching her.

He'd been listening to her end of the conversation. He knew she'd been talking about him and all sense of wicked play had disappeared.

"Are you sure?" Becca whispered. She pulled the sheet up so that it covered her, and Mish looked away tiredly, almost guiltily—as if he somehow knew exactly what Hazel was telling her.

"Honey, I used to work in the sheriff's office over in Chimayo. This license looked legit. It wasn't tampered with in any way that I could see. They have those fancy hologram thingies on 'em, you know, to keep people from messing with 'em." Hazel sighed. "You *were* planning to see him again, weren't you? That Mish? I *am* sorry about this."

"Thanks for calling," Becca managed to choke out before she hung up the phone.

Mish didn't look at her. He just sat on the bed, staring down at their clothes, still strewn on the floor where they'd left them last night.

"So. You want to tell me who you really are?" She'd meant to sound tough, but her voice shook slightly and ruined her delivery. "Seeing as how you're *not* Casey Parker?"

He looked up at her then, his eyes filled with regret and...shame?

Becca let herself get good and mad, fighting the tears that were on the verge of exploding from her eyes. Damn right he should feel shame!

"Maybe I should get dressed," he said, reaching for his clothes.

Becca scrambled out of the bed, pulling the sheet with her, and grabbed his pants away from him. "Oh, no, you don't. You're not going to leave before you at least give me *some* kind of explanation."

With shaking hands, Mish pulled on his shorts. Had he really thought he could have this woman without giving her anything of himself in return? Had he really thought he could hide here with her, safely cocooned from the real world, from the truth?

But the real world had reached out and somehow she now knew more about him than he did. How and what didn't matter. He should have known it would happen. He should have protected her from this.

And he would have, if only he'd stayed away from her. He should have been strong enough to resist the magnetic attraction he felt for her, that dizzying pull of longing. Instead, he'd given in to what *he* wanted, what *he* needed. And he'd hurt her. Badly.

Selfish. He was a selfish son of a bitch.

And in one brief moment, all of the magic of the night was gone, as if it had never existed, never been real. They'd shared something wonderful, something he'd longed to hold on to, something fragile and perfect that now lay crushed and broken at his feet. And he'd done that as surely as if he'd stomped on it with both heels of his boots.

"The real Casey Parker showed up at the ranch," Becca said, her voice thick with betrayal. "You had to have known that was bound to happen."

"I didn't," he said loudly, more forcefully than he'd intended. He stood up, pushing his hair back from his face, feeling as if he might be terribly, violently sick. Lord God, he'd been so selfish.

"You didn't?" Her voice rose, too. "Dammit, I *know* you're smarter than that. You *had* to know Casey would show up sooner or later."

He wasn't Casey Parker. He'd suspected that for a while. The name had seemed so unfamiliar. But still, he'd hoped.

God, he'd hoped. But hope wasn't enough. Not anymore.

So now what?

Although his back was to her, he could see her reflection in the big mirror that hung above the dresser. She was gazing at him with such hurt, such accusation in her eyes.

He still couldn't tell her the truth. He wasn't supposed to tell anyone why he was in New Mexico—he couldn't remember why, but he knew that he wasn't supposed to talk about it with a strength that was overpowering. Still, to walk away, leaving her to think that he'd purposely deceived her… He couldn't do that, either. How could he?

He stood there, stomach churning, sick to his soul, head bowed and shaking, unable to stay, unable to leave.

"You know," she said, her voice shaking, too, "if you'd come to the ranch and introduced yourself to me, if you'd been honest about who you were, I would have hired you. I don't understand why you had to lie."

What could he tell her? "Maybe I should just go. I can't tell you what you want to know."

Disbelief colored her voice. "You can't tell me your *name?*"

He glanced up and saw that she was crying. She tried to hide it by brusquely, almost savagely, wiping her tears away as she still clutched the sheet around her.

"Call me old-fashioned," Becca said sharply, "but I at least like to know the *name* of the men I've had sex with."

His name. Mish looked up, and came face-to-face with himself in that mirror.

He was still a stranger to his own eyes. Hard and lean and dangerous, with his morning stubble thick and dark on his angular face, his hair wild, messed from sleep, his eyes bitter, soulless, he looked to be the kind of man who would lie his way into a woman's bed and leave her with little regard for her feelings in the morning.

He stared into those eyes, praying for a glimmer of

memory, a whisper of a name. Some small fragment of truth that he could give her...

Mish.

Mission Man.

"Just tell me your name," Becca whispered.

He stared harder, fists tight, teeth clenched, hating himself, hating the stranger staring tauntingly back at him, no longer praying to God but *demanding* the answers he sought. Who the hell was he?

Mission Man.

An echo of Jarell's voice whispered the nickname, and his anger and frustration erupted.

"I don't know my damn name!" He exploded, spinning and hitting his reflection with his fist.

The mirror cracked, cutting his image in two. He hit it again, harder, and it shattered, the glass slicing his hand.

Becca backed away, shocked by his outburst, staring at this suddenly wild-eyed stranger whose blood dripped from his fingertips onto the carpeting.

"I don't know who the hell I am!" he shouted hoarsely. "I woke up nearly two weeks ago in a homeless shelter with five thousand dollars, a handgun in my boot, directions to the Lazy Eight with your name on it, and no memory of anything important—including my own name! You say I'm not Casey Parker? Well, guess what? This is news to me, too!"

Becca clutched her sheet around her, watching him, ready to run if he suddenly came toward her. Could what he'd just said possibly be true? Did he have some kind of amnesia? It sounded so amazing. And yet...

He was standing there, shaking like a wounded animal, his eyes filled with tears, unable to meet her gaze. "Just give me my pants, and I'll go."

"Where?" she asked quietly, her heart in her throat. She had been furiously angry with him, but if what he was saying was even remotely true...

He looked up at her. He didn't understand.

"Where will you go?"

He shook his head. He was so upset he couldn't even answer her. One of his tears escaped, and he wiped it away with a shaking hand. This couldn't be an act, it couldn't be. He was as upset by this as she was. More.

She didn't know much about mental illnesses, but it was possible this man she'd given a piece of her heart to last night was sick in ways she couldn't even imagine. If so, then he needed help.

And if not... He'd had a gash on his head when he'd first arrived at the ranch. It was mostly healed now, but what if the blow he'd received *had* taken away his memory?

She tried to imagine what that might be like, how terrifying and awful and strange. How completely alone he must feel....

Either way, she had to get him to a doctor. She had to convince him to go with her to the hospital.

"If you don't have anywhere to go, then it doesn't make sense for you to leave," she told him, keeping her voice low, as if she were gentling a frightened horse. The first thing she had to do was calm him down. Then she had to find out if he still had that gun he'd mentioned. Guns and high emotions never mixed well.

She stepped closer, holding out her own hand to him. "Come into the bathroom. Let me look at your hand. It's bleeding."

Mish looked down, as if noticing his injured hand for the first time. He looked at the mirror, looked at her. "I'm so sorry, Becca."

"Come on," she said. "Let's make sure you don't need stitches. And then we can talk and try to figure this out."

"I should just go. I'll leave money to pay for the mirror—"

"No," Becca said. "I want you to stay."

He started to argue, but she interrupted. "Stay," she said again. "I think you owe me at least that much."

Mish nodded. For a potentially crazy person, his gaze was remarkably steady now. "Becca, do you believe me?"

Becca turned away as she led him into the bathroom. "I'm still working on that."

CHAPTER TEN

BECCA HAD PUT CLOTHES ON. Jeans and a T-shirt. She sat across from Mish, her legs curled underneath her as she gazed at him.

Mish, too, had pulled on his pants. Like her, his feet were bare. The shirt he'd worn last night, the one she'd helped peel off of him, hung open as he gazed down at his bandaged hand and tried his best to answer her questions.

He'd told her about waking up at the homeless shelter, of the old man who'd named him Mission Man, of the way "Mish" had somehow seemed both wrong and right. He'd told her of his confusion and shock at seeing his unfamiliar face in the mirror. He'd tried to put into words what it felt like to remember nothing but trivial details of his past. And he'd apologized again for deceiving her.

She cleared her throat. "Before—you said you had a gun."

He glanced up at her and tried not to think about the way she'd looked, lying back, naked, on her bed. It was crazy. They'd made love twice, last night and early this morning, and he was still dying for her touch. He still wanted more.

Like *that* was ever going to happen again.

He cleared *his* throat. "Yeah. A small handgun. Twenty-two caliber. It was in my boot with the cash and that fax that had the directions to the ranch."

"Where's the gun now?"

"Back at the Lazy Eight. In my private lockup in the bunkhouse. I wasn't comfortable... I didn't think it was appropriate—or even legal—to carry it around."

Becca nodded, trying very hard not to look relieved.

Mish couldn't keep from smiling crookedly. "Makes you nervous, huh?" he asked. "The thought of me walking around with a weapon?"

She answered honestly, glancing involuntarily at the shards of broken mirror that still littered the dresser. "I'm sorry, but, yeah."

"You don't have to apologize. If our roles were reversed—"

"If our roles were reversed, *I* would have already checked myself into a hospital."

Mish shifted back in his chair. "I can't do that."

"Of course you can." She leaned forward. "Mish, I'll go with you. I'll *stay* with you. The doctors will—"

"Call the police," he finished for her. "They'll have to. Bec, I was shot. They'd need to report it." He hesitated. Lord, why not just tell her? He'd already revealed too much. "The truth is, I'm probably someone you wouldn't want to know. I've had these dreams..." Telling her about them in detail would be too much. The awful images already haunted the hell out of him—no need to haunt her as well. "They're...violent. *Really* violent."

"That doesn't mean anything. I've had violent dreams and—"

"No, this is stuff—at least some of it—I know I've seen. I've also dreamed of..." He couldn't look at her. "Prison. I've done hard time, Bec. I can't believe I would dream about it in that kind of detail if I hadn't."

She was silent.

"I think if I dig back and uncover my past, I'm going

to find out that I'm not a very good person," he told her quietly. "So let's go back to the ranch. Maybe if I'm lucky Casey Parker'll be there. I can give him that package that came for him, and ask him what his fax was doing in my boot—maybe find some answers. Then I'll take my things and clear out. And you'll be done with me for good."

Becca pulled her knees in close to her chest, encircling them with her arms.

"Or," he said, "if you'd rather, I'll leave now, find another ride back. I can arrange to be gone before you return on Tuesday."

He could walk out that door in a matter of minutes, and Becca would never see him again. And this was supposed to be something she'd *want?*

She felt her eyes fill with tears, and she blinked them furiously back. She stood up, unable to sit still another moment longer, wishing this room were bigger, knowing that even if it were the size of a stadium, she would be drawn toward him.

"Why didn't you tell me any of this last night?" she asked, forcing herself away from him, moving over toward the window. "We talked for *hours* at that party. I can think of ten different times that you would've had a perfect segue to this subject." She turned to face him. "'Funny you should mention your childhood in New York, Becca, because you know, since a week ago Monday, I can't remember anything about mine. In fact, I couldn't even remember my name until I came to the ranch and you called me Casey Parker…'"

His eyes looked suspiciously red, too. "Would you have believed me?"

"I don't know. I might've, yeah. I believe you now, don't I?"

"I don't know. Do you?"

She let out a burst of air that was nearly a laugh. "No. Yes. I don't know. I think, amnesia? But then I think, it sounds so crazy, it's *got* to be true." She couldn't figure out *why* he would make up this outlandish story. It wasn't to gain sympathy points to get into her bed. He'd already been there.

The truth was, she *did* believe him. She trusted him on a level that went beyond logic. Despite his conviction that he'd been to prison, despite his belief that he was some kind of criminal, Becca trusted him with every fiber of her being. And maybe that was just because of sex. Maybe it was just her hormones blocking all common sense. If love was blind, then lust surely was like being in a sensory deprivation tank.

But when she looked into Mish's eyes, she believed him, whether she wanted to or not.

Maybe he was a con man, maybe he was seriously mentally ill, maybe she was going to get badly burned. But she was damned if she wasn't going to see this through to the end, find the facts that would either prove her wrong and label her a fool, or provide the missing pieces in Mish's past. Either way, she'd come out further ahead than she would by walking away right now.

Or letting him walk away.

Becca turned back to the window, feeling a sense of calm at her decision, feeling the pressure of her impending tears lessen. "I'll call Hazel, tell her to page me if Casey Parker shows up at the ranch again. I'll have her offer him some kind of financial bonus if he'll stick around until we show up."

"He left the ranch?"

She looked up at the perfect blue sky, wondering at the sudden note of interest that rang in his voice. "Hazel said he got out of there pronto. Apparently he was ticked off by the fact that another Casey Parker had been there first." She turned to face him, certain she looked like hell, but grateful that at least she wasn't crying. "I think we should take a drive down to Wyatt City. Check out this shelter, try to talk to the men who brought you in."

Mish looked as emotionally exhausted as she felt. "We?"

"Yeah," Becca said. She crossed her arms so he knew she meant business. "Unless you lied and last night really *was* just a one-night stand."

He shook his head in disbelief. "Becca, didn't you hear anything I said? I'm probably one of the bad guys. I need you to stay away from me."

"Maybe," she said. "But what about what *I* need?"

WYATT CITY WAS AS DUSTY and run-down as Mish remembered it.

Except he only remembered it from the time he walked out of the First Church Shelter to the time he left on the Greyhound to Santa Fe.

It was one of those towns with a Main Street that hadn't had a face-lift since most of the buildings went up back in the late fifties, early sixties. It was crumbling. A true work in progress, as far as ghost towns went.

The old movie theater was boarded up, as was the Woolworth's. Both looked as if they'd gone out of business a decade or two ago, and the space hadn't been rented out since then. A liquor store was doing a thriving business, as was an adult-video rental place, and a bar.

"Have you considered the possibility that you lived here?" Becca spoke for the first time in what seemed like hours. She took a right turn on Chiselm Street, where a row of post–World War II adobe-style houses had been turned into offices. A palm reader. A chiropractor/

masseuse. A tax attorney. A tattoo parlor. "You might have an apartment somewhere in town. Or a room. Or..."

"Yeah," he said. "I guess it *is* a possibility." He didn't want to tell her about his hunch, his sense that he'd come to Wyatt City for a reason. A reason that he didn't know, but couldn't talk about just the same.

"Oh, no!" She pulled to the side of the road and hit the brakes a little too hard. She looked at him, her eyes wide. "You could have a *wife*. You could be *married*."

"I'm not," he told her. "I don't know how I know that, but—"

"You *can't* know it," she told him. "Mish, the only things we absolutely know about you are that you've never learned to ride a horse, you were here in Wyatt City for some reason two weeks ago, and that you aren't Casey Parker."

"If I *am* married..." He shook his head. "No, I know I'm not. I'm always alone. I live alone. And lately I work alone. I don't know how I know that, because I don't even know what it is I do." But he could guess. The list of possibilities was nice and short. Burglar. Thief. Con artist. Assassin.

"But if that's not enough for you," he continued, "then last night..." He squinted as he looked out of the truck's windshield at the setting sun glinting off the still hot street. "I don't know, I guess you probably could tell— it's been a long time for me. Since I was with a woman." He glanced at her, embarrassed to admit it. "Since I even *wanted* to be with a woman."

She laughed, a giddy burst as she tipped her head forward to rest on her folded arms on the steering wheel. "That's very flattering, Mr. I-know-damn-well-I'm-a-sex-god-but-I'll-pretend-to-be-humble, but the fact is, you can't *know* you're not married if you've got amnesia."

"No, there are some things I *do* just know. I know it sounds unbelievable, that I could know what size jeans I wear, but not even recognize my own face in a mirror. It doesn't make any sense, but Becca, I'm telling you, I *know*."

She was peeking out from beneath her arm, and he held her gaze. "And I'm not pretending anything," he added softly. "It *had* been a while for me. I wanted to make love to you all night long, but somehow the night got away from me."

Lord, what was he doing? She was wary of him, wanting to keep her distance. So why was he saying things like that, things that would draw her back into his arms?

Because he wanted her in his arms. And he had absolutely no willpower where this woman was concerned. He *knew* the best place for Becca to be was dozens—hundreds—of miles away from him, yet he couldn't stop himself from wanting to hold her.

She lifted her head, still watching him. He could see the heat of her attraction for him in her eyes, doing battle with her wariness.

He could see paradise lingering there as well, just a kiss and a heartbeat away.

He turned away. "The church is in this neighborhood, not too far from the bus station."

Becca hesitated, but he didn't look over at her again, and finally she put her truck in gear.

"JARELL? HE'S A POPULAR MAN these days," the woman who worked in the church office said with a chuckle. She pulled a file folder from a rickety old cabinet, and flipped through the pages. "He's a volunteer, so I can't guarantee his hours won't change, but let's see…" She frowned. "No, he's not working at the shelter this evening—actually, not until Wednesday night."

"Isn't there any way we could get in touch with him tonight?" Mish asked.

The woman shook her head, smiling apologetically at both Mish and Becca. "I'm sorry, we can't give out personal information about our volunteers. But there's a good chance he'll be in the kitchen tomorrow afternoon. There's a church dinner tomorrow night, and no one can make meat loaf like Jarell. At least not meat loaf for two hundred."

Tomorrow afternoon. Becca looked everywhere but at Mish. If they had to wait until tomorrow afternoon to talk to Jarell, that meant they'd have to spend the night here in Wyatt City.

She stood quietly aside as he thanked the woman, then followed him out of the church and into the hot evening air. They walked in silence until they got to Becca's truck, parked just down the street from the bus station.

Mish turned to face her. "When we left Santa Fe this morning, I didn't think quite as far as tonight. I'm…sorry. I'll pay for the motel rooms."

Rooms. Plural. Did he really want to stay in separate rooms tonight? Was it possible that, unlike her, he hadn't spent the entire day bombarded by vivid memories of sensations from the night before? Could it be that, unlike her, he wasn't dying for the chance for them to kiss again?

All day long, all she wanted was to take him in her arms and kiss him.

Becca closed her eyes. Please, God, let him be right. Have him not be married…

"We should go have dinner and—"

"Does it make sense," Becca interrupted him, trying to

sound matter-of-fact, when in truth her heart was pounding, "to pay for two when we're probably going to end up in one? Rooms," she added, probably unnecessarily.

His eyes looked luminous in the early evening light. "Do you really want that? Even knowing…who I am?"

She reached for his hand. "You say that as if you're convinced you're some kind of monster. Why? Because you were carrying a gun and you don't believe in banks? For all we know, your license to carry that gun was in your wallet, which was stolen. Yeah, the bullet wound on your head is a little harder to explain away, but it *is* possible that you were simply in the wrong place at the wrong time, isn't it?"

"Becca—"

"So, okay, you dreamed of prison. I've rented movies enough times to be able to have pretty vivid dreams of prison, too. Dreams are *dreams,* Mish. They're not the same thing as memories. I sometimes dream that my teeth are falling out. It happens to be a common stress dream, with no basis in reality, fortunately." She took a deep breath. "So, yes, I really want us to get a room. *A* room. A room with a shower, a pizza and a cold six-pack of beer. Let's lock ourselves in and forget about all this for a few hours. You know, for someone with amnesia, you're not very good at forgetting things."

Mish smiled, and her heart leapt. But then his smile faded. "What if it turns out that I'm someone terrible? What if I'm an assassin? A hit man?"

Becca had to laugh. "Only a man would what-if himself into the middle of a Clint Eastwood film. And that guy over there? See him? The one climbing into that van with the tinted windows?" She pointed down the street.

As they watched, a man with short brown hair and a barbed-wire tattoo encircling his upper arm, carrying

a cardboard tray with three large coffees, climbed into
the back of the van. Another man, this one a movie-star-
handsome blond, climbed out.

The blond looked as if he could make a fortune on the
rodeo circuit from just his smile, but he wore sneakers
on his feet instead of cowboy boots, and a baggy pair of
cargo shorts instead of jeans. His shirt hung open, revealing a chest of *Baywatch* quality. He made half circles
with his head, as if relieving the kinks in his neck as he
made his way across the street to the Terminal Bar. It was
named after its proximity to the bus station, no doubt,
rather than its dire medical condition.

"They're not just waiting for the bus from Las Vegas,
for the shorter guy's wife, Ernestina, to return from a visit
to her sister, Inez, who's a dancer at Caesar's. No, they're
probably sitting there, staking out the bus station on the
off chance *you'll* show up. Right?"

Mish looked at the man heading into the bar. His eyes
narrowed, and he looked closer.

"Mish." Becca pulled his chin so that he faced her.
She kissed him lightly on the mouth to get his attention
completely. "What if you're *not* a hit man? What if you're
the UPS man? Or what if you sell washers and dryers
at Sears? Or maybe you're extra-adventurous and you
specialize in overnight fresh fish deliveries to towns like
Las Cruces and Santa Fe?"

He smiled at that, and she unlocked the door to her
truck. "If you want, we can drive around for a little while.
See if anything sparks a memory."

Mish nodded, glancing at the van sitting in front of
the bus station. "Yeah," he said. "I'd like to do that."

Becca climbed into the truck and started the engine,
switching on the air-conditioning right away. God, it
was hot.

Mish swung himself in the passenger's side, picked her beat-up cowboy hat up off the seat between them, and put it on his head, tugging the brim low over his eyes.

And as they drove past the van, he slouched way down in his seat.

"TODAY I AM A VERY FOUNTAIN of information," Wes said as Lucky swung himself back into the van after making a quick pit stop at the Terminal Bar. "The captain called when I was taking a nap. I don't know how he does it, but somehow he always knows when I'm sleeping."

"That's why he's the captain and you're not," Bobby pointed out. "He knows when you are sleeping. He knows when you're awake..."

"What did he say?" Lucky asked. "Did he talk to Admiral Robinson?"

"He knows if you've been bad or good—no, wait," Bobby said. "That's Santa Claus, not Joe Cat." He smiled. "I always get them confused."

"Yeah," Wes said, "they're both so jolly. Well, Santa's jolly. Joe's not. In fact, he's getting pretty fed up and put out by the way the top brass are jerking him around. I don't know how many days running this is that first they tell him, yes, Robinson's on his way, only to call him later and say, no, he's been detained again."

"Any word from Albuquerque?" Lucky asked.

"Crash and Blue reported in. No sign of Mitch," Wes told him. "But he *was* there. At least the shop owner described someone who looks just like him, down to his pretty green eyes."

"That's good," Bobby said. "That's great. He's alive."

"Yeah, but the mystery thickens," Wes reported. "He spent nearly four hundred dollars. Bought himself a nice suit, a coupla shirts, some underwear. Total came to three and change, yet our boy used two of the counterfeit bills with two that were unmarked. What's up with *that?* And why's he buying a suit?"

"A few days ago, I wished I'd brought a suit with us from California," Bobby said. "Because I—"

"Had a date with the supermodel," Wes finished for him. "Yeah, rub it in."

"Okay, so maybe there's a woman involved," Lucky said. "We need to make sure we look at everyone passing by. Mitch could be with a woman."

"Or maybe he was just getting himself a disguise. If *I* wanted to disguise myself," Wes pointed out, "first thing I'd do is buy myself a suit. Make myself look like a business geek. No one would ever recognize me."

Lucky stared out the tinted window at the bus station. Mitchell Shaw was out there. Somewhere. Lucky had had a gut feeling that he'd come back for his "bag of tricks." But maybe he wouldn't. Maybe he and his new suit were long gone, the missing plutonium with him. Maybe the somewhere that Mitch was, was on the other side of the world.

"Did the captain give us any orders?" Lucky asked.

"Sit tight," Wes said. "Just sit tight."

"STOP," MISH SAID. "Bec, stop here!"

Becca slammed on the brakes.

The lengthening twilight was casting odd shadows in an alleyway that was probably poorly lit at best, even at high noon.

Mish climbed down out of the truck and went between two buildings, one brick, one wood. The pavement—what little was left—was pitted and cracked. The scent of rotting garbage filled the air. It was familiar, as was the latticework of the fire escapes that decorated the outside of the brick building.

Mish closed his eyes to see the image of those iron stairs and landings lit by a stormy night sky that flashed with lightning and...

Yes, he had been here before.

He knew without looking that a few steps farther in, behind the Dumpster, was a basement door—once painted a bright red, long since faded by the heat—that stood ajar.

"Mish?" Becca had parked the truck and now followed him.

It was getting darker by the minute, and he moved cautiously past the Dumpster, with its sound of rats scurrying away. He moved closer and...

A basement door.

Ajar.

Faded red.

"I've been here." He was certain now. He turned to Becca. "I remember..."

What? What did he remember?

He closed his eyes. Thunder and lightning. His clothes soaked almost instantly after the downpour started. He'd been following...

Following... Lord, he couldn't remember who he'd been following or why he'd been here.

"I had my weapon drawn." Somehow he knew that. He'd gone down the steps to the basement door, and he'd hidden deep in the shadows, his handgun held ready.

Nothing had moved. Nothing. The storm raged for many long minutes, and still he stood frozen, waiting, watching.

But the man he had followed and was waiting for to return—and it *was* a man—had vanished.

Finally, Mish had crept out. Up those concrete stairs and into the puddles of the alleyway.

Something had made him turn. Some instinct, or perhaps a sound he'd managed to hear beneath the pounding of the rain.

But he'd turned, and lightning flashed, and he saw the face of the man he was after for the briefest split second—before the muzzle flash from the man's handgun exploded his night vision, before the bullet from that weapon knocked him over and out.

He focused everything he had in him on that scrap of memory, on that split-second exposure of a face.

Forty-five to fifty years old, heavy set, graying beard, thinning hair. Small nose in an otherwise puffy face. He'd been up above Mish, on the roof.

Mish scanned the roof, scanned the windows of the brick building. He longed for the feel of a weapon in his hands—not that wimpy little .22 he'd found in his boot and left back at the ranch, but a *real* weapon. A Heckler & Koch MP-5 room broom. Or even an MP-4. Something with a real bite, something that would fit comfortably in his arms.

Then it hit him—he was actually standing here, wishing he had an assault weapon.

An *assault* weapon.

Who the hell was he?

"Mish, are you okay?"

Nothing moved along the roofline now, and Mish could see, even with the rapidly falling shadows, that it had been sheer luck that had enabled the bearded man to get the jump on him. It was also equally sheer luck he hadn't killed Mish.

Or maybe it wasn't luck. Maybe it was just ineptitude. Or amateurishness.

But if the bearded man had been a real shooter, he would've made damn sure he'd finished Mish off before he'd left the scene.

The scuff of a boot against the pavement made him spin around in a defensive crouch and...

Becca.

Her eyes were wide as she gazed at him, as he quickly straightened up.

"What do you remember?" she asked quietly.

"I wasn't here making a delivery for UPS, that's for damn sure."

CHAPTER ELEVEN

"PLEASE," MISH SAID.

His steak was as untouched as her grilled-chicken Caesar salad. Why had they bothered to come to this restaurant anyway, if neither of them intended to eat?

Becca thought wistfully of that pizza and beer she'd hoped to share with him, preferably while naked on a motel-room bed.

"You want me just to leave you here," she repeated. "To go back to the Lazy Eight tonight. Just…that's it? Good luck? So long? You're on your own? Thanks, but I'm no longer needed?"

It had been too many hours since Mish had gotten close to a razor, and with all that stubble on his face, he looked positively dangerous.

Except for his eyes.

Mish's eyes gave him away.

And his eyes told her he wanted her to stay.

But he leaned forward now, to convince her otherwise. "It's not as simple as what I do and don't need, Bec. For all I know, this guy—the man with the beard—is still somewhere around here. In town. Nearby. I don't know. But I *do* know that if I'm his target, I don't want you anywhere near me."

Becca sighed and gave up even toying with her salad. "So we're back in that Clint Eastwood movie, huh?"

"He shot me," Mish said flatly. "He looked at me, he aimed, and he discharged his weapon. And…"

It was her turn to lean across the table. "And *what?*"

He lowered his voice, looking away from her, the muscles in his jaw clenching. When he looked at her again, his eyes were bleak. "And if I had had the chance, I would've aimed and fired my weapon at him."

"Now, is this an actual memory we're talking about, or is this another of those things you just somehow *know?*"

"I'm sure you're very funny, but I don't happen to find any of this humorous," he said tightly.

She reached for his hand. "I don't mean to be such a smartass, I just…" She exhaled noisily. "Mish, I don't want to get in my truck and just leave you here. *I* still haven't given up on the UPS-man scenario."

He squeezed her hand slightly before he let her go, his eyes dark with regret. "I would have shot him, Bec," he said quietly. "And yes, that's a solid memory."

Odd, that part seemed to have been edited out of the version he'd first told her, after they'd left the alley and gotten back in her truck. Becca tapped her fingers on the table. "What else do you remember from that night?"

"I was carrying my .45—I don't know what happened to it. It must've been stolen with my wallet. The .22 in my boot was just a backup, but…I remember wishing I had an MP-5."

"MP-5?"

"Heckler & Koch MP-5," he told her grimly. "It's a German-made assault weapon. A machine gun. It's called a room broom, because you use it at a relatively short range to clear a room."

"Clear a room?" She was starting to sound like a parrot.

Mish nodded. "Yeah, it means just what it sounds like." He gripped his water glass tightly as he brought it to his mouth and took a sip.

"I have this recurring dream where I'm in a room," he told her. "Locked in with these other people. The door bursts open, and these men come in carrying assault weapons. There's a struggle, and one of the weapons—it's an Uzi. God, how do I know the names of these things?" He took a deep breath and when he spoke again, his voice was matter-of-fact. "In the struggle, an Uzi is kicked toward me, and I pick it up, and I use it to clear the room of the men with the weapons. One sweep with my finger on the trigger, and I kill them all. That's what it means to clear a room."

Becca shook her head, refusing to believe that could have happened—at least not as emotionlessly as he made it sound. "Mish, I know you're trying to prove that you're a terrible person, but you should hear some of *my* dreams. There's this one where I'm in a furniture store and—"

"I recognized the men in that van today," Mish told her.

That...van? She didn't say the words aloud, but she was certain they echoed on her face.

"The one with the tinted windows. Parked by the bus station?" he clarified. "I don't know where I know them from—both the shorter man with the tattoo and the man with the light-colored hair—but I definitely know them from somewhere."

Becca didn't understand. "Why didn't you say something to them? Approach them, find out who they are? Maybe find out who *you* are?"

"They were definitely running some kind of surveillance," Mish told her. "And I know you were joking this afternoon, but it's possible they are looking for me."

"Surveillance?" Becca was incredulous. "How could you know *what* they were doing in that van? You couldn't see inside. I'm sorry, Mish, but—"

"I didn't have to see inside. I knew there were three men, even though I didn't see more than two—because Tattoo brought three cups of coffee with him. Three *large* cups, which I took to mean they were planning to stay awhile. Blondie shook his muscles out when he got out of the van—they'd obviously already been there for some time. So long, in fact, he was in a rush to get into the bar and use the head."

"Use the...? What's a *head?*"

"Men's room," he said. "Lav. It's called a head on a ship." He rolled his eyes. "Great. Now I'm a sailor."

Becca laughed. She couldn't help herself.

Mish smiled, too, but it faded far too quickly. "Becca, go home."

She rested her chin in the palm of her hand, clearly going nowhere. "What if you don't remember anything else?" she asked. "What if the rest of the details of who you were don't ever come back to you?"

Mish shook his head. "I haven't really thought in terms of a worst-case scenario."

"Maybe," she said softly, "not remembering wouldn't necessarily be the worst-case scenario."

He gazed at her for a moment, clearly understanding what she was getting at. He'd thought it himself, many times. If he never pushed to find out the truth, if he just let go of whatever he'd done or been in the past, if he started over, from scratch...

"It would be kind of like being born all over again," Becca continued. "It could be a blessing. If you honestly think you did such terrible things..."

"You make it sound so tempting," he whispered. "But

I'm here. I can't leave Wyatt City without at least talking to Jarell."

"Ah," she said. "There you go. Now you know exactly how *I* feel."

She met his gaze staunchly as he searched her eyes.

After several long moments, he nodded. "All right. I'll get us two rooms for tonight."

He was determined to keep his distance. Becca nodded, too. She'd let him win that battle.

For now.

MISH FLIPPED THROUGH THE TV channels twice more, but it was just like playing a game of solitaire that had run its course. Nothing new or interesting had magically appeared.

An infomercial on selling real estate. A late-night talk show with some actress who had a body like a POW-camp survivor—emaciated and bony and completely unappealing, compared to Becca's soft curves.

Compared to Becca's lush breasts and soft thighs and...

Mish changed the channel, shifting uncomfortably on the bed, refusing to think about Becca, naked in his arms.

The movie channel was showing a romantic comedy about a man who, after only one glimpse of a beautiful young woman, knew that she was his destiny. From what Mish could tell from the few minutes he'd watched earlier, the hero was determined to win the girl's heart by any means, including outright deceit. He lied about his name, his identity, his profession, his past.

Mish watched for a few more minutes before turning off the set in utter disgust. He knew how the movie would end. True love would triumph and the girl would forgive the hero.

But real life didn't work that way. Real life was filled with unmendable hurt, with unforgivable wrongs, with irreparable damage.

And most people didn't get a second chance at *anything*.

He lay back on the bed, aching with an awful emptiness, staring up at the plastered ceiling, knowing full well that he was one of the lucky ones. He'd been given a second chance—a chance to detach himself from all of the wrongs he'd ever done. A chance to start fresh, to live clean, to do right.

So what was he doing? He was lying here, nearly jumping out of his skin, desperate to cross the motel courtyard and knock on the door to room 214.

Becca's room.

She'd wanted to spend the night with him again. She'd told him so. But he'd turned her down, obsessed with the idea of protecting her from himself.

He'd checked them in to their rooms, said good-night, and then he'd taken a long, cold shower. He'd shaved, too, although for what reason, he had no clue. He was here for the night. Alone.

And Becca was in her room. Alone. Way on the other side of the motel complex.

But now he lay here—alone—unable to think about anything but the softness of Becca's lips, the perfect fit of his body to hers, the sparkle of her eyes, the satisfied smile that curled her lips after he...after they...

Oh, Lord. He had to stay away from her. He *had* to.

Mish stood up, unable to keep from pacing. He was unable to stop himself from pacing right over to the TV where his room key sat, pocketing the key and pacing right out the door.

Room 214 was on the other side of the swimming pool, up on the second floor. He found the room without even counting windows—he already knew where it was. Behind the heavy draperies, he could see the glow of her light still on. She was awake.

Okay, he'd go over and knock on the door, ask her if she wanted to meet at the Waffle House for breakfast in the morning.

Mish crossed the courtyard, went up the stairs. He could hear the sound of a radio playing from inside room 214, heard Becca singing along. She had a sweet voice, low and musical.

He stood, leaning his head against her door, listening to her sing, and he knew without a doubt that he hadn't come here to talk about breakfast.

He'd come to stay until breakfast.

He couldn't do it. Try as he might, he couldn't stay away from her. Try as he might, he wasn't worthy of this second chance he'd miraculously been given.

Because here he was, yet again, right on schedule, giving in to temptation, choosing to do wrong instead of right.

He didn't know his name, but he knew with a gut-clenching certainty that before this was through, he was going to hurt this woman.

How hard could it be *not* to knock on her door? All he had to do was put his hands in his pockets or behind his back. And then he had to turn away, not think about the fact that she would probably greet him with a kiss, pull him into her room, surround him with the sweet scent of her freshly washed hair, the paralyzing softness of her smooth, clean skin. She would fall back on her bed with him, wrap herself around him and…

Mish couldn't turn away. And he couldn't keep his hands behind his back. He lifted one, about to rap loudly right next to the sign that said 214, but he never got the chance.

The door opened.

And Becca stood there, wearing cutoff jeans and a halter top that showed off a pair of smooth, bare shoulders that looked too damned good even when covered by a perspiration-stained T-shirt. She was carrying an open pint of ice cream, a plastic spoon stuck in the top.

"Mish! You startled me!" She was surprised to see him. And pleased. *Very* pleased.

"Yeah," he said, jamming his hands into his pockets and taking a step back from the door far too late. "Hi. Sorry. I realized we never talked about the morning. I didn't want to wake you up too early if you wanted to sleep in and…"

And she knew exactly why he was standing there, knew it had nothing to do with making plans for the morning. Mish could see her awareness in her smile, in the warmth of her eyes.

"I was just coming down to your room," she told him. She held out the ice cream. "I thought maybe you might want to share this with me. It's so hot tonight, and…"

And she'd intended to come to his room and share more than ice cream. He knew that, too. And she knew he knew…

"They were all out of cones," she said, "but I figured we could just spread it on ourselves. Take turns licking each other clean…?"

Mish laughed. He couldn't help himself.

"So," Becca said, her lower lip caught between her

teeth as she tried not to smile. "Are you coming in, or what?"

He was coming in. She knew it and he knew it. Mish lost himself in her eyes. "Why can't I stay away from you?" he whispered.

"Why would you want to?" she countered just as softly.

And as she reached for his hand and tugged him gently into her room, closing and locking the door behind them, Mish couldn't remember why he'd even considered staying away. She set the ice cream down on top of the motel television and he drew her into his arms. As she melted against him, he slowly lowered his mouth to hers and then, if he hadn't had amnesia already, he would have contracted a full-blown case of it right then as he lost himself completely in the sheer sweetness of her kiss.

As Mish kissed her, Becca tugged him toward the bed, afraid that he might come to his senses and walk out the door. She knew he was afraid of hurting her. She knew he wouldn't quite believe her even if she told him again that she wasn't looking for more than a low-maintenance, high-passion, short-term love affair. At this point, she wouldn't quite believe herself.

Last night had been incredible, even with the secrets that had hung between them. Tonight promised to be even more amazing.

Except tonight, she was the one with the secrets.

Mish's fingers were gentle as he worked to loosen the knots in her halter. His eyes were as warm as his hands as he pulled her top free. And as he drew in a sharp breath at the sight of her bare breasts, he made her feel like the most beautiful, most sexy woman in the world.

He touched her gently with his mouth and his hands, taking his time to look at her, to really take her in.

Becca tugged at the hem of his T-shirt, trying to pull it up, and he yanked it over his head. And then she was touching him, too, sliding her palms across his gorgeous tanned muscles, kissing him just as lightly, taking her time to look at him as well.

The bruise on his side was starting to fade. His muscles were amazingly well-defined, as if he had stepped out of an anatomy textbook. Or a J. Crew catalog. Arms, shoulders, pecs, he was sheer perfection right down to the six-pack of muscles that made up his abdomen.

But his eyes were as soft as his body was hard. And it was his eyes that held her captive.

All night long, he'd told her this afternoon. He'd wanted to make love to her all night long.

He lowered his head and lightly touched the tip of her breast with his tongue as he found and slowly unfastened the top button of her shorts.

All night long...

Becca pulled his mouth to hers and kissed him just as slowly, languidly, leisurely drinking him in.

It was as if the entire world had gone into slow motion, and with that, all of her senses had heightened.

She could hear the sound of their quiet breathing, the sound of her zipper being pulled down, tantalizingly slowly. She could feel the slightly calloused roughness of his fingers against her skin. The delicious chill of the conditioned air against the tongue-wetted tips of her breasts. The satin-over-steel silkiness of his back beneath her hands. The baby-smoothness of his cheeks against her face...

He'd shaved for her. He'd come to her reluctantly after trying for hours to keep his distance. And yet, he'd recognized the futility of his resistance enough to shave before coming to her room.

It was silly, really. That he'd shaved was no big deal.
It was simple consideration. A small sign of kindness, of
caring, yet it brought all of her emotions bubbling to the
surface.

He *cared*. She knew without a doubt that he desired
her, but to know that he *cared*...

Becca was in too deep. She was in serious trouble, if
the fact that this man had shaved for her was enough to
bring tears of joy to her eyes. But she couldn't stop what
she was feeling. It was far too late.

She was falling in love with this man without a name.
She was completely enthralled with the gentle warmth
of his eyes, with the way he truly listened whenever she
spoke, with the fact that despite the absolute goodness
that seemed to shine from within him, he was *not* an
angel. Despite his good intentions, he was drawn to her
as completely and powerfully as she was drawn to him.
And try as he might, as much as he wanted otherwise,
he hadn't been able to stay away.

He drew her shorts and her panties slowly down her
legs, and she took close to forever to help him rid himself
of his jeans. Then, skin against skin, she touched him,
breathed him, kissed him, completely on fire, yet preferring this slow, intense burn to a white-hot flash of flame
that would end far too soon.

No, she didn't want this to end.

She had no idea what tomorrow would bring, and
more than half hoped this Jarell from the homeless
shelter would provide no answers to Mish's many questions. His talk of machine guns had made her uneasy.
Those were the weapons used by the survivalists who
lived in military-style compounds in the mountains.
They were all-or-nothing organizations and Becca had

no desire to join one—no matter how desperately she loved this man.

Oh, yes, she loved him desperately. How could she have let that happen?

When she first asked him to have dinner, she'd imagined she'd love him just a little. A safe amount. Enough to justify giving in to this intense physical attraction, but not so much that she would feel this shortness of breath, this lack of control.

She'd wanted a brief entanglement with a handsome stranger. True, she'd wanted more than shallow sex, but she'd wanted nowhere near this Grand Canyon of emotional attachment.

But it was okay. It was going to be okay, because there was no way in hell Mish was going to fall in love with her. Becca could deal with a one-sided love affair. What she *couldn't* handle was hoping against hope that she had, in fact, at long last, found true love.

Because despite how much she hoped, true love didn't exist. And she and Mish would part, just later rather than sooner. And crushed hope was far worse than no hope at all.

Mish pulled back from their endless kiss, their languorous embrace, and as she gazed into his eyes, her heart twisted in her chest.

"I want you," she whispered, knowing he would misunderstand, but needing to say it, say *something*, all the same.

He kissed her again, then reached across her for the condoms she'd left on the nightstand. She closed her eyes, pressing herself against him, feeling the hard length of his heat parting her, dangerously close to penetration. She was more than ready for him, in every possible way.

It had to be biological—some kind of nesting instinct that was kicking in as her thirtieth birthday approached.

He pulled away from her to cover himself, and she resisted the urge to cling to him. She knew he would be back in a matter of moments. Still, she would use this as practice for the real thing, for when they would part for good.

He held her gaze as he came back to her, as he joined her in one slow, perfect thrust.

It was too good, too perfect, and Becca pulled him to her and kissed him, afraid of what he might see if he looked too close.

She shut her eyes and loved him.

All night long.

CHAPTER TWELVE

"Mr. Haymore?"

"Only folks call me Mr. Haymore be bill collectors and magazine salesmen." The tall African-American man stood at one of the sinks in the church kitchen. His back was to Mish and Becca, but he didn't turn around. He kept right on washing stalks of celery as he spoke. "If you're here on that sort of business, you might as well just walk right back out the door. You'll have to catch me some other time. But if you're here for something friendlier, call me Jarell, wash your hands and roll up your sleeves. I could use some help chopping this celery. Got two hundred forty people to feed tonight, and time's wasting."

Mish moved to the next sink over and started washing his hands. "Jarell. I spent the night at the shelter here two weeks ago. Do you remember me by any chance?"

Jarell's face broke into an enormous smile. "Well, I'll be! If it isn't Mission Man! Mish! You are looking *good,* my man! Out of uniform, but still doggone *good!* Staying clean, I'll wager." He held out a big wet hand for Mish to shake, then pulled him in for an embrace. "Glory be, it *is* a good day!"

"Out of uniform...?" The words had a strangely familiar ring to them.

"Yeah, you're here for your jacket, aren't you? I'm afraid it's pretty badly stained, though, and..." Jarell caught sight of Becca as he released Mish. "Hey, who's this?"

"Becca Keyes," Mish told him. "A…friend of mine."

She met his eyes briefly in acknowledgment of his hesitation, and he felt a wave of heat as a vivid memory of the night before flashed through him as clear as day. He could see Becca shattering as she sat astride him, head thrown back, breasts taut with desire as he, too, exploded in perfect slow motion. Friend, yes, but friend wasn't a big enough word for what she was to him. Except *lover* didn't quite cover the intensity of their relationship, either.

Jarell wiped his hands on a towel before enveloping Becca in a welcoming hug.

"Did I leave…a jacket here?" Mish asked.

"I knew you'd be back for it." Jarell picked up a knife and set to work chopping celery. "You were pretty out of it the morning you left. You were wearing it when you came in, along with a shirt, but they were both soaking wet so Max and I took 'em off you so as you wouldn't catch a chill. I apologize for not reminding you of that in the morning, although, like I said, I'm pretty sure the jacket's ruined." He set down the knife and wiped his hands again as he headed toward the office door. "I'll get that for you."

"Thank you," Mish said. His jacket. And a shirt. He had no idea what they would look like, but maybe—just maybe—they would trigger more memories.

Becca touched his hand. "Don't expect too much," she said softly.

He forced a smile. "I never do."

"Here you go," Jarell said, coming back into the room, carrying a plastic grocery bag. "If you get it cleaned, it'll keep you warm at least. Not that you're needing to stay warm with this heat wave we've been having."

Mish took the bag from Jarell, glancing inside. The jacket was black. From what he could tell, a plain suit jacket. Nothing special, nothing strange. He felt a rush of disappointment. Still, maybe Jarell could provide some other information.

Becca had picked up a knife and started chopping celery, earning one of Jarell's million-dollar smiles. Mish was afraid he'd cut off a finger if he tried to help, afraid his hands were actually shaking. Please, Lord, let him either find some answers or the peace to live with never knowing the truth....

"I was wondering," Mish said, "if that one night was the only time I stayed at the shelter, or..." He cleared his throat. "I know this sounds awful, but I was wondering if I spent the night here any time before that."

Jarell blew out a stream of air as he began cutting celery again. "Whew, it was a bad one, huh? Mish, I can't tell you how often I've seen it happen. A good man gives in to the temptation, takes a drink and ends up on a binge, God knows where." He laughed ruefully. "Then he spends the rest of his life unable to reclaim those days of blackout, always wondering just where he was and what kind of trouble he got into while he was gone." He sighed again. "As far as I was aware, the first time you used a bed at the First Church Shelter was the only time. The night you were brought in was my fifth night on in a row. Rico's brother got arrested down in Natchez, and I was covering for him, working more nights than usual. So unless you were drinking hard for more than a week, and sleeping somewhere else, which of course is entirely possible..." His eyes were dark with sympathy. "How many days of blackout you trying to recall?"

Becca was watching him, and Mish glanced at her only

briefly. He liked Jarell, but the truth made him uncomfortably vulnerable. He didn't want to tell anyone about his amnesia. "Too many," he answered vaguely.

"Hmm." Jarell frowned down at his celery. "Is it good news or bad news if I tell you a couple of men were in here a few days ago, flashing your picture around, looking for you?"

Damn. "One of them have barbed wire tattooed around his biceps?" Mish asked, managing to sound matter-of-fact. "Other one blond, dresses like he comes from California?"

"Barbed-wire tattoo, yes," Jarell said.

Becca exclaimed softly, and Mish looked up to see her nursing her finger where she'd nicked it with the knife.

"But his friend was Native American. Big man. Dark hair. Quiet. Reminded me of Chief from *Cuckoo's Nest.*" Jarell gestured with his head toward the sink. "Run it under cold water," he advised Becca. He glanced back at Mish. "They also wanted to know if you'd been here more than just one night. They seemed friendly enough…"

"But…?"

"But dangerous," Jarell admitted. "It was just a hunch, a gut feeling, but they were the kind of guys you'd want to make sure were playing on your team. Whether the game's softball or something else, you wouldn't want 'em to be part of the opposition." He paused. "You want to leave a message in case they come back?"

"No," Mish said. "Thanks, but I know where to find them."

"You want me to tell 'em you've been here if they come back, asking, or…?" The old man's eyes were knowing. He'd done his share of hard, harsh living.

Mish shook his head. "I'd appreciate if it you could

forget to mention we were here, but I wouldn't want to ask you to lie."

Jarell smiled. "Wouldn't have to lie. I'd just have to start spouting scripture. I'm sure you know what would happen then. They'd be done with their questions soon enough."

Mish laughed. "I'd appreciate it."

"No problem, my man."

Mish glanced inside the bag again. He wanted to examine the jacket and shirt more closely, but not here. Somewhere more private. Like maybe back in Becca's motel room. Maybe after they'd pulled the curtains and spent an hour or two naked....

He was staring at her. And she was gazing back at him, trepidation in her eyes.

She hadn't truly believed him when he'd told her about recognizing the men in the van. But she did now. And now she was realizing that—what had she called it?—this Clint Eastwood thing wasn't a movie, but was, in fact, Mish's real life.

Mish pulled his gaze away from her, and forced a smile in Jarell's direction, holding out his hand again. "Thank you so much. For everything."

Jarell slapped him five. "You're welcome so much. I'm glad I could be of help."

Mish opened the door to the parking lot and stepped back, waiting for Becca to go first.

"Just remember," Jarell called after them. "One day at a time, Father. Just one day at a time."

"FATHER?" BECCA SAID. Had Jarell just called Mish *Father?*

Outside the church kitchen, the early-afternoon sun seemed brain-searingly bright. Mish was scanning the surrounding neighborhood, as if searching for any sign of the tattooed man or his friends from the surveillance van. God, could those men really be looking for Mish?

Mish shook his head, obviously distracted. "He's full of weird nicknames."

She unlocked the passenger side door to her truck, then crossed around the front. "Why did he call you Mission Man?"

Mish reached across the cab to unlock her door. "I don't know." He glanced down at the bag he was holding before he went back to scanning the world outside the truck's windshield. "Do you mind if we go back to the room?"

"So we can pull the curtains and hide?" she wondered aloud as she started the truck and pulled out of the parking lot. "Mish, maybe you should just walk up to these guys, find out who they are and why they're looking for you."

He was silent, unwilling to give her a long list of reasons why approaching these men could be a terrible mistake. It was possible they had been sent to fix the bearded man's botched job. Maybe they would grab him, pull him into the van, drive him someplace isolated and pop him—plug two bullets into the back of his head. It was also possible that before they did that, they'd take him somewhere isolated and ask him questions he couldn't possibly answer, no matter the pain they inflicted upon him. And wouldn't *that* be fun?

But the thought that they might get their hands on Becca and threaten her safety to get him to talk made his blood run cold.

"Or maybe," Becca said, "we should just get our things, check out of the motel and go back to the Lazy Eight. You can work for me as long as you want to—as long as you need to. If you want, I could teach you how to care for the horses. I could teach you to ride. I could—" She broke off, as if suddenly aware of how desperate she sounded. "I like you, and care about you," she tried to explain. "You know that. I haven't exactly tried to hide that from you. All I'm saying is that if you *do* want to put whatever this is behind you, I'm here to do whatever I can to help."

Mish felt a rush of emotion that pressed behind his eyes and made his chest feel constricted. *I'm here...* He didn't have to be alone in this—he *wasn't* alone. Yet at the same time, he felt this odd mixture of disappointment and relief because she hadn't told him that she loved him. The disappointment didn't make sense—he was already terrified of hurting her, terrified of getting her inextricably involved in any of this, of putting her into physical danger.

And heaven help them both if she decided that she loved him....

"Thanks," he told her. "I just...I want to look at this jacket and shirt before I decide what my next move is going to be."

"I don't suppose there's a name tag sewn inside the jacket?" Becca laughed. "Probably not. It's probably been a few years since your mother sent you to summer camp."

Mish couldn't manage more than a wan smile. "Look, Bec, I know you need to get back to the ranch—"

"I can call Hazel, find out what the guest load is like, find out if I can take a few more days. Last I knew, the week was only lightly booked, so unless we've had a party check in at short notice, I won't need to get back right away."

She pulled into the motel lot and parked near her room,

turning to look at him almost challengingly. "Unless you still want me to leave."

Mish got out of the truck, unwilling to sit there on display, where anyone could see them. "I don't want you caught in the cross fire. If someone's gunning for me—"

"Then let's both leave Wyatt City." Becca had to run to catch up with him. "Right now."

He unlocked the door, and they stepped into the room.

It was welcomingly cool and soothingly dark after the harsh brightness of the afternoon heat. They'd left a do-not-disturb sign on the door, and the bedcovers were still rumpled from the night before, the colorful wrappers from the condoms they'd used still scattered on the floor.

Mish locked the door behind them, aware that they'd also locked the door the night before, aware that he wanted her again, just as badly as he'd wanted her last night.

More so.

And she knew it, too. She kissed him lightly, brushing both her lips and body against him in a message that was impossible to miss. And in case he *did* miss it, she said, "Why don't we wait to leave until tonight? We can take our time, take a nap—maybe catch a few hours of sleep."

Mish caught her, pulling her tightly against him, kissing her hard, letting her feel what she did to him. "Sleep?"

Becca smiled, glad he was no longer trying to ignore the attraction that sparked and ignited between them with little more than eye contact. "I did say *maybe*. But...first things first."

She pulled away from him, picking up the plastic

grocery bag from where it had slipped out of his hands and taking it to the little table by the window. "Oh, *this* is what I smell." She pulled the jacket out, held it up. It was stiff, encrusted with mud, stained and spotted. And it smelled *bad*. "Wow, if you smelled even slightly like this when you woke up in the shelter, I've got your nickname figured out. Jarell wasn't calling you Mission Man, he was calling you *E*mission Man."

She handed the jacket to Mish, who winced. "Whoa, man! I'm sorry—I can take this outside if you want."

"I can handle it. I work with horses," she reminded him as she pulled the shirt out of the bag. "You know, I was kidding about the name tags sewn in, but sometimes cleaners stencil part or even all of a customer's name onto the tail of a shirt."

Yet there was nothing there. The white shirt itself was unsalvageable, permanently stained dark brown in places from blood. Mish's blood.

He'd been shot and left for dead, bleeding in an alley. The thought made her a little light-headed.

"Check the pockets of the jacket," she told him, trying to sound as if searching articles of clothing for any identifying marks was something she did every day. "I didn't check the pockets."

"Empty," he reported. "But…"

Something in his voice made her turn toward him.

"I think there's something sewn into the lining. Here at the hem."

He held it out to her, and sure enough, there *was* something hard in there. Something small, but something that didn't bend.

"I have a Swiss army knife in my bag," she told him, but he'd already torn the lining open.

It was a key. An oversized key that might unlock a

hotel room or a locker, with the number imprinted right on it: 101.

Mish tore the lining completely out of the jacket, but there was nothing else hidden there. No notes, no messages, no nothing.

As Becca watched, Mish hefted the key in his hand. "How much do you want to bet this key fits one of the lockers at the bus station?" He sounded so grim, considering they'd just found a major clue.

"But that's great," Becca said. "Isn't it?"

He didn't say anything, and she realized, *bus station*. The men in the van had been parked outside of the bus station. Was it possible they knew Mish had something— a suitcase, a duffel bag—stashed in one of the lockers? Obviously, from the look on his face, Mish thought it was.

He picked up the plastic bag, ready to stuff the ripped jacket and shirt back in, but Becca could tell from the way he was holding the bag that there was something else still inside. He pulled it out. Like the shirt, at one time it had been white and…

Mish stared at it.

Becca stared at it, too, reaching behind her for the bed. She had to sit down. "Is that…yours?" she asked inanely. Of course it was his. He'd been wearing it. It was stained with his blood.

She'd never seen one up close before, but there was no doubt in her mind as to what it was. A liturgical collar. Some kind of clip-on version. The kind that a priest would wear.

A *priest*.

With any other man, Becca might have laughed at the absurdity of the joke, but with Mish, it just was possible.

And it all suddenly made sense. His quiet watchfulness. His compassion, his gentleness. His ability to listen.

Jarell had known, and had called him *Father*.

Mish looked stunned. "No," he said with conviction. But then he added a whole lot less certainly, "I don't think…"

He sat down next to her.

On the bed.

On the bed where they'd made love last night and again this morning and—oh, God, what had they done?

"Well," Becca said shakily, "I guess you were right about not having a wife." She laughed, but it was border-line hysterical and tears filled her eyes. She closed them tightly, forcing herself not to lose it. However upsetting this was for her, it had to be ten times worse for Mish. "Let's go to the bus station, find out if this key does fit one of the lockers. Okay? Let's go right now, see what's in there."

She didn't know what else they would find. God, what had she done?

"It doesn't make sense," Mish said, as if he hadn't even heard her. "If I'm a…" He took a deep breath. "I'm not. I *know* I'm not. Because why would I have a gun in my boot? How could I know so much about weapons and ordnance and… What about all this money I'm carrying? No. I'm not. I'm—"

"If you are a…priest…" She had trouble saying it, too. "*I'm* the one responsible for making you break your vows. I seduced you. This isn't your fault, it's *mine*." Try as she might to be tough, she couldn't fight her tears. They escaped and she dissolved. "Oh, Mish, I'm so sorry."

"Hey." Mish put his arms around her, pulling her close as she cried. "Shhh. Bec. This is going to be okay. I promise. Even if I *am* a…" He took a deep breath and let it out in a burst. "Look, what we've shared was amazing. It wasn't wrong. It was special and perfect and… It was a gift, Becca—something most people don't ever get to experience. And no matter what I find out about myself, I'm not going to regret it. I refuse to regret it. Not ever."

She lifted her head and gazed up at him, her face wet. And Mish's stomach twisted. Lord help him, he hated that he'd made her cry. "Do you remember *anything* about—"

He cut her off. "Bec, it's blank. I swear. If I remembered anything at all about *any* of this, about *anything,* I would've told you by now." He laughed ruefully. "I can't even remember the last time I went to church."

"You tried to stay away from me. On some level you must've known." Fresh tears flooded her eyes. "And I just wouldn't let up. I wouldn't take no for an answer."

"It's okay," he said desperately. "Please, don't cry. This *is* going to be okay."

"How can it be okay?" she asked quietly, "when I'm still dying to kiss you?"

Mish couldn't answer. All words deserted him. But he *knew* that—as much as he wanted to—covering her trembling mouth with his would not be an appropriate response in this situation.

But for several long seconds, as he gazed down into her eyes, he teetered on the edge.

Becca yanked herself away from him, out of his arms and halfway across the room.

"I'm in love with you, dammit," she told him fiercely, turning to face him, to glare at him. "How is *that* going to be okay?"

MISH WATCHED THE VAN FROM the roof of Jerry's Tire Center through a pair of binoculars he'd picked up at

Target, the last remaining department store in the dying town.

The van was still parked near the bus station.

And inside the bus station, through the window, Mish could see a row of beat-up lockers. Locker number 101 was down near the floor, four from the right end, about two and a half feet high and a foot and a half wide. The men in the van—Tattoo, California and the Native American man—had an unobstructed view of it.

Coincidence? Maybe. But Mish wasn't going to take that chance.

He had to get what was inside of that locker without getting caught. But how?

Create a diversion simply by walking by and letting the surveillance team get a clear view of his face? Lead them on a chase while Becca went into the bus station with the key and...

No. What if there were more of 'em? What if someone else was watching locker 101, too? Mish wouldn't risk putting Becca into that kind of potential danger. No way. Uh-uh. No thanks.

She loved him.

Mish couldn't remember the last time he'd felt both hot and cold simultaneously, the way he'd felt when Becca had let that little bomb drop. He couldn't remember ever both wanting and not wanting something—some*one*—quite so badly.

He had to get whatever was inside that locker. Now, more than ever, he *had* to find out the truth about himself.

He was going to have to evade the surveillance team in the van on his own.

And he knew just how to do it.

Funny, he knew all sorts of breaking-and-entering

tricks. He knew how to move silently, knew how to evade capture and escape detection.

But try as he might, he couldn't remember any but the simplest of prayers.

He was no priest.

But he just might be the devil.

CHAPTER THIRTEEN

LUCKY SAT IN THE VAN, drinking what seemed like his fourteenth cup of coffee in the past four hours, working hard to stay alert.

That was the hardest part of standing watch or doing surveillance. Staying not only awake but attentive.

He ran disaster scenarios—it was called war-gaming. He planned, down to the exact detail, what he would do should Lt. Mitchell Shaw suddenly appear, walking down the street. He planned what he'd do if Mitch just instantly appeared at locker 101.

He planned for Mitch to come exploding down from the low-hung, sound-deadening ceiling tiles, for him to grab his bag from the locker and be yanked by a rope back up to the bus station roof.

And he planned for his next phone call from Joe Cat.

Lucky had arranged today's schedule so that Bobby would come and relieve him in enough time for him to dash back to the motel and be ready and waiting for the captain's phone call.

With luck, Admiral Robinson would have arrived in California, and this entire mess would be cleared up with some simple explanation. Mitchell Shaw was following Gray Group procedures for going deep undercover— procedures that the admiral had failed to tell the captain about before he left. The possibilities were limitless.

And then he and Bobby and Wes could get the hell out of this dust bowl, and get back to the ocean. After this, they all deserved a silver-bullet assignment. Something that involved a lot of scuba diving in a location that looked a lot like Tahiti with crowds of beautiful women...

"Movement inside," Wes droned. "Heading directly for our locker."

The approaching woman had the shuffling, painfully slow walk of someone who carried seventy-five unnecessary pounds on legs that were getting too old to support that much excess weight. She was wearing a blue dress that hung down almost all the way to the floor from a rear end the size of a VW Bug. She wore ankle socks with a little lace trim and a beat-up pair of running shoes. She had a baseball cap on her head, straggly dark hair coming out the back, and she wore enough makeup to win first-runner-up in the Tammy Faye look-alike contest. She carried a black plastic trash bag—the ultimate in high-fashion luggage.

As Lucky watched, she did a U-turn away from the lockers and he felt himself relax. She went to the Greyhound counter instead and bought a ticket, taking her money from a bejeweled change purse and counting it out painstakingly slowly.

Ticket in hand, she struggled her way to the hard plastic chairs near the pay phones and wedged her enormous rear end into one of the seats.

There was no one else around. The next bus—the 4:48 daily to Albuquerque—wouldn't be ready to board for another twenty-five minutes.

Lucky swore aloud. "I actually know the daily bus schedule," he said when Wes looked up.

"I do, too." Wes grimaced. "Guess we could always get a job here in the event of more military cutbacks."

"Oh, sure," Lucky said. "I'm already looking forward to coming back to Wyatt City—but only after I'm *dead,* thanks. How can people live without an ocean?"

In the bus station, the woman with the trash bag pushed herself up and out of her seat.

"Got me," Wes said. "Speaking of the ocean, mind if I hop out and take a leak?"

The woman headed toward the lockers, directly toward number 101, and parked herself right in front of them. Her derriere was so incredibly *grande,* Lucky couldn't see what the hell she was doing there.

He swore again. "Wait," he told Wes. "I've got to get a closer look."

"At *her?* I'm sorry, I'm sure she's a very nice lady, but she's not exactly Mitch Shaw's type. I mean, we're supposed to keep our eyes out for someone he'd buy a new suit for. Someone he'd possibly sell out his country for and—"

"Wait here, because she's blocking our view," Lucky ordered, already out of the van. "I'll be right back." He headed toward the doors to the bus station, feeling every muscle in his body screaming from lack of exercise.

He walked past the lockers, past the heavy woman, into the middle of the room, then spun in a full circle, as if he'd come in and was now searching for someone. Of course there was no one around. Even the ticket-counter clerk had disappeared into the back.

Lucky moved toward the woman. "Excuse me, ma'am. Have you seen a woman with a baby?" He gave her his best sheepish grin. "I was supposed to pick 'em up an hour ago, and time just kind of got away from me."

Everything was cool. He could see as he got closer that the old woman was taking what looked like dirty laundry and a collection of old magazines from her Hefty bag and storing it in locker number 99. It was down low, right next to 101—which was still tightly shut and locked.

The woman looked at him and shook her head.

Blue eye shadow. Who the hell had ever invented blue eye shadow? Lucky didn't mind it so much when it was applied sparingly, but this woman's eyelids were nearly neon. And the fact that her face was powdered an almost solid pink sure as hell didn't help.

And hey, she smelled as if she hadn't bathed in about four months. Imagine winning the bad-luck lottery and riding in a bus all the way to Albuquerque next to that magic.

Lucky took a step back.

"No, sorry. Haven't seen anyone." She sounded as if she'd smoked three packs of Marlboros a day for most of her seventy years.

"That's okay," Lucky said, backing away. "That's... fine. Thanks anyway."

He pushed his way out the door, taking a deep lungful of the hot air reflecting off the sidewalk. It didn't smell too fresh either, but it was a definite improvement over what had last invaded his nostrils.

He climbed into the van and turned the air-conditioning up to maximum. "You can go on, hit the head," he told Wes. "She's just a bag lady."

"I coulda told you that." Grumbling, Wes left through the back door.

Through the windshield, through the bus station window, Lucky watched the aromatic woman close the locker, carefully pocket the key and shuffle toward the ladies' room.

And once again, nothing in the bus station moved.

Wes came back in one-point-four minutes, carrying several cans of cold soda, bless him.

The stinky bag lady didn't emerge from the ladies' room for another twenty-three minutes.

When she finally did, she was still carrying her plastic trash bag. She worked her way back to the lockers and planted herself in front of locker 99 again. She worked her magic, fussing with the trash bag for many long minutes.

Finally, when the 4:48 was starting to board, she moved away from the lockers, shuffling with her plastic bag toward the bus, leaving locker 99 empty and open behind her.

It could probably use a good airing out.

As Lucky watched, the woman went out the big glass back door and disappeared around the side of the waiting bus. He could see the bus shake slightly, and he could imagine her hauling herself up, one step at a time, trash bag clutched in her hands.

It was still early. There would be about ten or fifteen minutes before two or three people would make the last-minute dash for the bus.

Lucky settled back in his seat.

"So. Figured out what you're getting Ellen for a wedding gift yet?" Wes asked, clearly bored out of his mind.

"Yeah," Lucky said grimly. "I'm getting her an appointment with a psychologist because anyone who gets married at her age is obviously insane."

"Ah," Wes said. And wisely, he fell into silence.

Twelve minutes passed, each one endlessly long and desperately boring.

Lucky watched the lockers, watched the bus station, forcing himself to stay awake, to stay in battle-ready mode, war-gaming all the scenarios all over again. Of course, if *he* were Mitch, he'd wait until dark to show up. If he were Mitch…

There they came. A station wagon filled with young women. Three were going to Albuquerque, two were staying behind. Lucky watched as they bought tickets in a flurry of movement and chaos and big hair. Hugs. Kisses. Waving, the three travelers disappeared around the side of the bus, climbed on and…

It was only a matter of seconds before they came back into the station.

Lucky was too far away to read their lips, but their expressions and gestures as they spoke to their friends were obvious. They didn't like the way the 4:48 smelled.

Back to the desk, back to the clerk. Pointing toward the bus, talking, talking.

The ticket clerk shook his head, shrugged, pointed to the bus driver, a handsome young Mexican-American man who smiled at the women. And just like that, the mood changed from indignant to a little less uptight. Everyone flirted a little bit. The women explained about the smell—complete with the gestures, but with smiles, too, this time—and the driver nodded, flexed his pecs, straightened his shoulders and disappeared around the side of the bus.

The women hovered, fixing their big hair, adjusting their bras beneath their shirts, moistening their lips, waiting for their hero's return.

One minute turned into two into three…and then he was back, holding what looked to be a torn suit jacket between one thumb and forefinger, and…

A black plastic trash bag…?

"Oh, *damn,*" Lucky said, scrambling out of the van. He ran into the bus station, ran past the women and the driver, out the side door and around the waiting bus.

The door was open, and he launched himself up and into it and...

The bus was empty. It was absolutely empty.

He searched it, rushing all the way to the back, but the foul-smelling woman in the big blue dress wasn't on the damn thing.

He swore again, taking the stairs off the bus in a single jump, heading back into the station.

The driver had set the plastic garbage bag next to the overflowing trash can, and Lucky grabbed it, opened it and...

A giant blue dress. Little lacy ankle socks. A baseball cap. Old magazines, and a fine collection of rags.

And—all the way at the bottom—the key to locker number 101.

Wes had come inside, and he watched as Lucky grimly took the key and opened the locker.

Empty.

Mitch's so-called "bag of tricks" was gone.

"Son of a bitch!" Lucky swore. "*Son* of a bitch!"

The foul-smelling woman had been Mitch Shaw.

There was no point looking for him. A man who'd been trained in covert ops like Mitch would be long gone. Or hidden so completely even Lucky and Wes wouldn't find him.

Wes followed Lucky back to the van, climbed in silently.

"He looked right at me," Lucky fumed, as he started the engine. "He *had* to have recognized me. I mean, he *knows* me, we've sat in meetings together. What the hell is going on?"

"We have to call the captain," Wes said quietly. "I don't know, Lieutenant, but maybe we've got to stop thinking about Mitch as one of us, and start thinking of him as the enemy. If he *has* sold out…"

Lucky nodded. This wasn't going to be easy. Damn, telling Joe Cat that he'd let Shaw get past him wasn't going to be easy, either. "I never thought I'd say this, but I'm going to recommend to the captain that it might be time to get FInCOM involved."

BECCA DROVE NORTH ALONG state roads as the sun sat low in the sky.

Mish sat in silence next to her, the leather bag he'd found in the bus station locker at his feet.

He hadn't said more than twenty words to her since she'd dropped her little bomb back in the motel room. And two of those words had been an apology. Becca shook her head. She'd told him that she loved him, and his response had been *I'm sorry*. Still, she supposed that was a good thing. She didn't know what she would have done if he'd told her he loved her, too. It was too terrifying to consider.

The truth was, she didn't *want* him to love her, too. Even if he'd been just a normal ranch hand, just a regular guy, even if he hadn't come to her with amnesia and a bullet wound—yes, even a priest's collar—she wouldn't want him to love her, too.

Love was too risky. It was too uncertain. When she planned for her future, she didn't want to leave that great big unknown black hole of uncertainty gaping out in front of her, the one with the caption under it that read: *What If He Stopped Loving Her?*

Mish was sorry that she loved him, and she was sorry, too. But at least she knew what her future held in store for her. She knew that sooner or later—and probably sooner, from the way things were going—Mish would leave. And she would miss him. She already missed him. From the moment she'd seen that collar, their relationship had changed drastically, and she missed feeling free to touch him, to take his hand, to look into his eyes and dream about the night to come.

But there was no way she would do that now, not without knowing for sure who he was, *what* he was.

Their journey together had come to an end, and soon—possibly in hours—they would part. And she would feel like hell for a few weeks or months, until the day when she woke up and found she could think about him without aching. Then she would find she could wonder fleetingly where he was, and smile at the way he'd briefly touched her heart and her life.

But before that could happen, before she let him walk away, Becca wanted to know the truth. She wanted to know who he really was. She wanted to know what was inside of that bag.

Back in the motel room, Mish had beat a quick retreat after his apology, telling her that he was heading to the bus station. He intended to find out if the key they'd found in his jacket actually opened a locker there. How he was going to do that without the men in the van noticing him, he didn't say. He'd simply told her to meet him in two hours in the parking lot of the closest thing to an upscale bar Wyatt City had, over on the north side of town.

And then he'd left, taking his shirt, his jacket and that unmistakable, unforgettable collar along with him.

Becca glanced at him, glanced down at the bag at his feet. Supple, tanned leather covered a harder surface. It wasn't a gym bag as she'd first thought. It was some kind of hard case. And it looked as if he'd had it and used it for a long time. "Is there a reason you haven't opened that?"

He turned to look at her. "I'm afraid of what I'll find inside," he told her quietly.

Becca nodded, forcing her eyes back onto the road. "I am, too." There was a pull-off up ahead—an old abandoned gas station, the garage boarded up. She slowed and pulled into the dusty, potholed driveway, the truck bouncing until she stopped and put the engine into park.

She didn't turn off the engine. They both needed the air conditioner running.

She took a deep breath. "Mish, what happened between you and me... We're the only ones who know about it. No one else ever has to..."

She could tell from his eyes that Mish knew what she was doing. She was giving him permission to turn his back on her, to deny that their relationship had grown beyond the physical—or at least that it had for her.

"If we both agree it never happened," she continued, "then—"

"But it did happen," he interrupted her. "Bec, I know you think otherwise, but I'm not a priest. The collar was just a disguise. I'm...good at disguises. I know how to change the way I look so completely and...I wish I were a priest. Because then at least I'd have more options right now. I'd have the hope of someday having you in my life. I could make a career change." He tried to smile. "Take you up on your offer to teach me how to care for horses."

Was he saying...? "You'd want that?"

"I want *you*," he said simply.

Becca's heart nearly stopped. She'd said those exact words to him, and she'd meant...

"But it won't be easy to walk away from who and what I think I am," he told her. "It might be flat-out impossible. And I won't put you in danger. I don't really know who the hell I am, but there are people looking for me, Bec.

Dangerous people. And I want to be far away from you when they finally catch up with me."

She didn't know what to say, didn't know what to do. He'd spoken of "someday," implied they could have a *future*.

Becca turned away, suddenly wanting that future so desperately, her stomach hurt. Oh, that was bad. That was very bad. She couldn't have this man. And even if she could, she'd never wanted her happiness to depend on any one person. And yet here he was, saying that he would give up everything, if only he could, just to be with her.

"I know what's inside this case," Mish told her quietly. "I haven't opened it, but I still somehow know. I knew when I first saw it. It's got a combination lock, but that's not a problem because I know the combination, too."

He swung it up between them on the bench seat.

"There's a change of clothes inside," he continued. "Jeans and a T-shirt. Two clean pairs of socks. A pair of boots and extra laces." He spun and set the combination, and the lock popped open. "My H&K MP-5 assault weapon."

Mish opened the lid. Sure enough, the leather covered some kind of metal. This was no lightweight suitcase. This was heavy-duty. As Becca watched, he reached inside and took out something that was wrapped in dark fabric.

"And an overcoat so I can carry it concealed."

The dark fabric was, indeed, some kind of lightweight raincoat. And inside it was…

An extremely deadly-looking submachine gun.

"Oh, my God," Becca breathed.

"I'm not a priest," he said. "I wore that collar as part of a disguise. Are we clear about that?"

She nodded.

"Good." He smiled tightly. "No way am I going to have you spend the rest of your life thinking what we shared was any less than perfect."

Mish set the weapon down on the floor at his feet. He pulled a tightly rolled pair of jeans out of the case, along with another, smaller gun in a leather shoulder holster. Clips of ammunition—enough to outfit a small army. Boots, as he'd said. Rolled-up socks. A vest of some sort. A medical kit. A passport.

No, not one passport—seven. Mish had *seven* passports. As Becca silently watched, he flipped through them. His picture was on them all, but each of the seven names was decidedly different.

Becca had to ask. "Do any of those names—"

"No. They don't sound familiar. Not even the one with the Albuquerque address." Mish loaded everything back into the case. "I knew," he said quietly, "but I was hoping I was wrong."

Becca shook her head. "The guns don't prove anything. I mean, maybe you're a…a…"

"A thief instead of a killer?" he suggested.

"A gun collector."

Mish laughed, examining the machine gun before wrapping it in the raincoat again. "This weapon's sanitized—all serial numbers and other identifying marks have been filed clean. Same goes for the handgun. And I bet if we look at the .22 I left back at the ranch, we'll find the same thing." He closed the case, spun the combination lock. "Apparently I collect illegal weapons, which is, of course, illegal in itself." He set the case back down on the floor. "I want you to drop me at the next town and go back to the ranch."

Woodenly, Becca put the truck into gear. First he was a ranch hand who didn't know a damn thing about horses, then he was a hero who saved a young boy's life. Then he was a man without a past, without the faintest clue who he'd been and where he'd come from. Then he'd been a priest. She'd been so positive he was a priest. But no. He was, in truth, some kind of master of disguises, someone who needed seven passports and seven names and three deadly guns.

And two extra pairs of clean socks.

The socks gave him away.

Mish wanted her to believe he was some kind of a monster, and maybe he had, in fact, done some terrible things in his past, but he was, first and foremost, a man. A man she had only ever seen act gently and kindly.

She held tightly to the steering wheel. "You're going to Albuquerque to check out the address on that passport." She knew him well enough by now to know he couldn't let that go, even though it was probably just another false lead.

"Yeah. And no, I don't want you to drive me there." He knew her pretty well by now, too. "You can drop me at Clines Corners, but that's as far as I'll let you take me."

Clines Corners was on Route 40, right where 285 cut up toward Santa Fe. He'd be able to get a ride to Albuquerque from there, no problem.

Becca glanced at the clock on the dash. They were at least three hours from Clines Corners. She had a solid three hours to convince herself that the best thing she could do for both of them would be to say goodbye and let him go.

She knew it was the right thing to do.

So why did it feel so wrong?

CHAPTER FOURTEEN

THE DOOR OPENED, and the American leapt.

The assault weapon skittered across the floor, and Mish didn't think. He just picked it up and fired.

A spray of bullets, a spray of blood.

So much blood.

"Good job," the American told him through the blood that bubbled on his own lips.

Mish stared at the bodies, stared at what he'd done.

And on the floor, his father's hands started to twitch. Mish backed away, but he couldn't get far enough. He would never get far enough away. *Thou shalt not kill.*

The American's voice was tight with pain. "Way to send them straight to hell, Mitch."

Mitch.

He awoke with a start, drenched with sweat despite the truck's powerful air conditioner.

The sun had set, their headlights the only light for what had to be miles around. Becca's face looked ghostly in the dim glow from the dash. "You okay?"

He was still breathing hard, his hands shaking as he took his can of soda from the cup holder and took a sip. "Mitch," he managed to get out. "My name. I had a dream…"

"Oh, my God! Mitch," she tried saying it aloud. Laughed. "*Mitch.* Of course. No wonder Mish sounded so familiar to you." She turned toward him eagerly. "What else do you remember?"

Did he remember more than that one awful day? He tried to think back to the alleyway, to the man with the beard. But there was nothing there. No connection. He couldn't even grab hold of his last name. It was out there, but just beyond his grasp.

He shook his head. "I dreamed about... About my... father. He was shot. Killed."

"Oh, God," Becca breathed. "Are you sure it wasn't just a dream? Sometimes—"

"I don't know, Bec, it seems so real. I've dreamed about it a lot, although I didn't realize until now that he was my father. And it always happens the same way, as if it's a memory. I mean, yeah, some of it gets weird, like I know my father's dead, but then he stands up and it's pretty grisly..." He took another sip of his soda, trying to banish that image from his head. "I think it's more than a dream. I think some of it happened."

Becca glanced at him again. "Were you... Did you actually see him—his body—after he died?"

"I think I was there when he was killed."

"God, Mitch."

"I was fifteen." Mitch watched the lines on the road, brightly illuminated by the headlights but quickly fading into nothing as the truck moved forward into the night. How old was he now? Thirty-five was the number that came to him first. It seemed to fit. Twenty years since he'd first picked up a weapon and pulled the trigger and...

"Can you...tell me about it?" Becca's voice was so soft, so uncertain.

And ended a human life.

Mitch looked at her sitting there behind the steering wheel. She tried so hard to be tough and strong, when in truth the past few weeks had been devastatingly difficult for her. But her resilience shone through. She looked tired, yes, but gloriously undefeated, and Mitch knew without a doubt that she wasn't going to take Route 285 to Santa Fe and to the Lazy Eight when they hit Clines Corners.

No, she was going to stick with him. She was going to take him all the way, wherever he needed to go, and maybe even then some.

But it was only a matter of time before the gang in the surveillance van outside the Wyatt City bus station discovered that locker 101 had been emptied out beneath their noses. And it was only a matter of time before the search for him intensified.

And while Mitch still didn't know what he'd done to spark a manhunt, he did know one thing without a doubt.

He was *not* going to put Becca into any danger.

Even if that meant disappearing into thin air the next time they stopped for gasoline. Even if it meant leaving her without an explanation, without even saying goodbye.

He didn't want to do that. He didn't want to leave her wondering. He'd given her so little as it was.

Can you tell me about it, she'd asked. And he knew that this was really all he had to give her. This small piece of his past that he remembered, this awfulness, this terrible thing that—he suspected—had helped shape him into the person he was today.

"Yeah," he said. "I'd like to tell you. But it's pretty intense, so if you want me to stop…"

"I'll let you know," she told him, and he knew that was the last he'd ever hear of that.

"I was fifteen," he said again. "I don't remember exactly where we were, but we were overseas, I think somewhere in the Middle East. My father was a minister and he'd recently won this position as part of a multi-denominational peacekeeping group. It was a really big deal—he was so proud."

It was strange. Telling her about it was helping him to remember. He could recall the open airport where he and his parents had first arrived. He could remember the scent of exotic foods cooking, the swirl of colors and people. He remembered his disappointment when the hotel they were brought to was a tall, modern building rather than something ancient and mysterious.

"We'd been there for about two weeks, when my father took me to lunch at the downtown McDonald's. We were both dying for a Big Mac. I remember we'd ordered burgers from the hotel room service, but they were strange. My dad thought maybe they were cut with horse meat. And I remember my mother rolling her eyes, taking a bite and telling us it was just the local spices. But my father had the afternoon off, so the two of us took a bus from the hotel down to the market. He was...very charismatic. I remember he had everyone on the bus singing the McDonald's theme song. And most of the busload of people followed us into the restaurant, too. Some American businessmen. A group of tourists—mothers and teenaged girls from France, I think."

He could remember the menu hanging above the counter, the words both in English and something undecipherable.

"I didn't see them come in," he continued. "There was this loud noise—that was the first I knew of any trouble. The sound of weapons being fired. My father pulled me down, but it was over before it even began. Terrorists killed the security guards at the doors. They'd taken control of the McDonald's—the symbol for all things American. And we were their hostages."

The truck moved onward through the night. A sign appeared out of the blackness. Clines Corners, twenty miles.

Becca was silent, just letting him tell the story at his own speed.

"They took us into the back, out a doorway into the main part of the building. The guards there were dead, too. It was obvious this had been planned, that this attack hadn't been just a spur-of-the-moment event. They led us into a storage room that had been cleared out. There were no windows and only that one door—like I said, they planned it well. Some of the women and children were crying, and the terrorists seemed on the edge, too, shouting for everyone to be silent, and my father stepped forward.

"He tried to calm everyone down, started talking about the women and kids, trying to convince the terrorists' leader that they should let them go. And I remember…"

Is that your dad, kid?

"There was a man standing behind me. A black man. An American. He must've been in the McDonald's when we arrived—I didn't remember seeing him on the bus."

Tell your dad to back off. The American's eyes and voice had held an urgency.

"He told me to tell my father that these terrorists wouldn't negotiate, that they didn't respect his cross or his collar, that the fact that he was American put him in extra danger."

Tell him. Now.

Dad. "So I stepped toward my father, tried to take his arm and pull him back into the crowd."

His father had turned just a little, the sweat glistening on his brow. *Stay back with the others, Mitch.*

"He wouldn't listen to me." Mitch could remember his own fear. His sense of panic as he saw the intense concern in the American's face, saw the horror in his dark brown eyes. And he knew even before he turned back that his father was as good as dead.

"It happened so fast. The terrorist lifted his sidearm and fired. Two bullets. Right into my father's head. One second he was standing there, and the next…"

He'd crumpled to the ground, lifeless.

"It was so unreal," Mitch said, his voice tight with anguish. "It didn't seem possible that he was really dead. I mean, how could he be dead? He was *so* alive. But there was blood. I didn't know it at the time, but we'd been sprayed with it. All I could see was this pool of red on the floor, beneath him. I wanted to go to him, to help him, to stop the bleeding, but the American pulled me back, into the crowd. He put his hand over my mouth."

God, kid, I'm sorry. The American's voice had been nearly as rough as his hands.

Let me help him! Mitch had struggled.

"And he told me my father was dead."

Don't do this, the American had hissed.

"He told me if I made too much noise, they'd kill me, too."

I don't care! Mitch hadn't gotten the words out from behind the man's huge hand, but he knew the message had been understood.

"He told me to think about my mother, think about how she was going to feel losing both her husband and her son on the same day."

Stop being so damned selfish, boy, and you calm yourself down.

"He told me I couldn't help my father now."

"Oh, Mitch, I can't believe you had to live through that." Becca's eyes glimmered with sympathy.

"They locked us into that room," he told her, "and I sat on the floor, trying not to cry, trying not to look at my father. They just left his body there. One of the women had draped her scarf over his head and face, but…"

But that pool of blood had remained.

"The American was making a circuit of the room, trying to convince the others that we had to fight back, and that the moment to strike was as soon as the terrorists returned, as soon as they unlocked the door. He told us he knew about this group of zealots. He knew of their leader, knew that they weren't going to let any of us go free."

The American told them that when the terrorists returned, the killing would start.

"He said that he was going to fight. But no one else seemed up to it. Everyone was afraid. I was afraid, too."

But Mitch had looked at his father, at this man who had been so good, so strong, so caring. He'd been killed as if he were little more than a bug to be stepped on. And Mitch had looked up at the American.

I'll fight, he'd said. *I'll help.*

"Thou shalt not kill," Mitch told Becca. "If there was one thing my father believed more than anything, it was in nonviolence. Guns and weapons and war had no place in his world. But I wasn't in his world anymore. And I wanted to kill the men who had taken him from me."

The American sat down next to him. *Okay. Let's kill them, Mitch. You channel that rage, kid. Make it work for you.*

"The American man asked me if I'd ever fired an

automatic weapon." Mitch laughed. "In my house? I hadn't even seen one up close, let alone held one."

The force of the discharge pulls the muzzle up, the American had told him. *You've got to work to keep it down. And aim for the center of the body. Don't go for the head. It's amazing how often the enemy pops back onto their feet after a shot to the head with something as lightweight as a nine millimeter. And we don't want that, you copy?*

"He gave me a crash course in handling an assault weapon, and I pointed out that a lot of good it was going to do us to talk about firing one, since we didn't have one to fire." Mitch shook his head. "But he told me he had a plan."

"He told me about something called PV—*point of vulnerability,* and AV—*area of vulnerability.* He explained that there was always a point in which an attacking force was temporarily at their weakest. He told me when the terrorists came back, their PV would be when they first came into the room. And that's when we were going to hit them—when they were close together, coming through the door, when it was hardest for them to maneuver."

Mitch had looked at the American through the haze of anger and grief that seemed to rise like a mist from his father's prone body. "It seemed absurd. Out of a roomful of people, virtually sentenced to death, the only ones willing to fight back were this one older man and me. A kid who planned to major in philosophy and religion in college. I didn't know for sure, but up to that point, I had been pretty certain I would follow in my father's footsteps. I had this faith in God, and it seemed it was only a matter of time before I received the call and…"

He laughed again, but there was no humor in it. "I received a call that day, that's for sure. My father and his words and his faith couldn't save us—he couldn't even save himself. But with a weapon like those machine guns… Yeah, I received a completely different kind of call."

Becca reached across the bench seat and found his hand. He held on to her tightly, seeing the lights from the truck stop up ahead, and knowing it was just a matter of minutes now before he had to walk away from her for good.

"The American—I wish I could remember his name!— he was ready for them, and when the terrorists opened the door, he launched himself at them. It was a suicide play. He knew he was going to be shot. But he'd hoped to grab one of their guns and throw it toward me, and somehow he did. And when that weapon came sliding across that tile floor toward me, I didn't hesitate. And I left my father's world for good, Bec. I picked it up, and I fired. I leaned on the trigger, like the American had told me. I pulled the muzzle down, and I swept it across those bastards, all jammed together in that doorway, and I sent 'em straight to hell."

A spray of bullets.

A spray of blood.

So much blood.

Blood…

"I killed all three of them. And with the hostages armed on the inside, we held off the terrorists until the marines stormed the building. The American died on the way to the hospital. He and my father were the only casualties among the hostages."

"I don't know." Becca's voice was quiet in the darkness. "I might be tempted to call you a casualty, too."

"Yeah," Mitch said just as quietly. "In a way, I guess I died that day, too." He pointed to the exit that was approaching. "We could use some gas—and a cup of coffee would be something of a blessing right about now."

He could feel her eyes as she glanced over at him, and he carefully kept his gaze on the road in front of them.

In silence, she took the exit, braking at the Stop sign at the end of the long ramp. The truck stop was brightly lit, and she pulled into the parking lot, into a slot by the restaurant door.

She still had his hand, and when he would have turned away to open the door and climb out, she tugged him toward her. She pulled him into her arms, wrapping him in her sweetness and warmth.

"Thank you so much for telling me," she whispered, and she kissed him.

Mitch lost himself in the softness of her lips. That she would want to kiss him after all he'd just told her was amazing to him. And he knew more than ever that she wouldn't willingly go back to the Lazy Eight without him.

So he held her tightly and, without her knowing it, kissed her goodbye as gently as he could.

"I MET MITCH SHAW at his father's funeral." Admiral Jake Robinson sat at the head of the table in the Gray Group's makeshift temporary headquarters at Kirtland Air Force Base in Albuquerque.

After calling Captain Catalanotto, Lucky and his team had been ordered to Holloman AFB, pronto, where a special transport had been waiting to whisk them up to Kirtland. It was the power of the Admiralcy in action. When they landed, they were escorted posthaste from the transport to this office, where they were joined by the captain, and Blue McCoy and Crash Hawken, the two SEALs from Alpha Squad who'd been sent to look for Mitch in Albuquerque.

"The vice president of the United States was at the funeral, too," the admiral told them. "And he shook the kid's hand and told him he was very sorry for his loss, told him there was going to be a ceremony in Washington, and the president of the United States was going to present Mitch with a special version of the Medal of Honor.

"And Mitch looked him right in the eye and told him thanks, but no thanks. He didn't deserve it. His father did, though. His father had died believing in the power of good over evil. The way Mitch saw it, the Reverend Randall Shaw had died sticking to his belief that nonviolence was the only option. Mitch, however, believed that by killing those terrorists, he'd given in and used evil to fight evil. He didn't want a medal for that.

"I introduced myself to him," Jake told them. "I wasn't an admiral at the time, but I'd been heavily decorated from my time in Vietnam. Still it was obvious that he wasn't interested in talking to me—until I told him I was a friend of Senior Chief Fred Baxter, the man who'd died helping Mitch save those hostages' lives. After I told him that, he took a walk with me, and I had the chance to tell him that Freddie was a Navy SEAL, told him a little bit about what that meant. And I told him that Fred was getting a medal, too. Posthumously. And Fred deserved that medal, absolutely, without a doubt. Because Fred Baxter, like me, like most SEALs, believed in something just as absolutely as Mitch's father believed in nonviolence. Fred believed in the power of gray."

Jake looked around his room. "You guys know this. In our world there's no such thing as black and white. There's no clear line between right and wrong, especially when the outcome affects millions of lives. And so we operate in that narrow band of gray. Mitch was fifteen when he first stepped into that world.

"I don't know what he's doing right now," the admiral continued. "I don't know what the hell he's up to, but I can tell you with complete confidence, gentlemen, that he has *not* sold out, that he remains faithful to both God and country. He's worked closely with me since the conception of the Gray Group —in fact, he gave it its name. I trust him as I trust myself. There *will* be an explanation for his behavior, I guarantee it. I know you're not going to like this, but I suggest we sit tight, give him space to operate, and wait for him to contact us."

Lucky looked at Joe Cat, waiting for the captain to make an alternative suggestion. When he was noticeably silent, Lucky cleared his throat. "Admiral. Sir. Aren't we, um, forgetting about that plutonium floating around out there, about to fall into the wrong hands?"

Jake stood up. "Gray Group operatives have infiltrated an arms dealer's organization—the very one that will be attempting to broker the deal. The client's a political faction in an Eastern European country and we've been keeping tabs on them as well. The exchange was supposed to take place yesterday, but the seller cancelled at the last minute—which leads me to believe that the seller no longer has possession of the plutonium, and that Mitch Shaw does. But a new meeting's been set up for tomorrow. In Santa Fe. Which means that sometime before tonight and tomorrow, Mitch could well be calling in for some help. And gentlemen…" He looked around the table, meeting each of the SEALs' eyes. "When he needs us, we'll be ready."

BECCA KNEW WHAT MITCH was doing. She knew, without a doubt, that he was kissing her goodbye. If she let him get out of the truck, he was as good as gone.

She held him tightly, knowing that if she didn't speak now, she'd regret it for the rest of her life.

"Don't go." Her voice shook.

He didn't try to pretend he didn't know what she meant. "I have to, Bec."

She was glad he didn't pull back, glad he couldn't see the tears in her eyes as she did the one thing she swore she'd never do—beg a man to stay. "We can start over. Go away together. We can hide. There's got to be a million places two people can lose themselves in this country. No one will ever find you, we'll be careful and—"

"Spend the rest of our lives looking over our shoulders? That's no way to live."

Becca closed her eyes, feeling her tears escape.

"Please..."

"I can't. Not knowing who's after me, or why... It would drive me crazy. Bec, I have to find out who I am." He pulled away from her gently, opening the glove compartment and taking a folded piece of paper out. "I wrote this letter," he told her. "It's to Ted Alden. I've explained the situation as best as I could, and I've asked him to invest the money he wanted to give me in your ranch—the one I know you're going to buy someday. However he wants to set it up is fine. I want you to send this to him along with that check he wrote, okay?"

"No," she said. She wouldn't take it from him, so he put it back in the glove box. "No, it's not okay!"

He opened the door and stepped out into the night. "I love you."

It was what she'd both dreaded and hoped to hear. Becca squinted at him through both the glare from the overhead light and her tears. "Then how can you *leave?*"

He lifted his case up and out of the truck, his face in the shadows. "How could I stay?"

He closed the door, and Becca scrambled out of the driver's side, wiping furiously at her tears. "Mitch!"

But the parking lot was empty.

He was already gone.

CHAPTER FIFTEEN

MITCH COULDN'T SLEEP.

He'd toyed with the idea of not getting a motel room because he knew he'd never get his eyes shut tonight.

The Albuquerque address on the passport hadn't been real. Oh, it was a residential neighborhood, but—surprise, surprise—the house number didn't exist. And even though Mitch had walked around in the darkness for close to two hours, he hadn't felt even the faintest flash of familiarity from anything.

He'd walked back to the part of town that was lit by cheap motels, late-night bars and all-night coffee shops. He'd gotten his coffee to go, and paid the extra money for the motel room.

Not because he wanted to sleep.

Because he wanted to look through his suitcase again. See if there was anything he'd missed.

So now he sat on the sagging double bed, surrounded by the contents of his leather case. His...bag of tricks? *Grab your bag of tricks, Lieutenant...*

Lieutenant?

He'd set the weapons aside, but now he picked up the MP-5. His "room broom." It fit comfortably, easily in his hands.

His father would have been shocked.

He put it down, and unrolled his jeans. He hadn't had a chance to go through the pockets and...

He nearly missed it. It was a small photograph in the back pocket. The torn corner of a picture—just the head and shoulders of a man.

The face was shockingly familiar.

Shaggy hair, full beard, florid features…

Casey Parker.

The name came to him in a flash of certainty that chilled him to the bone.

Casey Parker was the man who had shot Mitch in that Wyatt City alley. He was also the man who had come to the Lazy Eight ranch, looking for the package that was supposed to be waiting for him there—the package Mitch had taken in his stead.

He still had the key that had been in that envelope. He was carrying it in his pocket.

Mitch took it out and looked at it again. It was, without a doubt, the kind of key a bank issued with a safe-deposit box. What was in that box, Mitch could only guess. Money, maybe. Or the take from some robbery. Jewelry. *Something* valuable. Something that had started all this. Something Parker had already tried to kill Mitch over.

And it was only a matter of time before Parker returned to the Lazy Eight, looking for this key.

He wouldn't find it, but he would find Becca.

All alone. Unsuspecting. Virtually defenseless.

Mitch threw his things back into his leather case and jammed his feet into his boots. He had to get to the Lazy Eight.

Before it was too late.

BECCA OPENED THE RANCH office early, just as the sun was coming up.

The sky was heavy with clouds. A storm was brewing.

Most likely it would rain hard and heavy starting sometime within the next few minutes and clear up before lunch.

She wished she could say the same about her own dark disposition.

She'd spent a restless night, tossing and turning in her bed, and she'd been exhausted when her alarm had gone off. But it was better to get up and get to work instead of hiding out by sleeping in. Besides, this way she'd be good and tired when tonight rolled around. And maybe she'd fall straight into a dreamless sleep without even thinking once about Mitch.

Hah. Fat chance.

But she had to stop thinking about him. It was entirely likely she would never see him again, so she'd better learn to stop thinking about him. She knew she could do it. And once she learned not to think about Mitch, well, then she'd be on her way to learning to live without him. She could do anything, if she put her mind to it.

And right now she'd stop thinking about Mitch by focusing on all the work she had to do to catch up around here.

The storm clouds were so dark, Becca had to turn on the light over her desk just to see.

She sat down, uncertain of where to start, and knowing without a doubt that such a dilemma wasn't worth crying over. Yet here she was, on the verge of tears. Again.

Damn Mitch.

And double damn herself for being so stupid as to fall in love with him.

Work had piled up in her in-basket over the days she'd been gone. Her email alone was enough to occupy her for most of the morning. She'd start with that. She scrubbed at her eyes and blew her nose soundly. She was determined to work in the office only until ten. If she could get enough done now, she'd give Belinda the morning off and take the guests on the morning trail ride herself, provided the weather complied. She could use some quality time with Silver and...

The office door squealed as it opened, and she closed her eyes, desperately hoping that whatever problem was walking into the office at 5:06 a.m. could be dealt with quickly and efficiently and...

"Becca, thank God."

Mitch? She turned around so quickly, she nearly fell out of her chair. It *was*. Mitch had come back.

As she stood up, he dropped his case on the floor and moved toward her, coming right up and over the counter that separated them. And then she was in his arms.

"Are you all right?" he asked, pulling slightly back to look down into her eyes. He touched her face, her hair. "Please tell me you're all right."

She nodded. Yes. Now she was very, very all right. "Thank you," she said, kissing his neck, his ear. "Thank you, *thank* you for coming back."

He caught her mouth with his, and the fire that raged to life between them ignited instantly. And as the entire world seemed to swirl and shift around them, as Becca melted against him, she wondered how she could even have *thought* she could learn to live without him.

And in that instant, she knew the awful truth. She'd found her true love. And he loved her, too. Given the opportunity, Mitch would stay forever.

Please, please, give them the opportunity...

He pulled away from her far sooner than she would have liked. "Becca, I remembered something."

She could tell just from looking at him that it wasn't something good.

"It was Casey Parker who shot me. I still don't remember why, but he meant to kill me. And I've got to believe that he'll be coming back here. He's going to want his key."

And Becca knew. Mitch hadn't come back to the Lazy Eight because he wanted to. He'd come because he'd had to. If he'd thought she was safe, she *would* never have seen him again.

But he *had* come back. And she had to make the most of this opportunity to convince him to stay.

Mitch released her, and she let him go, watching as he picked up the phone on Hazel's desk. "What's the sheriff's number?"

"It's right there," she told him. "On that list. Mitch, we've got to talk."

He found it and punched in the buttons.

"What are you doing?" she asked, realizing that he was dialing the sheriff's number.

He was listening to the phone ring, and he met her gaze only briefly. "Calling the sheriff."

"Obviously. Mitch—"

"Yeah, hi," Mitch said into the telephone. "I'm calling from the Lazy Eight Ranch. We've got a major problem here, and I was hoping the sheriff could come out as soon as possible...?"

He wanted the *sheriff* to come out here? If the sheriff got involved, then Mitch would...

"Well, let's start with attempted murder," Mitch said to whoever was on the other end of the phone. "Is that worth waking up the sheriff over?"

Mitch would have to admit to having amnesia. He would be investigated. His fingerprints would probably be run through the computer and...

And then they'd finally know who he was.

But so would the sheriff.

"We'll be waiting for him in the ranch office," Mitch said, and hung up the phone. He turned to face Becca, answering her before she even asked. "I'm turning myself in."

She shook her head, unable to say anything, unable even to speak.

"I thought hard about it the entire way out here. It's the right thing to do," he told her. "I should've done this weeks ago. I still don't remember much of anything, but that doesn't mean I shouldn't have to take responsibility for the things that I've done."

"You're jumping to conclusions here." She finally found her voice. "You may not have done anything wrong at all."

"How about possession of illegal firearms?" he asked. "We'll start there. Somehow I doubt we'll end there, though."

He went out into the main part of the office, walking around the counter this time. Becca followed. "You don't have to do this."

"Yes, I do." He pulled open the screen door. "I'm going to get my .22 from the bunkhouse lockup, so I can turn it in with the weapons in my bag."

The first crack of thunder rumbled in the distance, ominous and foreboding as Becca followed him outside into the eerie early morning light, and back toward the barn. The wind was starting to kick up, sending clouds of dust scooting across the dry yard.

"This is really the only way I can start over," he told her. "Yes, it feels like I've been given a second chance, because I don't remember my past, but it's not real, Bec. If I really want a second chance, I've got to do it right. And that means facing up to whatever I've done, and paying the price. Lord knows I don't want to go back to prison, but if I have to, so be it. Because when I get out—if I get out—*that's* when I'll be able to make a fresh start." He smiled at her, that crooked half smile she'd come to know so well. "Besides, I'd face more than hard time to be sure that you were safe."

Becca caught his arm. "That's why you're doing this, isn't it? Because you don't think I'll be safe from this Casey Parker if you don't."

He gently pulled free. "It's also the right thing to do."

Becca watched as he disappeared into the bunkhouse. "Dammit, Mitch!" She ran to catch up with him, following him inside, lowering her voice, aware that the other ranch hands would be rising soon. "You don't even know that Parker's going to come back here."

"Becca, go back to the office."

She rounded the corner that led to the common area and the ranch hands' private lockers, and stopped short.

Mitch was standing absolutely still, staring down the muzzle of a very, very deadly-looking handgun. It was bigger than the one Dirty Harry used in her favorite Clint Eastwood movies, big enough to blow an extremely fatal hole in Mitch, should the man holding it pull the trigger.

And the man holding it looked as if he'd enjoy doing just that. Big and beefy, he had at least five inches and seventy pounds on Mitch. But he was older, with a beard that was graying, and eyes that seemed almost lost in the fleshy folds of his face. Casey Parker. It had to be.

"She's not part of this," Mitch said to the man.

"She is now," he answered.

Becca saw Mitch's gaze flicker toward the lockup

where his handgun was stored, saw him reject the option of going for it, thank God. One gun was bad enough.

"You know why I'm here," Parker said.

"I guess you want the key." Mitch glanced at Becca. His eyes were filled with meaning, filled with a private message. *Be ready to run.*

"Good guess," Parker said.

And she knew exactly what Mitch was planning to do. Point of vulnerability. Just as the man he'd called "the American" had done, he was going to wait for Parker's PV and he was going to attack, giving Becca a chance to run to safety. And, like the American in his dream, it was likely that Mitch would be shot and killed.

Becca shook her head, just a tiny shake, barely discernible. *No.*

"Becca will have to go and get it," Mitch told the man. "I left it in the glove compartment of her truck."

Parker laughed. "Maybe we should try this again." He swung his gun so that it pointed directly at Becca's chest. "Give me the key."

Mitch nearly stopped breathing. He knew it didn't take much, just the gentle pressure from a finger, to end a human life. And as long as Parker had that gun aimed at Becca, it could happen. In half a heartbeat, she could go from living to dead.

Thunder rolled, closer still.

"My pocket," Mitch said through a throat tight with fear. "It's in my front pocket."

"Get it. Move slowly."

"Point the gun away from her first."

"Give me the key first," Parker countered.

Mitch did, holding it out to Parker on the palm of his hand. If only he could get him to come close enough...

But Parker laughed. "Toss it to me. *Gently.*"

"Point the gun away from her." Mitch knew it was futile. He knew Parker was going to keep that gun aimed at Becca until this was over. And how it was going to end, he didn't want to try to guess. The sheriff was due to arrive any minute, and he didn't even know if *that* would be a help or a hindrance. All he knew was that the next time Parker aimed that gun at him, he was going to rush him, take him down, take him out. Before the bastard had a chance to hurt Becca.

"Toss it," Parker demanded.

Mitch did. He watched the gun while Parker caught and examined the key, but although it swerved, it swerved only slightly.

Becca had been silent all this time, but now she spoke up. "Mitch doesn't remember you. He doesn't remember anything from before he was shot. He doesn't even know his last name. If you just leave, we won't tell anyone or—"

Parker laughed. "Oh, that's good. I suppose you'll give me your promise, too, huh? Well, for someone who doesn't remember, Mitch here has sure managed to screw me up big-time. No, we're going to go for a ride in your truck, Becca dear. Come over here."

Thunder cracked nearly overhead.

"Becca, don't move." Mitch knew that once Parker had Becca close enough to press the gun against her head, the man would never be vulnerable enough for Mitch to attack.

"Becca, come here," Parker said again. "Now."

He swung his gun toward Mitch, who knew this was it. It was now or never.

But before he could launch himself at the gun, Becca dashed forward and got in the way.

And *now* turned bleakly into *never*.

"Out the door," Parker ordered Mitch, Becca tight against him, the gun tucked up under her arm, nearly completely concealed from anyone who might be outside in the yard. "Into the truck."

It was starting to rain. Just a few big drops here and there from a heavy green sky that looked ready to open up. Lightning forked, making the air seem to crackle around them.

Becca's truck was parked near the office. Mitch took his time walking toward it, staring down to the end of the long driveway, praying for a sign of the sheriff's headlights through the unnatural early-morning darkness.

Nothing.

"Get in the truck—you're going to drive," Parker told him. "Keep your hands on the steering wheel where I can see 'em at all times. Take 'em off, and I'll shoot her right here."

Mitch got in and clung to that wheel. *I'll shoot her right here.* Instead of waiting to shoot her out in the middle of nowhere, where no one could see or hear.

Parker pushed Becca into the middle of the bench seat and climbed in behind her, his gun never moving from her. If he squeezed the trigger, a bullet would go straight into her heart.

"Start the truck," he ordered Mitch.

The keys were hanging in the ignition, where Becca had left them. Ranch rules—in case someone needed to move the truck fast. "I'll have to take my hand off the steering wheel," Mitch said. He had to get Parker to point the gun at him instead of Becca.

"Just one hand," Parker warned him. "Do it."

Mitch could feel Becca's shoulder pressed against him, her leg against his thigh. He started the engine, flipped on the windshield wipers and headlights, put the truck into gear.

"Head away from the buildings," Parker ordered.

Mitch pulled off the driveway, pointing the truck toward Finger Rocks, toward the dry riverbed. If it wasn't flooding yet, it would be soon. And maybe...

They drove in silence for quite some distance, the rain starting to fall harder now against the windshield.

Mitch glanced up. He could see Becca's eyes in the rearview mirror. She knew where he was heading, knew how deadly the arroyo could be.

"Don't get out of the truck," he told her.

Parker laughed at that. "You're in no position to be giving orders."

Mitch glanced into the rearview again, and she nodded. Her lips moved. *Love you.*

She thought she was going to die.

But she wasn't. Not if he could help it. Not even if he had to die himself to keep her alive.

"Stop up here," Parker finally said. "This is far enough."

Lightning flashed, and Finger Rocks loomed, still too far away. Mitch hadn't yet reached the edge of the dry riverbed. He could see up ahead that the water wasn't running. Yet. He just had to go a little farther...

The rain was starting to fall even harder on the roof of the truck, tiny bits and pieces of hail bouncing off the hood.

"I said, *stop.*"

Mitch took his time hitting the brakes, slowing to a stop. Any second now the sky was going to open up in a deluge so severe, visibility was going to drop to close to zero. In the meantime, he kept his hands on the steering wheel where Parker could see them.

"Get out of the truck," Parker ordered.

Mitch leaned forward to look at him across Becca. "I'm going to have to take my hands off the steering wheel."

"One hand at a time," Parker said. "Move slowly. Open the door. And then step back from the truck—keep your hands where I can see them."

Mitch knew what *he'd* do if he were Parker. He'd make Mitch back far enough away so that when he pulled his gun from Becca's side, Mitch would be too far away to be able to attack. And he'd shoot Mitch from inside the truck, make sure he was dead before pulling Becca out, thus completely eliminating his point of vulnerability.

"I love you," he told Becca, needing her to know.

"Lovely," Parker said. "Move."

Mitch moved *very* slowly as he put the truck into Park, still praying that the rain would help him out. *Please God...* If ever he needed a little divine assistance, it was now.

He opened the door and stepped out of the cab and moved back from the truck and...

God was on his side. Lightning cracked, thunder roared, and the rain came down as if someone had turned on a giant faucet overhead. Mitch was instantly soaked.

And nearly completely hidden by the deluge.

He heard Parker swear as Mitch dropped to the ground, scrambling swiftly and silently beneath the body of the truck. "Where the hell did he go?"

"I'm not getting out," Mitch heard Becca say, bless her. "You're just going to have to shoot me right here—and get the truck all gross and smeared with blood. And that'll go over really well with the state police when you're stopped for that rear taillight that's out."

He heard Parker curse. "You're getting out of this truck if I have to pull you out by the hair!"

Becca screamed as he did just that, but she knew that

she was right—he *wasn't* going to shoot her in the truck. He needed it to get wherever he was going. Probably only as far as to his own vehicle, parked somewhere outside of the ranch's fences. Still, the last thing he wanted to do was get her blood on his clothes. And he *was* going to kill her. She had no doubt of that.

The rain drummed on the roof, and the thunder cracking directly overhead was loud enough to wake the dead.

"Where did he go?" Parker demanded. "Where did that son of a bitch disappear to?" He pulled his gun out from her side to get a better grip on her and yanked her out into the rain.

This was it.

It was Parker's point of vulnerability. His gun waved in the air as she fought him, and Becca knew Mitch would be ready and waiting.

And he was.

He appeared with a flash of lightning, pulling Parker away from Becca, leaping on top of the man's gun as he wrestled him down into the arroyo.

The gun went off, and Mitch jerked—oh, God, he was hit. But he'd somehow managed to grab the gun and fling it, hard, into the rocks and rubble that made up the dry riverbed.

But it was dry no longer. The water was rising, and Becca peered through the rain as Mitch, despite being shot, splashed and wrestled with Parker.

"Get away!" he shouted, his voice barely audible over the roar of the rain. "Becca—take the truck and *go!*"

CHAPTER SIXTEEN

UP ON THE RIVERBANK, Becca stood still, frozen in the truck's headlights.

Dammit, why didn't she take the truck and get herself to safety?

Mitch fought Parker with a desperation, aware that his arm was bleeding, aware that the pain and the light-headedness he was already feeling from the shock were putting him at a disadvantage, aware that his opponent was trying to get to the place where they'd both last seen his gun bouncing off the rocks.

Parker was relentless, hitting Mitch hard, again and again, in the spot where the bullet had nicked him.

Nicked was an understatement, but Mitch was well aware it could have been far worse. A weapon like that, fired at close range, could blow a man's arm clear off. He'd been lucky.

He'd be luckier still, if Becca would get in that truck and drive herself to safety.

Instead, as he elbowed Parker hard in the face, he saw her begin to pick her way down the slope of the hill, *toward* them.

Dammit!

Lightning flashed, illuminating Parker's bared teeth as the man tried to grab Mitch's throat. And right then and there the world seemed to shift.

And for the oddest fraction of a second, Mitch was

back in that alleyway in Wyatt City, looking into Casey
Parker's eyes an instant before he fired the bullet that was
to wipe clean Mitch's memory.

And in that oddest fraction of a second, everything,
everything came rushing back.

Stolen plutonium. An unlikely lead in New Mexico.
Admiral Jake Robinson's covert Gray Group.

He was not a criminal, not a hired killer on the run
from the law! He was Lieutenant Mitchell Shaw of the
U.S. Navy SEALs.

There was no jail term in his future. There was only
hope and sweet possibility.

And Becca.

With a burst of renewed energy, Mitch fought even
harder.

BECCA COULDN'T FIND THE GUN.

She'd seen it fall near this tumble of rocks, but in the
pouring rain, it would have been hard to find her own
feet. And that would've been *without* the water starting to
rise. In just a few seconds it had gone from a slow trickle
to ankle deep, the current tugging at her as it rose even
higher.

The rain began to let up as swiftly as it had started,
but the gun was as good as gone, the water now up to her
knees.

She could see Mitch, still struggling with Casey Parker,
his shirt stained bright red with his own blood. He was in
serious danger of bleeding to death—that is, if he didn't
drown first.

Parker was tiring, but then so was Mitch. But at
least Mitch was on top—or at least he was until a current of water tossed them, pushing them over and Mitch
underneath.

Oh, God!

She could see Mitch struggling, fighting and splashing to get free, to get air. But Parker was so much bigger than he was. And Parker wasn't bleeding from a gunshot wound.

Becca charged toward them, splashing and stumbling through the water, stopping only to pick up a rock large enough to do some damage when it connected with Casey Parker's head.

But the water was still rising and before she reached them, she was knocked off balance. As she struggled to regain her footing, Parker was pulled under. With a swirl of bubbles, both men disappeared downstream.

Becca crawled to the side of the now swiftly flowing river, bedraggled and gasping for air, barely getting out of the way of a chunk of wood being tossed along by the water. She remembered the rainbow-colored bruise Mitch had received from what he'd called a "glancing blow."

As if Casey Parker and his gunshot wound weren't dangers enough, Becca knew that the river could kill Mitch, too.

She struggled out of the water, and ran toward her truck, water squooshing from her boots. She started the engine with a roar, and drove, following the bend in the riverbed, shading her eyes against the rapidly lightening sky, praying as she searched for any sign of Mitch in the raging current.

UNDERWATER.

It was the great equalizer in a fight that Mitch had been afraid he was starting to lose.

But underwater, the advantage spun once more in his direction. As a SEAL, he was at home beneath the water.

And Parker—judging from his current floundering—could barely even swim.

Mitch went with the force of the river, using it instead of fighting it. He could tell when Parker's air ran out. He could tell by the way the man was twitching that Mitch had to get him up to the surface, to air, quickly, or he'd die.

It wasn't easy pulling the heavier man out of the current and onto the rocky shore. And the water was still rising, so he had to pull him—with only one good arm—even farther up, away from the running arroyo.

Parker was breathing. But just barely.

He was out cold, thank the Lord. Mitch wasn't sure he had another fight left in him.

"Mitch!"

He turned to see Becca running toward him. Sweet Becca. With her angel's eyes…

"Thank God, thank God!" She scrambled down the hillside. "Where were you hit?"

"Just my arm. Only a nick." Lord, he was cold.

She was furious. "Only a…! Mitch, this is not *only a nick!*"

He'd lost a lot of blood. That would explain the cold.

"I'm all right," he told her. "Bec, I remembered. I'm a SEAL. A Navy SEAL. Parker has possession of stolen plutonium from a military lab. I've been working a covert op for months, trying to track it down. I'm one of the good guys."

She took off her T-shirt, which confused him for a moment until he realized she was using it to tie around his upper arm in a tourniquet.

"Can you make it to the truck?" she asked him, her voice sounding as if it were coming from a great distance.

Maybe he *had* lost too much blood. Mitch pushed himself up, forcing himself not to succumb to the blackness that was giving him tunnel vision. "What about Parker?"

Becca told him in a very unladylike way exactly what Parker could do with himself. "The sheriff can come back for him."

Mitch shook his head. "No. I've been after him for too long. Get the key from his pocket, Bec. At least let me tie him up."

He could see from her eyes that she was scared for him.

"Rope," he said. "Please. I've been after this guy for months. I can't risk losing him now."

"And I can't risk losing *you* now," she told him hotly. "You're it for me, Mitch. It's you or no one. If you die—"

"I'm not going to die."

"Promise?"

In his line of work, it wasn't good luck to make a promise like that. In his line of work, any kind of promise was hard to keep. But Mitch wanted to promise her everything he possibly could. "Marry me, Becca."

He'd shocked her. She stood up. "I'm getting that rope."

She vanished from the narrowing scope of his vision, and he floated—he wasn't sure how long, seconds probably—until she returned.

As Mitch watched, she hog-tied Parker with knots that would've made any sailor envious, then searched through the man's pockets for the key. She held it up for Mitch to see when she'd found it, then stuffed it into her own jeans pocket.

And then she was beside Mitch, hauling him up, nearly carrying him to the truck.

His arm was starting to hurt, and the pain sent him spinning as she did everything short of throw him into the cab of the truck. He felt her fasten a seat belt around him.

And then they were moving, bouncing, seemingly soaring across the rough land. His tunnel vision was getting worse, his world turning to shades of gray.

"Stay with me, Mitch," Becca said, her voice tight. "Talk to me. Tell me what you remember. Do you remember everything? Childhood? First kiss? Senior prom? Where you spent last summer's vacation?"

"I don't know," he said. "I think so, but…"

"Tell me what a SEAL is."

"We're good in the water." Lord, it was such a struggle even to speak. "We go away a lot. Away on missions all the time. Do things I could never tell you about. Leave again, too soon. Not sure—as your friend—I can recommend you marry me."

She laughed at that. "Do you come back?" she asked.

"Always," he told her. "For you, I'd come back not just from hell, but from heaven, too."

"I'm going to hold you to that. Dammit, don't you close your eyes!" She was crying. He hadn't meant to make her cry. "Mitch, we're almost there. I'm going to have the sheriff call for a medical chopper to take you into Santa Fe."

"Admiral Jake Robinson," Mitch managed to say. "Call him for me?"

"Admiral Jake Robinson," she repeated.

"He's—"

"I'll find him," she promised.

"Don't forget—"

"Parker?" she finished for him. "I won't."

"That I love you," he said.

Her laughter sounded more like a sob.

And there was shouting. Becca's voice, loud, calling for medical assistance. Hazel, shrill. The sheriff's deep bass.

And Mitch gave in to the darkness.

BECCA RAKED HER FINGERS through her hair as she hurried down the hospital corridor, trying to tame her curls.

There had been no room for her in the medevac chopper, and she'd driven halfway to Santa Fe. She'd left the sheriff standing in the driveway with Casey Parker in custody, changed her sodden and bloodstained clothes, grabbed her cell phone and headed into the city.

She'd connected with Mitch's Admiral Robinson on her first try. She'd actually called the Pentagon—it seemed like the best place to look for a U.S. Navy admiral. She'd been put on hold when she'd said she was trying to reach Robinson, put on hold again when she mentioned to the young but very efficient-sounding assistant who came on the line that she was calling on Mitch's behalf.

And ten seconds later another man had picked up the phone. She'd spoken to him for close to a minute before she realized she was speaking to the admiral himself.

She gave him the story in a nutshell—Mitch's gunshot wound to the head and the resulting amnesia. His search for his identity. Today's nearly fatal run-in with the real Casey Parker. She'd told him that Mitch had probably already arrived at the hospital in Santa Fe, that she was rushing over there now, via truck. She'd told him she was sorry, but she couldn't talk any longer, she had to call the hospital to make sure Mitch was all right, when he'd asked her the color of her truck and the route she was taking. He told her to watch the sky—he'd send an air force chopper to scoop her up ASAP.

The chopper had landed right in the middle of the state road. She'd locked her truck and gotten to Santa Fe in minutes.

The nurse in the E.R. hadn't given her any information on Mitch's condition over the phone and Becca was running by the time she reached his room and...

She stopped short.

The most gorgeous blonde woman she'd ever seen was sitting on the edge of Mitch's bed and holding his hand.

The most gorgeous blonde, nine-months-pregnant woman...

Oh, God.

She started to back away, trying to move silently, and ran into a very solid wall of a man.

"Hey." He, too, was blond—although his hair was more sunstreaked—and nearly as gorgeous as the woman. He was one of the men who had been in the van outside the bus station in Wyatt City. "Are you Becca Keyes? Mitch's friend?"

Mitch's *friend*. Becca nodded, unable to speak. It seemed that his marriage proposal had been a little hasty. Apparently he hadn't remembered *everything*.

He held out his hand. "Lt. Luke O'Donlon, Alpha Squad. My friends call me Lucky. Although I may have to give the nickname back after the hell of the past few weeks, the fact that Zoe Robinson isn't hovering anxiously at *my* bedside, and the added injustice that I didn't manage to meet *you* first."

He pushed her toward the door to Mitch's room. "Come on. We're all under strict orders to bring you right in if we see you."

"But—" Zoe *Robinson?*

"Ms. Rebecca Keyes," the man named Lucky announced loudly as if he were a very proper English butler.

"Thanks, Jeeves," Mitch said drily. He was smiling at her from his hospital bed. He still looked pale, but his arm was bandaged and he had an IV tube hooked into his hand.

And as Becca watched, the pregnant blonde moved gracefully from the bed, crossing the room to stand beside a uniformed man who couldn't be anyone other than Admiral Robinson.

But then Becca didn't look at anyone but Mitch. She crossed to his bed. "Are you all right?"

He held out his hand for her, and she took it. He tugged her down, and then he had his good arm around her.

"I needed a transfusion," he told her. "And afterwards, I felt so much better—"

"He tried to talk me into taking him back to your ranch," the Admiral interjected. "I'm Jake R—"

"Introductions later," his wife interrupted. "Everybody out."

Mitch's hand was in her hair, and she knew from his eyes that he was only waiting for the door to close before he kissed her.

But she didn't want to wait. She kissed him and kissed him, sweetly at first, then harder, deeper, infused with the fire his kisses always sparked.

When she pulled back, he was breathing hard. "I have to stay here overnight," he told her as if that were a total tragedy.

"I can wait," she told him. "I'm good at waiting."

She wasn't talking about just one night, and he knew it.

"There are things you need to know about me," Mitch said. "It wasn't fair of me to ask you to marry me before you know—"

"I know what I need to know." She pushed his hair back from his face. "You love me and I love you. Everything else is inconsequential." Becca laughed. "I never thought I'd get married, but..." She shrugged. "That was before I met you and discovered maybe true love isn't a myth."

He smiled at that, but his smile quickly dimmed. "I don't want to make you unhappy." He was so quietly serious, so intense.

"Good," she said. "Because it would make me really unhappy *not* to marry you. You know when I walked in here and saw what's her name? Zoe? I thought she was your wife."

He shook his head at that. "I told you, I knew I wasn't married."

"Yeah, but you also told me that you were this terrible criminal, and you'd spent time in jail and—"

"I *did* spend time in jail." He smiled at the look on her face. "It was part of a sting operation. I was trying to get close to the brother of a survivalist group leader. I was inside for nearly a month." His smile faded again. "See, these are the kinds of things that I do."

"Think," she said, "what fun it would have been knowing that I was there, waiting for you when you got out."

Mitch laughed. "I'm not sure *fun* is quite the right word."

"Yes," she said, "it is."

She kissed him to prove her point.

"We can make this work," she murmured. "I know we can. I've got forever—how about you?"

Mitch surrendered and kissed her. It was *definitely* worth a try. Because he loved her and she loved him. And like the lady said, everything else was inconsequential.

* * * * *